S.M. NAMKOONG

Ophelia

First edition

ISBN (paperback): 979-8-9932974-1-5
ISBN (hardcover): 979-8-9932974-2-2

Cover art by Jessica Cvilo

This book was professionally typeset on Reedsy.
Find out more at reedsy.com

And if thou gaze long into the abyss, the abyss will also gaze into thee.

FRIEDRICH NIETZSCHE

Contents

Preface

I'd like to extend my sincerest gratitude to the readers; thank you for picking up this novel and giving your support. All the characters and plot in this novel are a work of fiction. Please be advised, this book contains themes of attempted sexual assault, murder, suicide, emotional and physical abuse, alcoholism/drug abuse, animal death, and references to Christian ideology. These themes may be triggering for some readers, and I strongly encourage everyone to put their own mental health and safety first. I've done my best to approach these topics with care and consideration. There was no use of AI in any of the creative development, writing, or editing of this novel. Thank you once again for your support, and I hope you enjoy.

Prologue

"You must rest now, Evangeline."

Dr. Stevens leaned over the small figure in bed, tucked tightly in layers of blankets. He gently placed the back of his hand across her brow and frowned. *Much too cold.*

Despite the heavy blankets and a warming pan by her feet, the poor girl continued to tremble fiercely, as if she were out on a windy plain facing a harsh wind and not at home in her warm bed. Evangeline did not turn her head, but her eyes flickered to the doctor's. It shocked him how alert her eyes seemed, even as the rest of her body continued to fail her.

She moved her mouth as if to speak, but no sound came out. Her throat bobbed as she continued to try, but she could only moan lowly. The doctor smiled down at her and patted the rigid, cold hands that grasped the edges of the blanket tightly to her chest.

"All you need is a good, long rest, and you'll feel much better. You'll see. I'll be back first thing in the morning to check on you, alright?" He waited a moment for some acknowledgment, but the silent girl could only stare up at him. He nodded again and tilted his head. "Good night, Evangeline. Sleep well."

The doctor left the room, shutting the door after him. A moment later, the lock clicked softly. In bed, Evangeline exhaled lowly through her nose and did her best to try and tilt her head to face the door.

"Please," she finally gasped out in a low, breathy voice. Even in the quiet room, she had difficulty hearing her own voice above the

1

crackle of the fireplace. "Come back."

Despite how hard she tried to call out, Evangeline's rigid torso would not expand further, and every breath took more effort than she could afford to expend. Exhausted by her single, unheard plea, Evangeline relaxed back into the pillows. She focused only on breathing and remaining calm. She worked on wiggling her cold toes and flexing the rigid fingers that seemed to respond less and less every day. If she didn't look down every so often to check, she would swear they had disappeared altogether.

Evangeline closed her eyes and burrowed further under the blankets, but she couldn't seem to conserve any bit of warmth. She opened her eyes and peered at the wooden cross that hung on the wall across from where she lay.

"Oh God," she murmured only for her own ears. The cross began to tremble, shaking faster as her own prayers began to speed up. Her eyes widened, and her voice trembled. "-come to my aid! Come and meet me, angels of the Lord. Receive my soul and bring me to God. Lead me to Abraham. Give me my eternal rest, Lord. Please! Don't let her take me into the darkness. Please, let your light shine on me-"

The cross shook violently, banging against the wall until it fell, splitting down the center as it cracked against the floor. The moment it dropped, Evangeline's prayers stopped. The fireplace went out abruptly, as if God Himself had snuffed it out. She inhaled sharply, holding her breath until her lungs squeezed painfully.

The windows slowly opened as an unnatural wind entered the dark room. With it, Evangeline sat up in bed with a sudden ease and calm. Her face became blank, and her eyes stared out towards the dark beyond the windows as if someone were calling to her. She rose on silent feet, all her rigid muscles and aches forgotten. With a swift elegance, she shed her layers of clothes and threw off her thin, white nightgown before she climbed up onto the windowsill. For a moment,

Evangeline crouched there like a wild animal, and in the next, she jumped out and landed on the pads of her bare feet.

She straightened and stumbled forward through the back garden of her family home. Her feet dragged through the silt and tore up her mother's azaleas before she climbed over the stone fence that walled her family's humble property.

Evangeline paid no mind to the thorny bushes that scraped her delicate skin. Once she reached the rolling hills that led to the forest, her steps grew more determined and her pace quickened. Despite walking several miles and crossing hills, her breathing never labored.

At the bottom of the second hill, George Sullivan sat up a bit straighter from where he sat, rocking in his favorite chair on the whitewashed porch. Something moved in the distance, crossing in the peripheral of his vision. He set his drink and smoke aside to get a better look. He saw the illuminated figure of a young woman as she strode, naked, through the fields that abutted his own. He strained his eyes and stepped out for a better look.

"Is that-" he mumbled to himself. He raised his voice as he called out to her. "Evangeline? Evangeline, what are you doing, lass? Have you gone mad?"

He cried out her name several times over, but the figure never stopped nor reacted as they continued on their trek. Mr. Sullivan rushed back into his home and back out a moment later, pulling on his coat, with a blanket in hand. He ran as fast as his feet could carry him, but his bad knee began to give out, and he stumbled just as Evangeline reached the edge of the forest. He looked up from where he kneeled and reached out towards her one final time.

"Evangeline! Come back! Evangeline!"

She walked into the dark without a look back. Her feet bled as she stepped on jagged rocks and broken branches. She continued on as if it had been a journey she had taken several hundred times over.

When the moon reached its highest peak, Evangeline appeared in a clearing. The bright moonlight illuminated the dewy grass. The thick, dense trees seemed to part above, letting in the smallest opening to the heavens where the entire galaxy of the stars appeared like a window to another world. Silence settled heavily as the birds stopped cawing and the insects ceased chirping.

Whatever trance captured Evangeline lifted, and she let out a gasp. She took in deep lungfuls of breath as her head pivoted wildly around, taking in her strange surroundings.

"Where am I-"

A cold breeze hit her, and she noticed her nakedness. The cold and fatigue returned, and her legs trembled as she fought to remain upright. She stumbled where she stood, but a strong hand clasped itself around her neck from behind.

"Oh God!"

Evangeline had felt this hand several times before, but never got used to it. It was simultaneously soft as silk and as unyielding as steel. It never squeezed too painfully, but just enough to keep her exactly where it wanted her. Struggling was futile, but she tried anyway.

"Please," she whimpered lowly. The hand squeezed briefly, and it stole what little breath she had left. Evangeline gasped like a fish out of water as she tugged feebly at the hand around her throat. "Please, don't kill me. I don't want to die. Please, please."

"Shh," a low voice murmured into Evangeline's left ear. A second hand caressed Evangeline's cheek, tenderly like a lover. "Do not despair. It will be over soon. You're just not right, my dear."

Cold tears fell just as the hand stopped caressing her and clamped down over her mouth. Evangeline let out a pitiful cry, but it was muffled under the unyielding hand. Sudden terror gripped Evangeline's stomach, and her heartbeat picked up until it fluttered like the wings of a hummingbird. The hands around her face and neck began to squeeze, tightening like a boa constrictor.

Just when Evangeline thought the life would be pushed from her like the breath she struggled to take, the hands disappeared. The oppressive presence that seemed to gather behind her like a cloud, filling her lungs, vanished abruptly.

A hiccuping breath left Evangeline as she slowly turned her head sideways to look behind. Only dark trees stood behind her. She trembled again as another cold wind passed over her. She crossed her thin arms over her chest.

When she turned back, she let out a loud gasp as she looked into two bright eyes. The two pupils were so bright and all-consuming that the moon's light paled in comparison. Within that moment, Evangeline saw the beginning and the end. Whatever fleeting emotion of fear and pain left her, and all she could focus on were the two brilliant eyes that shone brighter than a hundred dying stars.

"Your eyes! God, your eyes."

Evangeline let out a low groan as a strong sting of pain erupted at the juncture between her neck and shoulder. Four sharp canines tore into her delicate skin as the little bit of blood she had left in her dying body was drained from her. That pain was fleeting, though, and then she felt nothing at all. She actually felt quite at peace.

Evangeline's body was laid gently on the cold forest floor. In her final moments, she mused internally that it seemed her own dying body was colder than the frozen ground below her.

Dying in such a way felt like how the ocean ebbs. Whatever life force made up Evangeline's soul felt like it had been pulled from her with every drop of blood. She felt nothing but comfort, like being slowly submerged into a warm bath. She turned her eyes up to the opening in the treeline and looked up at the galaxy above. The sea of stars twinkled at her and the bright, pockmarked moon peered down at her. The corners of her mouth tilted up as her suffering and weeks of torment finally came to an end.

"At last."

Chapter 1

Lawrence let out a low groan and pushed herself up onto her elbows. She rubbed a hand over her bleary eyes as she looked out the single window to her humble hut. The sharp breeze carried in the slight tang of saltwater, and she heard the booming crash of waves against rocks. The familiar noise lulled her to sleep at night and woke her gently at dawn.

She quickly rose from bed, the beams creaking with every slight movement. She rifled through her single suitcase she had yet to fully unpack, and worked quickly to dress herself. Before she stepped out, Lawrence looked back at the single-roomed pine cabin and gave it a once-over.

Each corner was devoted to some purpose: there was a cot in one corner with a thin hay mattress, a potbelly stove and chair in the other, and a half sink and cracked mirror in the third. She gave it a satisfied nod and turned to leave, letting the thin panel doors shut behind her with a clack.

Lawrence's seaside cabin stood at the bottom of a long trail that led up to a sharp drop-off known locally as Widow's Weep. She wrapped her thin coat tight around her as her long, black skirts whipped around her legs. She hunkered down and fought against the wind as she began her trek up. As the sun had yet to rise, Lawrence made the hike up in the dark.

As she walked, Lawrence tilted her head up and saw the top of the cliff several miles ahead. Just a little bit off the steep drop-off stood an imposing red mansion shrouded in darkness and covered on nearly all sides with thick, dense trees. Another sharp wind smacked her across the side, so she bowed her head and continued on.

She reached the first landing point and stopped to rest on a boulder; she watched as the dark night gave way to the brilliant, soft morning. Lawrence didn't even break a sweat; she had always had a strong constitution and was used to the exercise.

The sweet dew of rain on the pine needles and the salty tang of seaweed against the rocks filled her lungs with each deep breath. She looked out at the never-ending horizon of the sea, split only by a thin seam in the far, hazy distance. She raised her eyes to the east as the sun began to rise, ascending from the ocean's horizon. Lawrence sat in silent vigil as the rest of Maine's coast began to wake. After an hour or so, she rose from where she sat, brushed off her long skirts, and made the slow walk back down to her cabin.

When her little hut came back into view, she smiled and shook her head.

"Hello, Stinky Boy," she called out. "I know, I know. I'm late. Forgive me."

The black cat that lingered in front of her home meowed loudly as it brushed up against the door to be let in. It let out another yowl when she took far too long to obey. Lawrence let out a sharp bark of laughter and picked up the pace the last few steps.

She opened the door a crack, and the cat slipped in as if he owned the cabin. Lawrence followed after and immediately set to laying out a fresh bowl of water and leftovers for him to pick at. As he began to eat, Lawrence took a seat by the stove and tossed a few thin sticks of kindling into the opening.

"You know, I can barely afford to feed myself these days, much less your fat butt too."

Stinky Boy continued to eat, head lowered to the plate. Lawrence lit a match and tossed it into the oven. She then set a small kettle on top to make some coffee.

"You might want to consider pulling your weight around here," she said, continuing on. "It wouldn't hurt for you to run a broom around the place when I'm out."

Stinky Boy raised his head at that and looked decidedly unamused. He promptly went back to his food, and Lawrence chuckled to herself. Once the kettle steamed, Lawrence poured herself a watery cup of coffee and stuck her feet towards the warmth of the fire.

"We haven't been into town for a few days," she mused aloud, raising the cup to her lips. The cat raised its head. "What do you think?"

Stinky Boy slowly blinked, as if she had truly lost her mind. Its tail flicked back and forth as it sauntered once around the length of the cabin and then slipped out without a look back. Lawrence nodded her head.

"That's exactly what I was thinking too, Stinky Boy. Beautiful day."

* * *

The small, waterfront town of Bar Harbor lay nestled within Frenchman's Bay and directly south of four narrow fingers of water that sliced into the land like a grasping hand.

The coast had once been untouched and wild, with all manner of beasts wandering around the shores and lurking within the treeline. Now, a main street had been paved through the center, cutting through the wilderness like a giant gash. Pounded gravel and brick beat the wilderness back until the place resembled something like civilization. The city lines were placed like tilled plots made for seeds to grow, and sure enough, the town sprang up on its edges. It would continue to be built upon, added to, changed, and reworked for as long as humanity had a role to play.

Even as she walked down the dirt road, Lawrence tried to imagine how it might be altered in the coming years. How the world itself would be different once she was long gone. It sent a sudden jolt of fear through her, but she brushed it aside and continued on.

The bustling, lively town was entirely different to the quiet fishing port Lawrence had arrived at a couple weeks prior. Flashy cars rumbled down the dirt roads with towering trunks of luggage piled high and lashed down to the back. Lawrence watched families greet each other as they strolled down the street. Their clothes were all too fine compared to the locals', and Lawrence had no idea where they were coming from.

She entered the local post office and waved to the older man behind the counter. He shot her a smile and gestured her over.

"Morning, Ms. Stoner," Jeffery called out as she approached the single counter. He shot her a wry smile and winked. "How's the mansion with the ocean view?"

"It's a bit of a trek from the ballroom to my bedroom on the top floor, but I suppose we all must make certain sacrifices, don't we?"

Lawrence smiled as she laid out her postcard and a few cents for postage on the counter. Jeffery turned the card over and stamped it without a second glance.

"This one heading to Florence as well?" he asked. She nodded as a young boy appeared from the back room with a large stack of telegrams in hand. He ducked under the counter and put on his cap haphazardly. Jeffrey leaned around Lawrence to yell after him, pointing his pencil as he did. "Don't forget to pick up the outgoing this time, boy!"

The boy called out his affirmation as he dashed out. Jeffrey placed Lawrence's postcard in the outgoing pile. He turned back to Lawrence with an exasperated sigh.

"We've been sending out runners at least five times a day. I might as well take that door down to save the hinges from wearing out."

"Who *are* all those people out there? I thought I walked too far and ended up in the wrong town." Jeffrey snorted in amusement as Lawrence nodded over her shoulder to the busy streets outside. "This is not the quaint, *quiet* fishing town I was promised, Jeffrey."

"To be fair, it's still quaint, isn't it?" Jeffrey said with a tilt of his head. Lawrence raised a delicate brow, and Jeffrey shrugged his shoulders. "Well, it's the salmon run. You are witnessing the natural episode that occurs at the end of every spring here in Bar Harbor. The only thing that follows the thaw faster than the flowers are the rich folks coming back for the summer season."

"No kidding," murmured Lawrence, the gears suddenly turning in her head. "I got mansions all around me. I was starting to wonder who my neighbors were."

"Oh yeah. Henry Ford's son lives down in Seal Harbor. He's known to come up once in a while. I'd say we got about fifteen of the top twenty of the 'Forbes Rich List' walking around our streets. You want to make a change in Washington? You start in Bar Harbor."

Lawrence inclined her head and chuckled silently. "That's quite the little speech, Jeffrey. You should consider joining the tourist board."

"Eh," he shrugged, waving his hands. "My talents would be wasted on them. Besides, if I leave, this whole place will go up in smoke. Then how will the good people of Maine get their mail?"

"We shall have to give thanks to Providence every day for providing you to us," she replied dryly with another soft chuckle. Lawrence nodded her head in goodbye and turned to go. She stopped at the door and turned back. "The newspaper office is on this street?"

"Oh yeah, next to the tailors."

"Thank you, Jeffrey," she said, rushing out with renewed vigor.

* * *

The local paper's headquarters sat wedged between the general store and tailor's along the main street. Lawrence scrunched her nose at the stale, yellow air once she entered and spared only a passing glance around the tiny office. Boxes full of papers and files stood stacked up against the back wall as squirrelly men sat typing at their desks. Their eyes seemed to collectively raise and follow Lawrence as she crossed through the room.

A man there, a young clerk named William, took Lawrence's order for an ad and read it, glancing up at her occasionally until he was done. He smiled congenially and gestured with his pencil.

"You're a painter, eh?"

"Yes," replied Lawrence with a stiff nod. She shuffled in place, slightly uncomfortable under his assessing gaze.

"You don't look like a painter," he remarked offhandedly with another amused smile as he lowered his head to start filling out the paperwork.

Lawrence's jaw clenched tightly as she shifted again on her feet, crossing her arms in front of her. He was neither cruel nor mocking in his tone, but his words stung regardless.

"What are painters supposed to look like then?"

"I dunno," he said as he shrugged and licked at a stubby pencil, his eyes never raising from the work in front of him. If he noticed the sudden sharpness in her tone, he didn't show it. "Just not you."

She bristled again slightly at that and set her mouth into a thin line.

"I've been studying for over two years now, in Italy."

William raised his head at that and his brow furrowed slightly.

"That's in Europe, right?"

"Yes, it is," she answered evenly.

"I don't think I ever want to go over there." He shook his head with a disturbed look in his eye. He paused for a moment before he continued to fill out the form. "My brother died over there. Somewhere in France, it's called Saint-something. Saint Michel, I think. I don't remember."

"During the war?" she asked, suddenly subdued. He nodded his head with a neutral look on his face. She swallowed once and clasped her hands in front of her. "I'm, I'm sorry to hear that."

William smiled again, his kind eyes shining as he shook his head.

"He went and died in the mud in some foreign country. Got himself shot. What a schmuck, right?"

He chuckled lightly, but his eyes were pained. He cleared his throat and busied himself with the paperwork. Lawrence nodded in sympathy but said nothing.

"They told my ma he died like a hero, but I think we'd just prefer it if he was alive, ya know? I wouldn't want to die like that," he sighed. "I heard he gave those krauts a hell of a time, though; pardon the language."

"I don't blame you," she murmured, giving him a reassuring smile. "There's plenty of other places to go anyway, and much better ways to die."

William nodded in agreement, the skin crinkling around his eyes as he chuckled. He turned his eyes back to the paper, reviewing it quickly. He looked back up to Lawrence with a thoughtful look.

"You know, you may have an easier time finding work if you drop your card off at some houses. These rich folks might not be in the habit of looking in the ads for painters. Then again," he laughed, "What do I know about what rich folk do or don't do?"

"That's a bit forward, don't you think?"

She bit the inside of her cheek as her gaze lingered to the window and the view out to the street just beyond. William shrugged, tapping the pencil against the desk.

13

"Maybe, but you never know." He paused as he seemed to remember something. His expression immediately became serious, and he leaned forward. "If you do, though, I advise you stay away from Ashmore."

"Ashmore? What's that?" she asked, interested.

"It's the big red house near Widow's Weep. Maybe you've heard of it? It's on the main trail along the coast."

He reached into his desk and pulled out a map, pointing out where it was. They both bent their heads to get a closer look. Lawrence studied it and confirmed it to be the same house she saw on her morning walks. A strange feeling sizzled up her spine, and she inhaled sharply as William continued.

"I figured it was mostly abandoned by now, but the lamps came back on recently. No one's been able to talk about anything else for days. I'd just steer clear of it if I were you."

"Why's that?" she asked, cocking her head to the side.

"It's haunted," he stated, matter-of-fact and unblinking. Lawrence couldn't help but laugh a little at his seriousness. "And cursed."

"You're joking," she said as she huffed out another laugh. Uncertainty threaded through her as he continued to stare at her in complete sincerity. "You are joking, aren't you?"

"Mostly everyone thinks so too. You see, it's the three lamps outside the house. When they come on, bad things start happening." He leaned forward slightly, as if letting her in on a secret. "You know the last time those lamps came on was sixty years ago? I think it was in the winter of 1868. Maybe '69, I'm not sure. Shortly after they came on, a plague went through this town and three others in the area. The state quarantined us; they closed the trains and wouldn't let anyone leave. Almost a hundred people died before it just ended. Like that." He snapped his fingers, leaning back in his chair. "The lamps turned off, and people stopped dying. Like I said, cursed."

14

"Right," Lawrence said slowly, leaning away from William. Whether or not she was entirely convinced was made more plain by her disbelieving tone. "That seems more like a coincidence than actual evidence."

"Sure, but no one knows who the owners are either. They never come out." He then smiled as he remembered something. "When we were younger, my brother and I would dare each other to get as close as we could before we got scared. We'd always end up running away. It was a lot of fun, actually."

Lawrence grinned at William's faraway look as he reminisced about his childhood. His lower lip jutted out a bit, and she chuckled. When he looked back at her, his face flushed, and he quickly averted his eyes.

"What about servants?" she asked.

William shook his head. "There's this one old housekeeper who sometimes comes into town, but she's kind of gone around the bend. She talks nonsense to herself and then goes right back up the hill to the house."

"Well, I don't really believe in ghosts," Lawrence said with a little smirk. "Or curses, for that matter."

He finished up the paperwork and ripped out a little pink slip, which he then handed to her as a sort of receipt.

"Nobody believes in the boogeyman until they have a reason to."

"Thank you," she said as she took the receipt and tucked it into her pocket. She turned to go and was halfway out the front door when William came rushing after her.

"Hey!"

She turned just as he rushed to meet her, and he handed her the map from his drawer. She turned it over and saw he had marked the locations of houses with names.

"What's this?"

"Thought it might help you on your mission to try and make a dime in this town." He gestured to the houses and a few of the scribbled names. "These are the owners of the houses, and I put the butlers' names too, if I know them. Tell them William Ross sent you."

"Wow," she said, touched by the gesture. She met his eyes and nodded her head. "Thank you, William. Really."

"Don't mention it," he said, another flush creeping up his neck. "Your ad will be out in the next paper. Editions come out on Sundays. Welcome to Bar Harbor."

* * *

Lawrence took a slow stroll out of town and went down the main road in the opposite direction of her hut. The division between the estates and village was a stark one. The simple buildings and plain homes closer to the bay gave way to the wide estates and towering mansions that sat further apart the longer she continued on.

Grand homes occupied the land along the water's edge, carved out and claimed like pieces of pie. The newer ones closer to town were all whitewashed manors with long, sweeping driveways and well-trimmed lawns that stuck out against the natural dark foliage of the surrounding forest and land. The older estates closer to Widow's Weep were a bit older in style, but no less impressive; however, they seemed perfectly content in that and showed no interest in competing with their newer, more ostentatious neighbors.

Lawrence idly wondered why anyone bothered moving out into nature if they insisted on defying it at every turn. Those sorts of people saw the wilderness as something to be tamed, and it was hideous. Nevertheless, she kept her opinions to herself and hummed to herself as she trod along.

"Hello, good afternoon," she said to the housekeepers and butlers who answered the door. They all gave her a suspicious look, and before they could tell her off, she handed over her flimsy card and lowered her eyes in deference. "My name is Lawrence Stoner, and I'm an accomplished portraitist. William Ross referred me?" At the mention of his name, some eyes brightened, and hostilities were tempered. "I've just returned from Florence, where I studied under an Italian painting master. Perhaps you've heard of Roberto De Luca? No? Oh, well, he's quite a famous sculptor and painter. Anyways, if your masters have any interest in securing a formal portrait, I'd be honored to submit my name for consideration. Thank you very much. Have a good day."

She made a point not to linger and quickly moved on. She traveled from house to house without rest, and by the time she reached the end of the very long line of estates, a thin sheen of sweat covered her brow, and her shoulders heaved as she stopped to catch her breath.

Lawrence studied the map during her short rest and turned her eyes up to the final home at the top of the hill.

"Silly," she murmured to herself as her feet automatically moved forward towards Ashmore. She had never before trekked to the highest point of Widow's Weep, and as she did so then, she felt it appropriately named. All that separated the top from the over two hundred-foot drop into the gulf was a steep cliffside.

Ashmore stood in stark contrast to the other homes along the lane, new or old. The red-brick Georgian seemed almost modest in comparison, concealing itself within the trees around it. A thick forest of spruces and firs surrounded the perimeter and discouraged visitors of every kind. Off to the western side, Lawrence caught sight of a short trail that no doubt led to somewhere more intriguing.

She strode up the rocky path and straight up to the dark oak door. As she crossed the porch, she took a passing notice of the three lanterns out front that were indeed lit, flickering even in the bright afternoon. She knocked sharply three times and waited.

The door opened a sliver, and an old woman answered. She kept her silver hair in a tight, clean bun, and her black dress was hard-pressed, crisp, and terribly old-fashioned. Her eyes were the most prominent feature on her face, as they were large, wide, and cloudy. She stared directly at Lawrence with a hard frown and waited for her to speak first.

"Hello, good afternoon. My name is-" Lawrence began her speech in the most deferential tone she could muster.

"Go away," the lady whispered. Her voice cracked before she cleared it, coughing lightly.

"I beg your pardon?"

Lawrence leaned in a bit to hear her better. She forgot her prepared speech at the unexpected interruption. The housekeeper's head trembled as she tilted her head forward.

"Leave! We don't want anything you're selling. Go," she repeated in a hushed, urgent tone.

"Well, I'm not selling anything, ma'am. Not exactly. My name is Lawrence Stoner. Friends call me LJ. I'm quite an accomplished portraitist. I've just come back from rigorous study in Florence. If your masters would be interested in securing-"

"Aldane," the housekeeper whispered, interrupting Lawrence once again. "My lady's name is Aldane."

"Aldane?" Lawrence repeated. "Alright, well, if Mr. or Mrs. Aldane would be interested-"

"Oh no," said the woman immediately. "No man. No master."

The housekeeper shook her head at the mere implication. Despite her age, the woman's voice was strong and clear, like the deep-ringing gong of a bell. The old woman had a habit of tilting her head slightly sideways, which gave her an air of constant curiosity.

"How very modern," smiled Lawrence. "And you are?"

"I am Ms. Hettle, the housekeeper," answered the lady after a moment of hesitation.

Despite what the young man at the newspaper office had said, Ms. Hettle seemed quite alert. Even at first impressions, she was not at all how he described. Although her attitude was restrained, Ms. Hettle was not unfriendly. If anything, she seemed afraid. Though Lawrence couldn't understand what she could possibly be afraid of.

"Oh, I see," breathed out Lawrence with a smile. She held her hands behind her back as she shifted her weight back and forth. "Well, it certainly is a pleasure to make your acquaintance, Ms. Hettle. William Ross referred me."

At the mention of his name, Ms. Hettle neither stirred nor seemed to recognize who that was.

"Um, would it be possible to leave my card for your lady? Otherwise, I'd be more than happy to come back at their earliest convenience. I can bring some of my work. I live just down the trail."

Ms. Hettle listened quietly, wringing her hands and worrying her lip. Once Lawrence was done, she opened her mouth to speak, but then stopped short. She shot a nervous look back over her shoulder into the dark house, as if something were coming. She turned back to Lawrence, this time with a frantic, desperate look across her face.

"Please," she said, in a low and fervent voice. "You should go! Go far away."

"Sorry?" said Lawrence, taken aback by the sudden fear and urgency that gripped the older housekeeper. "What's the matter?"

"You don't want to leave your card here," warned Ms. Hettle. She shook her head again and gestured for Lawrence to turn back from where she came. "Go. Go!"

Lawrence remained stunned for a moment before she suddenly erupted into laughter and reached into her pocket.

"Oh, but I do!"

She held out the card with her information towards Ms. Hettle and placed it gently into her hand. The housekeeper reared back at the sudden contact and pushed Lawrence's hand away. She opened her mouth to convince her once more, but stopped.

As if someone had called for her, Ms. Hettle inclined her head slightly and looked back into the dark house, listening. She whimpered lowly and ducked her head down. Out of curiosity, Lawrence tried to look past Ms. Hettle's shoulder, but neither heard nor saw anything from within the darkness. Ms. Hettle turned back to Lawrence with a strange expression.

"Wait just a moment."

Before Lawrence could answer, Ms. Hettle quickly shut the door. She lingered on the porch for a few moments, waiting patiently, when something caught her eye.

Beyond the immediate trees around the main drive lay the short trail she had spotted earlier. It led to a hidden grove that covered a private pond and garden. The garden, despite being slightly overgrown and untamed, was otherwise magnificent. Nature was given free rein to run its course, and it stood out in sharp contrast to the well-trimmed bushes and manicured lawns of the other estates.

The pond housed a large, green gazebo with Italian columns and metal ivy and flower filigree. Marble statues of gods and tragic figures of myth all dotted the garden, their faces frozen in varying expressions of delight and sorrow, rage and horror. Each was so different in style and aesthetic to the other that it seemed certain their acquirer had traveled far and wide in their collection.

Lawrence went no further and stood in the center of the grove. She admired the dozens of camellia trees and each of their hundreds of blossoming flowers. She gazed at the flowering buds in wonder and touched the soft pink and white petals. Their delicate, sweet fragrance perfumed the salty breeze and was made all the sweeter by the slight dew leftover from the previous night that settled on their petals and leaves. It was a wonder that something as fragile as camellias could grow in an area that seemed suited only for the sturdier evergreens and pine trees that otherwise covered the rest of the state.

"Miss?" A voice called out from behind her.

Lawrence quickly turned and saw Ms. Hettle scurrying up towards her, pushing down her black skirts as they got kicked up by the wind. Her back remained slightly hunched as she walked, but she was sure-footed wherever she stepped.

"Over here, Ms. Hettle!" Lawrence called out, waving before she remembered it to be an unnecessary gesture. Ms. Hettle redirected and stopped a few feet off to catch her breath, patting her cheeks as she suddenly grew hot.

"You mustn't wander off!" She exclaimed between pants of breath.

"I am terribly sorry," Lawrence said, sincerely apologetic. She turned and gestured to the lane. "I was waiting and saw these lovely trees. I couldn't help myself. The garden is absolutely beautiful!"

"Yes, from what I remember, it was quite lovely," Ms. Hettle murmured as she folded her hands primly before herself.

"Have you been here that long, Ms. Hettle?" Lawrence asked.

"Since I was about fifteen, miss."

"My, you must know this place like the back of your hand then."

"Yes," she said, stilted and restrained as ever. There was something quite charming about the older woman, and Lawrence could only smile, amused. She turned her head back to the flowers to admire them for a moment longer.

"I really love camellias, so this is a wonderful surprise," Lawrence said after a few moments of passing silence between the two of them. "I adore them, but they're not really native to America. You can imagine my delight at seeing them here, so well taken care of."

The older lady's brows knit together, but she remained silent.

"There's a lovely little story I once heard about camellias that made me mad about them. Would you like to hear it? Well, I suppose it's actually quite sad. Anyway, there was a god named Te who fell in love with a mortal woman named Hemera. Te fell in love with Hemera after he saw her sleeping under a great oak tree. As she slept, he gifted her with hundreds of white camellias as a sign of his love. One day, Te left Hemera but promised to return soon. He did not understand, though, how fragile and brief human lives were, or are, I suppose. When he returned a hundred years later, oblivious and blissfully happy to return to his lover, he was shocked. Although he had not aged a day, his love had long passed on to the other side of the Great River. Out of grief and despair over his lost love, Te lay on the bank of the Great River and vowed never to rise from it again. As a god and an immortal, Te would never cross it the way his love had, so he simply lay at the edge, as close as he could get to her. From his body, a great tree of red camellias bloomed."

Lawrence paused as she thought back on the tragic story. She turned back again to Ms. Hettle, who remained silent.

"Sometimes I think about that. I mean, if the story is to be believed, he's still waiting for her, lying on the bank of that river. Quite sad, but lovely, isn't it?"

"Yes, miss," the housekeeper responded dutifully. It was clear that she was only engaging with her as much as was absolutely necessary. Lawrence chuckled again, not offended in the slightest. Ms. Hettle then stepped forward with her hand out. It had a slight tremor as she extended it, as if she had no wish to do so.

"I'll take your card, miss."

"Oh, is Mrs. Aldanes at home then?" Lawrence asked, intrigued.

"No," replied Ms. Hettle immediately. "No one's home. I'll take it."

"Oh, of course."

Lawrence handed over the card, which was then pocketed immediately. Ms. Hettle folded her hands in front of her again and bowed politely.

"Have a nice day."

She turned away and rushed back into the house, almost as if she were fleeing. Lawrence watched her retreating figure disappear into the dark entrance, and as her eyes rose to the great house, her gaze caught on the window in the east tower. She squinted, holding her hand up to shield her eyes from the bright glare of the sun. There, she saw a figure in the window.

Some dark, unmoving shadow stood a few feet from the glass. Although far away, Lawrence felt positive that whatever it was looked right at her. Her skin went numb, and the hairs on her neck rose. A strange sensation went through her like needles skittering across her skin that set her on edge.

She reasoned in her mind that it was not just her imagination. She fought for logic to win out over the irrational whisper of fear that overwhelmed all those clear thoughts. *There are no such things as ghosts.* When she looked closer, there was no questioning that it was a real person. Lawrence smiled in relief and waved. The figure continued to stand and stare, shifting slightly further back into the darkness. Something in Lawrence's gut twisted, and her hand froze mid-wave.

There was a loud pop, and Lawrence ducked down out of instinct. Down the road that had brought Lawrence up to Ashmore, a sleek, white car throttled noisily as it raced up. It sped up the path, kicking up the dirt into a large cloud that billowed out behind like a cape. It turned sharply and skidded up the drive on the estate closest to Ashmore. The engine let out another loud bang. A trio of young people in the car laughed loudly, singing at the top of their lungs. Lawrence felt a twinge of envy as she watched them go by, jealous of the company and the good time they were having.

Once they were out of sight, Lawrence turned back to the tower. The figure from the window had disappeared. Only the curtain swayed slightly in place.

For a brief moment, Lawrence wondered if she had truly seen what she thought she had. She chose not to linger on the property for too long and turned back to walk home before the sunset beat her to it.

* * *

The summer nights on the coast remained unforgivably cold, and every slice of wind managed to find its way through the slats of Lawrence's cabin. She lay dozing on the lumpy mattress of her cot, huddled under the thin, wool blanket in an effort to create a concentrated sphere of heat. Every so often, the firewood in her stove popped, and it helped draw Lawrence into the warm embrace of sleep.

For an hour or so, there was an undisturbed peace. First, the cot and wood ceased creaking, and silence descended. As if doused in water, the oven's fire extinguished and threw the cabin into absolute darkness. The door to the cabin shook slightly, as if someone were pressing on it from the other side. The handle began to jiggle and then went slack.

The door first pushed open slightly and stood ajar for a moment before it swung wide open without a noise. A gathered darkness outside the door moved through the room easily, floating towards Lawrence with intent. It lingered by her bedside for a moment as if looking down, assessing her.

A slender hand with sharp nails reached out towards Lawrence's covered figure and pulled back the blanket to expose her sleeping profile. It paused for a moment before it lay a hand across her brow.

The fingers traced along the soft outline of Lawrence's face to her jaw and continued down further to the valley of exposed skin at the hollow of her neck. It pushed down her nightshirt and tilted her face so the moonlight illuminated her more clearly.

"Is it you?" the low voice murmured. "Have I found you at last?"

The creature shrouded in darkness brought its head down to Lawrence's. The hands caressed Lawrence gently, and its lips placed soft kisses across her face and down her neck. When it reached the top of her left breast, it bared its teeth and bit down.

Lawrence awoke with a start with a pounding headache and the bright sunlight in her eyes. She immediately grabbed her chest and felt a sharp pain as she clutched at it. The pain quickly subsided to a dull throb that matched the slow beat of her heart. She rose from the bed on shaky legs and staggered over to her cracked mirror. She looked down at her exposed chest through the clouded reflection.

On her left breast, four small stinging marks lay across the top where blood had dried and crusted over. A thin line of dark crimson ran down to her belly. Her heart raced as she quickly wet a rag and cleaned herself with shaky hands. She concluded it to only be a spider bite. Once she was clean, she drank enough water and chewed on an old crust of bread until the nausea and lightheadedness subsided. She chose not to go on her walk for the morning and returned directly to bed.

"That silly clerk's stories got to me it seems," she murmured under her breath as she pulled the blankets tight around herself. "No such things as ghosts, Lawrence Stoner."

She continued to repeat it to herself like a prayer until she believed it.

Chapter 2

At the edge of town, the fishermen went out in the early morning to catch mackerel and bluefish in the bay. In the dusk, a thin layer of fog blanketed the pier and sea, uniting the two. All along the inlet, several boats dotted the calm waters, rocking as their sails shifted with the gentle breeze. Sailors and dock workers smoked by the water and drank their thin coffee in the quiet as they prepared to start the day.

Lawrence sat on a little stool at the edge of the dock with a small easel set up and a table of tools at her side. The sticky, cloying scent of turpentine intermingled with the tang of the sea. The wind, although chilly, invigorated her and filled her lungs with a crisp freshness.

She heard the faint sound of footsteps approaching from behind and turned to look. A young woman walked down the long pier with a cup of coffee in one hand and buttered cake in the other.

"You're back!" the woman called out to her as her cheeks flushed in the cold. Lawrence set down her brushes and pivoted in her seat with a warm smile.

Teresa worked at the local cafe where the dock workers and fishermen frequented after a long day's work. The young woman had short, blonde hair that framed her round face. In fact, everything about her seemed rounded off and soft, which gave her a vaguely cherubic impression. Once she came closer, Teresa blushed and nodded her head in greeting. She handed over the coffee and cake, which Lawrence took gratefully.

"I hadn't seen you for the past few days, so I thought maybe you were finished coming here," Teresa said, looking more at her feet than at Lawrence.

"I didn't realize you had noticed," Lawrence replied. Lawrence's own face heated, and she quickly raised the cup to her lips.

"Of course I noticed," murmured Teresa with another sweet smile. She kept her head down and stole little sideways glances at the easel. When Lawrence caught her eye again, the woman's cheeks flushed a lovely rose color. "That's very good."

Lawrence looked to where Teresa gestured with her head to the half-finished work on her easel.

"Thank you," she answered between bites of the soft, crumbling cake.

She swallowed it down with a gulp of hot coffee, a blessing in the chilly morning. She tried not to eat the cake all at once, mindful of savoring the first sweet treat she'd had after a couple of weeks. Until then, all her simple meals consisted of cold meat and simple soup.

"It's still in the early stages, though."

"Why's it all brown?" Teresa asked with a tilt of her head.

"That's just the underpainting. It'll look right once I add the rest of the colors on top."

"What's the point of doing that if you're going to paint over it anyway?"

Teresa's soft, sweet voice seemed no louder than a sigh. Lawrence couldn't imagine the woman ever shouting or raising it above a certain level. It suited her quite well in that way. Lawrence cleared her throat as she considered how to answer.

"Well, it, uh, it helps with everything, really," she replied. She leaned back and gestured towards the easel as she pointed out the separate areas. "It makes the dark areas darker and the light areas lighter. It ties everything together. Think of it like the foundation of a house."

Teresa nodded in understanding, glancing back and forth between the water and the captured scene on Lawrence's canvas. The way her eyes flickered seemed as if she were noticing certain details of the scenery for the first time as well. She turned to address Lawrence directly.

"Would you let me see it once you're done?"

"Really?" she asked, incredulous. Teresa smiled and nodded. Lawrence's heart did a light skip, and she smiled back, suddenly shy herself. "You'll be the first person I show then."

The girl lingered for a moment and looked down to study Lawrence with a pleasant smile. Dimples formed in her soft cheeks that reminded Lawrence of soft peaches.

"You're not from around here."

She said it for what it was, which was a fact. Lawrence only chuckled as she crossed her legs and looked up at Teresa, who stood a bit closer now. The woman tucked her hands under her arms and wrapped her thin sweater tighter around herself.

"Did something give me away?" Lawrence asked.

Teresa shook her head and the golden hair swayed violently as she giggled.

"It's a small town," she murmured. She stuck her hand out then in a move that was so sudden and outgoing, it caught Lawrence off guard. "Teresa Doley."

Lawrence grasped the warm hand in hers and gave it a solid shake. "Yes, I know. You told me."

"Oh!" Teresa gasped, her face flushing a darker hue of crimson as she tucked some hair behind her ear. "I'm terribly sorry. I must have forgotten. Yes, of course."

Lawrence laughed good-naturedly, flashing her a brilliant smile. "Allow me to put you out of your misery. You shared your name when

28

we first met, but I didn't have the chance to do the same. Lawrence Stoner. Friends call me LJ."

Teresa nodded gratefully and removed her soft hand from Lawrence's. She opened her mouth to speak, but a loud meow interrupted her. They both turned and watched as a familiar black cat sauntered down the dock towards them.

"God, you're a bloodhound," cried Lawrence as she leaned around Teresa to watch as Stinky Boy approached them. He wound his way through Teresa's legs and rubbed its head against the leg of Lawrence's easel.

"I see Hugo has taken a liking to you," said Teresa with a fond smile.

She crouched down to scratch him behind the ears, which he accepted gratefully. The cat displayed a gentler side to Teresa, which made Lawrence scoff in amused disbelief.

"Hugo," repeated Lawrence, incredulous. "This yowling, stinking beast is named Hugo? Is he yours then?"

Teresa laughed aloud in delight and shook her head. "'Fraid not. Hugo doesn't belong to anyone except himself. I just like to call him that since I think it suits him."

"I think a bath would suit him, or a quick drop in the bay," muttered Lawrence.

Stinky Boy seemed to understand as he tilted his head backward and meowed at her, unamused. Teresa giggled, covering her mouth with her hand to hide the slightly jagged teeth that Lawrence thought suited her and were quite charming.

The cat noticed the uneaten bit of cake still in Lawrence's hand and continued to stare at her, unyielding. She let out a loud sigh and handed it over, which he ate with gusto. Once finished, he trotted off and disappeared around a building corner. Lawrence watched him go and noticed someone crouched against a nearby building.

She stood then, squinting her eyes as she tried to make out the familiar-looking figure.

"Hello?" She waved her hand. "Ms. Hettle, is that you?"

The figure stiffened and quickly ducked away, disappearing behind the building. Teresa looked over her shoulder, but missed seeing the housekeeper. They both looked for a moment longer, but no one reappeared. Teresa turned back to Lawrence with a curious expression.

"Someone you know?"

"Not quite," admitted Lawrence. She let out an uneasy chuckle and shook her head. "My eyes must be playing tricks on me. More coffee, I think."

She took her seat again and raised her cup to her lips. Teresa resumed her place by her side. A moment of silence settled between them.

"So, is painting your hobby then?"

"Slightly more than that," answered Lawrence with a smirk.

"Work?" asked Teresa, brows raised slightly in interest.

"Well, I suppose it must be since I make my living off it. It's not much of a living, but it's better than nothing. Even the worst something is better than nothing."

Teresa laughed aloud again, and the apples of her cheeks rose as she did.

"I'm sure that's not always true." She hesitated and looked down at Lawrence with an expectant look. "May I ask you something?"

Lawrence nodded.

"What made you come *here* of all places?" Teresa asked.

Lawrence paused for a moment as she considered her answer.

"There was an old woman named Renata who took care of my painting master and his studio. She always stopped by in the late morning to leave food for him, and then for the both of us, once I joined. She would sometimes sit outside the studio crying, and one day I asked her what the matter was. Then, she showed me this flimsy card." Lawrence held her hand out, miming the act of how Renata had held the postcard to her then. "It was so worn and creased that I had no doubt that she kept it on her and touched it constantly to remind herself of it being there in her pocket."

Teresa listened, rapt. Her eyes never strayed from Lawrence as she spoke, and the edges of her mouth tilted up at certain points, sometimes in amusement and other times in sympathy.

"It was from her son, who had recently immigrated here. All she talked about was how wonderful and smart he was, but I knew she was worried. Whenever she drank, which was more often than not, mind you, she'd cry pitifully, wondering if he was alright. Anyway, I saw the card and it just took my breath away. I couldn't believe a place like that existed in my own country." Lawrence shook her head as her eyes glazed over, remembering the moment and the feeling as distinctly as ever. "The painted image was simple: a bright yellow sunrise breaking over the horizon and casting a brilliant, golden light over the deep purple-blue waves of the Atlantic. There was a lighthouse at the edge of a thick forest of trees, teetering precariously at the edge of a steep, sandstone cliff. At the very bottom, in simple typeface, it wrote: *The Beautiful Coast of Maine.* I don't know, I guess I felt like there was something impossibly hopeful about the image, and it was one of those rare times I felt touched. When one is searching desperately to be inspired in such a way, it's too good to simply walk away."

Teresa remained silent for several moments as a soft smile graced her equally soft face.

"You left because of an image on a postcard? That's quite romantic. *You're* quite the romantic, LJ Stoner."

There was no way for Lawrence to explain to Teresa that it was quite the opposite. She had left Italy in heartbreak, unable to associate anything with the place besides pain. She simply nodded in silent assent, though, as a lump formed in her throat.

"That's me," said Lawrence with a smile. "The romantic."

They chuckled together, and another moment of silence settled naturally between the two of them.

"Do you mind if I ask where you're from then?" Teresa asked, sincere in her interest.

"Indiana." Lawrence took another sip of the coffee that was already beginning to cool. "But, the studio where I studied was in Italy."

"Italy!" Teresa exclaimed, a bit of awe in her voice. "No kidding. That must have been something. How long were you there?"

"Just shy of three years."

"It must have been hard to leave then. I'm sure you laid down some roots," she said.

Lawrence hadn't really considered it, but she supposed it was true.

She suspected Signor De Luca knew she was planning on leaving him, as he had grown a bit harsher and colder towards her near the end. He lashed out for all sorts of different reasons, calling her a 'stupid American girl' and then sulking for the rest of the day before inevitably coming to apologize in way of leaving a small present for her. When the time came to leave, though, he stared at Lawrence with a lost expression and then gruffly reminded her not to be stupid and do something ridiculous, like forget to eat. He patted her head, gave her a gentle kiss on the cheek, and sent her on her way.

"I can't imagine going so far away," continued Teresa, breaking Lawrence from her silent musings. "I think I'll be here in this town until the end, cradle to grave, as they say."

"Well, it's a lovely town. There are plenty of worse towns, believe me. I come from one," Lawrence replied, some levity in her voice. "I can't say I'd even seriously considered returning to the Midwest." Lawrence turned to her then as an idea occurred to her.

"Seeing as that you're a local, I suppose you could tell me a bit more about this town."

"What would you like to know?" asked Teresa, eager to please.

Lawrence mulled it over for a moment, but she already knew exactly what she wanted to ask.

"What can you tell me about Ashmore Hall?"

Teresa seemed a bit hesitant, but finally shrugged. She hugged herself tighter, as if out of instinct to protect herself from even the thought of the place.

"My grandmother told me to never go up there and to keep our doors locked at night. People said witches danced on the cliff naked, practicing their craft and making deals with the devil in the moonlight."

Teresa grinned widely as she recounted all the ridiculous stories. She forgot to cover her mouth as she did, and Lawrence got to see her pretty, imperfect smile.

"Though, people nowadays don't really believe any of that stuff. At least, not the younger ones," she breathed out, laughing. "If you ask me, I think it's a big, old house owned by some rich fella who just doesn't have enough time or bodies to live in all his houses."

"You don't buy into all the superstitions then with the lanterns coming on?" asked Lawrence.

Teresa shook her head, knowing exactly what she was referring to.

"Not really. Anyone old enough to remember anything about the last time they came on is either mad or dead. The mad ones will say things that'll make your eyes roll to the back of your head."

They laughed once more together, and Lawrence regretfully finished off the last of her coffee. Teresa took the empty dishes from Lawrence, who thanked her again as she handed them over. Teresa tilted her head with a thoughtful expression.

"Though, I suppose with what's happened in Derby, maybe there's some substance to the stories."

"How do you mean?"

Teresa's face dropped, and she shook her head with a grim look across her face.

"It's horrible! This young man in Derby just passed. His name was Thomas. I didn't really know him all that well, but plenty of people in town did. It's terrible; he was only twenty-nine."

Lawrence sat in contemplative silence for a moment, hand on her chin. "Derby, how far is that from here?"

"About an hour or so. Faster by motor car, I'm sure."

"Do you know how he died?" she asked.

A small line formed between Teresa's brows as she frowned and puckered her lips. She did seem sincerely upset about the passing.

"Not quite. I just heard the details are quite upsetting. Something about a great loss of blood, and a sickness that affected his mind."

"Well, that is very sad to hear. We should all take good care of ourselves."

Teresa studied Lawrence for a moment and lingered by her side a moment longer than necessary. "Speaking of, you shouldn't stay out here too long; you'll catch something."

"I'm quite sturdy, and the coffee has warmed me up, which I thank you again for."

"It's no problem." She gave Lawrence a smile and turned to leave.

Lawrence watched her go, but Teresa made it only a few steps before she called out after her. "Actually-"

Teresa stopped and turned to look back in anticipation.

"I'd be interested to learn more sometime, if you're free. Would you be interested? We could get dinner at one of those nice cafes in town."

Lawrence's breath halted momentarily as she waited for Teresa's answer. Her heart beat rapidly, and she settled her hands on her legs to keep them from fidgeting. Teresa smiled brightly.

"That sounds lovely. I know a great spot."

"Swell, well, that sounds like a plan."

Lawrence waved goodbye as she resumed her seat. She calmed her beating heart, and something akin to hope flickered within her chest as she picked up her brush again and went back to work.

* * *

Lawrence returned to the pier the next day, and the next, and the following four days, but Teresa did not appear again. Nevertheless, she continued to set up in the same spot in the dark, painting and shivering until the sun peeked out over the horizon. She'd look over her shoulder every so often, expecting to see Teresa shuffling out with her tray and smile, but she never showed.

Lawrence felt the absence acutely, and bitter disappointment filled her. The next natural worry, though, was that something had happened. The next week, Lawrence sat at her easel as usual and simply stared at the canvas.

"Good morning."

Lawrence nearly fell off the stool as she stood abruptly, whipping around. The canvas teetered a bit as her leg caught on part of the stand, and she rushed to right it. Teresa stood a few feet away with a cup of coffee in one hand and a pastry in the other.

"God almighty, you nearly scared the life right out of me," Lawrence panted as she clutched her chest. She then let out a relieved chuckle once the excitement passed.

Teresa gave Lawrence a weak smile and held out the coffee and pastry, but her arms trembled and the cup rattled in its saucer. Lawrence studied Teresa closer then, and noticed the deep bags under her eyes. Her normally rosy complexion and full cheeks were ashen and hollowed. She looked beyond exhausted, and just standing there seemed almost a Herculean task for her.

"Teresa," breathed Lawrence, setting the plates aside. "Are you alright?"

"Yeah." Teresa smiled weakly. "I had caught a bit of a bug, but I'm feeling much better. Much better."

Her voice trailed off slightly as her eyes glazed over slightly. She suddenly refocused and smiled as best she could at Lawrence.

"I'm looking forward to our dinner tonight. Weatherby's and Maitlands is a lovely cafe. I've known the family who owns it since I was born. Would six work for you?"

"I don't know," murmured Lawrence, reaching a hand out slowly as if afraid a gentle breeze might blow Teresa over. "You don't look quite up to snuff. You know, we can always reschedule that. It's more important you get better."

"I'm better now," insisted Teresa. She shivered and wrapped her cardigan tighter around herself. A bead of sweat rolled down her temple, and she swallowed thickly. "I think I better head back in now, though."

"Teresa," Lawrence called out after her, but she continued to walk away. She only looked back once she was nearly off the dock.

"I'll see you tonight!"

Chapter 3

Lawrence sat among strangers in the bustling cafe. The noise and bodies kept her eyes and mind busy from her own thoughts. She chewed on her lip as her leg shook endlessly under the table. Her eyes continued to stray to the front door in anticipation.

She had arrived a bit early and took a table in the back of the room, appreciating that it was out of the way enough so she could observe the room more freely. She watched the couples sitting together, faces leaned in close enough to kiss. Groups of friends ate together, laughing uproariously and chatting loudly in competition with the other noises in the room. The ever-present smoke from cigars and cigarettes hung over the top of the room like a vague cloud.

Under different circumstances, Teresa would have been correct; Weatherby's and Maitlands seemed like a lovely cafe.

The first five minutes passed rather quickly, but each successive minute became slower. As she sat on her own, Lawrence suddenly felt a ridiculous sense of embarrassment. Once a full hour had come and gone, she made up her mind.

She began to gather her things and went to stand when a large shadow loomed over her. A hand appeared in her field of view and gestured to the chair meant for Teresa.

"Are you using this chair?"

Lawrence turned and looked up at the person towering over her. A big man, at least two heads taller than she was, grinned down at her. He had a great square jaw that reminded her of a boxer and sharp blue eyes with blonde hair gelled back flat. He had his coat slung over one arm and held his hat in the other. Once he caught Lawrence's eye, he immediately shot her a sly smile. She turned away and gestured vaguely towards it.

"By all means, take the whole table."

"You're leaving?" he said with a frown. "This place can't be that bad, can it?"

"No," she said with a polite smile. "Just heading out."

The man smiled again and held his arms out wide to keep her from leaving.

"Oh come, the night is young, and so are we. If you're not busy, and I can tell you aren't, you should join me. I'd be honored to have such lovely company."

Lawrence paused for a moment. Her immediate impulse was to refuse. She thought, though, of her disappointment at how the night was ending. The mere idea of returning to her hut and the solitude seemed unbearable. No doubt lying alone in the darkness would do nothing but invite parasitic thoughts to eat away at her mind. Teresa had looked unwell when she had seen her last. Surely, that was the reason why she hadn't joined. Then again, perhaps she had changed her mind in the end. Maybe Lawrence had said something wrong. The man leaned forward into her space, and she reared back as her wandering thoughts were disrupted. He had been trying to get her attention.

"Sorry, did you say something?"

"Apologies," he chuckled. "I didn't mean to bark at you like a dog. Then again, now that you're looking at me, I'm glad I did. Name's John Humphries; how do ya do?"

He held his meaty hand out, and it appeared before Lawrence like a serving platter. She took it politely and shook it. "Pleasure."

"You got a name, sweetheart?"

"Lawrence Stoner," she replied. "Friends call me LJ."

"Stoner, Stoner," he repeated aloud as he tried to recall if he knew anyone of the same name. "Where're your people from?"

"The Midwest."

"You don't happen to be related to Chivey Stoner, are you?" he asked.

"No, I don't believe so," she responded with a shake of her head.

"Too bad; he was a good chum of mine at Yale. Fantastic with a mallet. You watch?"

"Watch what?"

"Polo, of course," he exclaimed as if it were only obvious. Lawrence shook her head, and John frowned, clearly put off that he couldn't talk about the beloved sport any further. He shrugged and continued anyway. "It's a fantastic sport. They've got a little club out here that I'm a part of. We have games almost every week, and it's quite a good bit of fun. Anyone can come and watch the games. Maybe I'll see you around the pitch sometime, eh?"

Lawrence chose not to answer after he winked at her.

"Are you waiting for anyone?" he asked mildly as he gestured to the chair he had originally asked to take.

Lawrence's face flushed as she thought of Teresa, and she couldn't help but look one last time towards the door, as if expecting her to appear then. When she saw the empty entrance, she turned back to John. He promptly set his coat and hat aside and took Teresa's seat at her elbow.

"Please, join me," she muttered after he already took the liberty of doing so.

"Thanks, sweetheart."

He sat closer than expected, but she kept her mouth shut. She discreetly moved her chair a few inches away so their bodies wouldn't touch. They sat together for a few moments in silence, but she felt his gaze on her constantly. Her face grew hot under the direct attention, and John smiled in his misunderstanding. He leaned towards her and brought his mouth close to her ear.

"Ya wanna know what I was just thinking about?" he whispered. Lawrence looked sideways at him to continue. "Fate. You see, I usually come out to this dive almost every night. My first night back after two months away, and I meet a pretty gal like you. You know what I say that is? Kismet."

"Did you come alone too?" she asked as her eyes flicked over his shoulder, looking to see if anyone else in the room might be in his party.

"No, but I left the boys at the table once I saw you over here all on your lonesome. They won't miss me, and honestly, they might be more unforgiving if I leave you here on your own."

He chuckled at the thought and ran a hand over his perfectly set hair.

"Oh, I see," Lawrence replied with a polite laugh. She gathered her hands together in her lap. "You know, I was feeling rather lonely and sorry for myself just now, so the company is not half bad. It's nice to make a new friend."

"Like I said, kismet," smiled John. "You're not from around here, are you?"

Lawrence couldn't help but snort. Apparently, it *was* that obvious that she was an outsider. She shook her head in response.

"Just visiting?" he asked.

"I'm renting a little hut by the bay," she said with great pride.

"Alone?" he said, surprised.

Lawrence nodded, a placid smile on her face. Despite the struggles, she was quite content otherwise and proud to have a place on her own. John seemed less impressed, though, and continued to frown at the thought. He then shook his head.

"A young lady on her own? No, that's not right."

"I'm perfectly fine, I assure you."

"How far is it?" he asked.

"Not too far."

"What would your father think?" he countered, an arrogant smirk on his face.

"Considering he's dead, not much, I'd imagine," Lawrence snapped as she bristled in annoyance.

John paused for a moment and then abruptly laughed, reaching into his inner pocket for a cigar.

"You're not a member of the club, are you?"

"No, can't say I am." She set her lips into a thin line. "Should I be?"

"Well, that's no worry. We don't need to go there. It's boring anyhow. Full of stuck-up old codgers with sticks up their rears." He waved his hand as if erasing the idea away. He shot her a sly smile. "Besides, I know much better places."

"What sort of places?"

John let out another throaty laugh as he felt around his vest for some matches. It took a couple tries, but he finally lit his cigar and shot a wink her way.

"The fun kind, darling."

Lawrence arched a brow at that, but remained silent. She got the impression that John may not just be a brute by appearance alone. When he spoke or asked questions, it was harsh and direct, like being interrogated by a police captain. His eyes were sharp, and his gaze oftentimes lingered for too long. He exhaled sharply, tossing the box of matches onto the table between the two of them, throwing them away once they lost their immediate usefulness.

"So, what's a young filly like you doing out here, living on your own?" he asked, smoke blowing directly into her face. She waved it away as it stung her eyes.

"Painting," she responded primly.

"Painting?" he repeated. She nodded. "Painting what?"

"The landscape, mostly for now. I do portraits as well. I prefer them. I put out an ad for it last week, actually. I'm hoping to hear back from it soon."

"Oh, I doubt it," he laughed. The arrogance immediately irked Lawrence, and she clenched her jaw to keep from sniping back. He shook his head. "Who sits for portraits these days? Bit outdated, don't you think? Take two minutes, and you can have a photo. No painting will ever be as accurate as a photo. It's a dying art."

"Yes, but what photo will ever capture a subject's essence, its soul?"

John laughed, guffawing loudly so that even in the crowded, noisy restaurant, his voice carried like the dumb squawk of a bird.

"My goodness, what a thing to say."

Lawrence decided that John Humphries was as thick in the head as he looked. She began plotting the quickest and most painless way to end the night early and be on her way. The loneliness and silence of her hut may be preferred if this were the only alternative. John continued to speak, though, adopting a sudden, serious, thoughtful look.

"Don't think I don't appreciate the arts, though. Painting is a good hobby. I always think it's important for young ladies to pick up little skills like that. It's important they're not idle all day long, you know? Servants these days are not so common. Surely, a good, smart woman can finish cooking and cleaning within an hour or two, and what else will they do with the rest of their day?" He paused for a moment, as if waiting for Lawrence to answer, or more so, agree. However, when she did open her mouth to speak, he carried on like a steam train. "It's better they paint and sew and do those sorts of artistic things to keep themselves occupied rather than laze about in bed all day. Don't you agree?"

Lawrence only hummed in response. There was very little point in arguing with him, and it would only waste more time. She gave him a restrained smile, but it only served to give him the wrong idea by the way his own smile widened and eyes brightened. He leaned forward again.

"This place is awfully dull, isn't it?"

"I thought it was quite nice," she argued, just for the sake of it at that point.

"I've got a great idea!" he cried out as if the idea had just come to him. He slapped his hand down on the table, which rattled under the weight. "Let's go to a proper club and have a real drink. There's a fun little joint a little bit out of town. It's in the old rubber factory; keep that on the down low, though. It's certainly not the Palm Club, but it's a nice little place when you're stuck out here in the sticks."

Lawrence gave him a strange look because he laughed, clapping his hands together like a great ape. She was taken aback, but couldn't deny that her interest was piqued. She pursed her lips, and John took advantage of the moment.

"It's perfectly safe; don't have to worry about any coppers. Hell, half of the boys are there at night still in their uniform!"

"I don't know," she murmured, reluctant.

"Trust me, honey. It'll be a ball. We'll drop in, have a look around, and you'll be back in bed at a very respectable hour. Scout's honor." He held his hand to his chest with another boyish grin. "If you'd like, I can see to that personally."

She hesitated for a moment, considering what to say next. For some unknown reason, her refusal sat at the back of her throat. She had never broken the law before, but she was now seriously considering going to a speakeasy with a brute like John of all people. The longer

43

she took to respond, the bigger his smile grew. With a clap of his hands, he rose and gathered up his coat and hat.

"After you, sweetheart."

John found a cab with relative ease, and they traveled together to the outer limits. John paid for the ride, and Lawrence stepped out onto a dark and quiet street. The street lamps had long been extinguished for the night, and the sound of the ocean was now just a distant thing in the background. When she raised her head to look at the abandoned factory with all its dark windows and shuttered doors, Lawrence couldn't imagine any sort of bar or club actually being inside at all.

A breeze swept through, weaving through her hair and ruffling her skirts. Her skin prickled, and she turned to look at the dark street across the factory. She strained her eyes, searching the darkness, but saw nothing. John appeared, blocking her view, and took her by the elbow.

"This way," John gestured for her to follow as he went around the side of the brick building to a small alleyway.

They approached a door with peeling red paint. A man stepped out, cigarette in hand. He saw the duo and waved them forward silently, holding the door open and tilting his head for them to get in quickly. They crossed a dark hallway to another door at the end. Lawrence heard the faint bump of music and muffled thumping of dancing feet.

John knocked a couple times before it opened with a groan. A large, burly man who made John look petite peered down at the two of them with a suspicious look.

"You got the word?"

"Banshee, baby, banshee," John said with a smirk and far too much confidence to a man so much physically superior.

The man grunted and hesitantly stepped aside. John pushed forward first through the door. Another barrier of thick velvet curtains lay directly beyond, which he held aside for Lawrence.

Passing through truly did feel like stepping into another dimension. Lawrence stepped out into a lively underground club with a five-piece band and dance floor. Crumbling brick and broken glass had hidden its secret in plain sight.

The moth-bitten fabrics and rickety furniture left much to be desired, but nobody seemed to care. The state of the furniture was the last thing on anybody's mind there. It seemed the only place in Bar Harbor where the locals mixed with the rich without any pretense. Even those of greater, more well-established affluence, who otherwise looked down on the *nouveau riche* in every other situation, happily rubbed elbows with them without much thought otherwise. True to John's word, Lawrence even recognized a few officers she had seen in passing a few times.

Albeit a bit thrown together, the bar was noisy and lively and made her smile. They showed themselves to a table by the dance floor, and he held out the chair for her.

"What are you drinking?" he asked, coming close to be heard over the loud music.

"Oh, I don't really know," she stuttered, suddenly self-conscious at her own ignorance.

Years of abstaining from both drink and smoke showed itself in these rare occasions. John seemed to catch on and smirked.

"You did seem a bit dewy-eyed," he chuckled. "I guess my suspicions were correct. I'm not saying there's anything wrong with that, though. I like that. Other fellas might not, but I do."

He looked around the room as he spoke and gave an arrogant sniff. He turned back to her, hand on his chest, with a sincere look.

"I'm glad you're not like these other young women these days with their short hair and obscenely revealing dresses. Half of them look like boys, and the other half." He paused. "Well, I won't say, but it's unbecoming. They smoke like chimneys and every other word is a 'damn' or a 'shit'. It's very unladylike, and I don't care for it at all."

"How lucky for me," she muttered. She leaned in then to speak to him directly and he met her halfway. "I am being serious, though, when I say I'm a bit inexperienced. I don't drink."

"Don't worry, we'll fix that."

He laughed and waved his hand at the waiter. When the dressed-down man came by, John looked up, crossing his thick arms, as he considered what to order for them.

"Now, let's see here. No, not gin. I can't stand gin. It reminds me of this British shirt I went to school with, and I couldn't stand him. Champagne is what we need."

"We got a crate of 'em straight from France. Came in just last Tuesday," the waiter said as he jerked his head towards the back, no doubt towards where the crates were stored. John snapped his fingers at him.

"Get us a bottle and make sure to have another ready the moment it's empty."

John slipped the man a bill, who tucked it into his inner pocket. He gave the two of them a nod and hurried off to get the first bottle. Lawrence pressed her lips into a thin line during the entire interaction, but said nothing.

"That seems a bit much," Lawrence said, her brows knit together as she watched the waiter scurry off. "What was that for anyways?"

"Oh, you know," John said with a shrug. "Those types only pay attention if you make it worth their while. Nothing I can't respect."

Lawrence raised a brow at that. "I don't think we need an entire bottle for just the two of us. I don't know how much I can handle."

"Don't worry! I'm the best teacher there is," he said with a sly smile and another wink. He waved his hand. "Besides, champagne is weaker than water. You've nothing to worry about."

46

"Really? That doesn't seem true."

"Don't you worry." He put his arm around her shoulders and set his hand on her shoulder. He squeezed lightly. "I'll keep my eye on you."

She studied his face and he smiled congenially at her. He let go of her arm and leaned back in his chair, lighting up a fresh cigar. She turned to him then, leaning forward to be heard clearly.

"Isn't champagne typically drunk during celebrations?" she asked.

The band switched to the next song and the couples on the floor began to move wildly, swinging around in each others arms as they hopped and skipped around the floor to the frantic beat. They both had to nearly shout to be heard over all the noise.

"Of course!" cried John, a puff of smoke coming out of his mouth. He held out his hand and began to tick his fingers off. "There are a few rules: red wine with dark meat, white wine with fish, beer with your father, vodka with enemies, and champagne with lovers."

He wiggled his fingers and Lawrence's face grew hot. She averted her eyes and folded her hands neatly in her lap. John laughed uproariously in response.

"You're quite green, aren't you?"

"I don't know what you mean by that," she answered back, still avoiding his searching gaze.

"You're red as a tomato," he laughed. "It's very cute, though. It works for you."

"I think I'm just unused to how things are done here. Men don't normally talk to women like that. Where I'm from, we wouldn't even be sitting together like this without a chaperone between us."

"And I can respect that, but times are changing, baby. How in the hell are two young people meant to meet and get to know each other properly unless they're allowed to go out a bit, drink, dance, and fall in love?"

"Goodness, first the champagne and now this. We just met a few hours ago and now you speak of falling in love. How very un-American."

"Oh, I disagree. There couldn't be anything more American! We Americans are full of love. All of us are falling in love every minute. Look at this place. It's a country for lovers, made by lovers." He held his hands out as he looked out at the club full of couples. He turned back to her with a crooked smile. "Everyone thinks the French and the Italian are the lovers."

"Aren't they?"

"Hardly." He shook his head. "Any woman who has spent a night with a red-blooded American man knows there is no other greater lover in the world."

The champagne arrived, and John grabbed it from the waiter to open it himself. The cork popped, and the surrounding people clapped and whistled. John turned to wave and gave them all a roguish smile. He poured out two glasses and raised his in cheers.

"To a night full of promises!"

Lawrence took a tentative sip, and the sweet flavor filled her mouth. The bubbles tickled her tongue, and she felt the fizz as it settled and went down her throat. It wasn't as bad as she imagined, and the sweet flavor was actually quite delicate. She took another sip as John studied her.

"How's that?"

"It's quite nice," she smiled over the rim of her glass.

"Atta girl!" he cheered as he topped up her glass. "Now, I'm giving you a direct order to finish that glass and every other I pour for you, Stoner."

"I should take it slow," she said, shaking her head. "I've heard what alcohol can do to you."

"All it does is make us infinitely more interesting, beautiful, and invincible. We won't be able to keep our hands off each other once this bottle is done."

"That is indecent!" she laughed, suddenly swept away in the chaos and excitement of the night.

Her head began to swim and her muscles loosened. Although she might not normally have found it funny, she couldn't help but laugh in delight. It was exactly the sort of distraction she needed after her disappointment with Teresa, and she welcomed it gladly. She took another big drink as she shouted over to him.

"There is a lady present."

"Where?" he asked, craning his neck around as if searching for said lady.

"Oh!" she cried, laughter bubbling out of her again. "You're horrible."

With every passing glass of champagne, Lawrence's mood lifted just as John promised it would. They repeatedly held their glasses aloft and toasted each other and the night together. Random passersby would sometimes join in their toast, and absolute strangers joined in as they drank, laughing and cheering as if they'd been friends for years.

The two of them finished a bottle and then killed off another before Lawrence drunkenly agreed to let John take her out onto the dance floor. They moved in time with the other couples, swaying slowly to the music.

She placed her head on his shoulder and let his hand rest at the lowest part of her back. A numb, distant part of her mind warned her this was wrong, but she pushed the thought away. At the end of the slow dance, he leaned his head down to whisper something to her that she didn't quite catch and then kissed her. The kiss was nothing extraordinary, and that was all she needed to know.

Looking up into his green eyes, she smiled pitifully. "That's too bad."

"What's too bad?" he murmured.

She shook her head and rested it back on his chest. If the night proved anything to her, it was that some things simply cannot be forced. It might be easier, but it would be pointless.

The lights in the room elongated, stretching wide no matter how hard she blinked. Every step became unsteady, and the stifling air of the club suffocated her. The more she tried to settle her mind, it felt as if she would be sick at any moment.

A strong, prickling feeling hit Lawrence. It was the same sensation she had felt just outside earlier that evening. Goosebumps raised on her arms and the hair on the back of her neck rose. She lifted her head from John's chest and tried to look around the room for the source, but found nothing.

The sudden movement caused her to become lightheaded and she dropped her head back down onto his chest with a thump. She focused on her breathing and did her best to relax. She stepped away from John abruptly, untangling her arms from his. She staggered back and bumped into another couple.

"Sorry, sorry," she muttered. She stumbled off the dance floor, desperate for some fresh air.

"What's the matter, honey? Where are you going?" John called out after her as she rushed past the tables.

Lawrence staggered out into the alleyway, startling a few passing couples as she burst from the doorway of the building. She steadied herself against the wall as she took a few deep breaths of the cool evening air. Her flushed cheeks felt hot against the cold brick and she heard her own heartbeat thumping loudly in her ears. Panic and unease bubbled up in her throat. She bumped against the building and crouched down to steady herself. *Calm down.*

"Hey."

A hand reached out and grabbed her around the elbow. She flinched away out of instinct, but came face-to-face with John. She let out a sigh of relief. He studied her face with a frown.

"Why'd you run off like that?"

"Oh, John," she said, shaking her head. She swallowed and breathed out through her nose. "I don't feel very good. I think I overdid it. I need to go home."

"Come here," he said, nodding. "I'll take care of you."

"Thank you, thank you," she mumbled.

She let him take her by the arm, guiding her down the walkway. She leaned on him heavily and lowered her head to keep her eyes focused on the passing ground below. They took a sudden sharp turn into an alleyway and he steered her further into the darkness.

"Where are we going?"

Lawrence tried to slow and raise her head in order to look back, but he kept a firm hand on her arm and kept them moving forward.

"Just follow me," he assured her, patting her arm.

She tried to slip her arm out, but his grip was too strong. She let out a soft gasp as his fingers pinched into the skin of her upper arm.

In her drunken haze, her terror intensified and actually sobered her up significantly. She felt so keenly that she had made a grave error in trusting John, but it was too late. Any coherent thoughts or efforts to get away became muddled. She tried to pull her arm out of his grasp and dig her heels in the ground, but it was useless.

John halted suddenly and faced her. He laughed lightly as he touched her cheek.

"What's the matter, honey? You're shaking like a leaf."

"You're scaring me," she whispered.

He grinned at that and stroked her cheek once more. She felt the sudden urge to snap her hand out and slap away the smile off his smug face.

51

"What's there to be scared of, huh?" he asked under his breath.

He stood so close to her that his hot breath, rank with the smell of liquor and smoke hit her face. The urge to vomit came back tenfold. Her head reared back to get away from the smell.

"Just take a few deep breaths and close your eyes."

Against her better judgment, Lawrence did close her eyes and inhaled slowly. The world continued to spin and she swayed even as she stood in place. On the second exhale, she felt thin lips and scratchy stubble of John's chin against her face. She pulled back in shock, bumping into the wall. He gave her another smirk and leaned in for another kiss, but she turned her face away.

"Stop," she breathed out.

She tried to step sideways out of his reach, but he just followed her. He used his large frame to bracket her in against the wall and her breath stuttered.

"What's the matter?" he asked.

"I said stop," she repeated, her voice a little louder. She tried to push him away, but it was like shoving against a boulder, and equally as useless. "I don't want this. I-I want to go home."

At that, he pushed her further against the wall and her head banged against the brick. She let out a gasp as her ears rang from the impact. She began to struggle against his ironclad grip, wiggling like a small bird caught in a snare.

"Let me go!" she screamed out, but he clamped a large, sweaty hand down across her face.

"Be quiet! People will hear you," he grunted under his breath. He shook her lightly as if to shake some sense into her. "You let me kiss you on the dance floor; what's the big idea?"

She continued to fight against him, kicking and twisting under his body. He locked her in with his legs and lowered his head again. He kissed her neck and cheek and all she could do was scream out in

52

protest under his hand. Tears welled in her eyes. Stuck between his body and the building, she felt suffocated as if she were being buried alive.

A sharp whistle rang out out on the street and both of their heads snapped in that direction. As John's attention was momentarily diverted, his grip around her body loosened slightly. She took the opportunity and threw her head forward, connecting with his cheekbone, which gave a satisfying thud. His head snapped back, and he let go of her entirely.

"Bitch!" he cried out as he grabbed his injured cheek.

He raised his hand and backhanded her roughly. Lawrence's head whipped harshly to the side and her cheek stung. She fell to her hands and knees, but once he collected himself, John grabbed her around the shoulders and pulled her up again. She squeezed her eyes shut. The only thing she could hope for was just for it all to be over soon.

The heavy weight of John's hands on her disappeared. Without his overwhelming body over hers, Lawrence stumbled and fell backwards against the wall, sliding down until she fell into a heap on the ground. She looked up and saw John a few paces off, staring into the darkness of the alley from where they entered.

A long shadow fell from the end of the street to where they were. The wind stopped and all noises seemed to cease. Even the far-off crash of waves fell mute. A short breeze stirred. From the darkness, a figure formed and began to drift forward slowly.

"What the hell is that?" cried John, stepping back and raising his hands to protect himself. "Stay away from me!"

He let out a sharp scream before it was cut off abruptly.

John got sucked into the shadows, swept away as if he were nothing but a paper doll, bending easily as he folded into two. The ringing of his screams echoed in Lawrence's ears.

The wind returned, and the noises on the street resumed. Whatever darkness gathered in the alley disappeared, and Lawrence was alone. She saw no sign of John, or anyone else for that matter. She looked down and saw a single brown leather shoe on its side, along with a few drops of blood on the dark concrete.

Lawrence retched against the building wall and fell onto her side. She laid her head down and let the darkness overcome her.

* * *

Sharp brightness blinded Lawrence as if she were looking into the sun itself. For a moment, she believed that she had actually died. She felt terrible, though, so the idea was fleeting. Her head pounded and her throat was dry and sore, as if she had swallowed sand. After a long minute of trying, she gave up on trying to sit up.

Lawrence lifted her head and when she looked around, she realized she was back in her hut, alone and safe. She exhaled deeply and whatever strength she had in that moment left her. She closed her eyes once more.

First, a soft whimper escaped her. Once the first tear fell, the rest quickly followed. Sobs shook her shoulders as she struggled to breathe evenly. A long trail of tears streaked down the sides of her face and soaked her pillow. Something outside scratched at her door, pushing at it to be let in.

Lawrence rose and opened it a sliver, wincing at the bright sunlight. She looked down at Stinky Boy, who waited outside with the same imperious look on his face. Lawrence hiccuped and gasped, laughing suddenly at the sight of him.

"Oh, Stinky Boy," she sighed out, wiping at her ruddy cheeks with her arm.

The cat cried out again and she stepped aside to let it in. She laid out his usual water and food, and knelt to pet him. Another wave of tears hit her and she put a hand on his head.

"I'm glad you're here."

The cat peered up at her and blinked slowly at her. She pet him a bit longer and it rubbed its head against her leg.

Lawrence remained in bed for the rest of the day and spent the time doing her best to try and remember exactly what had happened. The sensation of trying to remember and coming up blank on certain details made her stomach twist. She remembered leaving the restaurant and going to the secret club, drinking and dancing, but the rest after remained hazy. A shiver went up her spine and a fresh wave of hot tears welled up in her eyes.

There was something else she remembered, but she wished she hadn't.

When she shut her eyes, all Lawrence could see was the way John had disappeared into the dark and his horrifying screams. His single shoe and the few splatters of blood imprinted itself onto her mind. Something had saved her that night, and although she felt terrified, she couldn't help but think it had acted as a sort of guardian angel for her.

"Don't be silly, Lawrence Stoner," she murmured aloud to herself as she stared up at her cabin roof. "He's fine. He's fine. Nothing happened. Ghosts aren't real. Monsters aren't real."

She continued to recite this assurance to herself like a mantra. No doubt the alcohol exaggerated the details of her memory, and John truly was fine. She placed a hand over her chest, feeling the soft skin and the four sharp bumps where scabs had formed over what she believed to be spider bites. Whatever monsters lurked in the dark paled in comparison to the one she faced last night.

Lawrence allowed herself the day to be weak and then rose the next day as if nothing had happened. She vowed to move on from the experience and never think of it again. She had brushed up gently against the robes of death, felt its icy breath against her cheek, and walked away. She would not question why she was spared, only that she had been. She would not waste her time by being idle or dwelling in the dark. With a renewed vigor, Lawrence set her mind only to work, and more importantly, of moving forward.

Chapter 4

"Please, please!" a voice whined out in the dark, pleading pitifully. "Please, no! God!"

In a heavily wooded forest, John crawled, dragging his bloodied, beaten body forward on his elbows. All his former charisma and confidence had deserted him, and he seemed like a scared child. He peered back over his shoulder into the dark forest behind and let out another childish cry. When he turned his head forward, he seemed to see someone and his eyes sharpened.

"You!" he shouted, raising a bloody finger forward. "It's your fault. It's all your fault! You'll get yours!"

Lawrence woke with a start, shooting up in bed as if she had been electrified. A sharp knock at the door sounded.

"Mail!" a voice called out from outside. "I'd have left it in your box, but you haven't got one!"

Lawrence exhaled lowly as she calmed her frantic heart. She worked to tie her long hair into a braid as she nudged the door open with her hip. Outside, the young boy from the post office stood with a single letter in hand. He tipped his cap at her and held the letter out towards her.

"Thank you," murmured Lawrence, her voice a bit hoarse. "You want some water?"

The boy smiled politely and shook his head. Lawrence watched the boy leave as she sat on the wooden chair outside her hut. She breathed in some fresh air and turned the envelope over.

The black stationery was small, but thick and fine quality. A red seal with an ornate crest pressed into wax kept the letter closed, and Lawrence's name in spidery, cursive writing covered the back.

She opened it up and glanced over the short message on the greenish-black card:

Miss Lawrence Stoner,
Ms. Ophelia Aldane requests the pleasure of your company for dinner on Wednesday evening, April 10th, 1926, at six-thirty p.m. at Ashmore Hall.

The stocky card held an embossed image of the same crest that was on the wax seal. She flipped the card around in her hand several times, but saw no other information. Not a single smudge of ink or mark out of place could be seen. She held it up to her nose and caught the faintest scent of jasmine.

Lawrence read and reread the card about four times before she set it aside. As soon as she did, she'd pick it up and study it again. She read the words, but could not comprehend their meaning. Of all the places, she had not expected her one and only invitation to have come from Ashmore. She accepted the information with a strange calm.

All Lawrence could think about was the mystery and intrigue that surrounded the house. It would be better not to go at all. If there really was something dark or evil within its walls, she would not come out once she went in. The way the whole town spoke of the place made it seem as if nothing but death and horror awaited her inside.

"Don't be stupid," she murmured to herself.

This was nothing but an opportunity. Lawrence had promised to focus only on work, and to move forward past the dark memory surrounding John. Besides, she would be a fool to turn down the one reply she had gotten. The prospect of possibly making real money cemented Lawrence's decision. Although she was unsure of what may come, she would deal with it once the time came.

There was no denying that the moment Lawrence laid eyes on the house, she was drawn to it. The camellia grove and hidden garden felt particularly special to her, and she desired to know exactly what and who resided within. Now, she had a name.

Ophelia Aldane.

Any worries Lawrence had were mere trivialities that could be set aside to abate her own curiosities. Once she made that silent acknowledgment, all her worries greatly lessened.

Stinky Boy suddenly dropped down from the roof and stepped closer to where Lawrence sat outside, leaned up against the outside wall of her hut. She noticed his approach and held the card out towards him.

"What do you think?" she asked in complete seriousness.

He took a single look at the card and hissed, back arching, as if he were insulted just by looking at it.

"Yeah, well what do you know," she muttered. She rose then, and brushed off her skirts.

The decision was made. Curiosity and practicality won out over all.

Lawrence couldn't help but feel, though, as if she were standing before a dark doorway. From beyond the threshold, a secret voice, one only she could hear, was calling her forward, enticing her to enter. The pull was so strong she had no choice but to go. While she could have let things continue on as they were, she despised the very thought of it.

* * *

The long days of summer had arrived to Bar Harbor, and even the cool coastal winds could not entirely relieve the residents from the heat. Lawrence had strolled into town and situated herself at a small tea shop along the street. A couple wicker tables sat out under pale blue awning, the fabric fading and yellowing at the corners.

She sipped at a tall glass of iced tea, content to watch the people and day pass her by. During her second glass, a terrible scream cut through the town.

The anguish and raw pain in the noise caused all the people in the street to stop. Heads appeared from windows and doors, bobbing back and forth in search of the source. Lawrence stood too, looking both ways down the street along with the others.

A young man staggered out of a building, his hand clenched to his chest. He fell against the side of the brick wall as he continued to wail. The bright, breezy day illuminated his tormented face. Tears fell down his ruddy cheeks as he tore at his hair, yelling wildly and incomprehensibly.

Another older man rushed out of the building shortly after, grabbing at the man's elbows and jacket and urging him to come back inside. Everybody continued to watch until the man was led away. Even then, his screams and cries echoed down the quiet street. Once he was entirely out of view things slowly returned to normal, but a strange cloud pervaded them all.

"Terrible tragedy."

Lawrence turned and met eyes with a young man at the next table over who shook his head in abject sympathy. Aside from his golden complexion and sturdy, varsity build, the man had natural good looks and a pleasant, easy-going manner that showed he had clearly been brought up in the comfort of wealth. He wore a long-collared white shirt tucked into high-waisted beige trousers. On the table sat a Panama hat along with cigarettes and a gold lighter. It was no doubt genuine gold at that.

The man held a paper in hand and used his head to gesture once more to the path where the anguished man had disappeared down to make his point.

"Local girl croaked. Complete mystery. She was right as rain a week ago, and now she's stone cold."

"How awful," she murmured. Lawrence chewed on the inside of her cheek and took a mindless sip of her watered-down tea.

"That poor boy you saw just there now was her dear older brother. If I'm not mistaken, he just got back from school," the man explained. His eyes twinkled slightly as he leaned closer and lowered his voice. "If you wanna know the real drama, though, you'll want to hear about the manner of her death."

Lawrence couldn't help but lean in closer, fully engrossed. "What about it?"

"She was found in the family garden, lying out in the bushes as if she were napping. Naked as a babe, pale as a ghost, and all her blood was gone!"

"What!" Lawrence cried, horrified. "What could have possibly caused that?"

The man shook his head and shrugged. There was no real way to make sense of such a strange death or the subsequent tragedy of a young life taken too soon. He personally chose not to dwell on such macabre things for too long. Lawrence tilted her head down at him.

"Did you know her very well then?"

"Very little." He shook his head. "I believe her name was Teresa. Her father won the local flower contest last spring. You just saw him, he was the old man consoling the brother. My friend's grandfather was the one who handed out the prize to him. Poor bastard."

She abruptly turned around to his direction again. "Teresa? Not Teresa Doley?"

Surprise crossed the man's face and his brows rose slightly. "Oh, you know her? Or, knew, I suppose."

Lawrence's mouth opened and closed a few times. No words or thoughts came to her. It didn't make any sense. It almost felt as if she had misheard him. Teresa's bright, lively face flashed through her mind. Her throat began to close up and her mind began to reel.

"Teresa died?" she repeated, more so just to herself than anything, but the man heard anyway and nodded in confirmation. She shook her head, unable to grasp the idea despite repeating it to herself. "She's dead."

The man studied Lawrence's face and frowned. He then pursed his lips as an uncomfortable expression crossed his face.

"Seems you *did* know her quite well. I'm sorry to have been the one to tell you. Really."

Lawrence looked at him, noting his apologetic look and nodded, giving him a weak smile. "That's quite alright. We didn't know each other that well. Just a bit. She was quite nice, that's all. We had made plans, and she didn't show. Makes sense now."

The man appraised Lawrence in an almost clinical sort of way, looking her up and down once, and then folded up his newspaper. He offered his large hand out to her, holding it horizontally as if expecting her to put something into it.

"Patrick Gannaway. I don't believe I've ever seen you around before. You're not a student, are you?"

There was a bit of arrogance in his eyes and in the way he lifted his chin as he spoke. He then smiled, and it was easy to imagine all the young women who would swoon if it were ever directed their way. It had very little effect, though, on Lawrence, who shook her head. He nodded, pleased.

"Good. I despise those who are younger and prettier than me. What do you go by, kid?"

"Uh, Lawrence Stoner. Friends call me LJ."

She took his hand and gave it a brief shake. Her eyes narrowed momentarily as she studied him more closely. All at once, she remembered and pointed to him.

"I've seen you before."

Patrick smiled another blinding grin and leaned forward. "Oh, really? You've seen me, and I haven't seen you. That's exciting."

"You don't happen to own a sleek little white car, do you?"

"I do indeed." Patrick's eyes brightened. "Say, you must live nearby. Do you mind?"

He asked as he gestured to Lawrence's table, rising from his own before she could answer. Nevertheless, she shook her head and cleared some space for him. He took the seat closest. Her shoulders tensed slightly as he did, but she said nothing. John's face flashed through Lawrence's mind and she stiffened slightly.

"You alright there, LJ?" He frowned as he looked over at her, and did genuinely seemed concerned. "You went all stiff."

Lawrence quickly shook her head and put on a placating smile. "I'm fine. Tea?"

"No, thanks," he said as he held his hand up. "So you're new to town."

"This town might be a bit too small," Lawrence snorted out a laugh.

He shook his head in response and crossed his sturdy legs. The expensive wool creased as he did, but he paid no mind to it. He took out a thin cigarette and offered one to her, which she declined.

"No thank you, I don't smoke."

As he lit his cigarette, he exhaled and set the case aside. "It really is. Small, I mean. Have you moved in nearby?"

"I took up a little hut near Egg Rock," Lawrence explained. Patrick's face distorted into a look of distaste and pity.

"What?"

"Must be a difficult place to live," he said. "You know, all those houses came in within the last five years? It's really done a number on the value of the land up here. Thank god we've got the nature reserve to keep them away. Sort of a natural Hadrian's wall, if you will."

"You're talking about the homes south of the park?" she asked.

He nodded grimly, and she understood. He was specifically referring to the property of newer mansions. He saw her expression and held his hands up in defense.

"I've nothing against them, not really," he explained. "They're just different. Once you spend any real time with them, though, it's clear as crystal that money just can't buy everything. Like manners. Some of them are absolute brutes, LJ."

"I see."

She nodded, but didn't understand. Money was money, and there were those who had it and those who didn't. It seemed an alien, curious concept to her how the length and duration one had held onto money mattered. However, it was not something she was in any great danger of needing to worry about anytime soon.

"And what is it you do down there in Egg Rock?" he asked smoothly with a puff of his cigarette.

"I'm a painter."

"A painter," repeated Patrick, who nodded his head, impressed. "I've met a few painters. All degenerates, of course. I'm sure that means we'll get along just swell."

He laughed, and Lawrence couldn't help but chuckle as well.

"What are you painting?"

"Well, mostly the land at the moment; however, I'm hoping to do a few portraits. I put out an ad and left my cards at a few houses."

"*Viel glück,*" he chuckled, raising his cup to her. "Which houses did you leave your card at? Perhaps I can give you some advice."

"Oh, that's very kind," she said, turning to him. "I visited most of the houses along the bay, I think. All the houses on Park and Ignatius. I went from the bottom of the hill up to Ashmore Hall."

At the mention of Ashmore, Patrick turned his head to her with a curious expression. Thinking he was just confused, Lawrence continued on.

"It's by the water over on Widow's Weep Cliff. The red one?"

"The red one," he repeated, laughing. The smoke curled around his face in long ribbons. "Well, as a matter of fact, I'm staying with a chum of mine practically next door. Maybe you know of the Sinclairs?"

Lawrence shook her head. "To be quite honest, I don't know many people east of the Mississippi, and my circle the last two years has been strictly Italian."

"Poor girl. Well, you're quite lucky to have bumped into me then." Patrick straightened a bit as he held his hand flat against his chest. "I suppose I'll take you under my wing. First order of business is introducing you to the Sinclairs. They're just good people through and through, Augusta and her grandfather, I mean. He's the big cheese in town. You know him, and you'll know everybody. He's the owner of Old Canary Green; it's spitting distance from Widow's Weep. Well, I suppose you've been if you say you left your card there. I wonder why he never said anything about it. They've got a wonderful little parcel directly south of the trail along the cliffs. Have you been yet? I go all the time; I'm mad for them. The trails, I mean."

"Oh, I take that walk from my little hut." Lawrence smiled, knowing exactly which trails he meant. "Although, not quite all the way up to Widow's Weep. And, I think I do remember the house. It was the lovely green one with the great big lawn and pool. Yes, I think I know what you're talking about now."

Patrick looked at her then with another disarming smile and seemed to realize something. He raised his hand to call over the waiter, who came shuffling over at great haste, and ordered fresh juice, two more glasses, and a few bits to nibble on.

He hadn't even bothered to look at any menu. Patrick seemed like the type who just ordered whatever came naturally to him in the moment, right off the top of his head. It seemed to work, though, as the waiter simply nodded and rushed off.

Patrick helped himself to one of the cookies laid out on the table and gave Lawrence a friendly wink as he did. He leaned back in his chair and twirled his lighter between his fingers.

"Auggie will love you; she's a peach. Gentle as a lamb, but a bit daffy. She's always complaining about the lack of society, but I don't know what's so wrong with me and Edwin. We're perfectly good boys. Speak of the devil."

Lawrence raised her head and followed where Patrick waved lazily to an approaching figure down the street. A tall, thin man with round wire spectacles and dark, coiled hair approached from down the sidewalk. He had a bit of a clumsy gait, like a newborn calf. He wore thick gray trousers like Patrick, but a proper shirt and tie under a white knit vest. The day was certainly too hot for the way he was dressed, and he seemed to be suffering for it. His eyes were dark and piercing, and they took up immediate attention on his otherwise sallow face.

The man weaved between passing pedestrians with a stack of books under his arm. He itched at his neck, where the collar rubbed against the skin, grimacing as he did so. He stopped in front of their table and mopped his brow with an old handkerchief from his front pocket.

"Geez, Pat, I'm soaking through my shirt. Let's grab Birdy and get going," he muttered as he undid the top button of his shirt. He then noticed Lawrence and tipped his head in silent greeting. He then nodded his head sideways at her to Patrick.

"Who's your friend?"

Patrick raised his hand and waved between the two of them.

"Edwin, meet LJ. LJ, this is Edwin Ernest, and he really is."

She smiled and laughed lightly as Edwin rolled his eyes, sighing and shifting the books to his other arm.

"One day, Pat, you'll have to hang that one up and find something new to say."

"Never mess with perfection." Patrick snickered to himself, pleased. He pushed out a chair with his leg for Edwin to join them.

As he sat, Lawrence observed Edwin more closely and compared the two friends as they spoke together. While perhaps not as conventionally attractive as Patrick, Edwin was at least a full head taller and more well-proportioned. The thick eyebrows over his spectacles gave him some charm and added character to his face. The tenor of his voice was low, bookish, and slightly condescending by default, so one always felt a bit out of depth when speaking to him.

"Shall we start? I think we've waited a respectable amount of time; I'm gasping!" moaned Patrick, slapping a hand down onto his friend's bonier shoulder.

The waiter arrived and set down more cups and fresh juice.

Patrick promptly tossed out the old tea from his cup and took out a small flask from his inner pocket. He tipped in some of the amber contents and handed it directly to Edwin, who drank it in a single gulp. He held the flask out to Lawrence with a suggestive shake.

Lawrence felt a bit of bile rise in her throat at the mere thought of drinking again so soon. She swallowed it down and shook her head with a soft smile.

Patrick chuckled. "Suit yourself."

Edwin shook his empty cup at Patrick to fill it again. Instead, Patrick leaned over to Lawrence.

"Didn't you say you were just in Italy?"

She nodded her assent, and he looked horrified.

"My god, at least tell me you had a bit of fun while you were over there," said Patrick. He took a look at Lawrence's face and just laughed again, hitting his knee.

"My god, no smoking, no drinking. What the hell do you do all day?"

"A great many things," she said, crossing her arms.

"Yes, a great many things. A great many things that can always be improved with a drink in hand. Don't you agree, Eddy?"

"On this particular issue, I'm inclined to agree with you, Gannaway. Just don't let it get to your already enormous head." Edwin turned his head slightly to regard Lawrence with a raised brow. "Whatever were you doing in Italy, may I ask?"

"Painting, or rather, learning to paint under a master."

"I see," hummed Edwin. "It's quite a beautiful country."

"So you've been."

He nodded. "Quite a few times."

"Why the devil would anyone want to leave America?" interjected Patrick, with an incredulous look on his face. "And where the hell is Augusta?"

He checked his gleaming pocket watch, snapping it shut. "It's nearly half past two already."

"The 'Sweetheart of Bar Harbor' is making her rounds," answered Edwin.

"Then, we'll need another drink. Or two."

Patrick tipped out the rest of his flask into both his and Edwin's cups. They clinked glasses before they both took their next sip. Lawrence kept looking both ways, sure that someone would see the men drinking in broad daylight. No one, though, seemed to care at all. Anyone who did see simply turned their head and continued on their way. Patrick lit another cigarette and looked to his friend.

"Say, did you finish your work, bud?"

"Yes, for today. All books but one I've ordered have arrived," confirmed Edwin, who patted the texts under his arm.

He held them close, as if they were terribly precious. Lawrence tried to make sense of the titles, but they were either too obscured or in an entirely different language. It seemed Edwin was a true academic, through and through.

"You checked in about the Doley girl, I presume," Patrick murmured, checking under his thumb nail. He shot a fleeting glance towards Lawrence, but his expression remained neutral.

Edwin nodded with a grim and disappointed look on his face. "I stopped in on Dr. Mordray to inquire after her. I've suggested a full autopsy of the body be performed. Unfortunately, it seems the family is quite against it. Religious reasons. They'd prefer to have her buried before the weekend, post haste."

"Yes, God is a bit tetchy about poking and prodding His dead," Patrick muttered into his cup. He cleared his throat loudly.

"Bit of a grim start to the season, isn't it, Eddy boy?" Patrick remarked languidly.

He seemed entirely detached from the idea of death, and his attitude was nearing boorish. His eyes, though, contained an irrefutable sadness that revealed his true feelings.

Lawrence clasped her hands tightly in her lap, but Edwin's eyes flickered over to her as she did.

"Didn't a boy in Derby also die recently?" Lawrence asked, recalling what Teresa had mentioned to her, particularly the details regarding his manner of death. Only Edwin nodded gravely. "It's not at all related, right?"

Edwin studied Lawrence, his eyes narrowing slightly. "A curious question to ask."

She turned away then, unable to stand the full brunt of Edwin's assessing gaze. "It's just that. Curiosity."

"Yes, a young man did," he said, chewing on his bottom lip as he thought. He cracked the knuckles in his left hand as he spoke. "There are certain paralleling factors in both the circumstances of the deaths and the conditions of the bodies that give one reason to believe there is some measure of correlation; the real question, though, is whether correlation relates to causation. With just two bodies, though, it's a bit difficult to say. At the very least, it'd be hardly advisable to try and come to any sort of conclusion. Data, after all, is the keystone to the arch of conclusive truth. *Veritas omnia vincit.*"

"English, you donut," teased Patrick, sipping at his drink as if he were on the back of a yacht.

Edwin turned to his friend with a bored, almost exasperated, look.

"Does having your family's name on a university's library mean anything if you refuse to actually go in one and read what's inside?" snapped Edwin in response. He waved his hand as he spoke. "It's not just a pretty marble building, you know. You may actually learn something for once, Gannaway."

Rather than take any offense, Patrick laughed uproariously, grabbing his chest as he coughed between the little spurts of laughter.

"How dare you, Ernest? Are you implying I got into Harvard because of my money?" He leaned forward with a dangerous twinkle in his eye and a crooked smile. "Them's fighting words, boy."

Edwin simply rolled his eyes as he pushed his glasses further up his nose, not at all intimidated or impressed by the promise of violence, playful or not.

"No, I am suggesting it was because of your *daddy's* money."

"Well, no one has ever accused you of being a liar, Ernest. And by God, your honor, a liar he is not," laughed Patrick, raising his glass in salute to no one in particular.

"How exactly did the boy in Derby die?" Lawrence pressed, fixated on what had otherwise become a forgotten conversation.

Edwin looked over to her, brows raised in surprise that she was still interested, and leaned forward. He pushed his glasses up again, and the gesture must have been some sort of invisible tell of his since Patrick groaned and leaned back in his seat.

"Well, he died after a number of weeks, which is quite unlike what happened to Teresa. However, it seems the changes came on rather drastically. One day, he was fine, and the next, he wasn't. He suffered terribly. By the second week, he could hardly sit up in bed. He said his arms felt like they were a million pounds being held underwater and tied to an anchor. He was as pale as a corpse and almost as skinny as one. He muttered nonsense all day long and only stopped once he slept. They thought it must be something like influenza, but he hadn't a cough or a high temperature. In fact, he was as cold as ice, and they found him wandering around outside at night! When he passed, they said it was a blessing."

"An interesting definition of a blessing," murmured Patrick, his cheeks turning slightly pink from the heat and drink.

Edwin looked sideways at him with a disapproving look, but continued on.

"Unfortunately, the Tillermans also refused to have a formal autopsy performed as well. Just like Teresa, most of Thomas' blood was missing as well."

"Goodness," Lawrence murmured, shaking her head.

It was a terrible way to go. Not that dying in any way is pleasant, but to suffer through an illness and die was perhaps the worst. She shuddered and wondered exactly how aware the poor man was of what was happening and what was to come. Did Theresa go through a similar fate too?

Patrick smiled and slapped his hand on Edwin's shoulder, which seemed to be a particular habit of his. "Enough of this dreary conversation, Eddy boy. Now, LJ here has been up to Big Red on Widows Weep."

Edwin's face changed in a moment. He was cold and analytical in one moment, but then bright and curious like a puppy dog in the next. He crossed his legs and leaned forward, eyes widening behind his spectacles.

"No kidding. Auggie said it was abandoned. No one's been around for decades," said Edwin as he perked up. He pushed back hair from his damp forehead. "How do you know the owners?"

Lawrence wavered a bit as she did her best to maintain eye contact with Edwin. There was something unnerving about his direct gaze, and it felt as if he were always searching for some kind of truth in one's eyes, even if it were a simple discussion about the weather. Lawrence felt the heat of that gaze as she spoke to him then, and she felt the admission that she had been invited to dine there on the tip of her tongue. She couldn't come to say it, though, and averted her gaze. She focused instead on moving her glass around.

"I don't," she explained. "I simply left my card at the house, that's all."

"What was it like?" asked Patrick.

"I didn't really see much, to be honest. I only spoke to the housekeeper," she said. "There is a lovely garden, though."

"Ah yes, 'Mettle Hettle'," mused Patrick with a soft grin. "The only woman with the guts and lack of brains to live in the Devil's Den."

"Patrick," chastised Edwin, shaking his head like a disapproving professor.

Patrick, unbothered, smoked his cigarette.

"She was quite nice," Lawrence argued. "Though perhaps a bit jumpy."

"Who can blame her?" Patrick smirked. "You know, the owners

are a bit of a hot topic around here, and the house has a bit of a reputation."

"Yes, I've heard."

"And what exactly is it that you've heard?" he asked with a raise of his brow.

"That it's cursed, and people have this sort of superstition around it. Bad things happen when the lamps go on, apparently. And then the usual with witchcraft and devil worship, of course."

"Of course," smiled Patrick. "Total hogwash, of course. They're royals, or used to be, at least."

"That's his theory," remarked Edwin in forced nonchalance, moving his thin shoulders up and down as he stretched them out. He turned his head away and observed the street and the people walking by.

"It's the generally accepted one," countered Patrick. He placed a hand across his chest. "I'm partial to the belief that they were once rulers of a relatively small, unknown land who were violently deposed or abolished from their kingship in some Russian Revolution-esque way. All the secrecy and insistence on keeping their distance from the rest of good society certainly reeks of shame, don't you think?"

"That's certainly what they say," murmured Edwin. He looked at Lawrence then with a less amused, almost bored expression. "LJ, you will learn very quickly that you cannot attend any dinner parties or enter any clubs in Bar Harbor without having to entertain the famous conspiracy surrounding Ashmore Hall at least once during the course of the night."

"Curious timing of events, though, isn't it?" added Patrick, absent-mindedly. "It looks like we've got our own boogeyman here on the coast."

He turned to Lawrence with another wink.

"New Orleans had the axeman, and London has Jackie Boy. Bar Harbor deserves some notoriety. The 'Red Ghoul of the Bay', or something like that."

"I'm sure it's just that," muttered Edwin, suddenly serious. "Unfortunate timing."

"There haven't been any other reported deaths in this town, have there?" asked Lawrence suddenly, her voice catching slightly as she asked. "Perhaps recently?"

The two men paused for a moment as they looked to each other and then at her. Edwin shook his head.

"I don't believe so."

"I see," she said, exhaling slightly with relief.

"Why do you ask?" he asked with great interest.

"No reason."

She glanced up quickly, meeting his eyes for a brief moment before she turned away again. Edwin continued to study her, and she felt his eyes on her, but she did her best to remain impassive and watch the passing pedestrians. Edwin opened his mouth, but was interrupted.

"Boys!"

A woman across the street yelled out and waved her arms wildly. She then ran straight across the road without looking either way. One car came to a screeching halt and swerved out of the way at the last second. They honked their horns loudly, and she yelled out an unladylike response that made Lawrence blush. Patrick laughed loudly, hitting his knee. Edwin only winced as he shot up out of his seat when the car came close to hitting her.

The woman arrived to the table and brought a breeze of freshness with the sway of her short skirt. She walked with great conviction and each step was powerfully confident. Uncaring of decorum or modesty, she spoke loudly and anyone within the vicinity heard exactly what she had to say.

She threw up her arms at the trio, the little beaded purse at her wrist swinging like a wild pendulum.

"There you two are!"

Augusta Sinclair was a beautiful woman. Her fiery copper hair was cut short and kept flat at the top. The ends flared out dramatically into wild curls that framed her sweet face, so it looked quite like a pyramid. Her voice was light and melodic, and she had a silly little laugh that tended to punctuate every other sentence.

Once Lawrence got to know her better, she came to understand that Augusta possessed the enviable and inimitable ability to cheer any unhappy person and diffuse the most difficult situations. It was not something easily taught, and more so a natural element of her personality.

"Auggie, meet our friend LJ. She's just come back from Italy." Patrick introduced the two women.

Augusta grabbed both of Lawrence's hands in hers and shook it emphatically. She shoved Patrick away from Lawrence's side and took his seat.

Lawrence's tense shoulders relaxed as the woman scooted in closer. She intertwined their arms together as if they were the oldest of friends. Augusta smelled distinctly of rose water and peppercorn, and it absolutely overwhelmed the senses. She pushed in closer with a bright smile.

"You don't say! Did you buy a place in the area? How grand. A young filly like you buying a big old house all on your own. How modern."

She giggled again and bumped shoulders with Lawrence. There was a slight gap between her teeth and Lawrence only remarked on how charming it made Augusta look.

"Italy, eh? Are you some Italian heiress then? You don't look Italian, but you may be a heiress. You've got the right disposition; I can already tell. You've got the chin of a rich gal. I would know; I'm practically an expert." She whistled as she looked Lawrence up and down. It was very unladylike, but it seemed to suit her. "Gosh, you're a dish; look at that waist. Look at those legs! Look, we've got the same profile. Don't we, Eddy?"

Augusta talked with little rest between each thought. She spoke loudly and fluidly, each word imbued with as much strength and sense of truth throughout, so even her opinions seemed black and white. Edwin seemed to seriously analyze the two women, and Lawrence felt her cheeks flush under the intense scrutiny. It was horrifying to be compared to anyone, much less someone like Augusta. While Lawrence turned her head down, Augusta raised her chin higher, turning side to side to allow him to get a better look. At last, he sighed, shaking his head.

"Hard to say, Birdy. LJ seems to have a more prominent nose. Yours is more pushed in like a pug," he said with mock seriousness.

Patrick snorted loudly and clapped a hand over his nose and mouth. He continued to snort as he laughed particularly hard, his shoulders shaking. Augusta glared at Edwin until he winked and smiled at her. She sniffed daintily and sighed, appeased.

Lawrence leaned into Augusta's side to address her directly, speaking lowly to her. "I've not bought anything; no, I'm renting a small hut in Egg Rock. I'm just a painter."

A thrill went through the boys as they excitedly repeated to Augusta all they had discussed up until her arrival. She asked the usual questions, and when she was caught up, she laughed uproariously with her head tilted back. Although Lawrence was no heiress or really anyone of any importance or wealth of any kind, Augusta didn't care a fig. She kept her arm wrapped tight around her new friend, and Lawrence liked her all the more for it.

As Patrick had no more to drink, Augusta naturally reached into her own bag and produced her own silver flask. The boys applauded her and she poured a little extra into their cups, which were now mainly liquor with only a little bit of juice. Augusta went to tip some into Lawrence's, but she quickly covered it with her hand.

"Incorruptible like a saint," murmured Patrick.

Augusta let out another silly giggle and overturned the rest of the flask into her own cup.

"She'll help keep our noses clean," Augusta agreed. She gave a little wink to Lawrence before she tipped back her drink.

"If we were any sort of decent people, we'd tell LJ to run as far as possible in the other direction," said Edwin with a shake of his head.

"Good thing we're not," laughed Patrick. He opened up his cigarette case and lit one for Augusta and then another for himself.

Augusta touched one of the bows that kept Lawrence's long hair in her braid and fixed it for her. She raised her downturned eyes to Lawrence and gave her a soft smile. There was something strangely familial about the gesture, and Lawrence felt her heat pang.

"So you're all alone in the world, living on your own in a little wooden shack by the sea?"

"I guess that's the up and down of it."

Augusta's eyes went dewy as she looked off in the distance.

"Gosh, how romantic," she said, sighing. "A real working girl, a starving artist who studied in Europe and came back to America to earn her way and make her name!"

She held her hands out like she was selling the next big film. She turned to Lawrence, then, with a pleading look. "Remember us when you're rich and famous, won't you?"

Lawrence laughed, "I'm in no serious danger of becoming either anytime soon."

"Oh, but you're the real McCoy, I can tell. You've got the aura. I can see it now." Augusta turned to the boys with another bright smile.

"Our little town is going to be immortalized by the famous painter, L.J. Stoner. They're gonna put a plaque up right there," she pointed to the wall above their heads. "Famous painter L.J. Stoner and friends once drank hooch and juice on this stoop."

"Personally, I'd like to see you paint the walls of Ashmore. It'll be like we have our own man on the inside," said Patrick.

"Why bother? No one's there," said Augusta nonchalantly as she focused on ashing her cigarette. Her response was too quick and for once her vibrant, upbeat attitude cooled.

"The lamps came on," Patrick pointed out. "Or did you forget?"

"I didn't forget anything," Augusta said, icily. She shrugged a delicate shoulder."Who cares if they're on? No one is home."

"Has no one really ever met them?" Lawrence asked. "Ever?"

Augusta shook her head, and her curls bounced around wildly. The two men merely shrugged and didn't seem too bothered by it. The three shared a strange look, and although fleeting, Lawrence noticed. Augusta giggled and waved her hand as if it hardly was a worry of hers.

"No sense of neighborly affection, I suppose. Lord knows if there's one or one hundred of them! I wouldn't care a wit!"

"Actually, didn't Pa meet one of them?" Patrick suddenly asked, but the way he did, it seemed clear he already knew the answer. Augusta shot him a deadly look, and there was a strained silence around the table.

Edwin cleared his throat politely.

"Pa is quite the patron of the arts, isn't he, Birdy?"

"Oh, absolutely!" clapped Augusta, her dark mood clearing immediately. "How exciting. Edwin you brilliant man, what would we do without you?"

Edwin blushed faintly at the praise, and Patrick snickered, nudging him lightly with the toe of his leather shoe. Augusta turned to Lawrence and squeezed her arm.

"Come to dinner over at ours as soon as you can. No, that's not quite good enough, is it? If you never set a firm date, no one ever commits. Come over on Monday for dinner."

"We're at the Astors on Monday," Edwin gently reminded her. "We should be free on Tuesday."

"Tuesday!" repeated Augusta, satisfied.

"In fact, you come on over whenever you're feeling blue," added Patrick.

There was a strange familial bond between the three of them. They had no qualms about speaking on behalf of each other. It tugged at Lawrence's heart as she wished she could have only a fraction of that sort of closeness to someone. She merely bit down on the inside of her cheek as she swallowed her sadness.

"Auggie's got a soft spot for anything in need of saving. We're proof of that." Patrick gestured between himself and Edwin. "Saved me from a dreadful season down south. Have you ever seen Florida skeeters, LJ?"

He shuddered at the thought.

Edwin raised his hand. "Egypt."

"Oh, but how amazing! Egypt!" gasped Lawrence.

"Yes, it is for the first few times, or a few dozen. It's just that they go every year!" Edwin exclaimed, exacerbated.

As Augusta giggled, smoke punctuated each laugh with a little puff that blew out of her nose and mouth. Patrick clapped his hand down on Edwin's back again.

"He's right, though," Augusta smiled as she leaned into Lawrence's side. She picked up a small lock of Lawrence's hair between her fingers. "You just come on over whenever you want. Day or night. Crawl down the chimney or sneak in through the window, for all I care! You can stay for as long as you like, if need be. I can't wait for dinner on Monday."

"I thought you said Tuesday?" said Lawrence.

"Did I?" Lawrence nodded and Augusta let out a little snort. "Oh, applesauce. I'm so silly. Sometimes it feels like nobody's home."

She giggled again as she tapped the side of her head and hiccuped slightly. Lawrence chuckled and patted the girl's hand gently.

"Mind you, I won't take no for an answer. Pa will want to meet you; he's mad about Italy. He's mad about Napoleon."

"Napoleon was French, Auggie," said Patrick. He yawned as he fanned himself with his hat, leaning further back in his chair.

"Really?" asked Augusta, raising her head from where it lolled to the side. "Well, then why was he mad about Italy if the damned man was French?"

"He said Neapolitan, I think," Edwin added from his corner.

"No, I can't believe it," frowned Augusta. "What in the damned hell even is a Neapolitan?"

"Do you perhaps mean Naples?" asked Lawrence.

Augusta's brows furrowed further in confusion. Edwin smirked into his drink and his thin shoulders moved up and down as he laughed silently. The drink had begun to affect him as well.

"What does Naples have to do with it?" asked Augusta innocently with a tilt of her head.

"I believe it's a type of sandwich the Italians eat," declared Patrick quite confidently with the same arrogant upturn of his chin. Only Edwin and Lawrence shared a brief look, but they remained silent.

"A sandwich," Augusta snorted, picking up a half-eaten cookie and popping it into her mouth. Between chews, "What a gas!"

Her bright smile fell a bit as she picked up her glass and realized it was empty.

"Oh dear, all out. There's nothing so sad as running out of drink. Don't you think?"

"Quite right," nodded Patrick.

The four of them stayed there for a little bit under the shade, chatting idly. The conversation ping-ponged around the table until Lawrence checked the time and declared she had to go.

"We'll drive you!" offered Augusta, tossing her cigarette away haphazardly.

Lawrence's eyes widened at the amount of cash Augusta carelessly threw down on the table. Augusta waved goodbye to the waiters and blew kisses to them all, which they received with pleasant smiles and kisses back.

The trio moved as a unit from the table to Patrick's car, and they pulled Lawrence right along with them. She piled into the back with Augusta while the two boys took the front. Lawrence couldn't help but brush her hand back and forth across the soft, supple leather.

The moment the engine roared, Augusta began to sing, chanting a bit off-key at the top of her lungs. She wasn't content, though, until the rest of them all joined in. Whenever the group passed another car, Augusta waved and greeted them warmly. They drove in merry company all the way down the lane until they dropped Lawrence off at her hut and went on their way.

All at once, things were suddenly silent and still once the trio had departed. Only until Lawrence was removed from their company did she have the chance to reflect. She nearly forgot all about Teresa. It had only been a few hours earlier that she had learned of her sudden, untimely death. Lawrence's stomach dropped and she felt a flush of guilt creep over her.

There was something undoubtedly dangerous about keeping company with Augusta, Patrick, and even Edwin. They all, except perhaps Edwin, were so unburdened that it was easy to get swept away by their frivolity.

Lawrence considered that she may simply be too old-fashioned for the progressive, fast-paced East Coast. Her outlook and general attitude were forbidding and a bit Puritan in their seriousness.

Certain topics, such as death, deserved a certain solemnity of attitude and respect; yet, it felt as if none of that applied out there.

In an act of penance, Lawrence sat outside her hut and thought only of Teresa, whom she had otherwise believed to be alive and well up until that morning. For all the faults and negatives she had imagined on the night they were meant to meet, Lawrence spent the rest of the night thinking of how good and sweet Teresa had been. It seemed death touched the ones who really deserved a little bit more time on earth than others.

Chapter 5

Fittingly, gray clouds gathered on the first morning Lawrence returned to the dock after learning of Teresa's passing. She stood at the edge of the wooden pier and looked out at the dark sea, watching as the boats swayed and the storm clouds promised nothing but tempestuous weather.

Nevertheless, she set up her easel and sat down. Great progress had already been made during her short acquaintance with Teresa, so only the finer details remained. A strange, grim determination settled within Lawrence that urged her to finish it as quickly as possible. Even as curious onlookers came up behind to look over her shoulder, Lawrence ignored them totally and didn't engage in any small talk.

The painting slowly formed before her eyes with the passing minutes and hours. Just like gold being unearthed from a muddy riverbank, being cleansed by the water as its brought up, the painting revealed itself: the rickety dock, the pale cornflower-blue sky and streaking, wispy clouds, and the stirring boats with their billowing sails on the midnight-blue waves .

On the day of her dinner at the Sinclairs, Lawrence sat for the last time. The wind sliced across the bay and cut through her thin coat, biting at the bare skin that she couldn't cover.

She added the last highlights and little details to the land and sea. White touched the tips of the sea foam, and stripes were added to the flags billowing in the imagined wind. This was meant to be the part she would normally spend the most time on, but the rough lines and shadows seemed more fitting for the rugged place and reflected what Teresa most likely looked out to every morning from her place of work.

Lawrence looked at her finished work, and no sense of pride or accomplishment filled her, as it usually did. Instead, a sudden wave of grief and sadness washed over her then and she cried quietly to herself. When her tears dried and her breathing evened, Lawrence stood and packed up her tools.

It took a bit of asking around and a short trip to the county registrar, but Lawrence knocked on the Doley family's door a little before tea time. The door opened a sliver and a pallid, thin woman with red eyes and a sharp, beakish nose appeared. Lawrence immediately recognized the same golden hair that had been passed down to Teresa.

"Yes, may I help you?" she asked in a feeble voice.

Even in this time of greatest adversity, Mrs. Doley maintained her decorum and manners.

"Hello, you're Mrs. Doley, correct?"

The woman nodded her head.

"My name is Lawrence Stoner. May I come in?"

Mrs. Doley hesitated a moment, but stepped aside, and Lawrence entered the humble family home. It was a single-story house with a modest sitting area and kitchen in front. A single table sat pushed up against the wall with a few chairs and a small sofa by the stove with well-loved pillows and hand-knit throws dressed over.

Lawrence quietly observed the few postcards and paintings on the wall, taking note also of the large cross that hung over the north wall. Although there was not much space, she could tell they were a once-happy family and it must have held a cheery warmth at one time. However, there was a clear sense of something, or someone, missing, and it simply felt cold and stagnant.

"Who's that Peg?" A weary voice called from the back.

Mrs. Doley didn't immediately reply, and an older gentleman appeared at the doorway connecting the front of the house to the bedrooms in the back. Their eyes met, and Lawrence immediately recognized the older man from the street from the other day. She nodded her head to him, but he simply stared at her.

He had a weather-beaten face and there was more gray than black in his thick head of hair and mustache. He had the stout, firm physique of a man who had worked the land since his youth. Any spark of life or youth in his eyes were gone, and he was aged at least ten years his true age. He shot a distrustful look at Lawrence, which reminded her of a scared animal.

"Good afternoon, Mr. Doley."

"Who are you?"

"Won't you please sit, Miss Stoner?" Mrs. Doley smiled politely and gestured to one of their nicer armchairs by the fire. "Can I get you some tea?"

"That's quite alright, Mrs. Doley; thank you. I've only just come to give something to you."

Lawrence handed over the covered canvas that she had in hand. Mrs. Doley took it, and after unwrapping it, swallowed thickly. Lawrence gestured to the work in explanation.

"Your daughter, Teresa, was very kind to me. We met when I was painting this on the pier. I promised I'd show it to her the moment I finished."

"Perhaps you have not heard," said Mr. Doley, his voice bitter and cold. "She's dead."

"Frances," murmured Mrs. Doley in a strained voice. She turned her red eyes to him in silent censure, but he didn't look at her. Lawrence only nodded in sympathy.

"Yes, I heard. My condolences."

"It's a very lovely painting," said Mrs. Doley, turning to Lawrence. She went to hand it back to her, but Lawrence shook her head.

"I'd like your family to keep it."

"We can't accept it," said Mrs. Doley.

Mr. Doley came forward from the rooms and stood behind his wife, inspecting the painting silently. He crossed his arms, and his lips were pressed into a thin line. He remained silent and withheld any opinions of her work.

"No, I must insist," Lawrence said. "You see, this pier was the exact view Teresa had while working in the cafe. I'd like for you to keep it. Please."

Mrs. Doley paused for a moment, her eyes shining, and all she could do was smile softly. She was a thoroughly gentle woman, and her grief was palpable. It caused a small lump to form in Lawrence's throat. Mrs. Doley turned and placed a hand on her husband's forearm.

"Please sit and join us for tea."

The three of them gathered in a small corner of the kitchen. A small plate of cookies and a pot of tea were laid out with three mismatched cups. Mrs. Doley poured, and they sat through a stretch of silence. Only the ticking of a small clock interrupted the quiet.

"Our eldest, Tom, has just returned from school, but he's out at the moment" Mrs. Doley whispered. "He's devastated. We all are, of course, but he's been hit quite hard. They had always been quite close."

"He's going to be somebody," Mr. Doley added gruffly, his eyes flickering momentarily over to Lawrence. She looked at him with touched surprise, and he grunted. "That's what Teresa always used to say."

He took a sip of his tea, his Adam's apple bobbing severely as he did.

"Yes, I believe I saw him in town," said Lawrence.

The Doleys raised their heads and shared a brief look. They knew exactly which moment Lawrence was referring to.

"It was a bit of a shock," Mrs. Doley said, clasping her hands together on the table. "We just can't make sense of it. She was smiling and laughing at dinner the night before...Well, before it started. She ate two plates because she was so hungry."

She shook her head, still confused by how it all happened. No doubt, she had replayed the night several times in her mind.

"It just doesn't make sense. Dr. Mordray-"

"The fraud!" muttered Mr. Doley. He sneered at the mention of the doctor's name and crossed his arms tight across his chest.

"Frances, what was he supposed to do?" Mrs. Doley wiped her nose with her handkerchief as she sniffed lightly. "She was already...gone by the time they got to her."

At the mention of Teresa's death, Mr. Doley lowered his head and coughed hoarsely. He quickly swiped the back of his hand across his face, turning away from the women as he did so. Lawrence caught the streak of tears that raced down his face anyways.

"The doctor said she had died rather quickly. Most of her blood was gone."

Mrs. Doley developed a far-off look in her eye as she wrapped both hands around her cup and recited what had occurred from memory.

"She looked like a little porcelain doll when we buried her."

Lawrence nodded her head, disturbed by the image, but she pictured it clearly. She saw Teresa's serene, soft face, her red cheeks and lips, as if she were merely napping. Her golden hair fanned out around her as she lay, tucked into her thin casket and wearing white robes like an angel. She shook the image from her mind and took a sip of her tea.

"I heard she was found out in the garden," Lawrence said. Mrs.

Doley nodded.

"She was lying in my roses." Mr. Doley spoke in a low voice. Lawrence turned to him, surprised by his admission. "They thought she had fainted, but she was stiff as a board. Not a drop of blood spilled, not a bruise on her."

Mr. Doley looked at her then with a peculiar look in his eye and an edge to his voice.

"I don't know what you've heard, but our sweet daughter was killed. Make no mistake of that. We've no evidence, but you ask anyone in town. They'll agree with us."

"Killed?" repeated Lawrence, incredulous at his confidence. He nodded his head. "Do you know who?"

"If I did, they'd not be alive now either; I can promise you that."

"Frances," Mrs. Doley whispered, her voice shaking. She turned to Lawrence with a pleading look. "We're not typically superstitious people, Miss Stoner. I mean, we are God-fearing folk."

"Of course," Lawrence said with a nod. "It is certainly odd. The circumstances. What would anyone want with that much blood, though? Is it truly impossible to believe it might have been a strange illness? I understand that might not be helpful, but-"

"Does a sickness make much more sense to you? Tell me, what sort of sickness does that to a healthy person over the course of a few nights? What sort of sickness, mind you, drains a person of all their blood?" asked Mr. Doley.

"I suppose that's true," conceded Lawrence.

"It's those damn lanterns." Mr. Doley shook his head. Mrs. Doley exhaled loudly, closing her eyes as she did. "Evil."

"You mean Ashmore?" asked Lawrence, surprised.

Mrs. Doley set her hand firmly on the table. Lawrence and Mr. Doley both turned to the woman, sobering once they saw the distressed look across her face.

88

"Frances, we'll not be getting into that now," Mrs. Doley said, her voice firmer than it had been as of yet.

Mr. Doley abruptly stood from the table. He returned to his room, and the door shut behind him with a loud thud. Mrs. Doley flinched slightly at the noise but gave Lawrence another polite smile all the same.

"Please forgive him. He's in pain, that's all. He doesn't know what to do about it."

"There's nothing to apologize for," Lawrence quickly said. "I'm sorry I shouldn't have-"

Mrs. Doley shook her head, silently telling Lawrence there was nothing to apologize for. They sat in silence for a moment before Lawrence reached forward and placed a gentle hand on Mrs. Doley's.

"What happened when she first fell ill?" she asked.

Mrs. Doley's eyes lifted for a moment and she looked to where Mr. Doley had disappeared to. She hesitated for a moment, and it seemed as if she would not say, but she licked her lips and began.

"She didn't come out for breakfast like she normally did," whispered Mrs. Doley. She kept her eyes firmly trained on the table, and her hands absentmindedly picked at the grain of the wood. "I went in to her room to wake her, but she wouldn't get up. I kept shaking her, and she was terribly cold."

She swallowed thickly and shook her head.

"We thought it was influenza, which still worried us, of course, but we didn't know any better. We called Dr. Mordray, and he simply confirmed our suspicions. Told us to give her lots of water, let her rest, and aspirin. It did help for a bit, and it seemed she was getting better. Then-," she said with a pause. Her dark eyes lifted to Lawrence's then with a disturbed look in them. "One night, I heard her through the door, speaking to someone. It sounded like she was begging. I had never heard my daughter's voice like that before. When I opened the door, there was no one there."

Mrs. Doley's expression grew haunted and her fingers began to pick at the wood furiously, scraping at it as if working to peel something off of it.

"What happened next, Mrs. Doley?" whispered Lawrence.

Their eyes met for a moment and Mrs. Doley shut her eyes, taking a moment before continuing on.

"Then it was the hallucinations. She kept saying there were demons in the walls that called to her. She said she saw eyes looking at her, spying. Next, came the sleepwalking. She'd crawl out of her bed and out the window like a wild animal, on all fours. We started tying her down to the bed to keep her put, but at night, all she'd do was thrash like a wild animal to be let free."

Mrs. Doley's voice cracked, faltering momentarily as she remembered the pitiful state her daughter had been in before her death.

"She began to grow so cold. Every day, she seemed to grow colder and stiffer, as if turning into a corpse before she truly became one. She kept telling me she was going to die, you know? You don't know what that's like as a mother. To hear your baby keep telling you that. It haunts me every time I lay my head down at night. I just see her apologizing to me, and telling me she'll wait for me at the Gates."

Mrs. Doley began to cry properly then and held a handkerchief to her mouth to keep the noise muffled lest Mr. Doley hear and come back out to investigate. She steadied her breathing and dried her tears.

"I failed her," she whispered. "I failed my daughter-"

"Mrs. Doley," said Lawrence, shaking her head. "You did no such thing."

"You don't understand," said Mrs. Doley, an expression of disdain across her face. "I kept things from my husband, and the doctor. It *is* my fault she's dead. On the first night, I helped bathe her, and I found four little holes right here."

She pointed to the base of her neck, where her throat met her shoulder.

Lawrence stiffened in her seat. She fought the urge to immediately touch the small dotted scars on her own breast. It felt as if they were burning then, but it was all in her mind.

"I thought they were nothing. It didn't make any sense. Even now," she said, lowering her voice even further. "I haven't said a thing. Maybe if I had told him, we could have done something. We might have stopped..."

Mrs. Doley's voice trailed off as her voice lowered.

"Stopped what, Mrs. Doley?" asked Lawrence.

Their eyes met once more and Mrs. Doley merely shook her head, refusing to say. After a moment, Lawrence nodded in understanding.

"I am sorry again for your loss."

Lawrence finished her tea and thanked Mrs. Doley again for her hospitality. She left the Doley house in the late afternoon. As she passed the front lawn, she looked to the side and saw the exact garden Teresa died in. She saw the roses. A lot of them had been torn up and uprooted, the fallen petals rotting on the ground. Several weeds had already begun to poke up through the neglected garden.

Although it felt like she had fulfilled the small promise she had made to Teresa, Lawrence felt hollow. She gave a final look back to the house and the heavy sadness that hung around it and left.

Chapter 6

Old Canary Green had been a part of Bar Harbor's history since the town's inception; the only other estate to have been erected earlier was Ashmore Hall. The great estate was practically an institution and a major hub of activity on the coast. Many a statesman or oil tycoon passed through its doors at least a few times during the season. 'Remove the front door and put in a revolving one instead. The grease on their palms should keep it running smoothly,' Patrick said as a suggestion, in which he was only half-joking. To be invited to dine at Old Canary Green carried a certain esteem that could not be easily bought or replicated cheaply. Only the shorter days of winter kept the busy doors shuttered.

The main house was a stately, faint green colonial with blue shutters and Doric columns that wrapped around the sides. A line of imposing trees neatly lined the property, planted as saplings back when the house was built. Otherwise, the front lawn remained wide open with beautifully trimmed shrubs and well-cultivated petunias along the gravel driveway and central fountain. In the back, a great pool had been cut into the ground, and a wide patio was installed that could hold at least a hundred people.

Augusta stood waiting on the drive and it seemed she had been waiting for some time. She paced back and forth on the walkway, barefoot like a wild child, with a little pink cocktail in hand. She spotted Lawrence and let out a high squeal, hopping around as she waved. The cocktail splashed as she did, but she paid it no mind. Her slinky green dress had a dangerously low back and beads that hung down in long arcs like waves. She flapped her arms as Lawrence approached, and the feathers stuck in her hair flounced around, making her look like a wild chicken. A big bangle of pearls and gold sat around her thin bicep.

Looking at how well she was dressed and all her fine jewels, Lawrence paused and looked down at her own simple black frock, which she kept aside for special occasions and funerals. Augusta took no notice though and let out a loud whoop.

"LJ, you've made it!"

She took her by the hand and practically dragged Lawrence straight through to the foyer.

As they crossed the threshold, a sharp scent hit Lawrence immediately. When she looked up, she saw a small bundle of herbs and flowers hanging over all the windows and doors. Each parcel had been tied off with string and bound to a rolled-up piece of parchment with foreign markings. She scrunched her nose up at the medicinal smell that seemed to create a wall around the property.

Furniture that had been passed down for generations, all situated with great care and kept in top condition, sat on Italian marble floors. Lawrence had very little time to take it all in, but could see it was all very grand. The level of luxury and richness of the furnishings truly did make it seem like visiting the palace of American royalty.

Augusta talked as they walked arm-in-arm, going on and on about this and that. Lawrence could hardly keep up with it all. Augusta's bare feet slapped noisily against the tiles as she threw her drink back in one go and smoothly handed the glass off to a passing servant.

"We're all absolutely dizzy with excitement that you're here." Augusta did tremble a bit as she spoke, her eyes glittering. "We simply don't know what to do with ourselves. Right in here."

A waiting servant nodded as the two of them approached and held open the door to the drawing room. The butler, Martin, announced the duo's arrival, and Augusta breezed in before Lawrence, clapping her hands.

"Look alive, look alive!" As she spoke, the beads in her dress clacked with every little movement.

Three men stood in the drawing room, dressed in tails, sipping their drinks and talking by the fire. Patrick turned to regard them first. He shot Lawrence a warm smile and stepped forward.

"LJ! Just in time."

Edwin stood by the fireplace in deep conversation with an elderly man. Their heads remained bent forward together, totally engrossed.

"Eddy, Pa!" cried Augusta, crossing her arms. "Where are your manners? Our guest has arrived!"

She waved her hand towards the two men, and they ended their conversation directly, putting on congenial smiles and turning to greet Lawrence properly.

The older man stepped forward and offered his hand in greeting to her. The wizened man had a thick head of shocking white hair and an impressive mustache that curled up at the edges. His bright, wide eyes held a gleam similar to the look young boys had when they had done something particularly naughty. He dressed finely and held himself in a proper, upright way, but a strange ornament hung around his neck: on dried twine, a small bundle of flowers, herbs, and a leather pouch hung like an amulet. Once Lawrence got closer, she got the same strong whiff of medicinal herbs she had smelled upon entering. If anyone considered it to be strange, nobody present seemed to notice.

"How do you do? Name's William Sinclair. Don't even think about calling me Mr. Sinclair, though. Nor do I care for William much either. You may call me 'Pa' as the others do if that doesn't offend you at all."

He beamed as he extended his hand out eagerly towards Lawrence, and her own tense shoulders eased a bit. There were always certain people where one is always better for having known them, and Pa fell squarely in that category. His brow quirked up as he looked her over.

"I hear you're Italian; how interesting. You don't quite look Italian, but things are a bit different over there, aren't they? Fascinating place."

"Pa, I said she was just visiting!" cried Augusta, followed by the titter of her airy laugh. "What was it again, LJ? Naples?"

"Florence," she corrected quietly.

Augusta giggled again as she fanned herself, accepting a new drink from one of the servants with a smile.

"LJ, nice to see you," Edwin said.

He gave a little nod of his head and a tight smile, but remained a bit reserved as he then turned his attention back to Augusta and her grandfather as they cleared up the little misunderstanding surrounding Mr. Sinclair's interest in Italy.

"Well, either way, we are glad you've agreed to join us here at Old Canary," said Mr. Sinclair with a grand sweep of his arms.

"We're dying to know," said Patrick with a coy smile. "Did you hear back on your ad? Perhaps from a particular place that rhymes with 'Dashfore'?"

"Gannaway," warned Augusta. Her face instantly darkened and she shot him a flinty-eyed look, but he simply kept his eyes elsewhere and sipped his drink without worry. He winked at Lawrence conspiratorially, and she fought to keep her face impassive.

"What's that?" asked Mr. Sinclair. A distant, far-off look came across his face.

"Nothing, Pa." Augusta quickly wound her arm around his and gave him one of her brightest smiles.

"If she so wishes, I am sure Miss Stoner will share with us later," added Edwin coolly. His eyes seemed to flicker over temporarily to Mr. Sinclair at the near mention of Ashmore Hall.

"You know how Pat is," said Augusta. She came around to Pa's other side and discreetly kicked out her leg to catch Patrick in the shins, who, in turn, moved out of the way in time with practiced grace. "Ignore him. He's just being an ass."

Edwin then cleared his throat.

"I hear a particularly nasty storm is coming," he said, smoothly turning the conversation over to a new topic.

Mr. Sinclair opened his mouth to ask another question, but the gong signaling dinner went off, and the party made its way through to the dining room. In the center sat a long oak table set with glittering candles and china plates with silver cutlery.

Patrick escorted Lawrence to her seat, held the chair out for her, and then took the seat directly to her right. Mr. Sinclair naturally sat at the head of the table, and the other two sat opposite Lawrence and Patrick. Augusta and Edwin faced the large windows to the dark lawn outside.

Once everyone was situated, three footmen and Martin began pouring out wine and serving the first course. They worked in a synchronized fashion that made it seem like a dance. Lawrence discreetly watched at how the others grabbed food from the offered platters and followed suit.

"So, LJ, we must know absolutely everything about you," declared Mr. Sinclair from his spot.

Whatever strange cloud had fallen over him moments ago seemed to have cleared. He draped his napkin over his lap and leaned forward to address her directly.

"Where is your family from?"

"The Midwest," Lawrence replied. "Loggers."

"Ah, steel!" Mr. Sinclair slapped a hand on the table and pointed to himself with his chest puffed out slightly. He then gestured between himself and Lawrence. "We're made up of the same stuffs then. Wood and metal have built this country up from nothing. You can't cheat your way in those things. It's either pure or it's not. That's what I like about it. I had a good feeling about you when I saw you. Your aura. It's pure. Augusta was right; she's a wonderful judge of character, after all."

"I told you!" remarked Augusta, leaning to Pa so they could observe Lawrence together. She gestured to the surrounding area around Lawrence's head. "All that silver."

Mr. Sinclair nodded his head enthusiastically. Lawrence's brow rose, but she said nothing. Patrick snorted lightly under his breath and shot her a knowing glance.

"Where did you attend school?" inquired Edwin, eyes focused on cutting the pork loin in front of him into equal, manageable bites.

"I attended a local girls school, but after my parents died, I went straight off to Italy. I ended up staying and apprenticing under a painting master."

"Sorry to hear that," murmured Edwin. He blushed then and quickly added, "Your family, I mean. Their passing."

"I'm more sorry about the latter part," drawled Patrick under his breath.

Edwin shot him an unimpressed look, but Lawrence laughed lightly and the slight wrinkles around Patrick's eyes creased as he smiled back at her.

"How did you afford to go?" asked Edwin suddenly.

When Lawrence turned her eyes to him, he reddened a bit further. He turned his eyes back to his food.

"Not to pry, of course."

"Did your family own a company?" Augusta asked with all sincerity.

Lawrence nearly laughed aloud at the idea, but shook her head.

"No," Lawrence said, still fighting the creeping smile that threatened to slip. "My family does not come from money. My father worked as a logger and my mother kept the home. They died rather unexpectedly, but had the good sense to take out life insurance. That set me up with some money, so I just decided to leave. I'd never been outside my own town before that."

She laughed suddenly as she remembered how she ended up in Italy anyways.

"I ended up just asking a random lady that was sat next to me at the station where I should go since I hadn't gone anywhere before. She looked at me like I had grown a second head. She told me, 'Rudolph Valentino just got back from his trip to Italy'. Said he stopped for three weeks in some city called Florence. 'If it's good enough for a fella like him, makes you wonder.' I guess that was enough to convince me, and I was there within a week."

The rest of the party listened quietly with thoughtful looks. Edwin was the first to speak.

"You left all you know, your entire world, and went off to an entirely different country on your own? Not knowing the language or anyone there to receive you?"

Lawrence hesitated. When spoken in that way, it did seem quite fantastical, and perhaps a bit foolhardy, but she hadn't considered it that way. She merely shrugged with a nod.

"So romantic," sighed Augusta, nearly melting as she clasped her hands together. "I could die!"

"A brave explorer more like," said Patrick, turning sideways to smirk and nudge his elbow towards her. "A true Lewis and Clark type. You got a lot more gumption than you look, LJ."

"And you have no interest in returning to your hometown?" asked Edwin, again with the serious, probing look in his eyes.

"If I hadn't gone, or perhaps if I went somewhere else entirely I could have returned home and been relatively happy. You see, it's terribly hard to return to the Midwest once you've been to a place like Florence." The others laughed lightly at that. Lawrence shook her head.

"However, no, I don't think I could," she answered, honest.

Edwin seemed placated by that direct answer and nodded his head once, as if he understood.

"Pa, why don't we ask Lawrence here to do your portrait?" Augusta clapped her hands. "We could sit for it together. Wouldn't that be nifty? A portrait of just the two of us!"

"Lawrence mentioned she left her card here," injected Patrick, spearing an asparagus smothered in Hollandaise.

"Martin, do you know about this?"

Mr. Sinclair turned in his seat to address the butler, who lingered by the back wall. He stepped forward with his hands clasped behind his back.

"Yes, sir. I believe it was placed on your desk, sir."

"How queer," he cried. He scratched his cheek as he pondered over it. "Can't say I saw such a thing. Then again, I'd lose my own nose if I could."

"It's a good thing we met you then!" Augusta smiled to Lawrence and then turned her eyes to her grandfather expectantly.

"So what do you say, Pa? It can be my birthday gift to you."

"I could never endure sitting for portraits," said Mr. Sinclair, shaking his head ruefully. He shivered at the mere thought of it. "I've only ever successfully sat for one with my parents. You'll see the evidence of that hanging over the sitting room fireplace. Ever since I was a little boy, I would always fidget. I had the most horrible time staying still. That only resulted in me getting boxed about the ears—rightfully so, of course, but it did leave a bit of resentment towards the activity. I haven't sat for one since."

Lawrence laughed. She had her fair share of experiences with unwilling, fidgety models. "Fair enough. It can be a tedious activity, for sure."

"Do you find it to be fulfilling doing portraiture? Surely, as an artist, you have your own interests and subjects you'd be more passionate about," said Edwin, his voice nearly as sincere as his eyes.

Edwin seemed satisfied, or at least content, that he had fulfilled his obligation of asking enough questions as was expected when in company. He turned to Augusta silently, who gave him a silent nod of approval.

"'What are men to rocks and mountains?'" recited Mr. Sinclair, cutting his pork and swirling it around in the dark gravy on his plate.

"What could be more interesting than people?" asked Augusta.

"Anybody who prefers staring at a basket of fruit all day to a naked model is a liar and a ringer," laughed Patrick, waggling his eyebrows.

"What say you, resident artist?" Mr. Sinclair mindlessly dragged a hand through his beard like a comb and twirled the edges of his mustache with a grin. "What is the verdict?"

"The cruelest thing in the world to a painter is a boring subject. The saddest thing is an ugly one," Lawrence said in a dramatic tone as she placed a hand on her chest. She turned to the Sinclairs then. "You two are neither; so I would be more than satisfied."

"Hear, hear." Mr. Sinclair cried happily as he slapped his hand against the table in applause. "Like I said, an excellent judge of character."

Lawrence then leaned forward to address Edwin directly across the table. "I don't believe you mentioned what it is *you* do, Mr. Ernest."

A series of groans and laughter went around the table as the rest of the party all reacted to the harmless question. Augusta clapped and laughed as she shot several shy smiles Edwin's way. Patrick shook his head as he wiped his mouth, and Mr. Sinclair only raised his cup once again to his lips, a ghost of a smile across his lips.

"They're all taking the mickey, LJ, and I'll kindly ask that you ignore them," Edwin stated, unruffled by the others around him.

"I don't understand."

"It's a bit of a running gag we have," explained Augusta. "We've asked him about it a hundred times or so, but he won't say what it is he does exactly. Even if he did, I don't suppose any of us would understand."

"The thing is, plenty of mates of ours have been in classes in university with Edwin. Hell, that's how we met," said Patrick as he stabbed a roaming potato on his plate. "It was in this dreadfully boring class. Do you remember?"

"History of religions," answered Edwin, immediately.

"That's right! History of religions," Patrick muttered, shaking his head at the memory. "A time killer, really."

"You all met in university then?" Lawrence asked as she gestured between Augusta and the two men.

"We've graduated," Edwin nodded, gesturing between himself and Patrick. "Augusta is finishing her final semester."

"We met Auggie through a friend's friend. A delightful Southern belle with an equally delightful laugh," said Patrick, discreetly braying like a donkey.

Edwin snorted, covering it quickly with a cough, as Augusta shot a scathing look at the two of them. Patrick continued on, relaxed.

"They're down at Wellesley, which is a lovely little convent out in the country that keeps respectable young ladies safe and well-preserved until they're ready."

"It's not a convent," muttered Augusta.

"Yes, well it might as well be," drawled Patrick.

He and Augusta stuck their tongues out at each other like bickering school children. Pa laughed good-naturedly, his eyes twinkling in amusement.

"It's one of the preeminent women's colleges in this country," said Edwin.

"Anyways, when the wallpaper starts to swirl and Auggie's about to start crawling up the wall, she nips up to us on the train."

"They're my heroes," declared Augusta.

"Now, back to what I was saying," said Patrick with a wave of his hands. He rubbed his chin thoughtfully as if he were a scholar. "You would think it rather straightforward to deduce exactly what it is young Edwin Ernest has decided to pursue as a career; however, the range and variety of classes young Mr. Ernest here took make it impossible. For example, exactly what sort of a career would require a young man to study both medieval and pre-Renaissance mythologies and folktales, along with advanced chemistry and international law?"

"I think he's a spy," said Augusta. "Or certainly well on his way to becoming one."

"He's an academic," stated Mr. Sinclair. "A lover of knowledge and a collector of facts."

"I think he's just confused," Patrick joked.

The others laughed. Edwin joined, but a half-measure too late. He looked at Lawrence again.

"LJ, I am guilty of one thing and one thing only, and that is of having a genuine interest in many things. God forbid anyone in this day and age should show any inclination towards academia; they will only be met with contempt and mockery. Pay no mind to them; I do not."

Patrick snorted. "Are you quite done with your tragic soliloquy, Shakespeare?"

"Well done, Pat; that's quite a big word for you," snapped Edwin in response.

He smiled though and the two men remained easygoing in their demeanor.

Augusta pouted as she cut into her food. "I honestly think it's a terrible waste of money to go to college, but Pa insisted."

"Yes, I do, and I still insist," Mr. Sinclair said, cutting in. "We've donated enough money to that damned place; a good education could hardly be considered an arduous assignment to them."

"I suppose it's not been all bad," nodded Augusta in almost immediate agreement. "I've made plenty of friends, so it's not been a total waste. Including these two knuckleheads. They're the best. The best friends a gal could hope for. They're practically like family, aren't they, Pa?"

"Certainly," nodded Mr. Sinclair.

It seemed clear to Lawrence that while status and financial assistance may have played a significant role in Patrick and Augusta's placement into their respective academic situations, Edwin had most likely been accepted on pure merit. While they were all wonderfully pleasant and welcoming, there was an undeniable frivolity and strange naivete in them all, even Mr. Sinclair. Lawrence expected for them to have been more worldly and discerning, but they were not.

"Edwin is the beloved second son," Patrick said. "I am merely the Cain to his Abel."

"Goodness," murmured Edwin, looking Patrick over with renewed interest. "Should I be worried, *brother?*"

Patrick shot a wink to Edwin as Pa chuckled.

"Pa and Edwin do get on so wonderfully." Augusta leaned over to address Lawrence and dabbed primly at the corner of her mouth with her ivory napkin. "They spend hours talking together and going over books."

"And ghost stories," included Patrick.

Augusta shot him a glare from across the table, her lips thinning as she did. Her fingers tightened around her fork.

"Patrick," Edwin said in a scolding tone.

"It's true, though, Eddy. Isn't that what you two talk about, Pa?"

Patrick turned to address Mr. Sinclair directly, who pursed his lips in thought. He then chuckled and used his cutlery to gesture towards Edwin and Augusta.

"These two are hesitant to discuss these sorts of things with new people. Then again, Mr. Ernest can generally be a bit reticent and withholding more often than not. Take no offense, LJ. Really, it has nothing to do with you."

"Oh, what a drag!" cried Augusta suddenly in a rush. "What a boring conversation; it makes me want to die. Let's not all keep talking about that all night!"

Her change in attitude was so sudden, but only Lawrence seemed a bit taken aback. All the others seemed quite used to it and carried on.

"You're right." Patrick turned to Lawrence suddenly. "LJ, have you heard that another man has died?"

"What?" she asked, her eyes widening. Her hand froze, fork still mid-air as her breath caught.

He nodded. "Though this one doesn't seem to match the others. Bit concerning, isn't it?"

"Patrick, this is really not an appropriate conversation to have at the dinner table, is it?" Augusta said.

Her voice although still sweet, had a sharpness to it. The withering look she sent him said plenty alone. He, as usual, ignored it, though.

"I knew John," Patrick said, continuing on. "Bit of a prat, if I'm being honest. Always went on about polo."

"We shan't talk ill of the dead," Edwin said, his voice grave.

"Indeed," nodded Mr. Sinclair in agreement. He leaned slightly to Augusta with a lowered tone. "Do we know them?"

"We met the Humphries last season. Helena and John Sr.?" Augusta said. "You know, the investor? They recently bought the Caldwell's old home?"

"Ah yes," said Mr. Sinclair, remembering then. He nodded. "Indeed, yes. A difficult loss to be sure. God help them."

"LJ, are you quite alright?" Edwin asked, head tilted forward as he addressed her.

"Dead?" Lawrence repeated, her voice barely above a whisper.

Her breath caught the moment Patrick mentioned the name. The table went silent as she felt them all turn to look at her. Her heart stuttered and her hands grew clammy. Although she had pushed all thoughts of him and the night away behind a wall, everything came flooding back as if the dam she had carefully constructed in her mind had erupted.

"Stars! You've gone all pale sweetie!" cried Augusta. She waved her hand to Martin. "Martin, do something! She'll simply collapse if we don't."

Martin hurried out of the room in search of something to aide Lawrence, but she held her hand aloft to show she didn't need it. She took a healthy drink of wine which brought some color back to her cheeks and steadied her nerves. She kept her eyes trained on the white tablecloth as the blood rushed to her ears.

"Did you know him?" Edwin asked gently.

Lawrence shook her head but kept her eyes down. She felt the heat of his gaze as he continued to look her way, searching.

"They're saying it was a wild animal," Patrick said, rather languidly. "Others think it might be the handiwork of a savage killer."

"Not here," lamented Augusta with a sad shake of her head. "Nothing like that ever happens here in Bar Harbor. This is such a good place; I can't imagine something like that happening. It's too awful; really, I must insist we change the subject."

"That's a good idea," seconded Edwin.

"What happened to him?" Lawrence asked, her voice still low and breathless.

Although she had no desire to know, she could not help the need to hear it for herself. The rest of the room went quiet, but Edwin cleared his throat.

"He went missing about a week ago, but he was finally found last night in the forest." His voice remained clinical and detached. "No one knows exactly what happened."

"He probably got fried and went wandering," said Patrick, swirling the wine in his cup around. "Probably ran into a bear."

"It's not related then to Teresa or the boy out in Derby?" asked Lawrence.

"No," said Edwin, carefully. "At least, it doesn't seem so."

"How do you know?" she asked again, insistent. For once she maintained eye contact with Edwin, determined to hear the answer.

"I don't think it's appropriate to say," replied Edwin.

His eyes flickered between Lawrence and the others in the room. The rest of the room, including the servants, waited with bated breath. Everyone seemed to lean in a bit, interested. He seemed to give in once he saw how Augusta waited to hear the answer as well.

"The, uh, the body was in quite a state when it was found. Quite different from the other deaths."

Lawrence paled once again and gripped the edge of the table. The room began to spin slightly and her breath caught once more.

"You seem quite affected, Ms. Stoner" said Mr. Sinclair.

His head tilted and his eyes narrowed slightly in interest. Augusta's eyes flickered around the room and her breathing sped up as a rosy color tinted her cheeks.

"Have you been noticing certain patterns too?"

"Patterns?" Lawrence repeated, taken aback.

Edwin's bushy brows quirked as he steepled his hands before his face.

"You knew him," he said definitively, saving her from answering Mr. Sinclair's question. Lawrence gave a subtle nod.

"We only met in passing," she confirmed.

Edwin nodded his head, but she got the vague sense that he didn't entirely believe her.

"When the lights go on at Ashmore Hall, the dead will surely follow," said Patrick in a sing-song voice.

He chuckled to himself, but no one else at the table seemed amused. He quieted then, coughing lightly as he took a healthy gulp of wine. The temperature in the room dropped several degrees, and Lawrence swore she could hear everyone's beating hearts and nervous breaths.

Augusta quietly picked at her nails, her eyes flitting sideways at her grandfather every so often. In turn, Edwin stared at her, brows furrowed as he chewed on his lip.

A strange look came over Mr. Sinclair's eyes, and his demeanor changed. Although he seemed unaffected at first glance, his jaw set and a tightness formed around his eyes where there were usually crow's feet.

A brief period of silence settled around the table. Lawrence focused her attention on the detailing of the napkin across her lap. Mr. Sinclair suddenly laughed then. Everyone around the table startled slightly at the noise.

"You know, I was just a young boy the last time those lights came on," Mr. Sinclair said. His voice became hollow as he recalled the memory. "I was out on the front lawn playing when a grand, black couch and four came up. My parents went out and greeted the lady in the back. I never spoke to her, but I saw her in the distance."

He stretched his hand out, gesturing far away. He cleared his throat lightly.

"Just a single woman in the back, dressed snout to tail in black with a long, dark veil over her face. I thought nothing of it, really, at the time, but then she looked right at me."

Mr. Sinclair pointed his finger right at Lawrence, as if the tip of his finger was the striking gaze of the woman. Lawrence inhaled sharply, holding it as she listened, rapt.

"I might be the only person alive who's seen her in person, but believe you me, I paid the price."

"How do you mean?" whispered Lawrence.

She momentarily looked away from Mr. Sinclair to gaze at the others. Augusta stared morosely into her drink, the edges of her plump lips pulled down. Edwin seemed to stare out at nothing, and for once, Patrick seemed contrite as he hung his head down and anxiously bit at his thumbnail.

"My parents died that season," explained Mr. Sinclair.

"I'm sorry to hear that," Lawrence said, a bit hesitant as she was unsure about the connection between the two. Mr. Sinclair gave her a sad smile and nodded, but shrugged.

"Pa," murmured Augusta. She shook her head and her fiery bob shook. "Please."

"Ma fell ill," Mr. Sinclair continued, ignoring his granddaughter. "Headaches and fainting spells came first. Then, it seemed to be a passing cold. The servants kept the fires burning morning to night, but she'd shiver endlessly. How she suffered, my poor mother."

Wetness gathered in Mr. Sinclair's eyes and he gathered his hands together to rest in front of him. His eyes hardened a bit.

"She certainly took her time with it."

"What?" whispered Lawrence.

"She killed them, you see. That woman."

Lawrence tensed, and the rest of the others shifted slightly in their seats. Augusta inhaled sharply as she gripped the edge of the table.

Mr. Sinclair carried on.

"I know it because I *saw* it. She didn't know I saw her, but I did." His voice lowered to a whisper like he was sharing a dark secret. "As a boy, I sometimes crept out of my room, and I'd go to my parents. It was almost like a little ritual we had. I'd creep up to my mother's side, and she'd open up the blanket and let me sleep there with them. Always got an earful from my father, but Ma didn't care. Neither did I. When Ma fell ill, though, I was directed to stay out of her room, and I did try. But, I missed her. So, when I couldn't bear it any longer, I went in. That was when *she* came."

"Pa," started Patrick. He laughed haltingly, tapping his fingers against the wooden table as he plastered a smile across his face.

"Perhaps we ought to let LJ get to know us a bit better before we share the whole backstory to the Sinclair legacy."

"You were the one prodding the issue, Pat," murmured Edwin.

Mr. Sinclair quieted then, and it did seem that he was prepared to drop the issue.

"I'd like to hear the rest," said Lawrence.

The others around the table turned to her in surprise. Mr. Sinclair raised his eyes to meet hers, and gave her a nod.

"When I went to my parents room that night, something was different," began Mr. Sinclair again. "I heard a strange noise, so I quickly hid in the closet. I waited until it felt like needles were in my legs. I felt silly, actually, for being such a little coward!" He laughed, but no amusement reached his eyes. "Then, everything went quiet. Quiet as the grave. First, the lamps went out!"

He snapped his fingers, and everyone around the table jumped a little at the sudden movement.

"Then, she came. The door opened, and all I saw was a figure of darkness."

"What happened then?" Lawrence asked, enraptured and horrified in equal measure.

Her mouth gaped slightly as she processed the idea of a young boy seeing his own parents murdered. A sudden awareness returned to Mr. Sinclair's eyes and he looked away.

"It killed them," he muttered. "Killed them both. In cold blood."

He exhaled and set his napkin on the table.

"Now, the lights are back on, and people are dying. She's back."

Augusta kept her eyes down and focused more on breathing steadily. She put her elbows on the table and set her head in her hands. Edwin leaned towards her and whispered something to her.

"Mr. Sinclair," Lawrence said, carefully. "Surely, it's not the same woman? You say the lights last came on when you were a child. It can't be the same person. That'd be impossible."

"What makes you think that?" he asked.

The corners of his lips turned down slightly as he stared at her in complete seriousness. Lawrence was at a loss for words then, her mouth opening and closing in an effort to answer. Patrick coughed lightly at her side.

"Apologies," he whispered lowly, just to her. She looked sideways and saw the sheepish, uncomfortable smile he shot towards her.

"So," declared Mr. Sinclair in a loud voice. He ran a hand down his white beard like a philosopher deep in thought. "What sort of creature disguises itself as a woman, kills nearly a hundred innocent people, only to return six decades later?"

"Pa," whispered Augusta, pleading. "Please stop."

"I agree, this has taken a bit of a dark turn," chuckled Patrick a bit awkwardly. "Let's not scare LJ off entirely."

"A vampyr," stated Mr. Sinclair simply.

"Christ," Augusta swore under her breath.

She pushed Edwin's comforting hand away from her, took a deep drink of her wine, and motioned for one of the servants to refill her glass. Patrick leaned his head closer to Lawrence's.

"We try not to humor these fantasies too much," he muttered, wiping his mouth. Edwin's head snapped up, having overheard him.

"They're not fantasies, Patrick," he argued.

Lawrence looked at him in surprise. Of all the people there, she was most surprised to hear the erudite scholar come to the older man's defense. He ran a slender hand down the front of his suit and smoothed out a few of the nonexistent wrinkles.

"It's just a theory, a hypothesis."

"If monsters and demons play part in theories, I beg your pardon, but they are categorically fantasies." Patrick turned to Mr. Sinclair at the head of the table. "My apologies, sir. I would never want to insult you or your grief, but I am a man of reason and science. Even the greatest of misfortunes and mysteries can be explained."

"Boys, this is why people talk about us!" cried Augusta.

She covered her eyes suddenly, and inhaled sharply. She wiped away a few errant tears from her cheeks, and Edwin's eyes softened as he turned to her. Patrick also quieted, and only Pa continued to smile serenely. He held his finger up and shook it.

"Mark my words, the men down at Rothsby's and the police and all of those idiots will say it's a disease. Some of the more educated charlatans will come up with very convincing explanations. Don't let yourself be fooled by any of it."

Mr. Sinclair pointed directly to Lawrence then with a glint in his eye. He gestured then out the window in the general direction of Ashmore.

"A vampyr lives up on that hill, and it has returned now. Just as horses and sheep abandon a pasture that's been picked clean of all its grass, she left once she had her fill. Now that the fear has all but been forgotten and the fat hens are all roosting, the fox has returned to the hen house."

"A vampyr?"

Lawrence was nearly breathless at the implication. Her mind went immediately to what Mr. and Mrs. Doley had referred to in the afternoon. While Mr. Doley had not made such strong accusations as Mr. Sinclair had, he had the same unerring belief that it was not a simple sickness that had killed his daughter either.

Edwin's eyes glittered as he listened intently. Patrick fidgeted and rearranged his cutlery, and Augusta focused on the wine in front of her. The old man was becoming excited, speaking louder with every passing moment.

"Consider the facts and the similarities between the recent deaths and the ones from sixty years ago: all victims followed a similar bout of sickness where the victims experienced chills, sleepwalking, and paralyzing limbs. In the end, most of the blood was drained from their body. Sometimes when something is so mysterious and inexplicable, there is no other logical explanation but the illogical!"

"Pa!" whispered Augusta urgently. Her eyes became watery, and her voice cracked as she held the napkin tightly in her lap. "Stop! Just stop!"

He ignored her, though, and held out the strange necklace around his neck and shook it about.

"Do you see this here? This isn't just for fashion, you know. It stinks like hell, but it keeps me safe. Safe from the things in the night that'd scare the Devil. I try to get Augusta to keep one on her, but she refuses. She still refuses."

"Do you really think a little bag of herbs and dried flowers will do anything to protect me?" muttered Augusta. Her mouth twisted and she shook her head, disgusted.

"It might," replied Edwin defensively.

When Lawrence turned her head to look at him, she found that he was already staring in her direction with a strange look across his

112

face.

Patrick suddenly threw down his napkin on the table. He laughed brightly as he spoke, running a free hand over his hair.

"That is enough! I think we've had enough of this. Poor LJ! How she must think of us. I promise, most dinners are not like this."

Mr. Sinclair leaned forward to address her. "I wouldn't say it if I didn't mean it. Do not go near that house. I strongly suggest you do whatever you can not to attract *its* attention. You're not safe, Miss Stoner. None of us are."

Lawrence's throat tightened as she remembered her invitation to dinner. She decided it best to omit that bit of information and instead laughed lightly, hoping to alleviate the somber atmosphere.

"It's too bad I've left my card there. I don't suppose there's some way to reverse what I've done?"

"I'll supply you with some talismans to protect you," answered Mr. Sinclair, sincere.

"Now, Pa, we agreed you wouldn't talk about these sorts of things in front of Augusta. You know she's sensitive," murmured Patrick listlessly.

"I am right here, Patrick!" cried Augusta. "Don't talk about me as if I'm not here!"

"Augusta, please calm-" Edwin began to speak, and as he did so, his gaze rose from the table to the windows behind Patrick and Lawrence that overlooked the front lawn.

At that moment, he locked eyes with something outside the window. His eyes widened, and his arm jerked forward in response. His wine glass clattered against the table and fell to the floor with a crash, splattering everywhere. The dark crimson color immediately seeped into the crisp, white tablecloth and the front of his suit.

He shot up suddenly, as if he had been shocked. His chair fell backward and crashed to the ground. The servants in the room all rushed forward to assist him, picking up the shattered glass and wiping at his ruined jacket.

"Good God, Edwin. What is it?" exclaimed Augusta, her eyes wide with worry.

She reached out a hand to him, offering it up in assistance. She forgot, in an instant, all about her own sadness and wanted only to help him. Mr. Sinclair rose and went straight to the window. He and Patrick scanned the darkness together, but found nothing.

"She's out there; I know it!" cried Mr. Sinclair.

Edwin quickly straightened and cleared his throat. He put his hand on his cheek, taking deep, even breaths.

"My apologies; I don't know what came over me. Forgive me."

"Eddy, you look as if you've seen a ghost!" cried Patrick.

"He's gone all pale, Pa!" exclaimed Augusta, thoroughly distressed. "Martin, see to Mr. Ernest."

Mr. Sinclair gestured to the butler, who immediately stepped forward with a ready arm. Edwin took up Augusta's glass of wine and finished it in one gulp. Some color returned to his cheeks, and his breath steadied.

"I think that's a sign we all ought to go through. Come along, children," declared Patrick.

The rest of them rose and left the dining room together. Augusta took Edwin by the arm and made up a seat for him by the fireplace. She continued to fuss over him, tucking him in and fluffing his pillow. Martin poured a drink of brandy water and served it to him, calling out to the footmen to bring a footrest.

Mr. Sinclair left the room with a quick step and a determined look in his eye.

Lawrence lingered by the back of the room and was soon joined by Patrick. He gave her a wink and chuckled as he handed her a cup of strong coffee. He had a cigar in hand that a footman lit for him.

He exhaled slowly, the spicy tobacco plumes creating a cloud around them.

"Never a dull moment," he murmured under his breath, so only she heard. They chuckled lightly together. "I wonder what he saw."

"So you believe he saw something?" she asked.

He gave her a sideways look that he was not entirely convinced. He then shrugged and inhaled again.

"I've known Eddy for a while now. He doesn't scare easy. I've only seen him go white like that once before, and he disappeared for a week."

"What happened to him?"

Patrick smiled, amused at his own story as he told it. He shrugged.

"We don't know. He won't say. Still won't say. Believe me, I've tried everything to get it out of him, but he's like Fort Knox. All I know is that he disappeared, and he came back a week later with a broken arm, bruises and cuts all over like he fought a hellcat, and a strange look in his eye."

"A strange look?" repeated Lawrence.

"Oh, yes. Like he had seen the Devil, or maybe God, and lived to tell the tale. He was back to rights soon enough, but I won't forget it. I don't think ever."

Lawrence looked sideways at him then. "But you don't believe all that nonsense they were talking about?"

Patrick hesitated for a moment and looked down at her. He stepped an inch closer and spoke quietly so only she could hear.

"You don't know what the rumor about the Sinclairs is, do you?" Off her look, he shook his head. "Of course you don't. Well, Pa's parents *did* die that night, but there's a bit more to it. Pa's parents were found the next morning in their bedroom, covered in blood. Now, it seemed that Mr. Sinclair, in his love for his wife and unable to see her in pain, decided to end her suffering. Then, in his grief, he took a straight razor and-"

Patrick made a quick gesture across his neck that shocked Lawrence, and she fought to keep her expression neutral. She looked sideways to where Augusta and Edwin sat, but they were engrossed in their own private conversation. She turned back to Patrick.

"Anyways, Pa was found the next morning in the closet. He believes wholeheartedly in what he saw, but public opinion, and evidence, say otherwise."

"You think his father did it then?" asked Lawrence. "You think he killed his wife, and then himself? And this," Lawrence paused. "-theory about vampyrs is just the grief talking?"

Patrick dispelled the heavy air between them with a chuckle that brightened his handsome face.

"I'll believe whatever you want me to believe, Stoner." Patrick bumped his shoulder with hers and gave her a cheeky smile. "But, yes."

Lawrence got the same sudden prickling feeling again on the back of her neck. She raised her head and looked around, but saw nothing. She turned back to Edwin on the couch and saw how Augusta doted on him. He was in another world, staring at the patterned rug with a serious, absent-minded look.

Mr. Sinclair re-entered the room with bundles of dried herbs and some iron crosses. He began to replace the ones above the windows and set more at the entryways to the rooms. Behind him, a few servants carried cups of salt and dutifully sprinkled it around the edges of doorways and windows.

Mr. Sinclair came to Lawrence then with a small pouch and held it out to her. "To keep in your home. Keep it on you whenever you leave."

She took it from him, and could already smell the pungent aroma.

She gave him a smile and nodded her head in gratitude.

"Thank you."

From the couch, Augusta watched the servants salt the room with a forlorn expression. She turned her eyes away and looked into the fire instead. Edwin placed a comforting hand on her shoulder.

"Augusta," Lawrence called out to her. She set down her cup and stepped towards her. "I am feeling awfully tired. Would you hate me if I left now?"

"Oh, of course not, darling!" said Augusta, perking up the moment Lawrence called her name.

Whether it was an act or not, she assumed her role immediately. Augusta looked to the clock that sat over the mantle.

"It's quite late; won't you just stay? We have plenty of rooms," she said with a pretty pout.

"I do appreciate it, but I must get going. I'm close by, so we'll see each other plenty, won't we?"

"Oh, loads for sure! I always throw a little party in the middle of the summer. You must come. I will be absolutely inconsolable if you don't. I'll throw myself off Widow's Weep. You must promise me you'll come. Oh, where's your coat? Martin, get Miss Stoner's coat! Did you have a coat?"

Augusta walked arm-in-arm with her to the front door. They argued, albeit politely, the entire way about how Lawrence would be getting home. Patrick and Edwin followed closely behind.

"I won't hear of it! Let Peter drive you over. You can't say no. I won't accept any other answer. It's no trouble at all. Besides, look how dark it is. It's far too late. Too dark and too late for a young lady to go home on her own. It's just not right. What would people think if we let you walk out in the dark like that? Now, I'm all for ladies' rights and whatnot, but this is just common sense."

"Really, Augusta. I'll be fine! It's just a quick little trot down the trail."

"Even then, something awful might happen, and I'll be beside myself."

Augusta shook her head, horrified at the thought. Despite speaking in extremes, Augusta was so sincere that one could never take any offense or believe any of it to be disingenuous. All Lawrence could do was smile and relent.

The front door opened, and the two women took a step out. Neither made it another step before Augusta let out a horrified scream at the top of her lungs. The men inside all rushed out until they were gathered together at the entrance.

Before them on the ground lay the corpse of a familiar black cat.

The air whooshed out of Lawrence's lungs as she stared down at it. She tried to inhale, but her lungs refused to expand. She finally let out a ragged breath and placed a hand across her chest.

"My god," she whispered.

The poor animal's throat had been torn out, and the gravel underfoot was irrigated with its blood. The body was placed on its back with the legs splayed out. The strange configuration of its body made it seem only natural to assume it had been placed purposefully.

Lawrence slowly went to her knees and laid a gentle hand on the soft fur of Stinky Boy's head. The people around her stared at the scene in utter silence. Augusta shuddered, and a few tears raced down her cheeks.

"Oh, poor boy," Lawrence murmured. "What did this to you?"

The dam cracked and Lawrence inhaled sharply. Hot tears fell fast as she began to fuss over the cat she had gotten so used to seeing around. Her shoulders shook violently as she hiccuped and sobbed. A gentle hand rested on her back. Edwin offered her his handkerchief, which she took wordlessly.

"How awful," Augusta hiccuped. She leaned into Edwin's side, where he tucked her in under his arm. Patrick lowered to a squat by Lawrence's side.

"Is- was he yours?" Patrick asked gently, his voice a low murmur. Everyone's gazes remained fixed on the cat. Lawrence shook her head.

"He didn't belong to anybody but himself," she said, remembering Teresa's words. Her tears slowed, but she continued to breathe shallowly, hiccuping every so often. Mr. Sinclair arrived on the scene and let out a loud sigh.

"It's happening," he whispered. He grabbed the amulet around his neck, and his eyes scanned the dark gardens and forests beyond the estate. "We shouldn't linger in the dark any longer than we need to. Miss Stoner, I must insist you stay with us tonight. Not safe."

Patrick grunted and quickly removed his jacket and placed it over the cat, so it was entirely out of view.

"A sobering reminder of nature and the circle of life to end our evening," he spoke smoothly. Edwin continued to stare at the little jacket-covered mound with great severity. Patrick then chuckled lightly as he tried to cheer the others. "Let us hope it is not some sort of omen."

The others ignored him as Augusta came to Lawrence's side and looped an arm with hers.

"I will show you to a room. You'll be right next door to me," said Augusta, her voice low and far away. She led Lawrence back inside.

The two of them crossed the front hall together and headed towards the grand staircase. As they did, Augusta leaned in to Lawrence's side with a strange look in her eye.

"I've a terrible feeling I'm going to go absolutely mad this summer."

Before they climbed the stairs to the rooms, Lawrence turned to look back where the front door remained open. She saw a young man cleaning up Stinky Boy, gingerly picking him up and depositing his body into a box. Patrick ambled back inside, puffing away at his cigar. Edwin and Mr. Sinclair remained outside, huddled together in deep conversation.

Chapter 7

Lawrence awoke before the sun and the servants, padding through the dark, cold house like a dormouse. She went out through the back patio and crossed the long yard, barefoot. The dewy grass soaked the hem of her skirts, but she paid no mind to it as she went to the property's edge by the water.

She craned her neck until she saw the top of Ashmore's roof in the distance on the top of the cliff. She waited for some sign, or to even feel the strange prickling at the back of her neck, but she felt nothing. Once the sun began to properly rise and she could no longer feel her toes, she turned and headed back inside.

"My goodness, LJ," cried Augusta upon entering the dining room. "What hour did you wake up?"

Augusta yawned widely as she crossed to the buffet set up along the back wall and piled her plate up with breakfast. She then sat down, settling the napkin across her lap. Her face held creases along her left cheek and brow where she slept particularly hard against the pillow. Lawrence stifled a light giggle.

"A little before sunrise," Lawrence replied.

Augusta nearly choked upon hearing that, staring at Lawrence as if she had grown a second head. The men filed into the room shortly after, greeting the ladies congenially. Once they had their food, they promptly sat and shook out their newspapers. Lawrence noticed they were short one person.

"Is Edwin not joining us?"

"Busy, busy," muttered Patrick, eyes never raising from his paper. "He's part mole."

"Sorry?"

"Mr. Ernest is in his study," replied Mr. Sinclair as explanation, looking out over the top of his reading spectacles. "He commits himself to his books, and we hardly see him. He'll come out when he's ready."

"Oh, I see," she murmured.

"LJ, you must stay and play a round of badminton with us," said Augusta. "We're going out this morning. You must stay."

"Oh, I don't-" began Lawrence. Augusta quickly waved her hands.

"Really, any answer besides 'yes' shall fall on deaf ears!" she cried. She turned in her seat. "Martin, do make sure the nets are set up!"

Augusta, Patrick and Lawrence moved to the back lawn after breakfast. The glittering pool water sparkled under the bright sun. A long table with sweet lemonade in sweating glass jugs, trays of pretty pastel cakes and uniform finger sandwiches were set out for them to pick at. Mr. Sinclair excused himself politely and disappeared back into the house.

Despite their pleading, Lawrence successfully avoided joining Augusta and Patrick's game of badminton and instead watched under the refuge of a large umbrella. At Augusta's request, a pad of paper and pencils were brought out for Lawrence.

"To document my sporting figure," she said with a dazzling smile.

Lawrence quickly sketched the scene, laughing as Patrick and Augusta posed dramatically for her. They got started with their game and she buried her head down to work. She absentmindedly fanned herself as she sweated through her top. She stuck the icy glass of lemonade up to her forehead. After a bright peal of laughter,

Lawrence raised her head.

Augusta danced across the impossibly bright green lawn, trimmed evenly across, as she returned a serve. She laughed again as she swung her racket; She expertly returned the shuttlecock that came sailing over the net towards her. Patrick stood on the opposite side, smoking a thick cigar as he volleyed it back lazily. The pair looked like a handsome couple, both dressed in white linen. Patrick's tanned arm flexed with every swing. He took the cigar out of his mouth and shot Augusta a blinding smile.

"Very good, Auggie. Very good. You're hitting on all six right now; keep that elbow up!" He called out to her, his voice strong with authority on all things athletic.

The whole scene was very picturesque and exactly what Lawrence imagined lovely summer days were meant to be made up of. She did her best to reflect the feeling in her crude sketch.

"LJ, are you absolutely sure you won't join us?" Augusta waved her racket at Lawrence, who smiled and shook her head. Augusta held her hand out to shade her eyes from the bright sun above. "Well, would you be a lamb and call Pa and Edwin out? We're going to have a little break once I win this game!"

"Chance'd be a fine thing," shouted Patrick.

* * *

Martin directed Lawrence to the library, but she took the opportunity to peek her head into random rooms on her way. When she showed herself into the library, it was empty. White, gauzy curtains moved gently as the breeze came in through the French doors. She lingered for a moment, turned to leave, but then stopped.

She inclined her head and took a few steps towards the walled shelves. Leather-bound tomes filled the wall from top to bottom, and she put her ear up against the cool spine of one. The soft mutterings of a conversation drifted through, muffled by the wall. Lawrence stepped back, scanning back and forth until her eye caught on one of the shelving panels, which angled out at a strange degree.

Lawrence peered behind the shelf and let out a little gasp. She tugged on the jutting section of wall and it pulled towards her, exposing a short, darkened hallway. At the end, a wooden door sat slightly ajar.

From where she stood, Lawrence could see what looked to be a hidden study. Lawrence took careful steps, mindful to stay within the darkness, and held her breath as she looked in through the small opening.

A small oak writing desk and Louis XV chair pushed up against the box window overlooked the back pool and garden. Towers of books and papers occupied most of the available space on the floors and tables. The short sofa in the center of the room had a thin blanket and pillow thrown across. On the coffee table, a tray of half-eaten breakfast and the morning paper sat in front of the smoldering embers in the fireplace.

Edwin sat hunched over the desk, with crossed legs and a solemn look on his face. He slowly wrote in a large journal which, as far as Lawrence could see, held long lines of cryptic, seemingly random codes in it. He leaned back in his chair to reference a textbook on wild cryptids from the East, dragging his long pointer finger as his lips mumbled along as he read.

On the couch, Mr. Sinclair sat in silence, peering into the dying fire as he smoked his pipe. The two of them sat in solid silence for a few minutes. Only the faint sound of Edwin turning the page and scribbling in his book disturbed that peace.

Lawrence raised her hand to knock and make her presence known, but Mr. Sinclair abruptly cleared his throat.

"Something must be done," Mr. Sinclair murmured.

Dark bags sat under his eyes and he dragged a weary hand through his beard. He crossed his legs, shook out the ash from his pipe, and helped himself to Edwin's leftover coffee.

"Pa-" began Edwin. Mr. Sinclair put up his hand to stop him.

"No, no, don't disagree with me," he said. "You know it's true, but you don't want to make the first move. I know you well enough now. You're on defense. You think I'm being daft."

"You must not, if you believe I would ever think badly of you," insisted Edwin. He continued to write, seemingly intent on distracting himself through the conversation if necessary.

"How many more will die this time, Edwin?" murmured Mr. Sinclair. His eyes glazed over as he looked into the dying fire. "No, no more. Something will be done this time."

"Something *will* be done," repeated Edwin, but his voice remained firm. He raised his head from his work, turning slightly to look sideways. "You're blinded by your own grief and need for revenge. As soon as those lights came on, you've thought of little else."

He sighed heavily and removed his glasses. He rubbed an ink-stained hand over his eyes.

"Forget about the danger you would be putting yourself in. You'd be putting Augusta at risk, William. Now that I would be unable to forgive even you for."

"She's at risk now," argued Mr. Sinclair. "She'd understand."

Edwin set his pen down, turning fully to speak directly to Mr. Sinclair. His face became blank then, devoid of any spark of anger or pang of sadness. He leaned heavily against the arm of his chair, recrossing his thin legs.

"She doesn't understand, though. It's been terribly hard on her. She is still a young woman in society."

Mr. Sinclair scoffed.

"I know what they all think of me, but I don't care. Who cares what *they* think?" said Mr. Sinclair with a sneer. He clasped his hands together as his voice lowered. "I know what I saw, Edwin. You believe me, don't you?"

"Yes," said Edwin, firmly nodding. "You know I do, Pa."

Mr. Sinclair nodded and looked down as he absentmindedly picked a piece of string off his trousers. He sighed deeply and let out a soft chuckle.

"You know, part of me wished my father *had* done it. I pray you never see someone you love suffer in such a way. It's not living." He shook his head. "I'd rather leave the party in dignity than linger in such a way."

"Pa, please stop talking about dying," pleaded Edwin. "It upsets Augusta, and it upsets me."

"I almost didn't believe it when I saw that thing," said Mr. Sinclair, continuing on as he ignored Edwin. "I don't think it expected my father to be there. He put up a good fight, but he was no match, of course."

Mr. Sinclair shook his head, his fist propping up his cheek as he recalled the memory.

"It was quick, which is its own small mercy, I suppose. It was strange, as if he were nothing but a pig being slaughtered. But with my mother, she took her time. I've only ever seen men savoring wine drink with less relish than that thing did that night when it drained my mother."

Edwin lowered his head. He swallowed thickly and turned to Mr. Sinclair in sympathy. Lawrence felt the hair on the back of her neck rise. She leaned in closer. Edwin sighed heavily.

"Let us suppose," began Edwin. "that it *is* the same creature that killed your parents. She may be much older and stronger than we are prepared to face."

126

Mr. Sinclair repacked his pipe and lit it, biting down hard on the wooden mouthpiece. He did not immediately respond.

"What have you found?"

"Very little," sighed the young man. "And my own personal experience is limited. In my one run-in, it was not anything like what the elders at the Symposium said it would be like. He was fast and unpredictable. He was perhaps stronger than most men, but he was large anyways, so it may have just been a coincidence. By the time we got to him, he had killed two sheep, three cows, five men, four women, and a young boy."

Lawrence's skin went cold and goosebumps covered her arms. She shivered as she listened to Edwin speak so impersonally about what sounded like a massacre. He spoke in his usual grave manner, but Lawrence felt nausea clawing its way up her throat.

"His wife told us he still visited her at night," Edwin continued. "The locals believed she was simply suffering from delusions, or grief. She kept the windows and doors open for him, waiting. At first, she thought it was just an apparition. I didn't understand why he didn't kill her. I assume it was because he still loved her."

"Beings like that can't love, Edwin."

"Perhaps," said Edwin, rubbing his chin. He did not seem entirely convinced, but held his tongue. He cleared his throat lightly before continuing. "She died, crushed in his arms. He had held her too tightly, and I suppose he didn't comprehend his own strength. I think he really did love her. I saw him try to cut his own head off afterwards; he was so miserable."

"They're irrational, emotional, and possessive perhaps." Mr. Sinclair tugged at his beard as he spoke, pensive as he thought things over. He turned to Edwin, then, out of curiosity. "Did you kill it?"

Edwin shook his head. "We followed him as he laid down to rest in a little cave. He lay in a little box, like a coffin. He had been dead for two weeks, but his body was as fresh as if he had just died that day. We tried to put a stake through his heart and cut his head off for good measure, but it was no use. In the end, all that came of it was that I lost a dear friend," he murmured, looking down. "I don't want to lose you as well, Pa."

"Son, we are men of science," said Mr. Sinclair. His eyes shined with love and warmth. He gestured with his hands as he spoke. "Despite what the world may think, we know the truth, and that comes with a price. You know as well as I that more than a few lives will be lost in that noble pursuit of extinguishing true evil."

"Is that why you do this then? To save other people?" Edwin asked, letting out a snort. He laughed bitterly. "I don't. I do it for my own selfish reasons. I saw what was out there, and it frightened me. Now, I only do it to save the people I love. Am I evil too, then, if I admit that?"

"You're not evil; you're honest. More honest than most." Mr. Sinclair exhaled a large cloud of smoke and gave Edwin a wry smile. "We all need that one person who makes saving the world a worthy endeavor. You *are* a good man, Edwin Ernest. Do not forget it."

Edwin remained pensive for a few moments as he considered Mr. Sinclair's words.

"I can be the lure."

"Certainly not!" cried Mr. Sinclair. "An unnecessary risk beyond necessity. If things do not go to plan, I will not let you risk your life over my own. I have lived my life. You should have a chance to live yours. If I die, Augusta will be alone in this world. She is the last Sinclair, and she cares for and loves you very deeply. You must look after her, Mr. Ernest. Promise me, Edwin."

Edwin hesitated a moment, but finally bowed his head and placed a hand over his heart.

"Yes, I promise."

"Good lad."

"LJ, are you in here?" Augusta's voice called out from the empty library.

Lawrence whipped around from where she remained hidden in the dark hallway. She watched as Augusta spotted the open door and headed towards it.

Within the study, Edwin and Mr. Sinclair both turned when they heard Augusta's voice and quickly straightened themselves out. Edwin turned back to his work while Mr. Sinclair rose to stand by the fire.

The short walkway contained a small broom closet. Lawrence dove into it, shutting the door just as Augusta entered and breezed by. She burst into the study a moment later.

"There you two are, holed away in the study like rabbits in their warren." Augusta's voice carried to where Lawrence hid. "Pa, have you seen LJ?"

"LJ?" the older man repeated.

"We sent her in awhile ago to get you two; she didn't find you?"

"Can't say she did."

Lawrence took the risk of pushing the closet door open a bit. She looked out from the opening and into the study. Augusta's back remained to her as she moved further into the room.

"Oh dear," Augusta murmured as she played with her bracelet, the beads clicking around as she did. "I do hope she hasn't gotten lost. Perhaps I shouldn't have sent her. Now, you two must come out and join us at once. Stop hiding away in this dark room at all hours of the day. Otherwise, I'll never forgive you. I'll carry it to my grave. I'm very good at carrying grudges to the grave. You know I mean it, too. Pa, it's tea time. Edwin, I won't hear your excuses. You two are joining us for tea, and that's final. Pa, you must find LJ."

"Aye aye, captain."

Mr. Sinclair emptied out his pipe once more and saluted his granddaughter. He slapped Edwin on the shoulder. He walked to the doorway but paused, turning to look back.

"Chin up, lad. You never know. We may be successful!"

Mr. Sinclair passed by Lawrence's hiding spot, humming as he walked, leaving only Augusta and Edwin together in the study. Augusta stood behind Edwin at his desk, who seemed wholly engrossed in his work.

"Martin said you went out again this morning," said Augusta, breaking the silence. "I wish you wouldn't run along the cliff trail. It's not safe. Especially with the winds and whatnot."

"Considering I'm not a piece of tissue," he drawled. "I think I should be relatively safe."

"You are nearly as skinny as one, so forgive me if I get confused," she snapped back.

In response, Edwin chuckled. He then paused and then tilted his head up at her.

"Are you having Martin keep tabs on me now, Birdy?"

Augusta said nothing and placed a hand across the back of his chair. As she observed them, Lawrence realized that they seemed like almost entirely different people. Augusta leaned over his chair to look at his work.

"What does it say?" she asked.

"If you read that book I gave you, you would know," he murmured back.

"You're very clever," she said, poking the side of his head. "I despise men who are overly clever. Makes me think they're compensating for something."

He laughed again, the sound low and resonating from within him. It was the first time Lawrence had seen Edwin smile so warmly. His eyes glittered as he looked up at Augusta with open adoration. He leaned back, crossed his arms, and cleared his throat lightly.

"So a man like Patrick would be your ideal type, then?"

"Oh, certainly," nodded Augusta. "Big, brutish, and a bit of a palooka. Just my type."

"Well, I know for a fact that you're not *his* type," muttered Edwin. He shut his notebook, setting it aside neatly for him to return to later. "You're worth more than he is, and you easily beat him at poker. No, not his type at all."

"I suppose I'll spend the rest of my days pining after someone who doesn't want me then," she said quietly.

Edwin looked sideways at her with a curious expression, but said nothing. She began picking at her nails, which she was prone to do sometimes when nervous.

"What were you and Pa talking about?"

"Do you want to know the truth?" Edwin asked.

He raised his head and they looked deeply into each other's eyes. She then smiled weakly with a shake of her head. She turned to look elsewhere, picking harder at her nails.

"No, I don't think so," she whispered. "I don't want to know at all."

He nodded his head then in complete understanding. She leaned closer to him and spoke under her breath.

"Will you tell me, though, if he's in danger?" she asked. "Will you keep him safe?"

Lawrence pitied Edwin. Burdened by his devotion to the family, he was stuck in the center of them. She watched a certain emotion flit across his face then, and he swallowed thickly. He didn't answer her, instead opting to give her a reassuring smile and a nod.

"You're being safe too, aren't you?" she asked.

"Oh, do you care for me then, Birdy?" he asked jokingly.

"Of course I do," she answered in all sincerity.

She placed her hand on his shoulder, which tensed slightly in response. After a moment, he placed his hand over hers and patted it. Augusta smiled brightly then and the somber, serious mood in the room was dispelled. She grabbed his elbow and dragged him from his seat. Lawrence quickly retreated back into the dark closet.

"Time for tea; we're late as is! Have I told you how things are getting on with the party? I'm going absolutely batty dealing with all these details. It's so hard to find good, reliable people these days. You'd think, honestly, that things would be ironed out. I mean, we have been throwing it for years now. What's the big idea? It's such a bother, especially getting good booze in. Margaret Kilmartin's cousin had a party, and she said half the hooch was just paint thinner and diesel fuel! They had a cracking time, but still. That's not the sort of soirée we're throwing here. It's awful. Absolutely awful. Anyway, you won't believe the fight I've had with the caterers. It's been such a palaver."

Augusta continued to chatter on. Lawrence heard as the two of them passed, the clicking of their shoes fading with time. She waited for a moment longer in the dark closet, releasing her breath once they were long gone.

Lawrence left the library, looking both ways down the empty hallway before she did so. Mr. Sinclair and Edwin's conversation continued to replay in her mind. She made it halfway down the hall before a voice called out to her.

"Miss Stoner?"

She turned and saw Mr. Sinclair at the opposite end of the hall. He stood with his hands in his pockets, a knowing smile on his face. His eyes twinkled as she approached and he held out his elbow for her to take. She took it and they began to walk side-by-side.

"May I ask you something personal?" he asked her suddenly. She nodded. "May I ask why you left Italy at all?"

"I thought I had said?" He shook his head. She took a moment to think, shrugging.

"I suppose I grew tired of the place. That's dreadful of me to say, isn't it? A poor girl from the middle of nowhere goes abroad and grew tired of it? It's obscene."

"Why should being a poor girl from the middle of nowhere have anything to do with that?" he asked.

Lawrence shook her head, smiling as she remembered how she felt when she had first landed there.

"It was truly as alien to me as if I had gone off to another planet entirely. The cobblestone streets and baked, yellow houses in towns older than anything I could fully comprehend. In the early evening, the elders would gather around rickety wooden tables, playing card games and moaning about pains no one else would understand."

Mr. Sinclair laughed at that, patting her hand in understanding. Lawrence's fond smile faded.

"Then, I got used to things. I stopped getting winded as I walked up the same hills every day. I saw the same people every day: the same workers who'd smoke on the same corner and talk about the same war, the women who breastfed their screaming, red-faced babies, and the same old men who sat around the cafe to play chess. Everything became an expectation."

"There is a curious blessing in that too, though, isn't there?" said Mr. Sinclair with a thoughtful look. "I have come to understand there's a certain privilege to boring routines."

"You'll understand then that the only natural conclusion I could come to is that the greater issue lay within me," said Lawrence, her head nearly hung in shame. "I had no purpose and the very idea of routine offended me; no amount of good food or beautiful scenery can resolve that. If a greater calling serves as the fuel to the engine of one's life, I worry I may never find happiness or be content in this life."

"Oh," said Mr. Sinclair with a sage smile. He patted her arm. "But you *are* still alive, Miss Stoner. Some people go out in the dark with shovels and lanterns to seek out purpose, while others find it as it arrives on the soft wing of a butterfly."

Lawrence returned his smile and leaned into his side.

"Don't worry. Since that time, I feel that a sort of calm has come over me. I'm not bothered by it now. I imagine it's the sort of strange sense of peace that eventually comes to people once they realize they are going to die."

"Are the general population as of yet not aware of that eventuality?" Mr. Sinclair asked with a curious expression.

Lawrence laughed and they reached the end of the hall. Before they turned, Mr. Sinclair stopped.

"You do have a purpose, Miss Stoner, and I believe your being here will make a great difference."

He looked at her in all seriousness. The sharp, herbal scent of his necklace hit her, and she looked at it. She had nothing to say in response to that.

"May I be forward just once more?"

"Of course," she said immediately, interested in what he had to say.

"You remind me of my late wife," he said. He looked over her face as if he were seeing his late wife through her. Lawrence smiled fondly. "I mean that as the greatest of compliments."

"That's not forward at all," she said. "What a lovely thing to say. To be compared to a loved one *is* such a compliment. Would it be too forward of me if I ask how she passed?"

"Oh," he said, his eyes glazing over slightly. His eyes lowered as a thin veil of wetness filled his usually bright eyes. "Perhaps the greatest evil of all. An unseen killer took her right out from under my nose! Cancer, in her pancreas."

He placed a hand over his torso where the organ lay beneath.

"Devious little illness. Works harder than the devil."

He laughed roughly and patted Lawrence's hand, who stared at him in sympathy. She nodded her head.

"She told me, 'Willie, you would have fought Death tooth and nail to keep me here, but it looks like the tricky bastard knew exactly how to get past even you.'"

"She sounds like she didn't need anyone fighting on her behalf, actually," said Lawrence. Mr. Sinclair let out a rough sound of agreement.

"We should go," he said, turning to continue on walking. "I believe the others have something set up. We're late, and I'm afraid my sweet granddaughter is quite insisting we be on time. Scarier than a yeti."

"Mr. Sinclair?"

He turned his head to her, expectant. She opened her mouth to speak, but nothing came out. When one had so many things to say and ask, it was strange how nothing came to mind. He smiled once more, patted her on the arm, and they continued on their way.

* * *

In the backyard, the trio of friends stood under a great oak tree at the far edge of the property. Augusta held a small bouquet of daisies, fussing over the flowers continuously. Patrick worked on shoveling out a small hole, cigar still in his mouth. Edwin stood off to the side, a rectangular box held carefully between both hands. Mr. Sinclair led Lawrence to them.

"What is this?" she asked.

Augusta turned and skipped forward. She smiled and grabbed Lawrence's other free arm, pulling her from Mr. Sinclair.

"We thought it'd be a mighty fine idea to come together and make something pleasant out of the rotten way things turned last night."

They stopped in front of the small hole, and Patrick stepped away.

He set the shovel up against the tree and wiped the back of his hand across his sweaty brow.

"I'm supposing we won't need all six feet for the cat."

"Yes, yes. We acknowledge your fifteen minutes of physical labor, Patrick. Well done," Edwin said drolly.

Patrick nodded and slapped his hand on Edwin's shoulder, coming to stand by his side. Edwin handed the box to Lawrence when she approached and gave her a subtle nod. She didn't have to look inside, knowing what lay within. Her throat constricted and she swallowed past the lump that formed. She held the box closely and placed a hand over the top.

"Well," she said.

She sniffed and looked around at the four of them with a grateful smile. She opened her mouth to thank them and express all she felt, but couldn't. Augusta squeezed her arm and nodded encouragingly for her to go forward on her own.

Lawrence kneeled by the small hole and set the box gently inside. She dropped a handful of dirt over the top.

"I'm sorry about this," she murmured to it. She raised her head to take in the surroundings with the great tree above and ocean a few yards in the distance. "Not a bad place to rest, though, is it?"

She got up and wiped at the fat tears that rolled down her cheeks. Augusta gave her a sad smile and hooked their arms together. Patrick wordlessly took up his shovel again and packed the dirt on top.

"The Lord is my shepherd, I lack nothing. He makes me lie down in green pastures, he leads me beside quiet waters, he refreshes my soul," Mr. Sinclair recited, looking up towards the Heavens.

"It's silly really," Lawrence murmured lowly to Augusta. She roughly wiped at her cheeks. "He wasn't even my cat. Not really."

"Don't be silly, Stoner," called out Patrick as he finished packing the dirt over the grave. He gestured to the small wooden cross stuck into the dirt. "You got a name for him?"

"Just, Stinky Boy," she replied with a watery smile. Patrick paused for a moment.

"Perhaps we keep it empty then," he said under his breath.

Augusta kicked him in the shin with a reprimanding look as Edwin shook his head. Lawrence couldn't help but laugh. Augusta stepped forward and set the daisies on the grave, rearranging it until she was satisfied.

As the others slowly walked away, Lawrence stared for a little longer. Someone stayed with her, and when she turned to see who it was, she was surprised to see Edwin.

"You have a big heart," he stated.

He had his hands clasped behind his back and looked at least twenty years his senior in that moment. He looked down at the fresh dirt on the grave with a pensive look.

"Augusta also has a big heart. It's what makes me worry. Those with big hearts feel each emotion more keenly, and tend to lose the most."

"Well, it sounds like she's in very good hands. I'm sure you will take good care of her."

"And who will take care of you?" he asked. Lawrence paused, unsure of how to answer. He nodded in understanding.

"You see, you needn't face everything on your own. The others have already taken quite a liking to you."

"I've been on my own for some time now," she said carefully. "I do appreciate it, but I think I'll be fine. I like to think I keep my head screwed on right."

He studied her and nodded. He pushed his wire frame glasses up his nose a bit further.

"All the same, may I offer some unsolicited advice? As a friend."

Lawrence schooled her face to remain impassive, but she wanted to smile at the idea that Edwin considered her a friend. She nodded and he stepped a bit forward.

"If you find yourself waking in strange places or finding strange marks on you, come to us immediately. Nothing will be too silly or small a concern. Do you understand?"

Lawrence nodded, a bit taken aback. She thought for a moment about confiding in Edwin about the invitation she had received or the scabs on her chest. Again, though, words failed her and she chose instead to remain silent. Edwin seemed content, having done his duty to warn her, and moved away. He began to walk back towards the house and looked over his shoulder a final time.

"Do not linger too long, LJ."

Lawrence stood under the tree for a bit longer. She brushed her long hair away from her face as it blew in the wind. She turned her eyes upwards towards Widows Weep as it stood off in the distance. She wiped away any errant tears and made the slow walk back to the others.

Chapter 8

Lawrence arrived to Ashmore promptly in time for dinner. She knocked three times and waited, fiddling with the edge of her black skirt as she did. The door opened a crack and Ms. Hettle's face appeared in the sliver of an opening.

"Is that you, painter?" she asked lowly.

"Yes, good evening," greeted Lawrence with a pleasant smile.

Ms. Hettle paused for a moment, murmuring something incomprehensible under her breath. It seemed for a moment that she struggled with whether or not to let Lawrence in at all. She finally sighed and pushed the door open further to let her in. She gave a little bow of her white head as Lawrence passed by.

"Follow me," Ms. Hettle murmured. "Don't wander off now."

The moment Lawrence entered, Ms. Hettle quickly closed the door. All the light from outside was shut out, and they were plunged into darkness.

"Ms. Hettle?" Lawrence called out, a bit alarmed.

She remained rooted to the spot, squinting as her eyes acclimated to the dimly lit mansion. A few candles lit the front hall and the wide entryway. Ms. Hettle appeared a few feet ahead and Lawrence quickly followed after her.

Two grand staircases led up to a mezzanine that wrapped around the top and overlooked the entrance below. Lawrence had only a minute to take it in, mindful to stay within Ms. Hettle's shadow.

The old woman knew exactly where she was going, where every door was, and exactly how many paces it was from one end of the room to the other. She moved at such a swift pace through the shadowy halls that she almost seemed like a floating specter herself.

The clicking of their heels echoed as they crossed the marble lobby. There was a strange staleness to the air within Ashmore; the air didn't seem to move at all. It was as if the rooms themselves were holding a collective breath, waiting and watching.

Goosebumps erupted up Lawrence's arm and a tingling sensation shot up her spine. She turned, peering uselessly into the darkness, searching for the pair of eyes she felt following her. She threw a glance over her shoulder every so often, but was met only with shadowy corners and empty hallways. Her shoulders remained tense and she clasped her hands tightly together to keep from shaking.

Ms. Hettle brought Lawrence to a set of oak double doors, engraved with intricate patterns that were impossible to make out in the darkness. The housekeeper pushed open one of the doors and a great flood of light illuminated the pair of them like they stood before the Gates of Heaven.

Lawrence quickly stepped into the brilliantly lit room, relieved. She looked over her shoulder at Ms. Hettle, who remained outside in the darkness.

"Stay here."

Lawrence turned to thank her, but the door shut quickly and she was left alone. She turned to take in the room. A pleasant fire crackled in the stone fireplace. She stepped closer to it, holding out her hands to warm herself from the chill that clung to her from the moment she stepped foot through the front door.

An enormous red and green Persian rug covered the floor. Rich chocolate mahogany walls with interior trim paneled each of the walls. Hand-painted murals occupied each inner panel, depicting what looked like scenes from the Inferno. All the filigree and detailing on the ceiling were detailed with gold, catching the firelight every so often. Two layers of thick curtains hung over the windows and matched the velvet, tufted chairs at the long dining table. Above the fireplace, a large clock on the mantle ticked methodically.

A long table meant for ten was set neatly for just two. Silver cloches covered fine china to keep the food warm. Lawrence placed a hand on the top of one, feeling the warmth still radiating from within. The two settings were directly opposite to each other in the center of the long table, one in front of the wide fireplace and the other in front of the long, covered windows.

Lawrence walked over to the windows and mindlessly pushed the curtains back. Only the dark waters of the Atlantic and the rugged coast could be seen. Rolling mountains of thick spruces and firs remained on the untouched, preserved land to the west. It seemed a terrible shame to keep the curtains drawn, but she moved them back nonetheless.

Lawrence took a seat at the table, facing the fireplace. Her eyes flickered from one detail of the room to the next. A strange sensation came over her then, and she felt separated from her own self. In that brightly lit room with the windows covered, it almost seemed as if time did not pass at all.

Wind whistled through the flue of the fireplace and a shower of sparks shot up as a log popped and fell in the grate. Lawrence heard her own heartbeat until it matched the staccato of the clock's ticking. The wood paneling in the ceiling creaked, moving as if the house itself were breathing. Then, in that loud silence, a quiet scratching.

It came from above, muted and far away. There were three, long scratches against the floor until it fell quiet. All Lawrence knew was that it distinctly did not resemble the scrabbling of small claws like a rat scampering through the walls. It was something bigger. Had there been any other noise or distraction, Lawrence would have missed it entirely. She tilted her head upward, listening. She waited for the scratching to return, but it never did.

A sudden shift in the atmosphere stirred the calm air. The same animal instinct that alerts grazing deer to the lurking presence of a shadowy predator in the nearby brush caused Lawrence to raise her head then. Directly behind stood a woman with one hand on the back of her chair, and the other reaching out towards her.

"Oh!" Lawrence's hand flew up to her mouth as she shot up from her seat.

She bumped into the table as she rose, and she nearly fell backwards into it. The crystal water glass by her elbow teetered dangerously. Just as it tipped over to fall, the woman's hand shot out and grabbed it. She righted it without spilling a drop on the pristine tablecloth. Lawrence barely had time to react and instead reached out to steady her chair before it fell. She clutched her chest and let out a choking gasp.

"I'm– I'm sorry, I didn't hear you come in."

"On the contrary, you must forgive me. I've startled you."

Her voice was low, like the distant rumble of thunder, and soft, like the underbelly purring of a feline. She peered down at Lawrence for a moment before she stepped away, walking round to the other side of the table to take her seat.

Lawrence settled back into her seat and reached for her water to distract herself. She glanced up through her lashes as the lady sat. Her heartbeat continued to thunder in her chest and her breath caught as she observed the woman across from her.

Ophelia Aldane was no old woman, as she somehow came to expect. She had strong, structured features and a regal face usually seen on old coins. Her high cheekbones gave her a sharp profile and her long nose curved down over her full lips. Her inky hair sat tightly set into a short, boyish bob that Lawrence had otherwise only seen on French models on the cover of magazines.

Whatever unease she had about coming to Ashmore ceased to matter. Seeing her in person was like turning the light onto a shadowy corner of the room, thinking the bogeyman was there, only to realize it was nothing at all.

How silly it all seemed then. Ms. Aldane was a being of flesh and blood.

She smiled tightly at Lawrence. Her dark, plum lips stretched back as she did, but her mouth remained closed. She draped the silk napkin across her lap and leaned forward, placing her sharp elbows on the table, fingers steepled before her feline face.

The orange hue from the fireplace cast a fiery glow around her and made it seem as if she were glowing, or burning alive. The two of them stared at each other for a moment in total silence.

"You've got glasses on."

Lawrence nearly choked the moment the thoughtless remark slipped past her lips. They had not met for five minutes altogether, and she simply made the first observation that came to mind.

Ms. Aldane did not seem to mind, though, and simply nodded. She spoke again in her low, cultured voice.

"Yes, I hope you do not mind. I have a strong sensitivity to the light. All kinds. I hope it is not too distracting."

"Not at all," assured Lawrence with a polite smile. She shook her head. "Please forgive my thoughtlessness. I can sometimes really put my foot in it."

Ophelia smiled again, little dimples forming in her cheeks as she did. Lawrence's own cheeks burned and she coughed lightly.

The sleek, round spectacles completely obscured Ophelia's eyes behind the opaque lenses. The thin, gold frames hugged her face tightly, and pencil-thin, straight brows framed the top. She observed Lawrence silently, her lips pulled back in her closed smile.

"Ms. Aldane-" Lawrence began.

"Ophelia," she insisted, corrected Lawrence gently. "You must call me Ophelia."

"Oh," Lawrence stuttered, laughing lightly. She absentmindedly brushed a hand over her unkempt bun. "Uh, well, I just wanted to thank you for inviting me to dinner."

"Of course, dinner." Ophelia shook her head as if she had forgotten. "Do not let me keep you."

She gestured to the plate before Lawrence.

They removed the covers to reveal golden chicken with buttery potatoes and crisp, steamed greens. Lawrence made a small noise of appreciation, but Ophelia seemed unmoved. While Lawrence picked up her fork, Ophelia instead reached into her pocket and produced the card Lawrence had left with Ms. Hettle. She studied it and set it down gently on the table.

"I do apologize for not meeting with you properly when you first came by to drop off your card," she said.

"Not at all," said Lawrence, cutting into her food. She kept her eyes down, but nonetheless felt the heat of Ophelia's unerring gaze. "You must be very busy."

"I confess I have not been *busy* for many years, but I do have a bit of trouble sleeping at night, so I end up sleeping through the day. That and I had taken a short trip to Derby shortly before you visited, so I was still recuperating."

"Won't you be joining me?" Lawrence asked, pointedly looking at Ophelia's untouched plate of food.

"I am not hungry. I had quite a large meal," Ophelia smiled, chuckling to herself as if it were some personal joke.

She raised her wine glass to her lips. Lawrence watched the muscles move in the slender column of her throat as she swallowed.

As Lawrence ate, Ophelia observed her closely. Whenever she lowered her eyes, Lawrence felt the same prickling feeling on the back of her neck and her skin grew hot. When she did look up, Ophelia's entire attention remained on her. She studied Lawrence with interest as she ate. She asked repeatedly if Lawrence enjoyed the food and if there were anything at all that she needed. Each time, Lawrence confirmed the food to be excellent and that she was perfectly content.

"And what do you think of my home?" Ophelia asked.

Lawrence dabbed at her lips with her napkin. She gestured her head around to the opulent room they sat in.

"It's very lovely. I admit I didn't have the chance to see much of it yet, but what I have seen is absolutely beautiful, like this room."

Ophelia took a look around herself. She turned her head to glance over the dark wood panels and murals along the walls, but only for a passing moment. One of her delicate brows rose and she hummed under her breath.

"Yes, well, it is kind of you to say so. I admit it's been some time since I've been back to this house. I'd nearly forgotten all about it, to be honest," she said. "A small chalet at the end of the world."

Lawrence stifled an amused laugh at the less than apt description. "May I ask what compelled you to come back then?"

"I was not entirely sure myself," Ophelia said slowly. She then looked to Lawrence with a downward tilt of her head. "But, I believe I may know the reason now."

Lawrence swallowed thickly and looked back to her food. She pushed some of the food around her plate.

"So, this home must have been in your family for quite some time?"

"Oh, for ages," said Ophelia, nodding. "Things were a lot quieter back then, and much more private."

Ophelia drummed her fingers across the armrest of her chair. She looked sideways and Lawrence appreciated her striking profile. Perhaps Patrick had been right, and Ophelia really was a descendant of royalty; she certainly had the right air to her. Lawrence cleared her throat lightly, and Ophelia turned her head back slowly.

"I had the great pleasure of meeting your neighbors, the Sinclairs. I had dinner at theirs a day ago."

Lawrence took the opportunity to meet the dark lenses of Ophelia's gaze. The unblinking black along with Ophelia's hollowed cheeks made Lawrence feel as if she were staring into a skull.

"I believe you may have met them before?"

She studied Ophelia's face closely, but her immediate reaction gave nothing away. Ophelia furrowed her brow as if in concentration and looked aside to try and recall, but she then shook her head.

"No, I can't say I have."

A strange sense of relief washed over Lawrence and a vice around her stomach she had not felt before, eased. The corner of her lips quirked up.

"Have you no interest in becoming more well acquainted then?"

At the mention of that, Ophelia's nose scrunched up as if she had smelled something foul.

"Not at all," she replied offhandedly. "I simply value my privacy. In small towns like these, privacy is a commodity more valuable than gold."

Lawrence nodded in understanding. It seemed perfectly reasonable and aligned with how purposefully detached Ashmore was from the other estates along the coast.

"Yes, I can sense how that may be true."

Ophelia raised her glass and seemed to study the floral design etched into the crystal. Her slender fingers wrapped around the glass and she tapped a long, tapered nail against it.

"I understand Mr. Sinclair lost his parents when he was quite young. Quite the *scandal*."

She seemed to suppress a smirk and covered her mouth with the back of her hand. Lawrence tensed momentarily, but swallowed quickly and focused again on eating.

"Yes, from what I hear, it was quite awful," she murmured. She raised her eyes to covertly study Ophelia, who gazed off to study the wall. "He wholeheartedly believes in his father's innocence, and I believe him."

Ophelia's form remained frozen as if she were a true statue. Her tapping fingers froze mid-air for a brief moment. Even Lawrence's own breathing paused. Ophelia then chuckled lowly and the tapping resumed.

"I see."

"Do you not-"

"Are you done?" Ophelia asked abruptly, looking pointedly at Lawrence's mostly empty plate. Lawrence nodded and Ophelia quickly rose, tossing her napkin aside.

Lawrence neatly folded her own and set it aside. She dutifully followed Ophelia through the double doors back into the darkness. She faltered for a moment as her eyes adjusted, but Ophelia stayed close and shot a coquettish smile over her shoulder. The way Ophelia moved, the serpentine sway back and forth and confident gait, reminded Lawrence of a jungle cat, a panther.

Ophelia led Lawrence out across the dark foyer, heels clicking against the marble tile. Small pools of candlelight created puddles of light across the floor, disrupted by their passing bodies and the long shadows that followed.

Past a second pair of double doors, the pair entered a library. The fireplace roared and the curtains remained tightly closed in this room too. Even in the limited light, Lawrence saw the towering ceilings covered floor to wall in shelves of books. A second floor walkway wrapped around the perimeter with a winding staircase against the wall. Two red sofas sat opposite to each other by the fire, and Ophelia gestured for Lawrence to take one. She crossed the room to a drink cart. She held a dark bottle aloft and shook it gently.

"May I pour you something to drink?" she asked.

Lawrence paused momentarily, looking at the bottle and Ophelia chuckled.

"I won't tell if you don't."

"Seems the 18th amendment is more of a loose guideline in this part of the country," Lawrence murmured with a dry chuckle. "And, no. Thank you."

"A passing phase," said Ophelia. "Once they see that people will always find a way to fuel their vices, the learned men of Washington will come to understand that simply regulating sin is far better, and far more profitable."

"A worrying thought," said Lawrence with a polite smile. "I'm glad the people were able to make their voices heard, and see their goals realized. Speaks favorably upon our government, doesn't it?"

Ophelia looked over her shoulder and leveled Lawrence with an amused look. She then nodded and said nothing further on the matter. Lawrence settled her hands in her lap and observed Ophelia's bare back as she poured her own drink.

"You don't keep much staff on," noted Lawrence. "Is that usual for someone in your position?"

"And what position is that?" asked Ophelia.

She then shrugged as she stoppered a crystal decanter of amber liquid.

"I prefer to keep things simple. Whatever I cannot do, I rely on the housekeeper. Otherwise, I am perfectly capable."

"Well, I imagined a lady such as yourself would have a house full of servants. I find it admirable, though, that you are so self-sufficient."

Ophelia sat opposite to Lawrence, crossing her legs at the ankles as she did so. The mahogany beads of her dress clacked with each movement, and the loose short skirts exposed some of her long, shapely legs. Lawrence averted her eyes quickly and instead turned her attention to the intricate pattern of the rug underfoot.

"I accept your admiration," said Ophelia. "Gladly."

Ophelia's slender hand wrapped around the glass and her nails occasionally tapped against the crystal. Her attention remained wholly focused on Lawrence and she continued to give her a thin, tight smile.

"Ms. Ald-Ophelia," Lawrence began.

"May I call you Lawrence?" Ophelia asked, interrupting her and her train of thought.

"LJ," Lawrence said. "My friends all call me LJ. I don't quite like the name Lawrence. I think it's too manly. I wish it had been something more feminine."

"I disagree. It's a beautiful name, and it suits you fine," she said, quite firm on the issue. "And I'd prefer not to be grouped in with any others. If calling you by your lovely name makes me singularly different, then all the more reason."

"Very well," Lawrence laughed, easily persuaded.

Something warmed within her to hear Ophelia express such interest to be special to her, even if it were only by the way she addressed her.

"If I may, I'm quite interested in knowing more about you, Lawrence. So won't you please tell me about yourself?"

Lawrence flushed, equally taken aback and flattered that someone like Ophelia would be interested in knowing anything about her.

"Well, I don't know what you would like to know."

"Everything. You must start before the beginning," demanded

Ophelia, entirely serious.

Lawrence laughed lightly, fidgeting in her seat at the overwhelming request. She suddenly grew unsure on how to relay her own history effectively, or objectively. She brushed a hand over her hastily done updo as she considered her words. Ophelia's gaze closely followed the action, and it felt as if she were just a bug under a magnifying glass.

"In all honesty, I can't really remember what my childhood was like," Lawrence began. "I mean, I can remember it, but it's just a sort of vague collection of memories. It's quite sad, isn't it? Either, I have such a lousy memory that I can't remember my own life or it was just really that uninspiring."

Although Lawrence laughed, Ophelia remained deathly still. She waited patiently, instead, for Lawrence to continue. Lawrence wet her lips.

"There's really not much to say. It's all rather quite boring, really. I grew up in the Midwest. Have you ever been?"

Ophelia shook her head. Lawrence nodded, understanding.

"I used to hate it when I was young; it disgusted me, actually. Just the wind and the never-ending flat land nauseated me. I had always been a bit dramatic." Lawrence smiled as she recalled her youth.

The memory of her family's small home and town in the middle of nowhere flashed through Lawrence's mind. Brief recollections of the local general store and the small chapel they attended on Sunday mornings, scrubbed clean and in their best clothes, came to the front of Lawrence's mind. Whatever had held her tongue until then loosened, and she spoke without caution.

"My father was a logger, and my mother stayed at home. They were good people. Good god-fearing, law-abiding people. Though, I know they were always a bit disappointed in me. First, for being a girl. They wanted so badly to have a son they didn't even consider any girl names. They just gave me the name they would've given me if I had been a boy." She paused then as her lips pursed slightly. "Then, I was an only child. You can only imagine how much more disappointing that was. I did have a younger brother once, but he didn't live for very long. I suppose it doesn't count then, does it?"

Her eyes flickered up momentarily and only caught the reflection of her own face in Ophelia's glasses. She had yet to move at all, and it almost seemed as if she were not breathing.

"Anyways, they died from an accident. I went to Italy shortly after and I studied under Signor De Luca in Florence, which is where I was until I came here. Anyways, I'm sure it's all a bit boring in comparison to your life, or any other life, really. You see, I've not done much."

After a short breath of silence, Lawrence's face heated. She had been asked a simple question about herself and she ended up sharing far too much. A hot flush of shame crept up her neck. Ophelia took a moment to consider Lawrence's words and tilted her head slightly, as if confused.

"You are not a disappointment, Lawrence. Quite the opposite," she stated firmly. Lawrence's brows rose, taken aback. The great sincerity with which she spoke, though, caught her off guard and she did not know how to react. "I cannot help but notice, though, that you did not really tell me much about yourself at all. For the parts you did, you were quite disparaging."

"That's just the Midwest in me coming out."

The expression on Ophelia's face twisted, and the corner of her lip raised slightly.

"An interesting American turn of phrase I am unfamiliar with, I think."

Lawrence laughed again, running her finger along the inner ridge of her palm. "It just means we don't really like talking about ourselves. Especially not in a positive way."

"I see," she hummed, tipping her glass up to her lips. When she was done, she licked her lips. "Why did you choose painting? Did you always dream of becoming a painter then?"

Lawrence gave her a wry smile and a shake of her head. "Not always."

"What made you want to become one, then?" Ophelia asked, pressing.

Lawrence "tsked" lightly under her breath, and crossed her arms. "I'm afraid that's a bit of a secret."

Ophelia smiled, the corner of her lip raising slightly and briefly revealing the tip of a sharp canine. "Is there any hope of you sharing it with me?"

"Maybe one day."

Ophelia hummed, intrigued. "I will have to work hard to gain your trust in this matter then. Very well. Tell me, at least, what it means to you now."

Lawrence considered simply telling Ophelia the truth, but decided against it. Even then, it was painful to even think about Domenica. She smiled and shrugged.

"I suppose I do it because I want to leave a part of me behind. Something to be remembered by. Maybe a hundred years from now, someone will see something I painted and will understand that part of me, and we'll be connected in that way," Lawrence said. "It's a terribly lonely thing to be alive. We only really know ourselves, don't we? It sounds like I'm just afraid of being misunderstood, and maybe that's a big part of it, but I think I'm mostly afraid of being forgotten. I'd like very much to be remembered. It's such a terrible tragedy, I think, to be alive and then forgotten about entirely." She paused a moment before continuing on. "I feel so much, and I can't bear keeping it all within me. I don't know how the others do it. Although, perhaps I'm going on for too long now. I have a bad habit of rattling on when given the opportunity."

Ophelia listened quietly until Lawrence was done. Although Lawrence chattered on, she never got the impression that Ophelia were bored or put off in any way. Although she had just chastised herself to maintain some self control, she forgot all about it within a few moments with alarming ease. Ophelia smiled her close-lipped smile.

"You are an artist. Only those who appreciate life can be artists. And you are wrong; you do not rattle. I am delighted and interested in all of what you have to say."

Lawrence's heart fluttered and she swallowed thickly. She stretched her legs out then, and Ophelia's head dropped slightly to take in the action.

"That's very kind, but I don't think I can accept such a lofty compliment," Lawrence said with a shake of her head.

"There is no need to be embarrassed. It is true."

With nothing to say in response, Lawrence ducked her head and turned her gaze towards the fire. She prayed the the warmth from the flames would excuse the constant redness that bloomed across her face. When she looked back, she kept her gaze firmly on the slender lines that made up Ophelia's throat.

"May I ask you something?" she asked.

Ophelia gave a little tilt of her head and nodded. She leaned forward and pulled a thin cigarette out of a little carousel on the table.

"May I ask why you invited me to dinner?" Lawrence asked, tentatively.

"Why, you left your card here, did you not?"

"Yes, but that was if you were interested in commissioning a portrait from me."

"What if I am?"

"Are you?"

153

Ophelia paused for a moment and brought the cigarette to her lips. "I'm not particularly interested in getting one, no."

Lawrence's heart sank and bitter disappointment filled her mouth. She nodded her head in understanding, but before she lost the opportunity entirely, she reached out to try and wrestle it back in her favor.

"I'm not very good with words, and this might be too forward," she said. Ophelia's head tilted slightly, but she made no move to argue. "I hope you may feel the sincerity with which I say this. I feel incredibly inspired by you. You've an exceptionally striking face, and I can only hope to do my best in capturing its essence beyond a simple likeness. I feel entirely confident that if you were to grant me this commission, it may very well be the best work of my life. I don't say that lightly."

Ophelia smiled and blew out a large cloud of smoke. "You flatter me."

"It's not just flattery; I hope you believe me." Lawrence leaned forward in earnest. "I could bring by some of my work so you could see my qualifications. I've finished dozens of portraits already. There's one I've done for the Contessa Michele in particular that shows some of the skills I've developed."

Ophelia waved her hands and shook her head. "There's no need for all that."

"I'd be more than happy to accommodate," Lawrence rushed out. "It's no trouble at all. Anything to put your mind at ease."

"There's no need, and you are wrong. You have quite the way with words. You're quite the salesman," she chuckled. "Well, of course I will give you the commission."

Lawrence stopped, unsure if she had heard correctly. Her mouth remained agape. "Really?"

"Of course. It was yours the moment I sent out that letter inviting you to dinner."

Lawrence sat back, unable to fully comprehend the rapid turn of events. She let out a short laugh of disbelief and ran a hand over her tangled hair.

She had meant every word. Even then, Lawrence felt a strange closeness and intrigue towards Ophelia, even though they had only spent a mere few hours together. There was something arresting about her smile and captivating about the way she spoke. Just as she had been captured by Domenica in the studio two years prio, she was suddenly as captivated by Ophelia. Perhaps even more so.

"Of course," Ophelia said slowly. "I do have a few conditions."

"Yes?"

"You must move into the house and live here as you work. Until the painting is done, I must ask that you not leave the grounds. You must cease all communication with the outside."

Lawrence's eyebrows rose at that, but Ophelia continued on.

"I'm afraid I must be quite firm on that. Of course, a room and all your meals would be provided. You will, also, be able to go out to the gardens."

"Not leave the estate at all?" repeated Lawrence. "No communication with the outside?"

Ophelia nodded her head.

"Of course, it's very generous of you to offer to let me stay here, but I don't know if I can accept that."

Ophelia's brow furrowed and her lips pressed into a thin line. She shook her head, as if she were merely relaying the orders of a higher being, and there was nothing she could do about it.

"You certainly must. Otherwise, I wouldn't be able to accept your working here if it meant you were always going in and out. Besides, you will be able to focus on your work much better." She then crossed her arms together as she leaned forward. "If I'm being perfectly honest with you, Lawrence, I have my own selfish reasons to have you stay.

155

I am a bit lonely, and I wouldn't mind having a companion with me. I hope that doesn't bother you."

In truth, it was the furthest thing that could have bothered Lawrence. But the idea she'd be forced to stay put in one place with no contact to the outside for what could be months was certainly daunting. She had no worries anymore regarding Ophelia or Ashmore, and she felt embarrassed for even seriously considering the ridiculous rumors she heard. Something, though, made her pause from immediately accepting. Ophelia seemed to notice and her lips pursed.

"You need time to consider," observed Ophelia, based on the wavering expression on Lawrence's face. "Perhaps, it is too much to ask."

"I don't want to seem ungrateful," said Lawrence, in a rush, worried she had offended.

"Nonsense," Ophelia said with the wave of her hand. "I understand, of course. It is a long time to commit to, and so much to ask of a young woman with many friends."

When she put it that way, it did seem silly to hesitate. She had no one to really contact, and Signor De Luca could go a few months without her letters. She thought of Augusta, Patrick, and even Edwin; were they really her friends? Surely a few days of being acquainted and a single dinner did not equate to deep friendship. They would not miss her. Teresa had passed. She had no one.

Ophelia remained stock still where she sat. Her lips remained pursed. Her manner immediately became cold, and Lawrence saw her fingers flex slightly as she waited for her response. They began to tap over her leg in the similar way a spider taps its many legs, testing the silken threads of its web for prey. Lawrence shook her head then, eager to bring back her pleasant smile.

"Of course not," she said. "Besides, I don't think it will take very long. I could be done by the end of the season."

Ophelia frowned slightly. "That quickly? Surely such a painting will end up taking longer than that."

"I shouldn't see why it should," Lawrence replied optimistically. "I work fairly quickly once I get going, and I'd have nothing but time to focus my energies on it. I should be nearly done by the end of August. I have full confidence in that."

Ophelia pouted but said nothing. She then smiled and stopped the tapping of her fingers against her leg. Lawrence's own tense shoulders eased.

"You've accepted me then? This is a night to celebrate. Let me pour some champagne."

"Oh no," said Lawrence, her stomach tightening at the thought of champagne. "Please don't. It'll be wasted on me, and I'll just feel bad."

"Then I need another drink to celebrate this occasion," replied Ophelia smoothly, rising to pour herself another drink. "After all, it's not every day I let someone in to my home. It truly is a momentous occasion."

Ophelia turned her back to Lawrence to pour herself another drink. Lawrence took the opportunity to stare at the expanse of smooth skin exposed by the low back of her dress. Her eyes trailed down the long line that curved down Ophelia's back, and she briefly wondered if she felt as soft as she looked. She cleared her throat lightly and turned her eyes away to look elsewhere. She settled on the intricate details carved into the granite fireplace.

"You know," Lawrence said with a light, airy laugh. "It's the funniest thing. Just this morning, I was so worried about meeting you. I was worried about coming *here*."

"Explain."

Lawrence realized then that she couldn't necessarily say exactly why it was that she was nervous without the risk of possibly offending her. She had no good reason, so she shook her head. Ophelia seemed to understand, though, and smiled.

"No doubt you heard all the rumors then," said Ophelia, resuming her seat. She lounged backwards, drink in one hand and burning cigarette in the other.

Lawrence only offered up an embarrassed smile and quick nod. Ophelia's own smile dropped and her lips thinned as her eyes narrowed. In the next second, she smiled again and shook her head.

"I forget what they used to say," she said. "Remind me."

"Oh, I don't- I don't remember."

"Yes, you do." Her voice was firm, but not unkind.

Ophelia tilted her head slightly, and resumed the tapping. This time, she clicked the nail of her pointer finger against the rim of her glass. Lawrence swallowed thickly, holding her hands together in her lap like an obedient student.

"There's a lot of stories," Lawrence murmured. "I've heard everything from it being empty to haunted or cursed. Some people think you're royalty. I've even heard some people say you're a supernatural being of some kind."

"Like the yeti?" Ophelia laughed as she asked.

"Or a vampyr."

At the mention of that name, Ophelia paused for a moment, her straight brows furrowing slightly. She sucked her cheeks in slightly, but said nothing.

"They say once the lanterns out front are lit, terrible things start to happen."

"Yes, and I suppose the recent deaths are not helping with that," Ophelia murmured, indifferent.

"Not really," agreed Lawrence. "Where common sense fails, madness prevails."

Besides not being particularly bothered by the deaths, Ophelia seemed more amused than anything. She snorted.

"Right. Witchcraft, devil worship, and whatnot."

"Errant nonsense, of course," said Lawrence.

"Of course," Ophelia agreed. "It takes far too much time and effort in order to properly worship the devil, or practice witchcraft. I'm rather an unindustrious and idle sort of being, so it would never work."

Lawrence let out a stuttering laugh at the joke, fiddling again with her hair, unable to comment. Ophelia, though, remained straight faced and interested in her reaction.

"I am curious," said Ophelia after some silence passed between them. "What your conclusion is. Your feeling."

"My feeling?"

"About the deaths. About me, this house."

"Well, I am sad about the deaths. It's horrible. Meaningless. Young lives ended so quickly. All that possibility gone."

Ophelia didn't seem quite so disturbed by the news, and her head tilted slightly to the side.

"Death is unprejudiced, yet reliable," she said flatly. "He comes for most in random and unexpected ways."

"Yes, I suppose so."

After such a remark, it was difficult to follow it up.

"What about me then?" Ophelia asked.

"Well, I don't know," said Lawrence with a shrug. "We've only really just met, haven't we."

"In regards to the rumors then," murmured Ophelia. "Humor me."

"I think you're very elegant and charming," said Lawrence, the hesitance clear in her voice. "-and clearly a woman of the world. So far you have been nothing but cordial and gracious to me, so I can only laugh at these ridiculous theories. I can only apologize for harboring any doubts, and I'm quite glad to be able to put ridiculous, unwarranted doubts of mine to rest," Lawrence said with a slight incline of her head.

Ophelia's delicate brow rose once more. Little dimples formed in her cheeks as she smirked.

"Good," she said. "I suppose we should discuss your staying, and working, here. I warn you, I never rise before noon."

"That suits me just fine. How about next week? I can move on Wednesday."

Ophelia immediately frowned. "You could move in tomorrow."

"Tomorrow!" Lawrence laughed. "Isn't that rather abrupt?"

"Do you feel it is?"

Lawrence mulled it over. Her stomach fluttered and her heart raced. It frightened her how quickly she had succumbed. Something akin to reason begged her to take a moment and consider things. She should wait to tie up her business on the outside and only move in once she was ready. She could write a final letter to the Signor and try to explain to the trio of friends her decision to move in. However, something stronger silenced all those perfectly rational thoughts. It was the same madness that caused people to walk into busy streets without looking and jumping from a high place without knowing if there's a safe place to land.

"I don't see why I can't move in tomorrow."

The effect was immediate and Ophelia's lip quirked up again. Her face brightened and Lawrence felt her heart tingle in delight.

"In fact, I think I've got a good idea for the composition already."

"Already? Why, we've only just met today."

"Well, I'm quite inspired," Lawrence confessed. "We've only met for a few hours now, and I feel it has only been a few moments. I can't understand how it's already nearing ten. That can only tell me two things: we shall be good company to one another, and we will have to put great effort into keeping track of the time."

160

Ophelia laughed good-naturedly and held her hands in her lap.

"Time only seems to march away from us when we'd rather it slow because we are enjoying ourselves too much. We do seem to get along quite well, don't we?" she asked, her voice low.

"Certainly."

"I have no doubt you will paint a wonderful picture."

"A small spark of hope in me has been fanned into a flame. I feel it stirring within me now, and I must do something or I shall burn up from the inside out."

"I confess that I'm delighted," said Ophelia, as she placed one of her hands across her chest. "And honored, to think I had any hand in inspiring anything so strong in an artist such as yourself."

"I have a very strange sense that if I were to look into your eyes, I would see all the world in them. I feel the weight of history and empires when I look upon you, and I will do my best to translate all that onto a mere piece of canvas. It's quite an undertaking, and it looms before me like a great mountain; however, I will simply focus on putting one foot in front of the other for now."

"You've got quite a way with words, Lawrence," Ophelia murmured in appreciation. "If you ever wish to put down the brush, may I suggest you consider taking up the pen? You may be talented in an entirely unexplored art."

Lawrence laughed, but it evolved into a yawn. She stifled it, but Ophelia immediately took notice and stood.

"You are tired; can I persuade you to stay the night?"

"Thank you for the offer, but I've got to rise early to catch the sunrise."

A brief, passing look of pain crossed Ophelia's face, but she composed herself quickly. She nodded her head and accompanied Lawrence to the front door. Ophelia turned to her then as she held the door open for her.

"Good night, Lawrence. I shall see you soon."

She held her hand out, and they shook. Ophelia's skin was cool and smooth, like marble. A momentary feeling of recognition went through Lawrence, but the moment was fleeting so she took no further notice of it. They said their goodbyes and Lawrence departed into the dark.

She crossed the porch and went past the lanterns that remained on through the day and night. As she reached the end of the lane, Lawrence turned back once to look at the grand house she would be living in shortly. She turned and continued to walk, but it wasn't until she turned the corner and the house disappeared entirely from view that the strange, prickling feeling at the back of her neck went away.

Chapter 9

"Now, you must remember these rules above all else: Never open the curtains, especially during the day. No leaving the grounds. You may go as far as the gardens, if you must. Under no circumstances are you allowed to enter the West Hall. My lady will not tolerate otherwise. Do you understand?" asked Ms. Hettle, stopping to peer over her shoulder.

Lawrence looked up at her from where she stood a few steps below on the grand staircase.

"Yes, of course," she said with a nod. She shifted the single valise in one hand and kept her bag of supplies in the other. Her easel remained strapped to her back, jostling slightly with every step up.

The rules outlined by Ms. Hettle were odd, but not something Lawrence chose to dwell on for too long. They were simple enough, and if that was all to be required of her to work and live in such comfort, she'd take no issue it with it.

Even in the daytime, the halls of Ashmore remained cool and dark. The pair crossed a lower landing where a large marble sculpture faced the entrance. Although Ms. Hettle continued on up the stairs, Lawrence stopped to admire it. A weeping woman hid her face in her cupped hands. At her feet lay a broken tree limb with fallen petals and a skull. Lawrence leaned in closer to get a better look in the limited lighting. The hard marble had been expertly carved; ivory marble had been carved to imitate supple flesh and soft, flowing fabrics.

"Look lively, miss," called Ms. Hettle from above.

Lawrence took a final look and took the stairs two at a time. They crossed the inner balcony that overlooked the main foyer, turning left down a long carpeted hallway. They stopped before a large door to the second best room in the house.

"My lady is in the best," Ms. Hettle explained, matter-of-fact. Her head moved subconsciously towards the opposite end of the house towards the forbidden corridor.

The lamps in that section of the house remained unlit so the entire hall was dark. Lawrence lingered in the doorway to her new room, staring towards the dark corridor in interest until Ms. Hettle cleared her throat. She turned her eyes away and quickly entered the bedroom.

By all accounts, her new bedroom was the finest room Lawrence had ever stepped foot in. Even finer than the grand room she had stayed in at Old Canary Green. How sad and small her hut by the water seemed at that moment.

She went first to the far wall where thick, velvet curtains were drawn over the windows. She paused for a moment and looked over her shoulder.

"I imagine I have the liberty of opening my own curtains, Ms. Hettle?"

Ms. Hettle paused, and considered it for a moment. "I suppose that should be fine."

Lawrence let out an amused huff and pushed back the curtains. She gasped in awe and pressed her face up against the glass. Directly beyond the windows lay the great expanse of ocean and sky. Lawrence imagined dark mornings with the thick clouds settled low against the rocks and late nights where the inky black sky mirrored the dark waters below.

Ms. Hettle puttered around the room, pulling out linens and tidying the already immaculate space. Lawrence walked around the large four poster bed and examined the murals on the walls. The light green paper displayed painted faces of impish nymphs and alluring naiads that bathed in little pools of crystalline water and frolicked under waterfalls.

"Are you hungry?" asked Ms. Hettle.

Lawrence's eyes flickered to the small clock on the mantle over the room's fireplace.

"Not quite," she answered. "When will Oph- Ms. Aldane be up?"

"My lady regretfully will not be able to join you today as planned," Ms. Hettle replied evenly. "She is quite tired from her travels so she will see you tomorrow afternoon. She wished to be fresh when she saw you again. However, she insisted you be made comfortable and that if you needed anything at all, to let her know."

"Travels?" repeated Lawrence. "She left and returned already? She must not have gone very far."

"Oh no," said Ms. Hettle, shaking her head. "Not far at all."

It seemed Ms. Hettle refused to speak any further on the subject so Lawrence simply nodded. She smiled brightly and held her hands behind her back.

"Well then, I would certainly like a tour, if possible."

"Tour?" stuttered the housekeeper. "I don't—I don't know about that."

"If you're too busy, I can go on by myself."

At the very mention of it, Ms. Hettle's body stiffened, and she shook her head furiously. "No, no, no. I'll take you. I'll take you."

Ms. Hettle dutifully walked Lawrence around the home, giving her a few moments to appreciate the finery and details before urging her along.

While all the rooms were age-old, they were well preserved and richly furnished. The presence of history and a certain cosmopolitan feel imbued the house as a whole: Persian and Turkish rugs carpeted every room, French oak furniture, that seemed to have been sent in a large set from Europe, sat largely untouched, and celadon vases and Ming dynasty jars decorated spare shelves. Even the flowers were of the rare sort, such as Dutch tulips and Japanese orchids, that kept the dark, stale rooms sweetly perfumed.

The duo crossed the first floor of the estate, looking first at the rooms Lawrence had already been in. In addition to the dining room, the western side of the first floor housed a drawing room and decrepit sun room. The latter was the only room of the house with windows that spanned the length of the walls, and no curtains in sight. Lawrence lingered the longest in that room, mentally planning on which areas to tidy up first.

At last, Ms. Hettle herded Lawrence into the library. She spotted the two red sofas she and Ophelia sat on the night prior. Lawrence's eyes then went to a small writing desk in the corner she had not previously noted. Beyond that lay a glass doorway that led out directly to the private pond and garden.

"I shall be back momentarily. Do not leave this room," warned Ms. Hettle as she turned on her heel and left.

Lawrence looked over her shoulder to watch the older woman leave, laughing softly to herself at the strange, charming woman.

As she waited, Lawrence strolled by the shelves, glancing briefly at the texts, some of which were as thick as her forearm. Lawrence continued to pace around until she stopped before a giant tapestry on the wall by the fireplace. She had not noticed it previously, but could focus on nothing else then. She frowned as she studied it. Within that time, Ms. Hettle returned and cleared her throat lightly.

"Miss, would you like to return to your rooms?" she asked. When Lawrence did not respond, she took a few tentative steps forward and tilted her head. "Miss? You are still in here, correct?"

"This tapestry," Lawrence mumbled, eyes glued it.

The tapestry in question took up most of the wall. Across a burning city, Roman soldiers grabbed women, pulling them about and hoisting their twisting bodies above them as they fought to get away. Sabine men lay underfoot, and children were pushed aside and disregarded. In the distance, Romulus stood at the entrance of a temple, placidly watching as his men carried out his orders. She turned her head and regarded Ms. Hettle's placid expression.

"It's the one up here on the wall by the fireplace."

"Yes, I am familiar with the one you are speaking of," she said. "You like it?"

"No," murmured Lawrence with a grave expression. "No, not quite."

"You object to it then," Ms. Hettle said with a little quirk of her head. "Does it offend you?"

"Oh, I don't know. I try not to share my opinion about the furnishings or art in a home that is not mine. Not good manners, is it?" Lawrence let out a sigh and shook her head. She crossed her arms as she looked over the artwork once more. "Though, I suppose it is the subject matter that bothers me. I don't blame whoever made this rug. Artists cannot be held responsible for the subject of their art. If they were, we'd have no art at all.

"Perhaps I cannot help myself because I am a woman, and I have a woman's sensibilities. I look at this scene, and I think of how those women must have felt. To see their loved ones killed and their children abandoned, to be abducted away from their homes, all in the name of war. How can others see it and not be horrified? Just war, they'd say," Lawrence murmured.

Ms. Hettle listened intently, remaining still from where she stood a few feet off. Her face remained impassive as she listened.

"It's all human nature, I suppose. When one is confronted so honestly by the truth of what we are truly capable of, we have the natural reaction of turning our faces away in shame. I think it's because we'd like to believe we are different, but we are unsure. Though, I'd like to believe differently. I'd like very much to believe that humans *are* inherently good." Lawrence laughed suddenly then and turned to face Ms. Hettle. "I suppose since it has evoked such a strong reaction from me, it is the greatest piece of art in this room."

"Yes, miss," replied Ms. Hettle, predictably restrained in her opinion as always. "Would you like to return to your rooms now?"

Lawrence studied the prim woman, suddenly curious. As someone who had been in Ashmore for decades, there was no telling how much Ms. Hettle could tell her about the house and its owner. If she were going to spend weeks there, Lawrence wished to be on good terms with its keeper.

"Ms. Hettle, won't you talk with me for a moment?"

"Is something wrong?" Ms. Hettle asked, the nervous tremor back in her voice.

"No," said Lawrence, infusing as much kindness and warmth as she could in her voice. "I just wish to have someone to speak with."

Ms. Hettle continued to hesitate. She lightly wrung her hands where she stood, her mouth pressed into a thin line. Lawrence then clapped her hands, which caused Ms. Hettle to startle slightly.

"Very well," she said, her voice full of mirth. "If I demand you sit and talk with me, then you have no choice in the matter and cannot deny me."

Whether the housekeeper could tell it was all in good humor, though, remained unclear.

"I wouldn't be comfortable sitting, miss," answered Ms. Hettle at last. She chose to stand behind one of the couches, her hands resting lightly on the carved wooden back.

Lawrence took her usual seat on the red sofa and crossed her legs.

"Very good," said Lawrence, settling her long skirts around her. "Now, are there any other people living here, Ms. Hettle?"

"No, ma'am."

"How about servants?"

"Just one, miss. She helps with the cleaning and cooking."

"Just one?" repeated Lawrence, incredulous. "Still amazes me how you're able to manage a house this size between a single servant and a housekeeper."

"We manage perfectly well, thank you," replied Ms. Hettle firmly, her cheeks flushing slightly and her thin lips settling into a tight line.

Lawrence noticed and only laughed in response, surprised and pleased by the sudden show of emotion from the otherwise humorless housekeeper.

"No, you're right. I really shouldn't have suggested otherwise," said Lawrence immediately. She raised her head and cast a cursory glance over the room. "Looking at this impeccably kept home is proof enough that you're more than capable. May I ask a personal question then, at the risk of possibly offending you further?"

"Yes, miss?"

"Are you unable to see at all?"

"I can see a bit, miss. It's quite like being in a dark hallway where there's a very small window of light at the end. When things are close, I can make out their shape and such. It's not all bad," said Ms. Hettle with a satisfied smile.

Lawrence immediately noticed how much younger she looked when she smiled.

"Has it always been like that, then?"

"Not always," said Ms. Hettle, shaking her head. "Sometime after my thirteenth birthday or so, it began to change."

"I see," Lawrence murmured, quietly considering how it must have affected the young girl. She was struck in a quiet, profound way by the housekeeper then.

Although her gaze had never moved from the woman, Lawrence felt as if a lens had been placed over her eyes which gave her a new perspective. At such a young age, Ms. Hettle had found the ability to not only move forward and be content, but to do so with great pride. Lawrence felt the weight of her own inadequacies and lowered her head. She cleared her throat lightly.

"If I remember correctly, you have been here almost since then. What can you tell me about the house?"

"Not much."

"Oh, you have no need to be secretive with me. Not anymore. I know all about the rumors and superstitions the locals have about this place. Don't worry; I don't believe a single word of it. Not a one. I'm simply interested in learning about the house itself, perhaps from an inside perspective."

Ms. Hettle paused for a moment as a thoughtful look crossed her face.

"It's just an old house," she murmured at last. "My mother believed in the stories. She used to tell me and my sister the same thing. Before I came here, people told me not to come. Shortly after I started, a terrible sickness ran through the town. My own family succumbed to it one by one. It was a vicious thing. No warning. In no time at all, those afflicted were dead. Before she passed, my sister begged me to come home, but I didn't listen. I said I was safe here. She didn't understand why I wanted to work and make my own way. She always told me to come and be with her, that she'd take care of me."

"You lost your sister?" asked Lawrence. Ms. Hettle nodded stiffly. "I'm sorry to hear that. I was an only child, and it was very lonely. How lovely it must have been to have a sister with whom you could confide and share all your secrets. Brothers are perfectly fine, I'm sure, but if I had any choice at all, I would pick a sister close in age to me. Yours sounded lovely."

Ms. Hettle smiled, reminiscing. In a moment, the smile disappeared off her face, and she grit her jaw. She shook her head and turned her face away.

"I don't want to speak about her anymore, if you don't mind."

"Of course," Lawrence said immediately, nodding. She absentmindedly tapped her fingers along her thigh, eager to move the conversation along. "What then can you tell me about your employer?"

"Nothing," Ms. Hettle answered immediately.

The speed at which she answered, though, gave Lawrence reason to believe otherwise. Whatever walls had been lowered between them until then shot back up. Lawrence huffed lightly.

"Oh, come now, Ms. Hettle. There's no need to be so guarded. No one is here with us!"

The woman seemed to consider it but looked over her shoulder and around the room. "I'm not so sure about that."

"What was that?"

"Is it your first time to Bar Harbor then?" asked Ms. Hettle abruptly, switching the conversation.

"First time to Maine, first time to the East Coast, really. I don't think New York really counts since I was only there for a bit before I left for Europe."

"You're very well-traveled." Ms. Hettle lowered her head and turned her face towards the fire, the bright flames illuminating the side of her sharp profile. "Quite like my lady then."

"I highly doubt that" Lawrence chuckled. "You must be quite well-traveled yourself then if you accompany Ms. Aldane on her travels."

"I've not left this house since I've come on," Ms. Hettle explained, indifferent. "I've given up all dreams of that a long time ago."

"This house has been left unoccupied for sixty years," said Lawrence, taken aback. "Are you telling me you were here on your own for all

171

that?"

"Sixty? No, it can't have been that long." Ms. Hettle did seem surprised by that.

"Yes, at least, Ms. Hettle," said Lawrence slowly.

The housekeeper remained quiet. Her head tilted back and forth. Although her mouth moved, Lawrence couldn't hear if she were saying anything.

"I imagine it must have been Ophelia's mother or grandmother you originally worked for."

"No, no," Ms. Hettle muttered under her voice.

Lawrence chose not to comment on that, believing she had misheard. It seemed Ms. Hettle was perhaps not as alert as she might have once been. There was the very real possibility that Ms. Hettle was simply confusing her current mistress with her former employer. Ms. Hettle fidgeted slightly where she stood. Lawrence opened her mouth to speak, but Ms. Hettle beat her to it.

"Let me get you something to eat. Yes, something to eat. You must be hungry. We do have a cook now after all."

Before Lawrence could stop her, Ms. Hettle scurried out of the room with intent. Rather than sit and wait again, Lawrence rose quietly and followed. She opened the doors slowly and removed her shoes altogether.

The housekeeper moved at an unbelievable speed, and once she crossed the foyer, Lawrence lost sight of her for a moment. She turned down a hallway, and Lawrence heard the noise of a door creaking open and shutting abruptly. The sharp and sudden noise in the otherwise silent house echoed loudly and she startled a bit at the sound.

Lawrence turned the corner, expecting a door, but came across a dead end. At the end of a short walkway was an alcove with a large painting and a few candles half-burning at its altar. She walked across the space twice, but Ms. Hettle seemed to have vanished into thin air.

Lawrence stepped toward the painting and observed it. There was nothing extraordinary about it; the subject was a stone bridge between a dark, ominous forest and a bright, Utopian field. As she got closer, she felt a soft breeze coming from behind the canvas and thick wooden frame. The candle flames closest to the edge wavered a little, matching the passing breeze.

Lawrence ran her fingers around the edges of the frame she could reach, looking. She pressed around the silver candlesticks until her finger caught on the handle of the left one. It was firm but gave way when she pushed hard enough. With a soft click, the painting within the frame gave way and pushed inward with a soft pop.

"Extraordinary," she murmured under her breath.

Lawrence peered into the dim interior and looked down a dark, drafty staircase. At the very bottom, a soft glow of light pulsated like a beating heart. Without a second thought, Lawrence pushed into the frame of the painting and entered, letting the canvas shut behind her.

As she descended, the light at the bottom grew, and Lawrence heard the telltale noises of a kitchen. A couple of hushed voices rose, and her curiosity grew. She took careful steps down, and when she reached the bottom of the hall, she listened mutely near the open archway.

"- asking questions," A voice muttered, filtering over the soft clinking of cutlery and chopping against a wooden board. Lawrence immediately recognized the shrill, tremulous tenor of Ms. Hettle. "I don't understand why she's here."

"I wonder why I'm here too," another voice muttered back. This voice was entirely new to Lawrence and decidedly firmer and no-nonsense.

"How am I supposed to keep an eye on her all day? I have my other duties to care for, especially now that my mistress is returned," whispered Ms. Hettle.

Lawrence could practically hear the old woman wringing her hands. The other speaker let out a sharp huff of annoyance.

"She's not a child, is she? Why should you keep an eye on her?"

"She might start wandering!" cried Ms. Hettle.

"Then lock the doors where she shouldn't go," the woman replied shortly. "I'm quite busy, Hettle, so if you've nothing more to say, perhaps you'll leave me be so I may finish my prep for dinner." The woman then sighed, and the sound of chopping ceased. "I'm not being paid to stick my nose where it shouldn't be. I stay down here; I don't ask questions, and once my job is done, I'm out of here. You've been here for decades; surely you know better than I."

"Yes, and I can count on one hand the number of weeks the Madame was actually in this house while I was here."

"Exactly!" cried the other woman. "More likely than not, she'll be gone before you can begin your count on the other hand."

"She's never invited any guests before, though. What if something happens to her? What should we do?"

"We should hang ourselves. What could possibly happen?" asked the woman in an exasperated voice.

There was then a pregnant pause, and Lawrence was tempted to peer around the corner at the risk of revealing herself.

"She's not safe here," whimpered Ms. Hettle. "It'll just be like my dear Helena!"

At that, Lawrence straightened up a bit, alarmed. As she did, she bumped against the wall, and the voices in the kitchen immediately quieted. Lawrence froze where she crouched, a mere few feet by the entryway to the kitchen.

"What was that?" whispered the other woman, her voice suddenly timid and low. All the bravado was gone in an instant. A chair scraped back.

"My lady, is that you?" Ms. Hettle called out.

When there was no answer, there was a quick shuffle of feet.

"I thought you said she would never come down here!" said the woman, her voice pitching despite how she worked to keep it to a low murmur.

"She shouldn't be up yet," whispered Ms. Hettle. "Stay put."

Lawrence rushed from her spot and backpedaled down the short hallway to the first open door. She threw herself in, heart racing in her ears. She peered out and watched as Ms. Hettle, tray of food in hand, hurried up the stairs.

Lawrence waited until she was gone before she finally exhaled. Only once her heart settled did she emerge. She crossed back through the short, dimly lit hallway in an attempt to get back upstairs when a voice called out.

"Who's there?"

Lawrence stopped, considered what to do, and then returned to the entryway of the kitchen. At the center of the wide room, knife in hand, stood a stout, young woman. The counter held a wide assortment of vegetables and meat, some prepped and others in wait. The cook looked at Lawrence with a disagreeable expression. She narrowed her eyes as she looked Lawrence up and down, her wide jaw clenched slightly as their eyes met.

Lawrence smiled and laughed as affably as she could.

"Apologies, I got lost and found myself down here." She let out another light, airy laugh. Lawrence looked at the knife in the woman's hand, which she continued to wield with a white-knuckled grip. "I don't believe we've met. Lawrence Stoner, nice to meet you. Friends call me LJ."

The woman studied Lawrence for a moment longer.

"Yes, I know," she said curtly. She seemed to realize where she was and who she was speaking to as she corrected herself by lowering the knife and quickly bowing her head. "My name is Greta, miss."

"Greta, nice to meet you. It seems I've given you a bit of a fright. I do apologize."

"It's quite alright. You better get back upstairs. I sent your food up with Hettle. She'll be looking for you."

"Yes, I imagine so. I'm getting the sense that she'd make quite a good dogcatcher." Lawrence chuckled. "The woman's got the nose of a bloodhound."

Greta's lip quirked slightly at that.

"This house is a maze. It took me a couple weeks when I first arrived just to get it straight in my head," she muttered, picking the knife up again and returning to her work. She kept her eyes lowered as she spoke.

Lawrence continued to linger in the doorway, watching Greta work. The soft chopping of carrots and potatoes was strangely comforting then, and the smells in the kitchen reminded Lawrence of her youth. She took a step forward and cast a glance at the preparations for the dinner of the day.

"So you're the one I should thank for the delicious food," Lawrence said, taking note of how quickly the woman moved within the kitchen. "I've only had a single meal, but I am sure I will be very well fed during my time here, like a goose before Christmas."

Greta's cheeks warmed slightly at the compliment. Her eyes flickered up to meet Lawrence's momentarily, but she kept her head down. Lawrence looked around the basement kitchen, where there seemed to be the most light and warmth in the entire house. Despite that, it was otherwise a small, sunless place hidden away below the house.

"Things are quite strange in this house, aren't they?" Lawrence said.

Greta finished chopping without answering and began wiping down the counter, tossing the refuse into a nearby bin. She was different to Ms. Hettle in more ways than one, but she seemed equally determined not to indulge in too much conversation.

In the way she worked and the manner in which she spoke, Greta was all around a bit rougher. Her cheeks were ruddy and her hands were coarse, but she had her own unique beauty that reminded Lawrence of the Tuscan women from the countryside—they'd work from dawn to dusk out in the wheat fields in their long patterned skirts and covered heads. She considered how to approach Greta as if she were a different animal to Ms. Hettle and took a step forward.

"Ms. Aldane seems to be a bit of an eccentric character. Though the line between the rich and deranged seems to get fainter every day," Lawrence said, laughing suddenly as she remembered something. Greta's brow quirked slightly at that. "I remember there was this one old lady that always visited the studio where I studied in Florence. Her name was Signora Matucci, and she was an incredibly rich widow. She always had her portrait done every few months, and never a more difficult woman have you ever met. You see, her ex-husband was a businessman with a penchant for French wine and women. There was actually quite a scandalous rumor that she had poisoned him. Anyway, she always came around with this big old parrot on her shoulder with a gold chain around its body. It was as red as a tomato and cursed all day long. Absolutely foul. Every other word was a 'damn' or 'shit' and it laughed like this, 'hah, hah, hah.'"

Lawrence did her best to mimic the parrot's thin, nasally laugh. Greta stopped working to listen, interested.

"The funniest thing was when it would sing. One time, no kidding, it sang this: 'Mary had a little lamb; her father shot it dead. Now it goes to school with her, between two chunks of bread.'"

Lawrence laughed again, and Greta chuckled. When she opened her mouth, attractive little lines formed at the corners of her eyes and Lawrence saw that she was missing the right canine in her smile.

Greta pushed her sleeves back, still chuckling heartily at the silly rhyme. She began to flour her worktable and threw dough onto the bench, beginning to knead. Lawrence remained silent for a moment, waiting.

"When you've worked in these houses for as long as I have, nothing is strange," muttered Greta.

Something changed within her, and it was like seeing a flower slowly bloom. Her shoulders relaxed, and she kept her chin up as she spoke, working without having to look at what her hands were doing. She looked up at Lawrence with a sly look in her eyes.

"There was this one family I worked for that lives not too far from here. Old money. Now, they were really off their rocker. I mean, their house was real swanky, and the kitchen was no joke, but boy, the people were goofy." She shook her head, still in disbelief over it. "Fordham Sr. married wife number five around the time I started. Mind you, she was five years younger than his own daughter."

"Good grief," murmured Lawrence. Greta nodded.

"That's not all," she said, her voice lowering a bit. "Once, the young missus wanted ox tongue. Did she want my braised ox tongue? No, of course not. She wanted the Westford Hotel's ox tongue down in New York. So, what do they do? They send a butler on the next train to go down to New York, pick it up, and bring it back for that evening, of course. Just one serving. Just for her. She didn't even touch it. Complained it was cold."

"What?"

Greta only nodded her head, narrowing her eyes at the ridiculousness of it. She threw the dough down once again, kneading it harder than necessary.

"That ain't even the tip of it honey," she muttered. "You won't believe some of the stories you'll hear working under the feet of some of these rich folks. The depraved things they do, the *illegal* things.

178

They get away with murder."

"I'm sure you're joking," Lawrence laughed, but at the sharp look in Greta's eyes, her laughter ceased. She shook her head, taking a seat on the stool facing Greta. "Why would they do anything of the sort? They've got everything, don't they? Why risk it?"

Greta shrugged, folding the yeasty, pale yellow dough that clung to the surface of the counter with every push and pull.

"I think it's because they got everything. When you got everything money can buy, you want things money can't buy. You want and want and want until there's nothing else. It destroys a person. It kills the soul, drying it up until it shrivels like a fruit in the hot sun."

"What does?"

"Wanting," replied Greta. "Desire, lust, greed. All of it. A man, with or without money, can still sin if, at the core of his being, all he does is want. The difference is if he can pay his way out of getting in trouble." She let out a loud sigh. "That's just my opinion. The real monsters aren't the ones who lurk in the dark. They're the ones strutting around in fine dresses and tails in their big houses with their big pockets."

"I take it you don't put much stock in the superstitions the locals believe about this house, or the person in it."

The look that crossed Greta's face only confirmed it as she pursed her lips and threw the dough down again on the counter. Lawrence smiled as Greta sighed. She sounded exasperated at the very thought.

"It's the 20th century, and people still think ghosts and demons are the cause of things. We're living in the age of science. It's embarrassing."

"You are a woman of science, then?" Lawrence inquired with a small smile, which Greta mirrored.

"Just facts. Evidence."

"Well, speaking from one fact-believer to another, perhaps you can provide me some objective information on this house and its owner?" Lawrence looked around, crossing her arms before her body. "I've been getting a lot of conflicting reports, and it's been hard making sense of it with what I know and what I see in Ms. Aldane."

"Aye, but it will be very quick," stated Greta, matter-of-fact. "An ad was placed a few weeks ago, and I was hired, and that was that. I thought it a bit strange that a fine house in Bar Harbor would advertise for work out in Cherryfield, but I didn't care to mull it over too hard. As for the lady, I've only seen her in passing once or twice. She's quiet, and she keeps to herself. She's never talked to me or looked at me. I'd be offended if I didn't honestly prefer it."

"What, not a single word? Not one?" asked Lawrence, taken aback.

Greta shook her head, shrugging. "She sleeps all day and paces around at night. It took me a few days to get used to it. It goes on all damn night. If we're lucky, she sometimes leaves, and we can get a proper rest."

"Where does she go?"

Greta shrugged again, indifferent. She put the dough into a bowl and covered it with a tea towel. "How should I know?"

"Aren't you at all curious?" asked Lawrence.

"I've worked in service for long enough. Odd people and their odd ways are the least of my worries. I don't need to be told twice to stay out of the way. In fact, I prefer it. At least this one is upfront about what she expects of us."

"Ah yes, the rules," mused Lawrence, slightly amused. She smirked and set her chin in her hand. "I suppose there's some comfort in knowing I'm not alone in them."

"Ms. Hettle holds all the keys so whenever I need to go and make up the fires, she always has to unlock the doors for me. What a bother! Except the West corridor. What bother is it to me if the lady doesn't want a warm fire in her room? I won't even account for the list of foods and herbs I've been barred from using." Greta raised her dark eyes to meet Lawrence's. "Maybe there is something to say for all those rumors."

Lawrence hummed under her breath as she studied the grain of the counter. She tapped her finger along the top as she thought. She felt Greta's stare as she let her mind wander. The woman chuckled lowly.

"Perhaps I've said too much."

"Not at all; you've only said as much as I asked you to." Lawrence rose from her seat with a smile. She nodded her head. "Thank you, Greta. It was a pleasure to meet you."

Greta nodded once in return and went back to her work. Lawrence left the bright warmth of the kitchen. The further she got from the kitchen, the colder she felt, and she immediately missed the earthy, spiced flavors in the air. Lawrence had gotten used to the dark and chill in the rooms above without even realizing it.

She emerged from the portrait doorway and padded softly across the hall. Ms. Hettle stood at the foot of the stairs, and when she approached from the side, her head turned her way.

"Miss Stoner? What are you doing coming from that strange direction?" She asked sternly, her brows furrowed together. "I was looking for you!"

"My apologies. I went out to look through the sun room and ended up wandering around a bit, but don't worry, Ms. Hettle, I did my best to behave myself."

"Oh, please tell me if you insist on wandering around on your own!" Ms. Hettle said quickly, frowning and gesturing with her hands.

"Is something the matter?"

"I just like to be kept aware, that's all," she sighed.

She seemed quite strung out, and Lawrence took some pity on her. She had no desire to make the woman's life any harder than it had to be.

"I can't do my job if I'm not aware."

"Yes, that's true, Ms. Hettle," Lawrence answered obediently. "I apologize; I hadn't considered that. I will make sure to keep you updated on my comings and goings."

"Very good. Your food is ready. Please follow me."

Lawrence ate her lunch alone, and she was again impressed by how delicious it was. Ophelia didn't eat much at all during their dinner. Perhaps she simply had very particular tastes. She thought about what Greta had said, and wondered if Ophelia was simply another one of those odd, rich folks.

In the room and in the silence, Lawrence took a quiet moment to appreciate how her luck had changed within a short period of time. She went from a small, lonely shack to a large mansion and company within a few days. She felt it important to remind herself of her good fortune and to be thankful.

When she was done with her food, Lawrence went out to the sun room. She looked out the dirty windows and considered the composition of Ophelia's portrait. Whatever she had in mind, she suddenly worried that she'd be incapable of properly producing it.

She considered something more stately: Ophelia sitting in a chair against a dark background, so all attention was forced upon only her. It would be appropriate and reflect the dignified air she had to her, but Lawrence rejected the idea almost as quickly as it had come to her. It didn't reflect even a small measure of how she felt when she saw Ophelia. Her mind went next to the gardens. She could set her against the lush greenery or within the grand gazebo in the pond; however, that too fell short of her expectations. What could be grand enough to capture all of who Ophelia seemed to be?

Under Ms. Hettle's close supervision, Lawrence wandered from one dark room to the next. She paced back and forth, crouching and sitting at different areas. She sat for minutes in one place before she'd abruptly rise and move to another.

Lawrence considered the time she'd have to paint. If Ophelia insisted on only joining her in the afternoons, they would have limited time. Even if they were allowed to open the curtains, it would be useless.

The daylight wouldn't suit Ophelia anyways. There was something expected, almost, about painting her within the shadows. Lawrence felt then that she had incidentally stumbled across the perfect setup.

The clocks around the home chimed all at once. The different bells and melodic tunes echoed out around the house like a haunting melody. 'Sunset', explained Ms. Hettle. They walked up the same steps together up to Lawrence's new room. At the threshold, Ms. Hettle stopped and reached into her pocket. She produced a small golden key and held it out towards Lawrence to take.

"What's this?" she asked.

"It's the only one for your room," answered Ms. Hettle in a low voice.

Lawrence took the key, pinching it between her thumb and forefinger.

"You should lock your door at night." Ms. Hettle's eyes trembled a little, and her face paled a bit, but she was otherwise firm and revealed little else. "You never know what goes on at night. I know I always feel safer with a locked door."

"How ominous!" Lawrence exclaimed, a laugh bubbling out of her. "You don't mean to say that anything might be trying to get in at night, do you? I suppose it'll be the ghosts in the attic or perhaps the mummy in the cellar!"

"You wouldn't be the first nor the last to experience one odd thing or another. This house has been around since before this country was born. Old as sin it is," remarked Ms. Hettle with a solemn look.

"The devil isn't some ugly, misshapen creature hoping to catch the ones that fall. He's beautiful like a dream and caresses your hand softly as he lures you into the dark."

"My goodness," exhaled Lawrence. She held the key tightly in hand and looked sideways down the dark corridor towards the West Hall. "Well on that pleasant note, I think I'll bid you goodnight then. Thank you again, Ms. Hettle."

"Good night, miss," Ms. Hettle said with a bow of her head.

She turned on her heel and walked off, silent as a mouse. Lawrence watched from her door as Ms. Hettle turned the corner and disappeared altogether. She stood in the dark, empty hallway for a moment and listened. She heard only the whistling of wind and the creaking of wood.

Lawrence shut the door after herself and looked down at the golden door handle. She glanced between the key in hand and the door before she let out an exasperated sigh and turned away without locking it.

"How ridiculous."

Lawrence prepared for bed, brushing out her long hair and slipping into her old nightgown. As she sat at her mirror, her eyes grew heavy. The muscles along her shoulders and back ached. She dimmed the lamps along the walls and slipped into the large bed that was two times too large for just one person. Lawrence shut the long curtains that ran around the sides of the bed to keep unwanted light out. The duvet was soft and thick, and Lawrence melted into it the moment she laid her head down.

Peace lasted but a moment.

A soft, whining cry like a wounded animal came from outside her door.

At first, Lawrence lifted her head, unsure if she had heard the noise at all. The second pitiful call caused her to sit upright. The skin along her arms and legs pimpled and she began to tremble.

With a slow hand, Lawrence pushed back the curtains to her bed. The firelight continued to glow, bathing the room in soft, orange light. Long shadows from the furniture stretched out across the room, and she felt as if every pair of painted eyes on the wallpaper watched as she slowly crept towards the door. She pressed her ear to it first, but heard nothing.

Lawrence carefully turned the doorknob and pulled her door open a fraction. It creaked slowly as she did, the light from inside pouring out to the dark hallway. She considered taking a light with her, but decided against it. She crept out of her room and looked both ways. Then, another pained, humming cry came from the dark West Hall.

Lawrence took slow, calculated steps down the carpeted hallway. Anytime her foot landed on a creaky panel, she froze. Her own heartbeat thundered in her chest with every step.

The West Hall was strange in its construction that the hallway contained only a single set of doors. Large canvas portraits and tapestries occupied every other space of bare wall. Lawrence stopped before the doors with her arm raised to knock. She paused for a moment, stunned by the complete silence. Only her own short breaths could be heard.

Another short whine, this time much closer, came from behind her.

Lawrence turned away from the doors and listened closely. The whimpering noise, muffled through the walls, cut off suddenly. There was no mistaking it, though. It had come from behind the tapestry on the opposite wall.

She looked over her shoulder at the closed double doors, and then back to the tapestry. It hung loose from the wall and depicted a blue Japanese god, sitting cross-legged atop a large mountain. A single bright moon rose high in the sky behind him, a bright ring of light around his head like a halo. Lawrence reached her hand out towards the rug.

185

Just before her hand went to pull it away, it was snatched away.

Lawrence gasped and turned, coming face-to-face with Ms. Hettle. The old woman's face twisted in fury, but her eyes remained wide in fear. The milky white seemed luminous in the dark hallway, and her eyes flicked momentarily to the tapestry. Ms. Hettle raised a single finger to her lips and shook her head. Her bony fingers gripped Lawrence's arm and she dragged her away.

Only once they were safe back in Lawrence's room did Ms. Hettle turn to her. "Three rules! Three rules, and you break one on the first night!"

"I'm sorry," Lawrence stuttered out, mindlessly rubbing her arm where Ms. Hettle had grabbed her. "I heard a noise! It sounded like someone in terrible pain. I thought it might have been-"

"Never mind what you thought!" cried Ms. Hettle. Even in her distressed state, she kept her voice to a restrained whisper. "I told you never to go to the West Hall! At night as well! My lady must be told of this indiscretion."

"No!" cried Lawrence.

Ms. Hettle raised her hands for Lawrence to keep her voice down. Lawrence leaned forward and grabbed both of Ms. Hettle's hands in hers.

"Please, Ms. Hettle. I apologize! I will never go back there no matter what I hear. If there's nothing to it, I shall forget it. Please, don't tell Ophelia."

Ms. Hettle's thin lips pressed into a line.

"Please Ms. Hettle," begged Lawrence.

She finally gave Lawrence a single curt nod.

"Very well," she said. "Quickly now, back to bed. Lock your door."

Lawrence followed Ms. Hettle to the door, thanking her and bidding her good night once again. Lawrence obediently locked the door once she left and rushed back into her bed. She snapped the curtains around her bed closed and laid her head down to rest.

At first, it seemed impossible to find any peace in order to truly rest, but with every passing moment of silence, Lawrence's mind eased and she slept soundly.

Chapter 10

Lawrence stood at the edge of the pond in the secret garden behind Ashmore. Mist covered the water's surface, settling over the lily pads and creeping up to the muddy bank. The early morning dew on the grass soaked the hem of her skirts and chilled her through her soft leather shoes. She held her hands behind her back as she quietly walked between the stone statues dotted around the flowers and shrubs.

She stepped forward to a stone bench eternally occupied by two figures in marble. A beautiful, young woman of alabaster grasped a dying figure of obsidian and kept it clutched tightly to their chest. A golden arrow pierced the figure in black through her breast. The alabaster woman's grief-stricken face turned upwards, mouth slack-jawed and brows furrowed as she cried out silently. The dying woman in her arms looked serene, a soft, placid smile across her smooth face, as if she were merely dreaming. Lawrence observed that particular statue the longest, turning around it several times.

As she walked the perimeter a third time, Lawrence passed by a section of brush along the edge that seemed dented. Only once she caught sight of it did she realize how out of place it looked to the rest of the thick bushes and trees that formed a thick, impenetrable barrier around the garden.

She stopped and took a step closer. Lawrence pushed away some of the overgrown brush and came upon a short dirt walkway. Even from where she stood, she saw a direct path to the exact trail she used to take on her early morning walks.

"Miss?" a familiar, shrill voice called out from behind.

Lawrence quickly let the branches snap back into place and walked away from the secret exit she found. She resumed her walk around the statues and approached Ms. Hettle where she stood.

"Good morning, Ms. Hettle," she called out jovially.

Ms. Hettle's head snapped to where Lawrence's voice came from and a bit of tension released from her shoulders.

"Oh, miss," she said. "There you are. You'll catch cold wandering around like a spirit! Come, breakfast is ready."

The events of the night prior went unacknowledged by the two of them. Ms. Hettle accompanied Lawrence to the dining room and hovered close behind as she dined. After enough time passed, the two simply carried on as if it had never happened.

"Is today the day?" Lawrence asked over her shoulder as she took a sip of coffee.

Ms. Hettle remained silent.

"Will your lady be joining me this afternoon?"

"Yes," Ms. Hettle replied stiffly. "I believe so."

"Perfect," Lawrence cried, standing from her seat. "Then, I will need to set up so we may start immediately. Idle hands are the devil's workshop, and whatnot."

Ms. Hettle grunted in response, following after Lawrence through to the library. The moment they entered, Lawrence stopped where she stood and let out a little gasp of surprise.

"Goodness," she cried. "What's happened there?"

"Ma'am?"

"The tapestry is missing," Lawrence said. "And by the looks of it, it was rather hastily torn down."

The blank wall by the fireplace was a few shades lighter than the rest of the wall, showing exactly where the rug had been. The rod and hooks that had kept it in place were bent like crooked twigs, as if a strong hand had ripped it down in one go. Lawrence went closer to inspect and saw loose threads littered at the foot of the wall in small piles.

"I nearly forgot," said Ms. Hettle from behind in a rush. "I had it taken down to be cleaned. Yes, that's all."

"Cleaned?" repeated Lawrence, incredulous. "Well, I'm afraid you've made a pig's ear of it, dear Ms. Hettle."

"Have I?" the housekeeper asked innocently. "Is it terrible?"

"Well, I'm not sure what we'll do about the rod on the wall, but it should be easy enough to clean up this mess down here."

"Let me," Ms. Hettle said, stepping forward.

Lawrence held her hand out and placed it gently on Ms. Hettle's elbow to keep her where she was.

"I'd feel better if you let me. I don't want you crouching so close to the fire," Lawrence said, assuring the older housekeeper. Lawrence crouched and quickly gathered up the loose thread and ripped fabric. She looked over her shoulder. "What will the lady think?"

"I imagine she's glad to be rid of it too," Ms. Hettle said. "Doesn't it please you? That it's gone?"

Lawrence stopped picking up the loose bits of thread and frowned at Ms. Hettle. "Why would that please me?"

"You hated it so," explained Ms. Hettle. "Now it's gone. Surely that pleases you."

"Well it doesn't really matter whether or not it pleases me," reasoned Lawrence, gathering up the bits in her hands. "But it is gone now, and that's that."

Once Lawrence had finished picking up the leftover bits of rug, she set to preparing for her work. Much to Ms. Hettle's distress,

Lawrence determined the library to be the best setting for her work. She set two ladder-back chairs directly opposite to each other, and took a seat.

Lawrence didn't hear her approach, but felt the change in the air, turning in her seat as the door opened. Ophelia glided in, skirts fluttering behind her.

If it were possible, Ophelia seemed even lovelier than Lawrence remembered. She seemed almost livelier, smiling demurely as their eyes met. She clapped her hands together and stopped a few feet off, posing and turning this way and that for Lawrence to get a better look.

"How do I look? Will this do?"

Lawrence took a moment to study her, rising from her chair and taking a step back. Ophelia had donned a dark navy day dress with a dropped waist and a long strand of pearls. Her signature glasses hugged her face tightly.

"I worry only that I may not do you justice," said Lawrence in a serious tone. Ophelia smiled again, dimples forming in her smooth cheeks. "A concern that only grows with every passing minute, I'm afraid."

"Flattery is unnecessary," said Ophelia, still smiling in a tight-lipped grin. She shook her head lightly. "You've already got the job, after all."

"Then, you may take comfort in knowing that my compliments are genuine." Lawrence gestured to the chair opposite her own. "Please."

Ophelia obeyed, settling smoothly into her chair like a queen on her throne. She folded her hands primly in her lap and looked around the library.

"Where are your tools? Are we not getting started today?"

"We certainly are," Lawrence said with a smile. She held her hands out towards her. "Do you mind?"

Ophelia's bronze skin chilled Lawrence to the bone the moment she touched her. Her own skin broke out in goosebumps and she fought the urge to shiver and pull away. She bit down on the instinct and gently guided Ophelia's arms to rest gently on the armrests. Lawrence tilted Ophelia's face, bringing her own face down as she did so.

They were a foot away from each other, and Lawrence's heart rate picked up. Her throat went dry as she looked down at Ophelia's smooth brow and full lips. Ophelia smelled of jasmine and smoke. The spicy, rich scent overwhelmed her senses and Lawrence felt herself growing a bit lightheaded at the heady scent.

She stepped away abruptly, turning her head away sharply. Ophelia exhaled lowly from behind, but said nothing. Lawrence went to stand a few feet away and bowed slightly at the waist with her arms crossed. She stared at Ophelia for a few minutes before she stepped forward and readjusted her slightly.

For half a dozen times more, Lawrence ended up clicking her tongue and shaking her head, unsatisfied. Ophelia never took any bother and listened obediently, posing as Lawrence surveyed her with a keen eye. Once Lawrence finally nodded her head in satisfaction did she take her own seat opposite.

Ophelia sat in stark profile to her. Her head was tilted slightly backwards, as if she were just turning to address someone behind her. Lawrence picked up her large drawing pad and settled it atop her crossed legs.

"Now, let's begin," Lawrence said.

She began the preliminary sketches, drawing up dozens at a time with slight changes between each iteration. She finished each quickly, taking no longer than a few minutes on each. When she was done with one, she ripped out the page and immediately started on the next. The finished sketches settled around Lawrence on the ground like a fresh blanket of snow.

"Have you gotten settled in?"

Lawrence peered up from her work and nodded subtly.

"Oh yes, Ms. Hettle has taken good care of me."

She ripped out the top page as she finished another quick sketch, but settled her hands across the top. She looked to Ophelia with a grave expression.

"I think the rumors are true though."

Ophelia tensed in the chair, her hands curling slightly around the armrests. "I'm sorry?"

Lawrence laughed abruptly. "I've been hearing some strange noises here and there. I'm pretty convinced now the rumors of your house being haunted must be true."

Ophelia let out a little snort. "Noises?"

Lawrence lowered her head back to her work, answering without looking up. "Yeah, just noises like groaning and scratching. I'm not sure."

"It's common in these older houses," answered Ophelia, pragmatically. "The wood beams and pipes are all older than can be believed."

"I'm sure," nodded Lawrence. "I heard you went away. How was your trip?"

"Productive," Ophelia said with a quick smirk. "I hope you forgive me for not greeting you when you first arrived, but I must confess I feel wonderfully refreshed."

"You certainly look it."

They settled into silence again as Lawrence resumed her work. In her element, Lawrence's mind went blank and she simply let her arms move like an automaton. She felt herself enter into a strange state of meditation and her heart slowed to a low thump.

"A little line forms between your brows when you concentrate," murmured Ophelia. Lawrence raised her head briefly, easing the expression from the taut look of concentration she had been holding for longer than she realized.

"I've been told that." She smiled. "I've also been told I sometimes stick my tongue out, like this."

Lawrence demonstrated, letting the pink tip of her tongue stick out between her lips. "Like a cat."

Ophelia chuckled lightly, and it was like the hollow ring of a brass bell. It was a delightful sound that instantly made Lawrence smile when she heard it. There was another brief moment of silence between them, with only the crackling of the firewood and the pencil scratching against the soft paper.

"Lawrence?"

"Hmm?"

"Will you tell me what brought you here?" Ophelia asked suddenly.

"Here?" Lawrence asked, raising her head briefly. When she saw Ophelia, she understood what she was asking. She opened her mouth to answer, but was interrupted.

"And be honest with me, please," Ophelia said. Her voice had become grave and Lawrence felt the full weight of her stare behind the glasses.

Lawrence thought for a moment as she continued to work. She had her own truths she kept guarded closely to her breast like playing cards; she was selective about what she shared and whom she shared it with. In this case, she opted for a half-truth.

"The honest truth? The decision was done rather hastily and I was perhaps not in the best state to be making such decisions, but I am here now."

Lawrence smiled tightly, the corners of her mouth lifting slightly as she forced it. Ophelia's delicate brow rose slightly, but she remained frozen in her pose.

"That's all?" she asked, her tone disbelieving and suspect. "You didn't answer my question, Lawrence."

"Well, I had a few reasons. I didn't have anything left for me there." Which was true. She let out a low sigh. "And, I missed America. I didn't really think about it that much. I just got up and left. I suppose I was desperate to get out."

This was also true.

"So you did not enjoy your time while you were there?"

"I wouldn't say that," Lawrence said in immediate defense. "I was very well taken care of, all things considered. Then again, although Signor De Luca was a terribly wonderful painter, he was an amazingly awful mentor. He was a real tyrant and completely useless anywhere but the studio. He had this long, crooked nose that he always looked down at me from when he yelled at me, and he always called me a stupid, American girl."

Lawrence chuckled lightly at the memory despite what she said. She dabbed the corner of her eye with the edge of her sleeve.

"I complain about him a lot, but he was actually a wonderful man. He taught me everything I know, and I adore him. I did my time, though. I'd be happy if I never set eyes on that blessed Duomo again." She paused for a moment, ripping out another page that was complete. "Although that might not be entirely true, I forgive and forget very easily. I'm sure in about a month or so I'll forget all about everything bad that's happened in the past two years and beg to go back."

"I certainly hope not," murmured Ophelia, her ruby lips pressing together. "I will have to entice you by any means necessary to get you to stay."

Lawrence didn't have anything immediately to say to that, and hid her reddening cheeks by lowering her head to feign work. She cleared her throat.

"I have no intention on going back anytime soon. I've quite fallen in love with this place. I'm most looking forward to being here once the days grow shorter and colder."

Lawrence could already imagine the change. In her mind, she saw the rolling mountains of spruces and oaks losing their vibrant green to make way for the brassy orange and yellow of fall. In winter, the needled branches would slump and bend once the thick piles of snow packed on their limbs, making them bow and twist under the weight.

When Lawrence looked back to Ophelia, they simply stared at her with a soft smile. She cleared her throat.

"I actually worked on a painting before I moved in here, a landscape."

"Did you abandon it?" Ophelia asked.

"No," Lawrence said with a shake of her head. "I finished it."

"Where is it? I'd like to see it."

"I gave it away."

"Gave it away?" repeated Ophelia, the corners of her lips turning down. "Not for free, I hope."

Lawrence laughed. "Afraid so."

"Now, why on earth would you do that?" she asked in all seriousness.

"It was for a good reason."

Ophelia didn't say anything, but tilted her head slightly. Lawrence felt her silently prod her to continue on.

"Well, you know those unfortunate people who passed recently?" Lawrence asked. Ophelia nodded her head subtly. "I knew one of them. Her name was Teresa."

"Teresa?" Ophelia repeated the name as if it were an interesting revelation. Her lips pursed and her fingers drummed against the armrest of the chair. Lawrence nodded.

"Yes, she worked at a cafe and would always bring me out hot coffee and cakes."

Lawrence paused for a moment as she thought about Teresa. She turned her head back down as she suddenly became overwhelmed by an unexpected rush of emotion. A thick knot of emotion swelled up in her throat and the corners of her eyes pricked with unexpected tears.

"You liked her?" Ophelia asked quietly.

She shook her head. "I barely knew her."

"You have a certain look in your eye. You think quite fondly of her."

"Yes," Lawrence confessed, nodding. "She was very kind. Life is unfair. People like her die for no reason, and the worst ones refuse to die."

Ophelia nodded sagely in agreement.

"Anyways, I went to her parents and I gave them the painting."

"Did you think it would help them?"

Lawrence shook her head. "Not necessarily. Teresa had asked me to show her the painting once it was done. After she died, it felt like I had to give it to them. It felt right. I'm not sure why."

"That was a silly thing to do. What good would a painting of a pier do for them now?"

Lawrence was about to disagree wholeheartedly; however, she stopped. She looked up at Ophelia with a curious expression.

"I don't think I mentioned it was a painting of the pier."

"You must have," replied Ophelia.

"I don't believe so."

Ophelia's fingers suddenly ceased tapping along the armrest. She then turned her head down. "I didn't realize it would affect you so. Her death."

"I actually had plans with Teresa that night," said Lawrence. "I was quite upset when I thought she had simply not turned up at all. I was being quite silly that night. Then, I learned she had passed and it made me feel even more silly and guilty. Actually, the worst part was seeing her parents. Just seeing how it left them."

Ophelia remained still, but her lips thinned slightly. She turned her head sideways, exiting the pose to look into the fireplace. "You artists are all the same; you're all feeling and no sense. Giving away your painting for free."

Lawrence laughed good-naturedly as she ripped out a page and started again on a new sketch. Through time and practice, she had unknowingly developed skills and was moving at a rapid pace. She smudged out a section she disliked with the heel of her palm and drew over it.

"It's interesting; before I came here, I never really considered myself an artist. Yet now, I've been reminded of it constantly."

"Why on earth would you not consider yourself one?"

"Well," Lawrence started. "I suppose it's because I've not really been successful in any way. Only really successful people can decide what they are."

"Is the intention not enough for you?"

"A fish can dream of flying, but until they do, they are simply a fish."

"You are young," argued Ophelia. "You have time enough to learn how to fly, so to speak."

"Time may not be the issue," Lawrence sighed, itching her temple and giving Ophelia a contemplative, sad smile. "True accomplishments of worth could take a lifetime or a day. I've lived at least a quarter of my life already. How do I account for the last two decades? For the time I have had, what do I have to show for it? I would have thought I'd have accomplished something great by now, but every year that passes, I only grow older. I fear I've just finished the quarter of my life with the most potential, and now I am only in that terrible transition to the end. I may die and not have done anything great to be remembered by."

Ophelia frowned. "It seems important to you to be remembered."

"I suppose so," said Lawrence with a chuckle. Ophelia did not join her. "Vanity is my sin."

Ophelia's face was thoughtful as she turned her head away once more to let Lawrence continue on with her work. Lawrence lowered her pencil and looked to Ophelia. She then glanced to the pile of sketches around her.

"I think that's enough for now."

"Done already?"

"Already? It's been at least a couple hours. Besides, I've got what I need to get started," she said with a definite nod. "Would you like to see?"

Ophelia rose from where she sat, rising smoothly like a phantom. She glided over to Lawrence's side and lowered her face to look at the sketch pad.

Black charcoal crossed the paper in strong lines. The coal stood stark against the white, and although the sketch was done quickly, each line had been placed exactly. Ophelia's rendered likeness was made up only of long, arcing lines that gave her a fluidity like flowing water. Ophelia traced her own face, her finger following the serene expression to the sharp collarbone.

A cold hand landed on Lawrence's shoulder and the chill went straight through her blouse to the bone. Ophelia's hand was heavier than it looked and she gave Lawrence's shoulder a slight squeeze.

"You've immense talent, there is no doubt of that. Come sit with me."

The two of them took their original seats from the first night they had met. As soon as she sat, Ophelia lit a cigarette and leaned back to observe her. Lawrence fidgeted slightly, unsure of what to do with herself under the full weight of Ophelia's undivided attention.

"Lawrence," Ophelia began, picking at some imaginary lint on her skirt. "Something you mentioned before has been stuck in my mind, and I wish to discuss it further with you."

Lawrence couldn't help but chuckle. "There's no need to be so formal. Please, feel free to ask whatever you wish."

"Are you unhappy?"

Lawrence startled a bit, taken aback by the sudden question. No one had ever asked her such a thing before. She ran her thumb along the inside of her finger as she considered her answer.

"What a question," Lawrence said with a sigh. She looked towards the fire, watching the flames flicker and dance about within the marble mouth of the fireplace. "I don't know. Why?"

"From what I've heard, you wish to leave behind some sort of legacy. I want to know what would make you happy then. Is it fame, or money? What would satisfy that desire you have?" Ophelia asked earnestly, as if she herself wished to help Lawrence achieve it.

Lawrence struggled to understand why Ophelia seemed so singularly focused on this issue. Ophelia continued with her probing.

"What would you have to accomplish then to feel that you had succeeded?"

"I don't- I don't know." Lawrence crossed her legs and uncrossed them again. "I feel so strongly that my life has purpose, but I don't know what it could be. Should I aspire to be great so that I may be remembered long after I am gone, or would something modest be enough? Say I were to settle down, have children, and just live as a mother and a wife. Perhaps I would be happy. Or, should I sacrifice all that at the risk of dying a spinster, unknown and unloved? Even if I were to *become* great, what purpose does that serve? I will die anyway, and it won't matter much then, will it?"

"I feel that you are grappling with a much stronger beast than you think," mused Ophelia after a moment. "The purpose of life. How envious we might be of the simple ant, who goes about its day with a clear motivation. It lives and dies within a few short years, but its purpose is simple. Its entire *raison d'être* is so deeply ingrained in its being that it knows nothing else. If its colony is threatened, it throws itself in the direction of danger, uncaring of the consequences to its own life. What bliss." She exhaled, and the smoke of the cigarette filled the space between them. "But you are not that simple. You are not as simple as other humans, either. By asking yourself the question, I'm afraid you've answered it as well. You see, the very fact that you are grappling with the decision between the normal expectation of what you should do with your life and something else means you desire that other road."

"I would hate to put my ladder up and make my way to the top only to realize I've put it up on the wrong wall."

"Regret is a horrible thing to feel and incredibly human."

"You say that as if you have none yourself," laughed Lawrence. "Regret is only natural. Are *you* happy then, Ophelia?"

"I will be," she replied simply.

Lawrence's brows rose in surprise. "You seem remarkably self-assured of that. Please share your secrets with us mere mortals."

"I am happy now," she smiled. "I am here with you; that makes me happy."

"Now you are the one flattering me."

"No, no," Ophelia said, shaking her head. "I only ever say what I mean. Especially with you, you can be sure of that." Ophelia put out her cigarette.

"You must be hungry. Come."

Again, as Lawrence dined, Ophelia mostly watched. It seemed her fork never returned a second time to any part of her food, and she chose mostly to drink her wine. They sat together a little longer, and once the moon had fully risen, Ophelia accompanied Lawrence up to her bedroom. She stopped Lawrence before she went in.

"I do hope you will enjoy your stay here," Ophelia said, placing her hand on Lawrence's forearm.

She stepped closer, tilting her head down slightly. Lawrence raised hers and her breath caught as Ophelia stood a breath's distance away.

"I mean it, Lawrence. If there's anything you need, or wish for. You need only ask."

"I-"

"I wish to do right by you," Ophelia said, her voice a low whisper. "It's what you deserve. I will treat you only with the utmost respect and admiration. I hope you understand that, Lawrence."

Lawrence exhaled and found it impossible to speak. She merely nodded and Ophelia returned it with a curt nod of her own. She let go of Lawrence's arm, turning on her heel to walk off. Lawrence watched as Ophelia disappeared down the dark hallway. Her arm continued to tingle as the warmth slowly returned. She slipped into her room and locked the door, but kept the key in the lock as she settled down for the night.

* * *

The curtains around Lawrence's bed shifted before a slender hand appeared from within. It mindlessly pushed away the fabric until a small window of space appeared. Lawrence pushed herself out of bed, stumbling slightly as she stood upright. Her eyes remained closed and she breathed deeply, even as she continued to dream.

Lawrence pushed off her nightgown from her shoulders until it pooled at her feet. She staggered forward to the window, pushing on the glass until it popped open. The cool sea breeze entered, blowing back some of her long hair. The clear, bright moon sat at the highest point of the sky, casting a light glow over all it touched.

She unlocked her own bedroom door and walked through the dark home with soft footsteps. Lawrence appeared outside, her nude body illuminated by the moonlight. She wavered for a moment, but continued on. She plodded across the front lawn, crossing through the flowers. She trod on them carelessly and kicked up the wet dirt with every step. She went on her mindless trek, sure-footed but blind. It seemed she had a clear destination as she made her way to the green gazebo in the pond. Once she reached the center, she stood alone, swaying slightly.

She waited, and waited.

Although it seemed she stood there for a long time waiting in the darkness and cold, the time passed quickly.

In the blink of an eye, she was no longer alone.

A cool, firm hand wrapped around her eyes. The other arm went around her center. Someone held her close from behind.

Lawrence remained asleep, breathing deeply, stuck between dreams and reality. In her mind, she floated peacefully on her back in a shallow pool of water. She felt no fear, even though the water grew darker and the waves became wilder. Lawrence remained unaware, cast out as she was in a wild sea of danger.

The arm around her center moved, gripping her waist tightly. Along the spot where Lawrence's neck met her shoulder, a soft pair of lips kissed her. Even in her dreams, Lawrence caught the fragrance of smoke and jasmine as it enveloped her. It surrounded her like a cloud, impossible to ignore and all too familiar.

A sharp sting and prick like needles pierced the thin skin. She struggled for a moment, but was kept firmly in place by the steel-like arms banded around her.

From within her dreams, Lawrence felt a sharp tug that pulled her down under the water with a quick jerk. She fought against it, but it continued to pull at her. She went further down, deeper and deeper. The tugging sensation drew from some well deep inside her, as if her own soul was being tugged out.

"Miss?" A voice called out.

It sounded muffled at first as if being shouted through a thick wall of cotton, but it grew clearer with every passing second.

"Miss!"

Lawrence froze, slowly waking. Her mind grew clearer with every passing second, and panic blossomed from within her core. She began to blink faster, and her breathing became stuttered.

She let out a loud gasp suddenly, as if resurfacing from water. Lawrence staggered forward and spun around wildly, but found herself alone in the green gazebo.

She continued to search the darkness all around her, her skin prickling from the cold and the unsettling feeling that she was still not truly alone.

Lawrence raised her eyes up to the full moon, which began to warp and waver in her eyesight. She swayed where she stood, suddenly feeling lightheaded. The cascading ocean waves in the distance continued to crash against the cliffside, providing a steady beat that mimicked her heart. Between the sharp exhales of her breath, the summer crickets chirped loudly.

"Oh, miss! What are you doing out here!"

Ms. Hettle arrived to Lawrence's side, practically crashing into her. She quickly wrapped her up in a robe, tying the sash tightly.

"You'll catch death!"

Ms. Hettle let Lawrence lean on her as they stumbled back towards the house, the two of them staggering forward in the dark. Ms. Hettle made no mention of the mud caked up to Lawrence's shins as they crossed the foyer and went up the stairs.

When they reached Lawrence's room, Ms. Hettle stopped momentarily. She reached a hand out, feeling. The door remained wide open as Lawrence had left it, and she let out a low sigh.

"Come on dear."

Lawrence sat by the fire as Ms. Hettle rubbed a warm rag over her legs. She opened up the robe to guide Lawrence back into her nightgown. As she did, she placed a hand on Lawrence's shoulder. Her face screwed up in confusion. She pulled her hand away, bringing it up to her nose to smell. She let out a little gasp as she placed her fingers against the long trail of blood that went down Lawrence's front.

"Is something the matter, Ms. Hettle?" Lawrence asked in a bleary voice.

Her eyes began to flutter as she fought sleep. She could barely keep her eyelids open and a bone-deep weariness set in that caused her to slouch where she stood.

"No, no," rushed out Ms. Hettle in a tremulous voice. She did her best to keep her voice steady, but it shook regardless. "Everything's perfectly fine. Let's get you back into bed this instant. You must be freezing."

"I feel a little odd," Lawrence murmured. "This is a very strange dream."

Ms. Hettle quickly wiped Lawrence down as best she could, bringing her face close to make sure no traces were left behind. She pressed the rag firmly against Lawrence's neck until she was satisfied.

Ms. Hettle asked no questions and tucked Lawrence back into her bed. She continued to mutter to herself, same as always. The parts Lawrence could make sense of sounded distinctly like a portion of a prayer she had a distant memory of hearing once many years prior. She wondered idly why Ms. Hettle was praying for protection against the Devil at that moment.

Ms. Hettle continued to linger by her bedside, as if on vigil. Lawrence opened her mouth to try and thank her, but no sound came out. Her eyes remained closed, and she heard the distant noise of a door opening and closing. Thereafter, she slept dreamlessly.

Chapter 11

A sharp ray of light woke Lawrence. She let out a low, discontented noise and pushed herself up. The sudden movement caused her head to spin, and she fell back onto her pillow with a crash.

"Good god," she murmured.

She rubbed at her eyes and looked around. The curtains to her bed remained wide open and the bright daylight poured into her room. She went to look at the clock, but stopped as her eyes landed on the small coffee table.

The largest arrangement of camellias sat gathered in an ornate vase. It seemed like an entire tree's worth of flowering buds had been picked for her. The sweet perfume of the flowers hit her. The normally adored scent was overwhelming and turned her sensitive stomach. Lawrence turned her head away towards the open window as the breeze came in.

When she sat at her vanity, Lawrence's eyes widened at the watery, diluted streaks of blood that had dried across her skin. Four, new distinct scabs stood out, crusted over in dried blood. She placed a gentle hand on it, flinching slightly at the soreness. She let out a sharp exhale, dropping her hand into her lap.

Lawrence leaned forward to the mirror, studying herself. Her face seemed a bit grayer than normal. The normally smooth skin around her cheeks seemed a bit more sallow as well. Faint bags formed under the thin skin under her eyes, highlighting how exhausted she felt.

It took her a bit longer than usual, but she brushed and plaited her hair. She dressed in her usual long black skirt and work blouse and slowly trudged down the long flight of stairs.

Ms. Hettle found Lawrence sitting on her own in the sun room, basking in the light like a lizard. She kept her face pointed to the warmth, eyes shut as if napping. Ms. Hettle gave a timid knock against the door to signal her arrival. Lawrence slowly opened her eyes and turned her head. Ms. Hettle stood at the entrance, tray in hand.

"Good morning, miss," she said. "Normally you're out roaming around as you please before the morning light. I hadn't thought to look for you here."

"Ms. Hettle, good morning," Lawrence said in a breathy voice. She rose slowly and gripped the back of the chaise tightly, her knuckles turning white. "I don't feel quite right this morning."

Ms. Hettle came forward, setting the tray within Lawrence's reach. She guided her to sit once again.

"Now, none of that," Ms. Hettle said in a comforting tone. She patted Lawrence on the shoulder and poured her a steaming cup of tea. "I've brought you pastries with jam and fresh butter. Now, you just have a few bites of that and you'll be right as rain. That's all."

Lawrence smiled weakly and nodded. She reached out and grabbed one of the rolls, bringing it up to her mouth. She chewed slowly, savoring the sweetness that did seem to perk her up a bit. She finished the rest of it and drank some tea.

"There," said Ms. Hettle. "I bet you're feeling better already."

"Ms. Hettle," said Lawrence, her voice serious. She grabbed the old woman's arm until she came down to her level on the chaise. "I had the strangest dream last night. I need you to tell me if it was real or not. Please."

"Dream?" repeated Ms. Hettle, her brows furrowing.

"Yes," said Lawrence. "I had the most peculiar dream, and I woke up with blood on me. I think something bit me last night. Feel."

Lawrence lowered the neckline of her blouse. She grabbed the housekeeper's hand before she could protest and placed it against the four small scabs that lined the outer edge of her neck. Ms. Hettle quickly pulled her hand back, as if she had been burned by the touch.

"Oh," Ms. Hettle said, laughing lightly. "That-that is nothing! Silly girl. You slept with the window open and a bug got in, that's all. You must remember to keep the windows closed. They'll get anywhere if you let them, even the second floor."

"No," said Lawrence, shaking her head vehemently. "The windows were firmly shut when I slept. I swear. You must tell me, Ms. Hettle. Did you find me sleepwalking?"

Ms. Hettle hesitated for a moment, but patted Lawrence's hand.

"Don't be silly, girl. You were in bed all night. Promise."

Lawrence's brow furrowed, almost disappointed by the answer. She let out a shaky breath, nodding. She let Ms. Hettle go and rose as well.

"Very well. Thank you, Ms. Hettle. I suppose I should get started on my work."

They walked together, and Lawrence stopped her, remembering.

"Thank you, though, for the flowers. You really shouldn't have. What would your lady think?"

"Flowers?" repeated Ms. Hettle, stunned. "What flowers?"

Confusion and concern swept through Lawrence, but she merely shook her head. She then smiled.

"Oh, nothing. Must have been part of my silly dream. Forget I said anything."

By the early afternoon, Lawrence felt a bit of energy return to her. At Ms. Hettle's cajoling, Lawrence finished another two sweet rolls before she insisted on starting her work.

She pushed past the slight ache in her body as she laid out a tarp on the ground. She set out small pieces of framing wood and unrolled her duck canvas. The taupe cotton canvas was one Lawrence regularly used; she always enjoyed the weave of the cotton and the way it felt as she worked. She knelt on the floor as she began to construct the large canvas she would use to paint Ophelia's portrait on.

She pulled and strained her muscles as she held the canvas taut, keeping it pinned as she nailed the corners and folded back the excess into neat layers. Although her body protested, Lawrence ignored it and continued to work until the canvas was done. A light layer of sweat covered her for work that normally came so easily to her. When she stood the frame upright, the height of it came up to her chest.

Another wave of dizziness struck then, and Lawrence rested on the floor, leaning against the edge of the sofa until it passed. She took even, steady breaths as the room spun around her.

"Steady on, Stoner. Keep your head on."

Lawrence positioned Ophelia's chair and set up her easel opposite. A small table provided by Ms. Hettle held all her tools and brushes with paints and jars for thinning out the oils. Under the careful supervision of Ms. Hettle, anything that could potentially be touched by paint was removed or pushed out of the way.

Before lunch, Lawrence sat before the giant, blank canvas. She observed it as it remained untouched and considered all its potential. Her eyes continued to roam over the linen until it was all she saw.

"My goodness. Busy, busy."

Lawrence nearly jumped as Ophelia's silky voice came from directly behind her. She hadn't heard her enter, nor had she realized that she had begun to doze off again. The canvas remained untouched. She looked to the clock above the mantle and saw then that several hours had passed seemingly in the blink of an eye.

Ophelia had on her usual sunglasses but wore a different day dress where the neckline sat low below her sharp shoulders. Glittering emeralds and rubies sat around her delicate neck and dotted her slender fingers. Ruby earrings dropped from her ears like fat teardrops of blood.

"Ophelia," Lawrence said, rising from her chair.

She grabbed the back of it to steady herself. Ophelia studied her, frowning as she looked her over.

"I didn't hear you come in," Lawrence said, running the back of her hand over her damp forehead. "Forgive me. I must have dozed off."

"You look a bit peaky, my dear. Sit, sit."

Ophelia guided Lawrence over to the sofa by the fire and sat by her side. Lawrence breathed heavily and Ophelia gently brushed a sweaty tendril of hair off her face. She gathered one of Lawrence's hands in hers, pressing her thumb down onto the center of her palm. Lawrence's breath hitched in her throat.

Ophelia turned her head slightly until their faces were just a few feet apart. Lawrence breathed in and was immediately transported to her dream. Her eyes widened slightly as she studied Ophelia, but simply saw her own stunned reflection in the dark tint of the glasses.

"What?"

"Your smell," Lawrence muttered. "It's very distinct. Jasmine and something smokey."

"As is yours."

"What do I smell of?"

"Like orange blossom and ferns, caraway seeds and pepper. It's becoming my favorite scent."

Lawrence's cheeks heated and she swallowed thickly. The sweat across her brow cooled and she shivered as Ophelia continued to hold her hand.

"Yours reminded me of something."

"How interesting," Ophelia said with a tight-lipped smile. "Something *good* I hope."

"Actually, something very strange that happened last night," Lawrence said with a shake of her head. "I dreamed that I sleepwalked. I went out to the garden, all the way to the gazebo. Ms. Hettle found me."

"Really?" Ophelia asked in interest. Her head tilted slightly like an inquisitive cat. "Do you remember anything else from this curious little dream of yours?"

"Yes," Lawrence said with a nod. "It was incredibly vivid."

"What do you remember?" Ophelia asked with the quirk of her brow.

The air between them grew thick. Lawrence looked away from Ophelia, brushing her free hand across the back of her brow.

"Nothing actually, I just remember it being vivid. I remember smelling the sea and the dirt, and something else. Someone behind me, I think. Silly."

"Dreams have a funny way of telling us the truth. That which we may not know, or something we know so deeply that we do not know it at all."

"Do you really think so?" Lawrence asked keenly, turning back to Ophelia with a practically manic expression.

She reached for the top button of her blouse and began to undo it. Ophelia's brow rose, but she remained still. Lawrence revealed the top of her chest, showing Ophelia the scabs and dried blood she had yet to wash off.

"This is real. Ms. Hettle thinks it was a bug. I've seen it before though."

Ophelia quietly studied the exposed skin in silence. She remained still, raising her hand and reaching out as if to touch. Her shoulders tensed and her nostrils flared slightly as she traced the faint blood. She abruptly stood from the sofa and walked away from Lawrence. She left the library, returning shortly after with a bowl of water and a rag.

"What's that?" Lawrence asked. She reached out to take it from Ophelia, who then held it out of her reach.

"Please," Ophelia murmured, kneeling before Lawrence where she sat. "You've had a terrible shock, and you've bled. Let me take care of you. I want to."

Lawrence went to argue, but stopped. She lowered her arm and nodded mutely. Ophelia dipped the rag in the warm water, but waited.

"You'll need to remove your blouse further," she said.

"What?" Lawrence repeated, her voice pitching in surprise. "What for?"

"Oh, come now," Ophelia teased, the corner of her mouth quirking up as she looked up at Lawrence.

It was an entirely new vantage point for Lawrence, and her eyes flickered momentarily down the front of Ophelia's loose dress. She saw the briefest flash of bare skin and something lace that sent her heart racing. Lawrence quickly averted her eyes, but felt her skin heat. Ophelia placed a gentle hand on the outside of her thigh.

"We are only women here. There's nothing to be ashamed of."

Lawrence thought about it for a moment before she slowly raised her hands to the buttons. She slowly undid them as Ophelia watched like a hawk. The blouse pooled around her waist until she was only in her long cloth brassiere. Ophelia placed the warm towel against her chest and began to clean.

Lawrence focused on breathing as Ophelia made slow, methodical strokes over her skin with the soft cloth. Streaks of water ran down her chest, soaking the thin fabric of her top. It stuck to her skin like papier-mâché. Lawrence held her breath as she raised her head. Her eyes rested on the bare patch of wall by the fireplace.

"I wonder when the tapestry will be back."

"What tapestry?" Ophelia asked as she continued on with her task. Lawrence raised her arm to gesture, but Ophelia didn't stop to look.

"That nice tapestry that used to hang by the fireplace, of course."

Only then did Ophelia's hand stop. Lawrence momentarily glanced down at her to study her reaction, to see if she revealed any inkling of knowing. Ophelia turned her head slowly, pivoting it upwards to Lawrence.

"Nice?" Ophelia repeated in disbelief.

"Oh yes," nodded Lawrence, emphatic. "Quite an interesting moment in history. I quite enjoyed looking at it. When Ms. Hettle told me she had it taken down to be cleaned, I was quite dismayed."

Ophelia's brows pinched together, framed by the metal filigree of her spectacles. She then suddenly laughed, resuming her work. "Why are you lying, Lawrence?"

"I'm not lying."

"Yes, you are," insisted Ophelia. Her voice lashed out slightly, as if she were bristling at the mere idea of being challenged in such a trivial matter. She once again stopped her work and looked up at Lawrence, her mouth set in a firm line. "Don't lie to me, Lawrence."

"Did Ms. Hettle tell you then?" Lawrence asked in a quiet voice.

Ophelia chose not to answer. Lawrence heard only her own thudding heartbeat and the soft crackle of fire as they stared at each other. Due to her stony composure, it was impossible to tell what Ophelia was thinking. Lawrence felt a chill and crossed her arms in front of herself, suddenly feeling exposed.

"The flowers," Lawrence murmured. "They were from you, weren't they?"

"Naturally," replied Ophelia immediately, deliberate and composed

213

as she tilted her head away.

How easily she confessed! Lawrence paused for a moment; her lips parted as the next words failed to form on her lips.

"Who else would they have come from then?" Ophelia asked with an amused chuckle. "Hettle? The cook?"

"Why?" Lawrence asked, confounded.

Ophelia inhaled, raising her hand to brush another stray hair away from Lawrence's temple. She then smiled gently until little dimples formed in her hollowed cheeks.

"The tapestry bothered you," Ophelia said simply. "And you adore camellias. That is why."

"You would only know those things if Ms. Hettle told you," Lawrence pointed out. Ophelia nodded her head once.

"Is she spying on me then?" Lawrence asked petulantly, her eyes narrowing slightly.

Much to her surprise, Ophelia laughed good-naturedly. She set the cooled rag aside and placed a gentle hand on Lawrence's arm, trailing down it until she clasped Lawrence's hand tightly in hers. She gently guided Lawrence's arm away until she was no longer covering herself.

"She reported back to me, yes," Ophelia said in a soothing tone that didn't quite seem to suit her. She remained on her knees before Lawrence like a humble supplicant. She then lowered her head in humility.

"I find it difficult to lie to you, so I won't," she confessed. "I did ask Ms. Hettle to tell me what you had talked about with her. I wanted to know what you like and dislike. I only did it so I could understand you better, and I only did those things, perhaps a bit overzealously, to ingratiate you to me."

Lawrence sat in silent contemplation for a moment. She considered her feelings. Perhaps she ought to have been more bothered,

214

concerned even, but she felt none of those things. In truth, she felt a warmth in the pit of her stomach burying itself like a small seed. It began to grow, unfettered, until it bloomed into joy, and something hideously similar to hope. She swallowed thickly, considering how to move forward.

"At the pier," Lawrence said, at last. "That was her, wasn't it? Did you send her out to spy on me even then?"

Ophelia's lips pursed. Her hand that rested on the sofa cushion by Lawrence's leg began to drum.

"Would it bother you if she did?"

"That's how you knew about the painting," Lawrence said with a dry chuckle. "Of course. Poor Ms. Hettle, trekking through the whole town to chase after a poor, uninteresting painter. You could have spared her the trouble."

"I will confess," Ophelia said with a smirk. "I looked forward to her reports. I savored every little bit of information like a child with sweets."

That too filled Lawrence with pleasure, and she felt her cheeks warm. She looked down and noticed most of the blood had been washed, but the water had soaked through her top until it was nearly sheer. She quickly covered herself once more. Ophelia misunderstood, and her brow creased in concern.

"Does that bother you?"

"What?"

"I hadn't meant to offend you, Lawrence. Really."

"Oh, no," she said quickly. "Strangely enough, that doesn't bother me at all; but, Ophelia, if you have any wish to know something about me, you need only ask me yourself. I welcome that more than having it being parroted back to you by someone else. As for the tapestry and flowers, there is no need for such gestures. I am more than grateful simply to have your patronage."

Ophelia frowned at that. "Seems quite cold, and impersonal."

"Friendship then?"

"A good start."

"If we are friends then," Lawrence said with a sudden shyness. She gestured to the scabs around her throat and then lifted her hands. "May I show you? Only in the interest of having you understand my earlier anxiety. As you said yourself, we are just women here after all."

Ophelia's jaw tensed, but she nodded. Lawrence undid the top buttons of her brassiere and lowered it until the top of her breast was exposed. Ophelia stilled for a moment, and her shoulders tensed slightly.

Whether or not she saw what Lawrence had wanted to show her was unclear, so she pointed to the faded marks on her breast where she had been bitten before. The skin close to her nipple was several shades lighter where it began to scar. Ophelia then turned her head away slightly, as if disinterested.

"It's the same," Lawrence murmured in concern. "That's why I don't think it was a dream after all. It can't just be a bug. What if it's something *else*? Shouldn't I tell someone?"

Ophelia raised her hands and brought it up to Lawrence's exposed chest. She traced a cold finger around the old bite mark, and Lawrence's skin felt electrified at the cold touch. She held her breath as Ophelia traced the shape, letting her finger drag perilously close to the edge of the exposed nipple. She then righted Lawrence's top and helped button it back up with a placid smile.

"Wandering pincer beetles," Ophelia said at last.

"I'm sorry?" Lawrence asked dumbly.

She watched as Ophelia set aside the rag and bowl, and rose from her position. She turned her back to Lawrence and took a seat on the sofa opposite. She lit up a cigarette, shrugging as if it were nothing at all.

"I've seen those types of bite marks a few times before. Hettle is right. Keep the windows shut tight at night."

Lawrence nodded obediently. She quickly dressed once again, pulling on her blouse. Ophelia kept her gaze fixed pointedly at the fire as she did.

"Thank you," Lawrence said at last. Ophelia turned her head at that, raising a brow in silent question. "For helping wash the blood off. I am glad we are friends, Ophelia. Truly."

Ophelia smiled, and she didn't bother hiding her teeth when she did. The fire illuminated her brilliant smile, and the double canines along the top row of otherwise perfect teeth gleamed in the light.

"Me too."

Lawrence squinted her eyes slightly to get a better look. Ophelia quickly shut her mouth again and pressed her lips together. Lawrence shook her head.

"Your smile is beautiful, Ophelia."

It was slow, but Ophelia's lips pulled back again, and Lawrence saw the bright ivory teeth and the sharp canines. She felt a dull throb in her breast, and her mind immediately went to the bite marks she received in the night. She felt a chill at the thought and her breath caught. She then returned the smile back. Lawrence refused to even consider the dangerous thought that entered her mind unbidden, and was sure it was all just a coincidence.

Chapter 12

"May I ask you a question?"

Lawrence's head poked out around the side of her canvas. She held one of her long, thin brushes in her mouth like a horse's bit while she held another mid-air. The great canvas she had constructed days earlier stood several feet up in the air when up on its modest, wooden pedestal.

Lawrence paused her work for a moment, setting down her brushes on her work table at her side. A dirty rag covered in smudged fingerprints in old paint sat slung over her shoulder. Ophelia sat posed in her seat just as Lawrence had positioned her originally. She remained in place, but turned her head slightly to '*tsk*' lightly at Lawrence.

"I've told you to stop asking me that. Simply ask me."

For the past several days since first sleepwalking, Lawrence rose early before the dawn and would putter around in the garden among the sculptures. Although she did not have the courage yet to step beyond the boundary, she would simply check to make sure the little exit she had found was still there. She'd step away, letting the branch snap back into place, and go on her way.

Lawrence found a special refuge in the garden, spending most of her free waking hours by the pond or under the gazebo. It felt like its own sort of oasis, as the gazebo itself was contained within the private pond. Lilies crowded the shimmering surface, and the reedy edges played host to all sorts of creatures. Sometimes, when the light was just right, it would reflect off the pond, and soft sparkles of light would dance across the metal frame of the structure and the soft petals of the flowers.

Ms. Hettle would then collect her for breakfast, and she'd work on her own until Ophelia joined her in the late afternoon. Ophelia seemed able to sit for hours without budging at all. She never complained of sore muscles or lack of entertainment. She'd keep her gaze fixed on Lawrence and watch in silence as she worked.

During these brief evening sessions together, they would speak, chatting about nothing at all or things that Lawrence had never quite considered thinking about before. The very nature of their conversations was that they moved easily from one thing to the next like water traveling in the uninhibited flow of a brook. Societal rules and expectations were always checked at the door and abandoned when it was just the two of them.

Lawrence breathed out a light laugh, pulling the rag from its resting place to wipe at her hands once again. She leaned back in her stool and studied the canvas. A slightly crude version of Ophelia stared back at her, outlined in burnt sienna and crisp white. She leaned out over the side of her easel once more.

"Have you ever been married?"

"Not in this lifetime," Ophelia replied with a smirk and a deep chuckle that was low and percussive, like the low tapping of one's palm against a drum. Lawrence frowned, crossing her arms in front of her.

"You have no interest in getting married, then?" At the subtle shake of Ophelia's head, Lawrence continued. "May I ask why?"

"Why should I want to get married?"

Lawrence shrugged. "Well, you are rich, well-educated, and

219

beautiful. You could marry anyone you'd like," she said observantly.

Lawrence turned her head slightly, looking between Ophelia and the crudely painted canvas.

"Do you have no wish for children, then?"

Ophelia grimaced, the corner of her lip quirking up in a slight sneer. The flash of white teeth caught Lawrence's eye before they disappeared once more. Ophelia shook her head.

"I couldn't imagine anything worse, no."

Lawrence laughed, amused by the flat and horrified tone in Ophelia's voice. She held her arms out. "Love and companionship, then. A great partnership to know and be known fully by another."

"I am very open to both," said Ophelia with a slight smirk. "I've yet to meet any *man* able to provide either to me."

"*Ma dai!*" Lawrence murmured.

She brushed away some dust from the canvas. She pulled her chair further out from behind the canvas to converse with Ophelia more directly. In turn, Ophelia turned in her own seat and relaxed from the rigid pose she had been holding for several hours. Lawrence stood and brought over a cigarette for her, knowing she would want one.

"I've no objection to men in general," Ophelia said. "But, they are generally quite stupid."

Lawrence struck up a match to light the cigarette for Ophelia, ducking her head down as she laughed. She wiped a stray tear that fell from the corner of her eye and returned to her seat.

"Well, you're certainly not afraid to speak your mind. The more and more we speak and spend time together, you defy any and all opinions I form of you."

"I wasn't aware you thought of me so often."

"I've thought of little else, if I am honest," she confessed.

Ophelia grinned wide, pleased by that particular confession. Lawrence crossed her legs at the ankles, taking the break to stretch out the aching muscles in her lower back.

"However," Lawrence began again. "I admit my imagination did go a bit wild. At the expense of little to no information, the missing details were filled in by my errant mind."

"An old, boring relic of a woman with a snobby, aristocratic husband and a wild brood of brattish, undeserving children?"

"I hadn't considered children, and no, nothing quite as bleak as that," Lawrence said. "Don't you feel some pressure or obligation to continue your family's legacy? Who will inherit this great house? Do you not have any fears for the future?"

Ophelia immediately shook her head, and the little teardrop gems dangled wildly around her face.

"What is there to fear? If my only reasons to have children are those things alone, I think I have made a fine choice in abstaining," replied Ophelia breezily. The corners of her lips turned down. "Don't tell me you're interested in that sort of life, Lawrence. I had gotten the impression you were above it all. If not, you will resort to settling, for you will have to settle once you've chosen a man. No one will be truly worthy of you. See, this is how I imagine you, Lawrence, and it's how I see most women. You are a bird, wild and beautiful, soaring in the sky and living by the rules of nature and your own mind. Soon enough, a man will come by, exclaim how lovely you are, and make vows and oaths that he must have you, and he will capture you. Once you've been caught and forced down into the marriage bed, with a delicate chain around your lovely ankle, your only purpose will then be to produce undeserving, ungrateful, screaming brats for their equally undeserving, ungrateful father. As an added insult, on top of it all, you will take his name so that all of you, everything you were and will be, will simply become a reflection of him. That will be your reality until either you or your miserable husband dies. Is *that* the legacy you wish to have?"

Ophelia's face twisted into an expression of derision and disgust as she spoke. Lawrence listened with a soft smile and absentmindedly tidied her work table, prepping more umber and swirling a few brushes in thinner. Her brows rose and fell as Ophelia spoke. She turned back to Ophelia with a peaceable smile.

"I suppose that's life, though, isn't it? We are the outsiders, Ophelia. Should we really cast judgment on so many women who may not have had a choice? Or, further still, they may be happy. If that is the legacy that fulfills them, who are we to judge? If anything, we are the worse off." Lawrence sighed as she leaned back, occasionally taking the time to observe her progress. "It doesn't need to be so horrible. If I loved some…one very deeply, it could even be quite nice."

Ophelia scoffed at that and put her cigarette out with a flourish. She crossed her arms, tapping her fingers along the outside of her arm.

"Times are changing, Lawrence. Women in this day and age can do so much more. Undoubtedly, we were all set back several centuries with the crusades and such, but there's no need to tie a rock around your ankle and jump into the lake, so to speak."

"Oh, are you an atheist now as well?" Lawrence asked with a hearty laugh. She shook her head. "Good grief, who exactly have I agreed to stay with this summer?"

Ophelia smiled as well, but this time her lips parted slightly, and Lawrence once more caught the bright, pearly flash of her teeth. A shiver shot down her spine, and she quickly rose from her seat. She turned her back to Ophelia, pretending to busy herself with her paints and brushes.

"You're not religious, are you Lawrence?"

"I'd say I am," Lawrence answered immediately, turning her head slightly to look over her shoulder.

Ophelia smirked in response. Lawrence hesitantly continued on, struggling to find the right words.

"However, I suppose I could do better about my prayers. Are you really not then?"

"Heavens, no," Ophelia answered sharply. "Religion is used on people the way blinders are put on horses. It's a hammer used by malicious, self-serving individuals and a panacea by the stupid and obstinate."

"You don't believe that, surely."

Lawrence frowned, turning momentarily to look at Ophelia, who held her head high and stared back, apathetic.

"Do not feel compelled to simply say what you've been trained to say. I urge you to speak your mind freely when you are in my company. I want nothing more, and I encourage you to explore other avenues of possibility in all things. Try for a moment to imagine what the purpose of religion is, and now look at our reality. God and the belief in God have killed more people than any *monsters* have."

"That's blasphemous, Ophelia," Lawrence murmured, albeit half-heartedly. "God is not a cure-all, and religion does not always have all the answers. Any evil conducted in the world by men is by those who have perverted its true meaning. If anything, it is something we should aspire to, surely."

"If it can be so easily twisted and manipulated, changed, and adapted to suit men, no matter how evil they may be, what purpose does it serve? Every hundred years or so, its meaning changes. What we value changes. The meaning of the word changes. It all changes," muttered Ophelia, her voice turning bitter at the end.

Lawrence didn't have an answer then, and she began to feel a bit out of her depth. At Ophelia's direction, she sat and meditated on her true feelings. She considered how she truly felt, compelled by Ophelia's brazen honesty and confidence. There was certainly some taboo to it, but it was at the same time thrilling.

Lawrence remembered cold Sunday mornings, shivering next to her mother as they sat in the pews of the small, unheated church in town. As they sang hymns, their breaths came out in puffs, trembling with every warbling, wavering note. The backs of her hands still bore the white scars of being rapped over the knuckles repeatedly with rulers as she did her best to recite passages she never cared to remember. Her family always prayed over their food before every meal, but all Lawrence could remember was murmuring the words half-heartedly, anxious to get on with eating. Ophelia watched as Lawrence remembered, and her smile grew.

It did feel as if she and Ophelia were good friends who had merely been reacquainted and were now settling back into the comfort of an old friendship. It was a potent thing—to be fully seen, acknowledged, and cared for—and something very easy to covet and depend on. Lawrence rolled up her shirt sleeves, ready to go back to work.

"I suppose I am comfortable admitting, in present company, that I find very little comfort in God. Although He is meant to be the ultimate source of that, I'm not quite sure why. I suppose I must not be doing it right, or there is something wrong with me."

"You are, putting it simply, not simple. That is why you feel that way. Nor is anything wrong with you. Not believing in God does not make you evil, my dear," said Ophelia. Her mouth was set in a thin line, and her hand curled around the armchair of the chair. "Life is short. Do not let archaic, man-made rules of propriety and middle-class morality prevent you from being totally and truly happy."

"What a conversation we are having." Lawrence began to chuckle, shaking her head. "However, it's been exceedingly easy to be frank and forthcoming with you, as if we have known each other for far longer."

Ophelia seemed to perk up at that and leaned forward in her seat. "Do you mean that?"

"Though, I suppose that's how the new ladies are. They're all very progressive, and I am stubborn in my old-fashioned ways."

Ophelia scoffed. "Even us poor, feeble ladies can now vote. What is so wrong with us discussing these things freely?"

"Yes, I suppose you're right." Lawrence nodded, biting her lower lip as she thought. "However, I don't know how I feel about that. I don't know much about politics or laws. Do most regular women? I can't imagine they do, so I don't think I, personally, am qualified to vote."

"You *are* qualified, Lawrence, because you are a human who lives and knows her own self and experiences. Why should women who know little about politics have any less say than men who know very little? I won't have you say these things in my presence about not being qualified. How ridiculous."

Lawrence could only nod. That seemed to be Ophelia's ability; she was incredibly persuasive and determined in her convictions. Even if Lawrence did not already feel submissive in her presence, Ophelia seemed able to lay out her thoughts clearly in such a way that it was easy to always nod and agree.

"Yes, I suppose that's true," she said immediately. "Do you mind?"

Lawrence picked up her brushes once more and resumed her work. The sketch underneath slowly faded, covered in sepia and thick, shapeless blocks of dark paint. From an untrained eye, it seemed as if no work had been done at all, but Ophelia seemed to know better. When Lawrence finally declared they had done enough for the day, she rose from her seat and came to stand behind Lawrence's stool.

Lawrence felt her heartbeat pick up as she felt Ophelia's hovering presence and the soft smell that lingered whenever she passed. Her skirts hit Lawrence's leg, the beads clacking and the satin rustling. Ophelia lightly placed a hand on Lawrence's shoulder.

"You *are* fast," she murmured.

Lawrence inhaled deeply and tilted her head up sideways with a polite smile. "I meant it when I said I was motivated."

Ophelia tilted forward at the waist to inspect the canvas more closely. She leaned down over Lawrence until the side of her chest rested over her right shoulder. Lawrence nearly jumped out of her seat when she felt Ophelia's chilly hand trace the edge of her shirt collar.

She held her breath until Ophelia pulled her hand away with a small smirk.

"Any more bug bites? I'd be happy to check."

Lawrence shook her head with a chuckle. "Must have gotten in through the windows like you said."

"Good. No more mysterious dreams then either?"

Lawrence rose from her seat and threw a cover over the easel. "Happy to report none of the sort whatsoever."

Ophelia stepped away and went to the drink cart, as was usual for her. When she turned back, she held two glasses in hand and held one out towards Lawrence. She shook the glass lightly, gesturing for Lawrence to take it. After a moment's hesitation, she did, but made no move to drink. Ophelia noticed, tilting her head silently in question.

"It's complicated," Lawrence offered up by way of explanation.

She looked down at the amber liquid in the crystal and immediately caught a whiff of the sharp scent of liquor. Lawrence no longer gagged at the scent, but unwanted memories kept her from indulging. She took her seat on the sofa, balancing the whiskey glass on her knee. She had to distract Ophelia, and suddenly laughed.

"There was this older man who sometimes came into our studio. Count Giramondi had a portrait done every year. When I first met him, he was quite good to me, and I even ended up selling him a painting I made of some opera singers. Anyway, he was a very devout man, and he told me never to drink or smoke. He said the moment I started, I would start my journey down a road I'd never be able to come back from. I just abstained to humor him, and then I just kept going."

Ophelia's head tilted. "Are you superstitious or incredibly honorable?"

"Neither, really."

The corners of Ophelia's lips turned up. She raised her own glass to her lips and spoke into the glass. "You're not telling me the truth."

"Sorry?"

Lawrence's head whipped up. Ophelia shook her head at her, as if in disappointment.

"You are lying, Lawrence. I don't like it when you lie to me."

Lawrence stared back, and she felt her stomach drop. Her spine straightened as she set the untouched glass aside entirely. Although she raised her chin, Lawrence's face paled and her eyes quivered.

"I don't know what you're talking about."

"You *do* know," Ophelia replied in a low whisper.

If it were at all possible, Lawrence felt the heat of her stare through her glasses. Her skin broke out in goosebumps and sweat gathered at the nape of her neck. She began to breath heavily.

"It's nothing," she replied, waving her hand to move on from the topic.

"If it's nothing, you will not mind telling me then."

"Why does it matter?" Lawrence cried out, her voice rising as she lashed out.

Her hands trembled until she grasped them tightly in her lap. Lawrence's vision tunneled. She felt panic clawing its way up her throat. She inhaled sharply and looked to Ophelia, who remained eerily serene.

"I am grateful, really, of the opportunity to work and live here in your company, but I won't sit by as you call me a liar. You say you wish to be my friend, but you press me for details on things you don't understand. At the end of the day, you are my employer, Ms. Aldane. Nothing more."

Ophelia's lips pressed into a thin line and the muscles along her shoulders tensed. Lawrence watched as they pulled together, taut like a tiger before it pounced on its prey. She inhaled deeply as her fingers began to drum on the sofa cushion. Her jaw clenched, but she remained silent. With every passing moment of silence between the two of them, Lawrence felt her bravery and indignation leave her. She opened her mouth to quickly apologize.

"Nothing more," Ophelia murmured under her breath.

Lawrence winced at the hurt tone, swallowing thickly. She shook her head, but Ophelia continued on.

"I see how you feel. You only needed to have let me know sooner to spare me this embarrassment."

"Ophelia-"

"You're frightened," Ophelia observed with a subtle tilt of her head. "Frightened and feeling sorry for yourself. All you talk about is being afraid, but you won't do anything about it. You're afraid of being forgotten. So what? Do not let yourself be forgotten so easily then! You are afraid to be alone? Then, let yourself fall in love. You keep shying away when doors are opened to you because you're too afraid to see what's on the other side! Then, when you are alone, you cry and wonder why it had to happen to you. You revel in being part of the crowd, the flock!"

"I am not afraid," Lawrence argued, her voice no higher than a weak whisper. "You have no idea where I've come from, and how I've gotten here. It would all be easy for me too if I came from this!"

Lawrence gestured to the grand library in the large mansion. Ophelia remained calm, but shook her head.

"That is a sheep's mentality, Lawrence. You are not one of *them*. I thought you were an artist, Lawrence. You said it yourself you want to be remembered! How can you ever possibly dream of attaining anything like greatness if you despise being honest with yourself? God forbid you do, you will have to actually have some courage."

Lawrence looked at her, mouth opening and closing in insult. She went to respond, but Ophelia pointed up to her.

"You know it's true, Lawrence. Don't you dare try and lie to me again. You cannot help it. You were trained from birth to think and act this way. All I am trying to get you to understand is that you do not need to keep these shackles on yourself. Just try. Try! Do not be a coward, Lawrence."

"How dare you!" Lawrence cried, rising from her seat.

The heat rose in her cheeks and she clenched her hands into tight fists. She pointed down at Ophelia where she continued to sit, who in turn, tilted her head up to gaze at Lawrence.

"You're a hypocrite. You judge me that I'm not being honest, but you've been anything but! I don't know the first thing about you. You leave whenever you damn well feel like while the rest of us stay here under lock and key! Why don't you ever eat with me? Why is no one allowed in your part of the house? Why do you wear those damned things all day long?"

"Ask," sighed Ophelia. "If you're really so curious, ask me then."

Lawrence's shoulders rose with each heavy breath. She stared down at Ophelia, but couldn't bring herself to say. At last, Ophelia chuckled and Lawrence hated it. It set her teeth on edge and made her want to storm out of the room. Ophelia rose and came to Lawrence's side. She placed a gentle hand on her shoulder that sent a shiver down her spine.

"I only push you because I can see your potential," she murmured. She leaned in and brought her lips closer to Lawrence's ear. "You do not need to be afraid with me."

Despite her words, something within Lawrence disagreed. Ophelia walked around Lawrence and went to stand by the easel. An idea struck Lawrence, and she went to the nearest window.

"What are you doing?" Ophelia asked, turning.

"I am not afraid. I'm tired of the dark!" cried Lawrence.

She yanked on the thick tapestry, using all her strength to pull. Ophelia's mouth opened once she understood what Lawrence meant to do. She took a half-step forward with her arm outstretched.

"No! Don't!"

Lawrence drew back the curtains fully. Ophelia immediately rushed backward as if touched by fire. She crashed into one of the side tables, falling backward. She let out a cry and threw her arm over her face.

"Ophelia!"

Lawrence rushed forward as Ophelia pushed herself further back into the shadows. It was as if she were physically repelled by the afternoon light. Ophelia took the glasses off for once and covered both eyes with her hands, pushing the palms deep into her eyes as she groaned out in pain. Lawrence dropped to her knees and drew her into her arms.

"Ophelia! My God!"

"The light," Ophelia shuddered.

Lawrence immediately rushed to the windows and snapped the curtains close at once, drawing the room into darkness once again. Her eyes worked to adjust to the darkness, and when she turned to look for Ophelia, she found her pushed up against the far wall. Ophelia had returned the glasses to her face, but two dark tracks ran from her eyes.

"Your eyes!" Lawrence cried in despair. "You're bleeding! Ophelia-"

Lawrence went to help her up, but Ophelia held her arm out to stop her. She turned her head away, quickly wiping at the dark blood that ran down her cheeks.

"Leave me be."

"Ophelia, I'm sorry. I-"

"Get out!" she screamed.

Lawrence jumped slightly. She lingered for a moment longer, as her feet refused to move. Ophelia noticed and sneered at her.

"I said, get out!"

Lawrence quickly turned on her heel and left the library. Ms. Hettle lingered outside in the hallway, wringing a rag between her bony hands. Once Lawrence appeared, she straightened up a bit and took a timid step forward.

"Madam? Is that you? Are you quite alright, my lady?"

Lawrence didn't answer and went forward, rushing past her and up the stairs. She didn't stop until she reached her room and shut the door behind her.

She paced back and forth until night fell. Every so often, she would go to her door, intent on finding Ophelia to apologize, but then she would step away. Ms. Hettle came by a few times to coax her out to eat, but Lawrence refused to move from her spot. She sat in one of the armchairs by the dying fireplace until she eventually fell asleep, curled up by the dying fire.

When Lawrence woke the next morning in the dark room with her numb toes and red, runny nose, she felt as if she had run several miles. She struggled to move from the chair for several minutes, even though she was desperate for a drink of water. She finally sat up and stumbled over to her vanity.

Lawrence regarded her ashen complexion in the mirror. She had been foolish and she'd be lucky if she didn't catch a cold. It felt as if she had already. Her thoughts immediately went to Ophelia, and she only wanted to see her to apologize for what she had done. Lawrence was so distracted, she didn't think to examine herself more closely. Perhaps if she had, she would have noticed the fresh pair of marks along the right side of her breast.

Chapter 13

A sharp wind cut through Lawrence the moment she slipped out the side door to the garden. She wrapped her thin jacket tighter around herself, considering momentarily on simply returning inside.

It had taken more effort than she cared to admit, dressing and taking the stairs down. After waking and floating between the warm waves of sleep, Lawrence finally pushed through the numbing lull of sleep and dressed for the day. She tiptoed through the dark house, mindful to avoid the planks she knew creaked loudest.

Once outside in the garden, Lawrence headed to the bench of tragic lovers, crossing past the statue to the small opening in the hedge she had found. She brushed aside the first barrier of branches and cast back a single look to the house. It would only be for a little while, and she'd be back before anyone would have to know.

She had not seen Ophelia for days after their fight in the library, and Lawrence felt lost. She needed to clear her mind, and knew that walking the familiar trail would do that. Without another thought, she pushed through and left Ashmore's grounds.

Lawrence joined with the path quickly, taking its direction up to the highest point of Widow's Weep. She had only ever traversed the first leg of the winding trail that hugged the coast and merged again at the edge of the park. The gravel pressed through her soft leather boots, stinging the soles of her numb feet. Her reddened cheeks stung, and she felt her lips crack. She grew winded after walking a few minutes, and a cool sheen of sweat covered her brow.

"It seems I've grown lazy," she huffed out under her breath. "This won't do."

She stopped by the edge for a moment and inhaled deeply. The crisp, salty breeze filled her lungs until it hurt. After being sequestered away within Ashmore, breathing only the stale air, it felt as if she had escaped from the bowels of a mausoleum. She closed her eyes and listened to the sound of the waves and whistling wind as it soothed something unsettled within her.

"LJ!" A faint voice from behind called out.

Lawrence turned and saw a figure further down the trail, waving madly. They began to trot forward and once they got closer, she smiled and waved back enthusiastically. Patrick strode forward, dressed in a thick wool coat and Homburg to keep the chilly wind at bay. He sidled up next to Lawrence with a beaming smile, but it fell once he got a better look at her.

"Good grief, Stoner, what are you doing out here in that rag?"

He stuck his cigar in his mouth and undid the red scarf around his throat. He quickly tied it around her head and neck with a smile. He then gestured with his head towards the cliff's edge, where they were stood close to.

"You weren't going to jump now, were you?"

"What?" She looked down at the steep drop with a horrified look. He laughed once he saw the look across her face. She shook her head with a bemused grin. "What a thought to have so early in the morning."

"You're up mighty early, LJ. I'm not interrupting your witchcraft, am I?"

"I'm all done casting my spells now, so it's fine."

She smiled up at him, and he returned it. Once he studied her face

234

a bit closer, though, he frowned slightly.

"Stoner, what's the meaning of this?" he said, gesturing to her dark under-eyes. "You look like you're about to cross the river, kiddo. You're not feeling under the weather, are you?"

"Oh, just a little tired, but nothing serious," Lawrence said, smiling.

"Well, you lean on me," he said, offering up his elbow for her to take. "I won't let you eat dirt."

They began to walk side-by-side up towards the top of the cliff. Patrick's broad body kept the wind from getting at her. She ducked her head down lower into his scarf, smelling his cologne and the smoky scent of his cigar. She tilted her head up and sideways at him.

"What are *you* up so early for? You don't seem like the type to beat the sun."

"What can I say? I'm a man of many surprises."

He smiled as a thin, wispy line of smoke left his mouth, streaming behind them like the exhaust from a train as they walked.

"Believe it or not, the house can get a bit stuffy. And they're all so" —he gestured with his hands as he spoke, his face contorted into something akin to exasperation— "it's nice to have a moment of peace when I can have it."

He sighed and tossed the cigar over the side of the cliff. Lawrence perked up a bit as she remembered something. She leaned into his side.

"I nearly forgot! I've got quite the secret. You'll absolutely die once you hear what it is."

"Well, come now, don't keep me in suspense here now LJ," Patrick said. His eyes glittered, practically giddy like a small child on Christmas day. "Is it something juicy?"

"Oh yeah," she said, her voice low in a conspiratorial whisper. "I've moved into Ashmore."

Patrick turned to her sharply, eyes wide. He remained momentarily stunned into silence. "What?"

"Yes," she said, laughing between breaths. "I was invited to dinner and she offered me a commission for a portrait."

"Who?"

"Her name is Ophelia. Ophelia Aldane." Lawrence squeezed Patrick's arm, shaking her head. "Really, Patrick, you should meet her. You all should. She's nothing like what the others think."

"Good Christ, you're being serious, aren't you?"

Patrick sounded astounded as he shook his head, looking out to the lightening skies in the distance. She nodded, and he let out a sudden boom of laughter. He tipped his head back and his whole body shook with it.

"Lord, you're actually living there. My god."

"It's really not as scary as everyone makes it seem. Just a bit dark."

"Dark?" he repeated.

"Ophelia's a bit sensitive to light so we have to keep the curtains drawn at all times."

Lawrence quickly hung her head in shame as she remembered what she had done so callously the other day. She remained quiet as Patrick continued to mull over the news.

"*Ophelia,*" he muttered under his breath, chuckling. "What bull."

"I'm serious!" she cried. "She wears these dark glasses. It's a big problem for her. I thought it was just a preference, but it's real. Trust me."

"You do understand this is all absolutely ridiculous, LJ, right? I mean it'll be absolute mayhem once Pa finds out."

They shared a quick look of understanding.

"Is there nothing you can do?" Lawrence asked. "Help them understand that there's nothing wrong with Ophelia or her house."

"Good grief, I wouldn't even know where to begin. It's like learning the Easter Bunny is real." He chewed on his lower lip for a moment.

"What is she like?"

Lawrence debated on how to answer, brushing aside some stray hair.

"Incredibly worldly. I don't know, but she's just different. I'm not doing her any justice, but she's wholly unlike anyone I've ever met before. I wish there were a way you could all just meet."

"Fat chance," he murmured. "You can imagine how well that would blow over."

Lawrence pouted, shivering again despite being tucked up against Patrick with his warm scarf around her. She began to pant a little in her effort to keep up with his long strides. He seemed to take notice and slowed down to match her pace. He held his hands out in defeat.

"Look, I'll see what I can do, but I've been working at that particular knot for a long time. Honest to God, I have half a mind not to tell them at all."

He bumped up against her, hands shoving deep in his pockets, as they fought against the wind.

"Don't worry, Stoner, I'm on your side here. I'd be interested in meeting the mysterious lady and finally putting a rest to all these ridiculous stories."

"You won't stand a chance against her," she said playfully, arching a brow.

"Oh hoh! Don't intrigue me any further now, LJ."

He smiled, the left dimple in his cheek appearing as he did. Even in the dim light of the early morning and sleep still in his eyes, Patrick still had a boyish, vivacious energy.

"To be honest, I was actually going to come and visit you at your little hut pretty soon."

Lawrence looked to him in surprise. "Visit me? Whatever for?"

"To convince you to come and stay with us at Old Canary, of course."

He paused for a moment, but continued once he saw the confused look on her face. He grimaced.

"Another man has died, and another has gone missing. It just didn't feel quite right knowing you were off living on your own."

"What?" Lawrence cried, stopping their walk altogether.

She struggled to breathe evenly, but whether that was due to the walk or the news was unclear. He took his hat off to run a hand through his hair, his lips thinning as he nodded.

"It wasn't here," he supplied in some effort to comfort her. "Still, Fort Haven is only about fifteen miles from here, give or take. Eddy heard the news first and told us. Once Pa found out about it, the two of them went off together into his study like squirrels burrowing into an oak tree."

"What about Augusta?"

"She's rather more like an ostrich when it comes to these sorts of things; she'd rather stick her head in the sand than think of anything remotely unpleasant."

"I can't blame her," she said, nodding. "Who wants to think about such horrible things?"

"Yes, but you do understand what this means, then?" Lawrence shook her head. "Diseases and animals kill, yes, but not kidnap. This is starting to look distinctly human, or inhuman, depending on how you want to look at it."

"Oh," she whispered, turning her eyes towards the sea. "Goodness."

Patrick grunted in understanding. They shared a moment of silence as they looked out to the never-ending sea.

"Of course, there are those who don't think it's necessarily something human either."

The two shared a look, and he laughed softly. The humor didn't reach his eyes as it normally did.

"Yes, I know you think they're crazy."

"I didn't say anything of the sort; don't put any words in my mouth and more lovely than ever. Her skin seemed to glisten like dark honey and her short, dark hair was lustrous, even in the dark.

Ophelia ignored Ms. Hettle and fixed her attention on Lawrence. She waved a hand. "Leave us, Hettle."

Ms. Hettle immediately bowed and rushed out of the room without another word. Once it was just the two of them, they gazed at each other for several moments.

"You are not feeling well?" Lawrence asked at last. "You look incredibly well. Better even."

Ophelia shrugged, remaining silent. Lawrence waited for her to speak, but she said nothing. She took a step forward, placing her hands across her chest.

"Ophelia, I am so sorry for what I did. I never meant to hurt you. I was being a child. Lashing out at the one person who deserves it least of all. Of course you are my friend, Ophelia. What would I do without your friendship? You gave me a chance when no other person on this entire island would! Please, will you forgive me?"

Ophelia remained still for a moment longer. She looked down at her hands and spoke in a low whisper. "You hurt me."

Lawrence took another step closer, frowning. She would have done anything then to show how sorry she truly was.

"Ophelia, I'm sorry! I hate myself for what I did to you. Really."

"You don't have to apologize out of fear of losing the commission," Ophelia muttered in a pettish tone. "I'm not that cruel."

"What?"

"You were right. I granted you the commission of a painting and the offer of living here with me, but have asked for far too much in return. Let us move forward in complete understanding of who we are to each other."

"No," Lawrence said, immediately shaking her head. The pit of guilt in her stomach grew as she felt it drop in fear. She stood before

Ophelia and held her hands out before her. "Ophelia, please. Don't do this."

"I am not doing anything," Ophelia replied breezily. "Now, please excuse me. I shall join you to continue our work tomorrow."

As she turned to go, Lawrence felt the anxiety of watching Ophelia leave grip her. She suddenly grabbed Ophelia's hand. There was something unspeakably powerful Lawrence felt as she took hold of her. Quite like grabbing the trunk of a great oak, nothing would have moved Ophelia if she did not let it. Lawrence fell to her knees.

"I'm sorry! Please, Ophelia. Please don't leave."

Tears unexpectedly fell as she continued to beg. The corner of Ophelia's lip quirked up for one moment, but then disappeared. She went down on her knees and faced Lawrence, watching as she cried.

"Don't cry," she cooed. She brushed the back of her hand across Lawrence's cheek. "I forgive you. Let us forget all about this silliness then. Agreed?"

Lawrence nodded her head immediately. Ophelia grinned. She brushed away another few errant tears.

"Do you care for me then, Lawrence?"

Lawrence nodded again, but Ophelia shook her head.

"I want to hear you say it."

"I care for you, Ophelia. Of course I do! I care so much that, that it hurts!"

Ophelia grinned wider when she heard that. She sighed and held Lawrence's face in her hands.

"And I feel the same," she said in a low voice. "You understand me, Lawrence, and I understand you. No one else will understand you the way I do. Do you agree?"

Lawrence agreed heartily.

"It's just you and me here. Ashmore can be our little place where we don't have to pretend. No more pretending," Ophelia said. "Now,

now," chided Lawrence.

He shook his head anyway. "You don't have to. I know it, and we know it. Everybody on this damned coast knows it. It's not easy, but they're family to me, and I don't mind that it's not easy. They believe what they believe."

He turned to face her then with a grave expression. It was by far the most serious Lawrence had ever seen him.

"All I care about is making sure they don't get too out of hand, and do something silly like get themselves hurt, or worse. That extends to you too now, LJ. Sorry to say," he said as he smiled again. The lines around his eyes crinkled. "You're a part of this circus now."

As the sun rose, the land transformed before their eyes. Rich, coppery rays overtook the bleak, gray dawn of the early morning. Lawrence inhaled sharply, suddenly feeling an unexpected hot prick of tears. At that moment, she felt glad she had defied Ophelia's rule and left as she would otherwise have been alone in the dark. Patrick grunted, chuffed.

"Not bad, eh?"

Lawrence turned sideways as he looked down at her with a knowing smile. "Yeah, not bad."

They began to turn around, retreating back down the path towards the long stretch of houses along the coast. Patrick maneuvered his way around Lawrence so he stood closest to the edge on their way back as well.

"You know," he said, picking the conversation up again. "You didn't actually tell me anything besides the fact that the house is dark and that you're absolutely infatuated with this Ophelia person."

"Infatuated?" she cried softly, laughing.

"Yes, I'm feeling a bit jealous actually," he said with a pout. "I've changed my mind. Don't tell me. I've no interest whatsoever in hearing how splendid of a time you're having over there with your interesting, *worldly* friend."

Lawrence chuckled and wound her arm through Patrick's. "'How many fond fools serve mad jealousy!' No, there's nothing like that. You three were kind to me first, and I'll never forget that. I'm just excited about the work, that's all. I've never lived anywhere so nice."

"I'll count that."

"There are only two servants in the entire house: Ms. Hettle and a cook, Greta. They're quite nice, but a bit like skittish horses. One can't move too quickly in there, or they'll all go bolting for the hills."

Patrick let out another raucous laugh. "Right off the edge with the lot of them."

"We've all got this list of rules we have to follow, which, mind you, I'm breaking one of them now by being out here."

"Oh really?" he said, smiling devilishly. "LJ, I knew I had a good feeling about you. You absolute rogue."

"You're my co-conspirator now. You won't go ratting me out now, will you?"

"Oh, this is getting me all 'tickled with excitement', as Auggie would say. You know, I'm the very best at keeping secrets. I haven't even told anyone that Edwin still sleeps with a tattered piece of fabric that was once his 'blankie'."

Lawrence arched a brow at him, shaking her head in disbelief. Within a few short moments, Ashmore was within a short distance and Lawrence stopped.

"Well, Stoner," Patrick said. "I imagine we'll be crossing shadows out here again. I'll see you around, won't I?"

She smiled and nodded.

"Good, good."

She went to untie the borrowed scarf, but he stopped her, placing a firm hand over hers to keep it tied.

"Keep it. And get yourself something warmer to wear, for God's

sake. Go straight home and rest, young lady, that's an order."

Lawrence raised her hand in salute and bowed her head obediently. "Yes, doctor. Right away."

Lawrence parted from Patrick, stopping momentarily at the hedge to watch his disappearing figure. He continued to amble down the path, arms held behind his back. She lowered her head and returned through the hedge.

When she appeared back in the garden, Lawrence untied Patrick's scarf and hid it within the branches. It felt natural to immediately hide all evidence of her secret trip out, but a slight twinge of guilt wormed its way into her gut.

The house remained quiet, nary a soul awake besides herself. She continued to pause and listen, waiting for Ms. Hettle to come flying out of some dark corner, as if knowing she had broken one of the rules. Lawrence's heart continued to pound furiously in her chest, and only quieted once she felt sure no one had caught her.

Even after she returned, Lawrence struggled to catch her breath. Her whole body ached more than it ever had from a simple walk. She lounged across the sofa in the library, warming herself by the fire until Ms. Hettle found her and gently woke her for another solitary breakfast.

* * *

Lawrence sat at her spot before the easel, waiting. Her eyes flitted once again to the clock above the mantle. Another ten minutes had passed. She spent the last several hours watching the small increments of five and ten minutes go by. Ophelia had yet again not come down to join her.

Ms. Hettle entered the library, and Lawrence immediately rose. "Well?"

"She's not feeling well," Ms. Hettle responded in a slow, measured way that made Lawrence want to shout. She approached the housekeeper and ran a hand through her messy hair. The neat updo she had pinned into place that morning was nearly undone. "She may join you tomorrow."

"No," Lawrence cried in a rush. She grabbed Ms. Hettle by the elbow, ignoring as the older lady let out a small noise of shock and tried to pull away from her grasp. Lawrence held on tight.

"Please, Ms. Hettle. Please, let me go and see her. It's been nearly a week!"

Ms. Hettle vehemently shook her head. "Absolutely not. My lady would be furious with me if she knew I allowed you anywhere near that part of the house."

"I don't care!" Lawrence cried, throwing up her hand. "I'm going up there and you can't stop me."

Panic flashed across Ms. Hettle's face and she held her arms out wide to try and stop Lawrence as best she could. Her head tilted back and forth, listening.

"Miss, please! It's forbidden."

Lawrence went to step around the housekeeper. "Stand aside, I'm going to see her."

"You can't!"

"Goodness," a voice called from the doorway.

Both Lawrence's and Ms. Hettle's heads snapped towards the door where Ophelia stood. Ms. Hettle immediately straightened and lowered her head.

"What is all this ruckus about?"

"My lady," Ms. Hettle bowed, lowering her voice in deference. "I am so sorry we've disturbed you. Please forgive us."

Lawrence looked sideways to Hettle and then fixed her attention on Ophelia. Despite supposedly being unwell, Ophelia looked fresher no more tears or you'll tear my heart right into two. Let me kiss you."

Lawrence felt her heart arrest for a moment as Ophelia came forward without another thought and placed her soft, cold lips against her cheek. Her lips lingered for a moment and she placed another quick kiss before she pulled away. She smoothly rose from where the two of them had knelt on the floor and held her hand out for Lawrence to take.

Once Lawrence stood, Ophelia pulled her into a close hug. She wrapped her arms tight around Lawrence. Immediately, Lawrence shivered as it felt like being stuck in an ice box, but she nonetheless reveled in being in her arms. Ophelia brought her head close.

"Never lie to me, Lawrence. Do you understand?"

She then held Lawrence out at arm's length to study her. She smiled softly, as if no one else existed, or mattered.

"If you let me, I could give you everything. Everything."

She let her go, and Lawrence immediately wrapped her arms around herself. Wherever Ophelia would go, she would follow. That was all Lawrence could think of as she took her seat by the fire to try and chase away the lingering chill deep in her bones.

* * *

Lawrence slept soundly as one might, but the strange chill that had touched her that first night she had wandered out to the garden continued to plague her. Even wrapped in her thick duvet with the fire roaring, it wasn't quite enough. Still, she rest peacefully, hidden away behind the curtains of her bed like a butterfly in its cocoon.

The fire went out in a rush, sputtering for a moment as a line of smoke wafted up in a thin line. Darkness and quiet settled over Lawrence's room like a heavy blanket. Only her soft, steady breaths could be heard otherwise. The windows of her room began to tremble.

The panes of glass shook, rattling within the frame until it seemed they would shatter. They continued to shake until at last, the windows pushed open in a rush. The sudden whoosh of wind and sound of crashing waves filled the room. The curtains around Lawrence's bed whipped up into a frenzy in the wind.

Lawrence appeared from within her bed in the same mindless state. She rose from the soft mattress and removed her nightgown in a single movement. She trudged forward to the window, leaning out and tilting her head as if listening for something. Her mouth moved slightly, muttering under her breath. She then placed her foot on the windowsill and pulled herself up. Lawrence balanced precariously on the edge of the windowsill, balancing on a thin ledge of a few inches between the safety of her room and a twenty-foot drop to the ground outside.

The knocking sounded far away. It continued. It grew louder, becoming clearer until it was all she heard. Whatever Lawrence had been listening to, faded to the background. The doorknob jiggled, and the knocking at her door continued, insistent.

"Miss?" a low voice called through the door. More knocking.

Lawrence blinked a few times, waking. She let out a loud gasp and immediately gripped the edge of the window, staring down at the dark drop in front of her. She stumbled back, nearly falling on her back as she rushed to get back inside.

She stumbled forward and grabbed her robe, tying it around herself. She continued to shake her head, waking from the deep sleep she was just roused from. Lawrence stepped forward to the door, opening it a crack.

Through the small sliver, she saw Greta's ashen face.

"Greta?" she whispered out.

It was strange to see the young woman anywhere but the kitchens. Not unlike seeing a creature of the sea walking around on land. Dark circles lined Greta's eyes and she continued to grip the edges of her dirty apron.

"What are you doing here at this hour?"

The cook looked a bit at a loss for words. She shot a furtive, fleeting glance over her shoulder into the dark hallway. Greta took a step closer to the door and brought her face closer to Lawrence's.

"Please let me in."

Lawrence nodded and opened the door further. Greta stepped in and Lawrence quickly shut it after her, locking it for good measure. When she turned to regard the woman again, she found her standing at the center of her room.

"Your fire is out," she pointed out.

"Oh, it is," Lawrence said, noticing it for the first time herself.

"Ms. Hettle doesn't know I'm up here talking to you. I figure..." she gulped. "I figure you're the only one in this god-forsaken household I *can* talk to."

"What's happened?" Lawrence asked.

"It's *her*," Greta whispered, eyes wide with fear. "There's something seriously wrong in this house. She's not normal."

"Greta, what are you talking about?"

"I went into her room," she confessed. They kept their voice low like they were whispering in a confessional. "Her *real* room."

"Real room?" repeated Lawrence. "What are you talking about? What were you even doing? You know we're not allowed there."

"I know." Greta gulped. She reached into her skirts and revealed a black key. "I took it from Ms. Hettle."

"Greta!" Lawrence cried out, shocked by the young woman's actions.

"I know what I heard. You heard it too! I've been hearing noises like that ever since I came to this damned house. I'm not crazy. I refused to believe it was something ridiculous like ghosts, so I thought I'd just go and see for myself. I wasn't stupid," she bit out, her eyes sparkling even in the dark room from her excitement. "She left tonight. Who knows where she's going off to? I didn't know when I'd ever have a chance again. So, I went up after the old woman went to bed."

"And?" asked Lawrence, fully absorbed now in Greta's story.

Greta looked into Lawrence's eyes then. She seemed lost, still reeling from whatever it was she had seen or found. She shook her head.

"I didn't go in. I couldn't see a thing, but I know the smell of blood. I'd know it anywhere. It reeked in there. There was nothing but the smell of death in that room."

The air evaporated within Lawrence's lungs. She exhaled sharply and spoke in a gentle, reassuring tone.

"Greta—" she began.

"No!" the cook cried, backpedaling as she held the black key tightly in her hands. Her eyes widened further until Lawrence saw the full whites around her dark pupils. "I know what I smelled. I can't stay here any longer! I'm telling you, there's something seriously wrong with that woman. I'm-I'm leaving."

Greta began to look around wildly, as if searching for a way out just then. She grabbed Lawrence's hands and held them tightly in hers. In direct comparison, Greta's hands were rough, calloused by work, and warm. Even for the few moments she held her hands, Lawrence felt herself slowly warming for once.

"Greta, calm yourself," she said, doing her best to soothe the woman. "Don't act brash now."

"We're going to die here!" she cried out in a barely contained shriek, covering her face with her hands. "They were all right about this place!"

"Greta, you're basing this off what you *believe* you smelled. We have no real knowledge that it's really anything. Let me speak to her, I'm sure there's an explanation."

"Look at this," Greta said abruptly.

She reached into her pockets and produced a small, worn photo roughly the size of a small postcard. The edges were creased and a corner had been dog-eared. It looked to be an old-style of photography with sepia tones and a faded vignette around the edge.

In the photo stood Ophelia. There was no doubt it was her. Even in the aged photo taken from a distance, Lawrence recognized her at once. By her side stood a young man, and a young woman sat in front of the two of them. They all bore the same striking elegance and poise that Lawrence had only yet seen in Ophelia.

All three figures wore sunglasses and maintained neutral, haughty expressions as they gazed forward to the camera. Lawrence looked it over closely, bringing it closer to discern the finer details. No doubt it was quite old, but just how much was unclear. Even the dresses and outfits they all had on seemed quite old-fashioned. It looked as if they were in front of some river in a desert region.

"Turn it over," Greta whispered.

Lawrence obediently did so. Spidery writing in an elegant hand covered the bottom in dark ink: *Cairo, 1856.*

Lawrence looked up to Greta, who stared at her expectantly. Lawrence lowered her eyes to the impossible date and read it over again. She did the math in her head and then once more. She felt the small whisper of doubt in her mind. It couldn't possibly be true. A chill wormed its way down her spine, and she lowered the photo.

"Don't you see? Do you understand now? We can't stay here!" cried Greta. "What more evidence could you need?"

"There's an explanation," Lawrence whispered, more to herself than Greta. "There's an explanation. There must be."

"Oh, you dimwit! Fine, be next. What do I care!" Greta grumbled out.

She tried to snatch the photo back, but Lawrence pulled it away from her reach. Greta stared at her with a shocked expression, as if Lawrence herself were morphing before her eyes, or revealing herself to be something she hadn't expected. She took a few stumbling steps back.

"Greta," Lawrence called after her, but the cook held her hand out to keep some distance.

Greta reached the door and unlocked it quickly. She threw Lawrence a final look of disappointment and distrust over her shoulder before she slipped off into the dark hallway.

Lawrence held the photo in hand and continued to stare at it. She brought it over to the nearest light and flipped it over several times, searching for something. Without another thought, she stuffed the photo into her nightstand drawer and shut it firmly.

She had defended Ophelia blindly, as if it were the most natural and immediate thing she felt she had to do. She hated the very idea of people misunderstanding or accusing her, but she couldn't help but feel as fear snaked its icy hand around her neck. Even Greta, solid, unshakable Greta had been rattled.

Lawrence shuddered as she got back into bed and pulled the blankets tighter across her body. She undid the rope around her robe and tied one end to the headboard of her bed. She tied the other around her wrist, making sure the knot was impossible to undo easily. She couldn't bring herself to think of what Greta had to say about Ophelia, nor about how she had woken suddenly from her dreams, naked and standing at the window as if she were about to jump. She continued to turn in her bed until she simply fell into her dreams.

Chapter 14

The two women turned their heads as the door to the library slowly opened. Ms. Hettle's shocking white hair appeared first as she stuck her head in.

"Hettle, I thought I told you never to interrupt us," Ophelia bit out.

Lawrence instinctively lowered her own head at the cool, autocratic tone. She shot a sideways glance towards the housekeeper, her brush frozen mid-air before the blocked out canvas.

"I apologize, ma'am," Ms. Hettle stuttered out, keeping her head bowed. She hesitated a moment, as if wondering whether to continue on at all. "The police are here."

Ophelia remained silent for a moment, but then rose from her seated place and clasped her hands together.

"I see. Well, let them in, of course."

Lawrence lowered her brush, face paling. She swallowed thickly as her heart began to race. Ms. Hettle disappeared for a moment before the door widened. The policeman entered shortly after, a wary look on his face.

It seemed entirely strange and unsettling to see a new person within Ashmore, as if the house itself was a living organism of some kind and a foreign body had invaded. They were all keenly aware of the infection and watched his every movement as he strode into the room.

The officer came alone, dressed in a charcoal suit rather than the expected uniform. He was a stout, middle-aged man with a thick beard and belly. He took powerful steps that caused the nearby furniture to tremble in his wake.

He removed his hat as he approached, tucking it under his arm as he tilted his head in greeting to the women. His eyes glanced over Lawrence and when they settled on Ophelia, he continued to study her. He seemed in equal measures taken with, and aback, by her.

"Afternoon, ladies," he said, his low voice was raspy and hollow, as if echoing out through a smokestack. He had a slight accent, but not one Lawrence could immediately place. The words curled and rolled around his mouth as he spoke. Ophelia stepped forward with an affable smile.

"Good afternoon, officer." She gestured to the table where a pot of tea and cookies sat untouched. "May I offer you something to drink?"

He held his hand up in refusal with a smile that sent the corners of his impressive mustache up.

"Thank you, ma'am. I am sorry to call on you two abruptly like this this afternoon. Are you the owner of this house, ma'am?"

"I am," answered Ophelia. "Is something the matter?"

The officer's lips pressed into a thin line. "Are you two the only residents in this house?"

One of Ophelia's thin brows rose and she crossed her arms. Her slender hands tightened around her own forearms as she looked the officer over.

"I don't believe you introduced yourself, *officer*."

"Detective," the man corrected. "Detective Declan, ma'am."

"Detective," Ophelia repeated. "Please state your business, detective, and speak plainly."

The man looked up with a grim expression. "I am sorry to say, as I have no wish to offend. It might be quite shocking to such young, refined ladies such as yourselves."

Ophelia snorted softly, and Lawrence stifled her smirk as she shot a sideways glance at her. The detective didn't seem to notice.

"There's been a murder."

"Oh?" said Lawrence. She tilted her head as if in interest, but her voice remained flat. The detective turned and fixed his attention on her then.

"So, is it just you two ladies here in this house?" he asked again.

Lawrence turned to Ophelia, allowing for her to answer.

"We are," Ophelia answered firmly.

"Your names?" he asked as he reached into his inner pocket and produced a small notepad. He flipped to a new page to take record.

"Ophelia Aldane, and this is my companion, Lawrence Stoner."

At the mention of Lawrence's name, the detective's head rose, and he made eye contact with her. She felt as if he looked right through her then. He scribbled something down on his notepad.

"What would we have anything to do with a murder now, detective?" Ophelia asked, holding her hands out as if the mere idea was simply laughable. She smiled her usual close-lipped grin and folded her hands neatly. "We don't even know who the poor victim is."

He raised his head again to address Ophelia. "His name was John Humphries."

At the mention of his name, Lawrence felt the blood freeze in her veins. She inhaled sharply and struggled to exhale at all. The officer closely watched her reaction.

"Miss?"

The detective stepped forward with a hand extended to offer aid, but Ophelia smoothly blocked his way and stood between the two of them. She gave him a polite, saccharine smile.

"You must forgive her," she explained. "She's got quite a delicate condition. I believe you were right, officer. This may have upset her, after all."

"I thought he was found," Lawrence whispered. She trembled against her own volition, and she wrung her hands to try and keep still. "They said it was an animal."

The detective and Ophelia both turned to look down at Lawrence where she remained seated. Ophelia's jaw ticked slightly, but she remained quiet. The detective nodded, confirming that it had indeed been the initial conclusion.

"The Humphries disagree with the official investigation carried out by the police force. They feel the whole thing was rather rushed and not looked into as thoroughly as it should have been. Naturally, as is well within their right, they've decided to bring in a second opinion. At least, to put their own minds at ease and for a sense of closure. I intend to deliver that, to the best of my ability, God willing, of course."

"Yes," drawled Ophelia. "God willing."

"What, what does that mean?" Lawrence asked, her hand still hovering close over her mouth as she felt the nausea making her head swim.

"He's a private investigator, dear."

Ophelia reached down and gripped Lawrence's hand, patting it. The cool touch sent an involuntary tremor through Lawrence. Despite that, she held on firmly as if it were her life preserver. Ophelia turned to address the detective then.

"If you'd like, detective, we may leave my acquaintance here so she may settle her nerves, and I will answer any and all questions you may have."

"Actually," the detective said. "I'm here to speak with Miss Stoner."

"Me?" Lawrence asked, paling a bit further.

"Yes," he said, flipping to an old page in his notepad. "A few patrons at Weatherby's and Maitlands have confirmed seeing you with Mr. Humphries having dinner together several weeks ago. Does this sound accurate to you?"

"Well, yes," she answered, nodding timidly. "But-"

"And you were then seen leaving with him shortly thereafter, correct?" he asked, staring her down. She felt pinned under his unforgiving gaze like a mouse being pressed down under the claws of an eagle.

"Um-"

"Where did you and Mr. Humphries go to after dinner, Miss Stoner?" Detective Declan pressed on, adamant to get his answer.

Ophelia smoothly stepped in front of Lawrence then, providing a shield between her and the detective.

"Detective, it is my understanding that as you operate in an independent capacity apart from the police, you have no actual legal authority to be here and to question my companion in such a way."

Ophelia remained still, her head tilted up as she addressed the man without a single wobble in her voice or tremor to betray if she felt at all fearful as Lawrence felt.

"As an act of good faith, however, I will gladly answer any questions you may have for me."

"I see," Detective Declan said, his eyes narrowing a fraction. "Besides your housekeeper, what other staff do you have on property?"

"Just a cook."

"I see," he muttered, returning to his notepad to write his notes. His eyes ventured around the room, taking in all the luxurious furnishings and rich details. "Have they both been with you long?"

"Ms. Hettle has been on this estate for decades," Ophelia said. "The cook joined us a few weeks ago. You'll have to inquire about the details with my housekeeper. She handles all that."

"I see, and your acquaintance?" he asked, leaning over to try and catch Lawrence's eyes again. "From my understanding, you were living on your own not too long ago."

"Yes, I've come here on a commission," explained Lawrence, gesturing to the canvas and the general supplies around her.

The detective took a step forward to get a better look at the portrait. He frowned as he assessed it, calculating how long it might have taken for her to get to its current state.

"I had heard of Mr. Humphries' passing," Lawrence said, eager to be of some help despite the fear she felt. "However, that was the first night we met, and I had not seen him again after that. That's all."

The detective nodded his head and jotted down a few more notes. The more he wrote, Lawrence felt the pit in her stomach grow. Another wave of nausea hit her. Ophelia's hand found her shoulder and squeezed. When Lawrence looked up at her, her face remained serene. The detective looked at Ophelia then, his eyes narrowing slightly.

"Have you any history with the deceased, ma'am?"

Lawrence expected Ophelia to say she hadn't, but she merely shrugged her shoulders and sniffed primly.

"I would not speak ill of the dead."

"In the interest of the investigation then," said the detective.

"I've not met him, but I've heard he was quite a brute. Particularly to young women. I'd hate to make baseless accusations, but I heard he drank quite regularly and in excess."

"That is an interesting accusation," the detective said, stepping forward. "John Humphries was universally regarded as an upstanding citizen and a gentleman in every sense of the word. He was a regular patron to several charitable institutions and participated actively in local government. I understand he was quite a favored choice for Municipal Treasurer of Bar Harbor. Therefore, I'd be interested in knowing where your own widely deviating opinion comes from."

Ophelia remained stoic, silent for a few moments. The tension deadened the air in the room and it felt as if two great adversaries had finally met. She then smiled tightly.

"I am aware of what drink can do. Even the gentlest lamb of a man can become a faithless heathen with a single drop."

Lawrence couldn't help but snap her head to her in that moment. Nothing she said matched what she knew of Ophelia and her true feelings. How easily she lied. When she looked back at the detective, he seemed equally skeptical. His eyes narrowed, but he nodded.

"That's very true, ma'am," he said. He turned his head towards Ms. Hettle, who lingered near the back of the room. "Would you and the other servant be open to some questioning as well?"

"My servants never leave the house, officer," Ophelia said. "They will provide very little, I'm afraid."

"Right," the detective sighed. "Well, just as a matter of procedure, then."

Ophelia remained silent a moment. Her fingers drummed along her arm as she thought. She then turned her head sharply.

"Get the girl."

Ms. Hettle bowed lowly and left, doing so only once she got the order from her mistress. Lawrence's hands began to shake so she gripped them tightly in her lap. Sweat gathered on her brow and each breath became shallower.

"Easy," Ophelia murmured low under her breath just to her. Lawrence raised her eyes, but Ophelia continued to stare ahead, watching the detective as he paced back and forth.

"Close your eyes and count to ten."

Lawrence did as she was told, and the sharp pain in her chest began to subside. Ophelia continued to rub her hand discreetly, which warmed Lawrence's chest.

Within a few moments, the door opened and Greta entered the room with Ms. Hettle close on her heels. She and Ms. Hettle stood together in the center of the room, a few paces away from where

Lawrence sat with Ophelia hovering by her shoulder. Greta couldn't help but stare openly at Ophelia, so much so that she nearly missed the detective's questions.

"Do either of you ladies know John Humphries?"

"No, sir," Ms. Hettle answered immediately. When Greta didn't answer, the housekeeper nudged her gently.

"Oh, uh, no. No, sir." Greta stuttered out. She averted her eyes from Ophelia and kept her eyes trained down as Ms. Hettle did.

"Really?" Detective Declan said, taking a step forward towards Greta. "You are Greta Byrne, are you not?"

Greta's head snapped up. She looked between Ms. Hettle, who kept her head bowed at all times, and Lawrence. She even spared a passing glance to Ophelia, who remained stone-faced. She cleared her throat.

"Yes, I am."

"You worked for the Humphries for a time, did you not?"

"Well, yes," stuttered out Greta. "But just for a stint a few years back. I was hired on for the season and brought back temporarily when they hosted a few other families at the house."

"So, it would be reasonable to assume you knew the Humphries quite well?" the detective asked, coming even closer to bear down on Greta. "Therefore, you would certainly know the eldest son, John Humphries. So, I ask again, did you know John Humphries?"

"Not really," she whispered. "I didn't know any of the family well. I doubt any of them'd even know me if we brushed elbows passing each other down the street. That's the God's honest truth."

"Well, you certainly must have heard *of* him then. I find it hard to believe you lived within the same house for several months and did not form an opinion."

Greta remained silent, and Lawrence saw the girl physically bite her lip to keep from talking.

"So," the detective said, continuing on. "What sort of man was John Humphries? Was he the type to go fast? Did you ever see or hear of him giving trouble?"

A look crossed the cook's face for a moment, but she smothered it down with practiced calm. When she raised her head to answer, she pasted on a practiced, polite smile and shook her head.

"Not at all. He's always been a well-respected member of society. A model citizen."

"You swear by that?"

Greta fidgeted as the detective stared her down. She swallowed and rocked back and forth on her feet. Satisfied, the detective gave her a close-lipped smile and closed his notebook with a snap.

"Very good," he said. "I'm glad to hear some measure of truth lives in this house. Well, I think that will be all for now. I do appreciate your cooperation."

"Ms. Hettle." Ophelia simply called her name and the housekeeper immediately bowed and ushered Greta out of the room as quickly as possible. Once they were left alone with the detective, Ophelia turned to address the detective.

"Thank you for coming by, detective."

He turned to face Lawrence and Ophelia with a calculating look on his face. "I'm sure you can appreciate my great interest in helping find closure for the Humphries. I would be grateful for your cooperation in this."

"No doubt," agreed Ophelia. "I'm sure every ounce of your concern is being well-compensated for."

The detective's eyes narrowed imperceptibly and his face reddened. He turned to leave the room, but stopped by the door and turned to address Lawrence directly.

"That poor man was torn apart, limb from limb. Whoever did that to him was a right brute. As God is my witness, I shall bring that poor man justice. Miss Stoner, may I suggest you not leave Bar Harbor anytime in the near future? I'm sure we shall meet again."

"Hettle!" Ophelia called out past the detective through the door. "Please show the kind detective out."

He turned without another word and left. Once he was gone, Lawrence let out a heavy breath and held her head in her hands. Lawrence felt Ophelia come to her side and crouch in front of her. When a gentle hand landed on her shoulder, Lawrence jumped slightly. She then raised her head.

"Will you tell me?" Ophelia whispered. Lawrence's brows rose in question, but Ophelia shook her head. "You turned pale as the dead when that man's name was mentioned."

Lawrence shook her head immediately. "It's nothing."

Ophelia hesitated, then removed her hand. "You promised, Lawrence."

Lawrence hesitated to say. Ophelia let out a sad sigh and went to stand, but Lawrence grabbed her wrist to stop her. She pulled Ophelia down to the seat next to her, grabbing her hands and gripping them tightly. She leaned forward, keeping her voice low.

"You must promise you won't ever tell anyone."

"To my grave."

Lawrence nodded once, swallowing as she gathered her courage. Her eyes shifted restlessly.

"On the night Teresa died, I told you I had been a bit silly. Well, John had introduced himself to me in the restaurant when he saw me on my own. I didn't think much of it and thought he was just trying to be pleasant. We sat together and then he brought me to one of those secret clubs where they serve drink."

Ophelia listened quietly, her expression unreadable. She rubbed her thumb over the back of Lawrence's hand in a comforting gesture.

"I see," Ophelia murmured. "And what happened then?"

Lawrence hesitated and cleared her throat lightly as she struggled to go on. She lowered her eyes.

"I had too much to drink. I was being a fool, and making a fool of myself. He promised he would take care of me."

Ophelia's brows knit together over her sunglasses and a tight-lipped frown formed. Her shoulders went rigid, but she remained silent as Lawrence continued on.

"He led me into an alleyway. I tried to get away, but he hit me. I don't remember what happened, but something, or someone rather, saved me. I thought it was just a dream. What I saw—" Lawrence held herself as she shuddered slightly, remembering "—wasn't real. It can't have been real."

Ophelia leaned closer into Lawrence's side and brushed the hair away from Lawrence's face gently. As the tears began to fall down her face, Lawrence hiccuped and struggled to breathe evenly. Ophelia gently hushed Lawrence as she continued to pet her.

"Lawrence."

"He's going to find out I was there," Lawrence murmured. "They're going to think I had something to do with his death! I don't know what happened to him!"

"Lawrence."

"They said he was torn limb from limb! Oh, god!" Lawrence cried out as she dropped her head into her hands once again. Her shoulders continued to shake as Ophelia wrapped an arm around her and pulled her in close.

"It sounds to me like he got exactly what he deserved," she murmured lowly.

Lawrence inhaled sharply, her breath coming out ragged. She wiped away a few more errant tears. Ophelia held onto her tight and placed a gentle kiss on the side of her head which sent Lawrence's heart skipping.

"Do you trust me?" Ophelia asked in a low whisper.

Lawrence studied Ophelia's face, eyes flitting back and forth as she took in every bit of her features. She then nodded and Ophelia smiled until the dimples formed in her cheeks. They were close enough that Lawrence could clearly smell Ophelia's signature scent, which soothed her like a calming drug. Ophelia intertwined her fingers with Lawrence's.

"No one will ever hurt you like that again. I promise."

Lawrence raised her eyes and looked into the dark lenses of Ophelia's glasses. Through them, she saw only her own distorted reflection with her ruddy cheeks and tear-stained face. Ophelia raised her hand and cupped Lawrence's cheek.

"You must trust only in me. Believe me when I say that everything is going to be alright. If it's not, I will fix it," she said.

Ophelia rose from the sofa, walking to the drink cart and pulling out a bottle from the inner cupboard. She poured out a small measure of wine and returned to Lawrence's side. She took a sip and then held it out for Lawrence to take.

"The best thing to do is to forget it ever happened. Think of it only as a bad dream."

"A bad dream?" she repeated. Ophelia nodded. Lawrence took the offered drink and looked at it. Ophelia came closer.

"The difference is that you are safe with me. I will never harm you."

"Yes," Lawrence said. "I trust you."

She took a small sip. The sweet wine filled her mouth and immediately warmed her cheeks. She took another gulp, and her heart's frantic pace calmed. Ophelia smiled. This time, Lawrence clearly saw the sparkle of her teeth and the unmistakable sharp double canines.

* * *

Lawrence sat dangerously close to the fire, having pulled her seat nearer to feel its warmth. No matter how close she got to the flames, it seemed she continued to carry a slight chill within herself. As some feeling returned to her fingers, she flipped through the pages of her old portfolio.

She looked sideways and glanced momentarily at her setup. Ophelia's chair sat empty. Her side table with paints and brushes sat at the ready, cleaned and lined up like neat soldiers. She normally never worried about it, but it seemed Ms. Hettle couldn't help herself and reset the space every night. The easel was covered with a cloth, the vague outline of the large canvas pushing at the edges.

Progress had been made, and the portrait's foundations were laid. Over the first wash of brown color, Lawrence had painted in large blocks of dark shadows and stark white. Over the coming days after the detective had come and gone, Lawrence began on Ophelia.

For now, only a vague idea of a person could be seen. Rigid blocks of a torso, angular limbs, and a stiff head were all that existed. For every minute and hour she sat in front of the canvas, she worked away at each section, softening and rounding the image out like she was polishing a precious stone. Only she could see the potential of what lay within, and Lawrence felt like a Forty-Niner working away, believing wholeheartedly that just a bit more work would reveal shimmering gold ore.

She turned back to her old work of sketches and small practices in still life that her old master had drilled her to practice for endless hours. It was a fascinating thing to see, how her progression could be so plainly laid out from the earliest sketches of crudely drawn apples and wooden mannequins to her first nude models and expansive countrysides.

When she came across the first of many sketches of Domenica, Lawrence felt the familiar twinge that went through her chest.

Months had gone by, and she was still plagued by the pain. When would it end? Her eyes stung and she felt a knot form in her throat that was hard to push past. She quickly closed the book and set it aside.

"Don't sit so close, or you'll erupt into flames," Ophelia said from directly behind.

Lawrence shot up from her seat. The sudden rush caused her to become dizzy and she staggered to the side, grabbing the sofa to steady herself.

"God, Ophelia," she gasped. "Your steps are far too quiet. I didn't hear you coming at all! How long have you been standing there?"

Ophelia chuckled and walked over to the table where tea was set. She picked up one of the cups and inspected the inside of it, pouring herself a cup once she decided it clean enough. Lawrence looked to the clock on the mantle, noting the hour.

"You're up quite early today."

"It's the weather," Ophelia said. "I adore the rain."

True enough, a clap of thunder boomed and a torrent of rain pelted against the side of the house. Lawrence huddled deeper into her throw blanket. The windows rattled and it felt as if the house itself were being shaken.

Ophelia threw herself down on the sofa next to Lawrence, their bodies nearly touching. She looked over to Lawrence, wrapped up in blankets, and frowned.

"My dear, are you still feeling cold?"

Lawrence looked down at her numb fingers that gripped the edges of the blanket. "It must be the weather. It's not helping. I'll be alright. I just need a bit more time to get warm."

Ophelia suddenly rose and left the room. She returned a moment later with a stack of blankets. She wordlessly tucked Lawrence in with a smile.

"There'll be none of that. I'll have Hettle get the cook to make you something to warm you up." Ophelia nodded her head to the discarded folder by Lawrence's side. "What's that?"

"Oh, just some of my old work."

"May I?"

She held her hand out for it. Lawrence's cheeks flushed a deeper red and she immediately placed her hand over the top. Ophelia waited until she finally conceded and handed it over, wordlessly. Ophelia scooted closer, opening it for the both of them to look over it together.

"Oh, no," Lawrence said, chuckling. She tried to push the book away from her. "I can't stand the embarrassment. Can't you look at it on your own and never bring it up again?"

"Don't be silly," Ophelia said with a teasing smile.

She took her time with each page, looking over each as if they were all individual masterpieces to be examined and studied carefully. Lawrence fidgeted in her seat, constantly fighting the urge to snatch the book away and lock it away somewhere. Her cheeks continued to blaze and she no longer felt the numbing cold that had been bothering her before.

When Ophelia reached the first nudes, she took even longer in her analysis. When Domenica's section came up, Lawrence held her breath as her shoulders tensed. Ophelia remained silent, but studied the myriad sketches and portraits. Her head tilted at times and she continued on until she reached an anatomical study of Domenica lounging on her side.

Each line outlined Domenica's soft skin and the taut muscle of her flexing legs. Her long hair pooled around her head, tangled up between her slender fingers as her head tilted back in a frozen laugh. Lawrence had used a gentler hand, though, to sketch her full breasts that fell naturally to the side.

"You've drawn this woman several times," Ophelia murmured.

"What is her name?"

"Domenica," whispered Lawrence.

"You love her," she stated.

The casual way Ophelia had stated it caused Lawrence to turn sharply to her. Her heart jolted, and her mouth gaped like a fish as she struggled to answer. She didn't know where to begin. She began to shake her head and laugh.

"Of course not. She's just a model, a friend," she explained, rushing through her explanation. "What a thing to even say."

She took the book from Ophelia's hands and shut it, tying the silk ribbon around the center. She held it tightly over her torso like a shield.

"You draw like someone in love," Ophelia murmured. "I apologize if I've misunderstood, but it seems quite clear to me. Do you really think I'd see you any differently, or expel you from my company?"

She laughed at the thought and the tinkling sound soothed Lawrence. Ophelia reached out and tentatively took Lawrence's hands in hers. When Lawrence raised her head to look at her, Ophelia gave her a soft smile.

"So, was I right then?"

Lawrence paused. Her instinct told her to lie. It urged her to. All she had to do was reaffirm her lie, and that would be that. But when she looked at Ophelia then, she made a decision. It sent her heart racing and she felt sick, but exhilarated at the same time.

"Yes," she whispered.

Ophelia nodded, as if it were the most obvious thing in the world. She cleared her throat lightly. "Did she reciprocate?"

Lawrence's shoulders relaxed as another spasm went through her chest. She absentmindedly picked at her nails and swallowed thickly.

"I thought so." She coughed lightly and bit down on her lip. "She got married."

Ophelia hummed lowly in the back of her throat and inhaled deeply. "Then she's a fool."

"She's not," Lawrence said immediately, defensive. They sat in a brief moment of silence until Lawrence sighed. "You asked me once why I became a painter. It's not at all interesting. It's actually quite stupid. It was my last night in Italy. I took a long walk, turning down alleys and streets I didn't recognize just for the sake of it. By chance, I passed Signor De Luca's studio. I saw *her* through the window, and I felt like I couldn't breathe."

She held her hands up in front of herself, remembering the moment exactly.

"She was modeling, and she saw me through the window. She smiled at me, and I stayed."

"She smiled at you?" Ophelia repeated in a soft murmur. Lawrence nodded.

"I went back every day for a week until he let me stay. Gave him the rest of my money too."

"Is she the reason you came back?"

Lawrence nodded. "Part of it. You see, I'm not some deep person who had some artistic calling from the start. I was just aimlessly drifting and landed into this because I fell in love. Isn't that very stupid?"

Ophelia reached to the coffee table where a small carousel of cigarettes sat. She took one and lit it, exhaling smoothly. She offered it to Lawrence to take.

"You know I don't smoke."

"Try it," Ophelia said with an encouraging nod of her head. "They're perfectly harmless, and they're quite soothing, actually. Once you get used to them. I think you'll quite enjoy it. I think you need it."

Lawrence grabbed the cigarette, holding it awkwardly between her fingers. She inhaled and felt the sharp sting of hot smoke fill her nose.

It burned and she immediately coughed, tears filling her eyes. Ophelia laughed lightly, patting Lawrence's thigh. A wave of lightheadedness hit Lawrence, and she was glad to be sitting; otherwise, she was sure her knees would have buckled.

"I see you were not grossly trivializing your innocence," Ophelia said with another light laugh. Her hand continued to linger on Lawrence's thigh. She picked up Lawrence's skirt and felt the fabric between her two fingers. Her brow raised and she stared at it in quiet displeasure.

"Is something the matter?"

"No wonder you're always cold," she said. "This is far too thin. I will have to see about acquiring you new clothes."

"Please, Ophelia, you would only make me uncomfortable. I assure you, I'm perfectly content to continue dressing as I do," Lawrence said, doing her best to try and dissuade Ophelia.

"Nonsense," she said with a flick of her hand. "Besides, I know the perfect dresses that would look absolutely darling on you. It will only take a few weeks at most."

"It wouldn't suit me," Lawrence insisted. "Besides, I could never allow you to pay for anything I could not pay for myself."

"Nonsense," Ophelia said with an air of finality. "I'm a rich, lonely woman. Who else should I spend my money on than a dear friend who is more than deserving? No, I must insist you let me take care of you in this way, or I won't be satisfied."

"I will fight you on overindulging and spoiling me in any way I don't deserve," Lawrence warned with a grin.

"Hah!" Ophelia laughed. "I welcome you to try. I am a prize champion in that regard."

They set Lawrence's portfolio aside, and Ophelia never asked about Domenica again. The two of them continued to sit together, and Lawrence was only too acutely aware of Ophelia's close body. She imagined what the color of her eyes were. They must be a deep, dark hue that matched the midnight color of her hair, or perhaps they were something more unique and striking. That would suit her just as well.

There had never been anyone like Ophelia, and surely no one would compare who came after. She was unshackled and wholly confident in her sense of self. If she were the sun, Lawrence was just a small planet, eager to be in its presence and drawn to it in every way.

"What are you thinking about so seriously?" Ophelia asked her then. She had her head propped up on one hand as she held the cigarette in the other.

"I was just curious where you're from. You're certainly not American."

"Certainly not," she affirmed immediately.

Lawrence let out a small laugh.

"It doesn't matter," she said with a shrug. "It's nowhere you'd know. The place I come from has been forgotten entirely. Quite frankly, I don't think I could show you exactly where it was if you showed me a map to point it out."

Lawrence frowned. "How sad. Surely you must miss it."

"Not at all. I've gotten used to adapting to the changing times. I've quite forgotten all about it."

"Well, I could believe that. You're quite fashionable," Lawrence pointed out.

Ophelia smiled her closed grin again and placed her cool hand on Lawrence's wrist. She kept it there and seemed to press her fingers on Lawrence's pulse, feeling each steady beat of her heart.

"Not to mention progressive. I think you'd give those suffragettes a run for their money."

"Those bullish women terrify me," Ophelia shivered. "Luckily, I have the means to put myself where they can't get at me."

269

Lawrence laughed aloud at that. Ophelia handed back the cigarette to her. She had been right, as usual. The coughing and dizziness passed quickly enough, and now it was lovely and smooth.

"If you don't have a home, where do you go all the time?" Lawrence asked.

"Anywhere I want to," Ophelia answered. "I've been all over the world, and in the end, a place is a place."

"You don't have any city you're particularly fond of?"

Ophelia merely shrugged and shook her head.

"Do you?" she asked, mindlessly tracing shapes on the inside of Lawrence's wrist. Lawrence struggled to focus, but shook her head.

"I've not been to enough places," she said. "I think New York would be a wonderful place to go. I've read so much about it in magazines, and I've only really seen it in passing when leaving and coming back from Europe."

"I have a small home in New York," drawled Ophelia. "I can't recommend it."

"Why not?" Lawrence exclaimed, surprised.

"Because it's absolutely filthy for one thing. As to the people, half of them are arrogant, *nouveau riche* charlatans who have no real taste and no manners to speak of, and the other half are just bodies. They're like rats in the way they fill up every space and spill out from the overflowing buildings. No, it's a dreadful place, my dear, and I can't emphasize that point enough."

Lawrence giggled and hid her mouth behind her hand as she shook her head. "Do you have such strong opinions about everything, Ophelia?"

"There's nothing worse than sitting on the fence. Pick a side and defend it to the death, even if you are wrong. A woman with conviction in the wrong beliefs is infinitely better than a woman with none at all. They are not even humans; they are spineless hag fish."

"I must be a hag fish then," Lawrence mused.

"Nonsense; your only fault is that you are young and naive," Ophelia said with great conviction, waving her hand away as if brushing the thought out of the air. "I shall introduce you to life, and you will certainly learn to make your own decisions."

"And if they are in competition with your own?" Lawrence asked. "You won't resent me for that?"

"On the contrary, it will only make you all the more dear to me."

Ophelia rose from the sofa and crossed to their setup. She carefully removed the cloth covering the canvas and studied the progress with a neutral expression.

"In my history, I have found that disagreement and discourse add something of great substance to a relationship."

"I can't agree," said Lawrence. "Friendship demands a certain amount of accord on some foundational beliefs, so there is a greater sense of harmony."

"Look at that, we're already disagreeing, and look at how much closer we have become."

Ophelia smirked and Lawrence shook her head in amusement. She returned to Lawrence's side, sitting even closer than before. A thoughtful look crossed Lawrence's face.

"You don't think any less of me then?" Lawrence whispered, almost afraid that if she were to raise her voice too high, it might change Ophelia's mind after all. "What *are* you thinking?"

Ophelia brought her face closer to Lawrence's.

"I think that woman was a fool, and I am grateful to her. Otherwise, you would not be here, and I think everything has worked to bring you here to me. Of course I don't think less of you. You're all I think about, and you're everything to me."

Lawrence pushed forward first, bringing her face in towards Ophelia's. Their breaths intermingled. Ophelia raised her hands and embraced her closely. Just as Lawrence's lips grazed Ophelia's, a loud thump overhead caused Lawrence to turn away. For a flash, Ophelia's lip curled in contempt at the interruption.

A low groaning came through the floorboards, like the pained moan of a dying animal. The noise was so clear that there was no doubt it had really happened, and was not simply Lawrence's imagination.

Lawrence immediately rose from the sofa, the blankets pooling on the floor around her feet. She continued to stare up at the ceiling, as if waiting for the noise to happen again to confirm what she heard. Ophelia remained seated and didn't react at all.

"There!" Lawrence cried out. "That noise!"

"Hm?" Ophelia asked indifferently. "What noise?"

"Surely you heard that! There must be someone upstairs, or something fell! Don't you think we ought to go check?" asked Lawrence, grabbing Ophelia's hand. The muscles in her arms and legs spasmed as she felt the anxiety stringing out her nerves.

The door to the library opened wide and Greta appeared, eyes wide as saucers. She met Lawrence's stare, and then looked at how tightly she and Ophelia's hands were clasped together.

"That noise!" Greta cried. "It sounds like someone crying out in pain!"

"I heard it as well," said Lawrence, releasing Ophelia's hand and taking a step forward to the cook.

"You!" Ophelia barked out.

Lawrence and Greta both froze and turned to Ophelia, who faced the cook with an incensed look across her features. She nearly bared her teeth at the woman and her hands curled up into tight fists.

"How dare you come up here and enter this room uninvited," she spoke in a low, deceptively calm tone. "Get back downstairs this instant."

Greta let out a shuddering breath and turned to go. She stopped and turned back to give a half-bow. "Apologies. Apologies."

She quickly left the room, letting the door shut after her with a thud. Lawrence forgot all about the noise above, and turned to Ophelia with a confused expression.

"Why are you so harsh on them?" she asked in a quiet voice. "She didn't do anything wrong."

Lawrence couldn't make sense of it. It almost seemed unreal to her. Ophelia had only spoken to her in soft voices with sweet smiles. She had teased and pushed her, and occasionally let some of her impatience slip, but Ophelia had never barked at her or stared with such unveiled hostility. It surprised her to such a degree that it felt like a cold wash of water being thrown over her head. Ophelia didn't turn to look at her.

"Where in God's name is that old bat?" Ophelia muttered to herself as she stalked towards the door. Lawrence turned to watch her go.

"Where are you going?"

"Don't you have work to do?" Ophelia grumbled over her shoulder as she opened and slammed the door firmly behind her.

After several minutes passed, Lawrence moved from her spot to the easel. She removed the cover and took a seat, staring at the canvas. She shouldn't have said anything. That was the only conclusion she came to. She resolved to apologize, to do anything to have Ophelia smile at her again.

Lawrence picked up her palette and brush to work as Ophelia suggested she do, but all she could do was sit and stare.

Chapter 15

The warm summer rains continued through the week, breaking but for a single morning. Lawrence snuck out into the dark as the gray storm clouds gathered in the distance. For once, the weather outside matched the chill within the house.

The grounds were soft and gave way easily with every step. The sweet scent of flowers and moss carried over the breeze as she made her way to the trail. Before she left the garden, she pushed back the branches to her little hiding spot. She stared at the empty space for a few minutes.

Patrick's scarf was missing.

She looked around for a minute longer before continuing on. Had she misplaced it? Surely Ms. Hettle could not have found it. Lawrence ruminated on the issue as she exited from Ashmore and went out on the trail.

Patrick stood waiting by the edge, a lone figure in black. His hat sat low and he kept his hands stuffed deep into his coat pockets. His face brightened once he saw her.

They met and Patrick affectionately rubbed the top of Lawrence's head.

"You holding out Stoner, yeah?" he asked with a smile. "Looks like you could do with a bit more rest. She working you to the bone?"

"Not at all," she said with an easy grin.

Lawrence felt like she could finally breathe as they walked up the trail. All that had accumulated within her felt like it had been released at once. She didn't think about strange noises, sleepwalking, or inexplicable impossibilities like photos over half a century old. She focused only on her walk with her friend, and the invisible hand that kept an iron grip around her lungs loosened.

"I've got a present for you," he said.

Patrick reached into his coat pocket and produced a thick envelope. He handed it over and took out a cut cigar next. He cupped his hand around the end and lit it with his signature golden lighter. Lawrence opened the envelope, looking it over. He gestured with his cigar.

"I've taken the liberty of filling out the RSVP for you. I figured you'll be there, and there's really no acceptable excuse for you to miss it."

"Patrick," Lawrence said with a shake of her head. "You know I told you about Ophelia's rules. There's no chance she'd let me leave for a party of all things."

Lawrence studied the rich, creamy card with the embossed letters and gold emblem of the Sinclair family crest. It was to be a costume party to be held within a week's time. All sorts of promises of fun and everlasting memories were included in the regular instructions on how to get to the house and when to arrive. She tried to hand it back to Patrick, who shook his head vehemently. She sighed and tucked it into her pocket.

"What a crock of shit," Patrick muttered.

Lawrence looked at him, unused to his sudden gloomy mood. He walked ahead of her, stopping only to regard her with a look of distaste.

"What sort of autocratic nonsense to dictate what you can and cannot do? She sounds like a real pill, that one."

"That's not fair, Patrick," said Lawrence. "Don't talk about her like that."

"What?" he asked, turning to her with an incredulous look. "Don't feel like you have to defend her. Just be honest. She can't hear you."

"I am being honest," she argued. "It's complicated. She just wants privacy, that's all."

"Privacy?" cried Patrick. He shook his head in disbelief. "She's keeping you locked up in that house and under her thumb. You look paler and sicker every time I see you! That place is no good for you."

"You don't understand!" she cried, turning away from him. "None of you do. You wouldn't be saying the things you do if you just tried to see it from her perspective!"

"LJ!" Patrick exclaimed, stopping Lawrence's breathless speech. "I'm just saying this because we're concerned. That's all!"

"We?" she repeated, eyes widening.

Patrick froze, a guilty look crossing his features. He averted his gaze and ran a hand through his hair. She took a step back, shaking her head.

"Patrick, you didn't."

He stood silent, head bowed and tail tucked like a dog that knows it had done wrong. Lawrence abruptly turned and began to walk back towards Ashmore. When Patrick realized she was no longer there with him, he turned to look for her. She had already put a considerable distance between the two of them.

"Oh LJ, come on," he called out after her. "I'm sorry! Come back!"

She continued on anyway, ignoring his pleas to wait for him.

"LJ!" he called out after her. "Lawrence, let me explain! It was an accident! I never meant to tell them. I begged them not to do anything!"

Lawrence rushed forward, hurrying the rest of the distance back to Ashmore. She dived through the hedge and entered back into the secret garden.

She entered Ashmore back through the sun room, doing her best to tame her windblown hair by patting down the flyaways that had come undone from her braid. She took a moment to collect herself. Her ears rang with the sudden, all-encompassing quiet of the house.

Lawrence mindlessly crossed the room to head towards the library, but the moment the door opened, a hand reached out and grabbed her by the shoulder. Lawrence was pulled into the darkness of the house with an unnatural speed. By the time she had realized what had happened, she was already pushed up against the wall.

"Ophelia?"

"Where were you?" she ground out, bringing her face close to Lawrence's.

Ophelia gripped both of Lawrence's shoulders tightly, keeping her pinned up against the wall directly outside the sun room.

"Ophelia!" Lawrence whispered. "What are you doing up?"

"Answer me!" she snapped. She sneered at Lawrence, who clearly saw the double set of fangs along the top row of Ophelia's teeth. Lawrence gasped, still unable to answer. "You disobeyed me! You left me! How could you!"

"Ophelia, stop," she whispered. Ophelia continued to tremble in fury, and Lawrence shook against the wall. "Stop, you're hurting me."

"Me?" Ophelia seethed. "Who were you with? What's their name? Are you already tired of me then, is that it? You think you're going to leave me?"

"No, of course not!" Lawrence cried, tears threatening to fall. Ophelia paused when she saw her tears, but her face remained stony.

"I just went for a walk. That's all! I just needed fresh air, Ophelia. Please, I'm sorry! Please forgive me."

Ophelia scoffed. She turned her beautiful face away from Lawrence's. "You're lying, again."

"Ophelia, please!" Lawrence cried. She reached out for Ophelia's arm and tried to bring her back. "I'm not lying! Please, stop!"

Ophelia came closer, placing her arm next to Lawrence's head, caging her in against the wall. She brought her face closer to Lawrence's until they were a breath's distance away from each other. Lawrence held her breath as her heart pounded in her chest.

"You're not lying?" she asked in a low purr. Lawrence could only nod. "Are you sure you want to stick with that answer?"

Lawrence nodded immediately. "Of course."

"And you weren't meeting with anyone?" she asked in the same dead, dangerous voice.

Lawrence hesitated for a moment, but shook her head. Ophelia brought her face even closer, so their breaths mixed. She tossed a familiar red scarf towards Lawrence, who caught it out of the air.

"Try again."

Lawrence held Patrick's scarf in her hands. She opened her mouth to answer, but a loud bang caused her to jump. The loud banging continued, followed by a flurry of raised voices and shouts that echoed through the home. Ophelia remained frozen, her face an inch away from Lawrence's.

"God's sake!" she growled out, banging her fist against the wall.

Lawrence shrank away as Ophelia turned on her heel and headed to the front hall. As Lawrence looked over her shoulder, a hole had been punched in to the wall where Ophelia's fist had been. The thick wood had splintered easily, cracking like flimsy twigs under the force of her blow. Lawrence let out a shaky breath and pulled herself upright, hurrying out to the foyer.

"I demand you let us see her this instant, or we shall come back with the police!"

Mr. Sinclair's voice boomed through the empty house, echoing off the marble floors. He continued to demand from outside the front door, blocked mostly by Ms. Hettle, who barred the entrance with her frail body.

"Sir, I must please ask you to lower your voice!" Ms. Hettle cried out, holding her arms out between the open door and frame. She moved her hands out in front of her as if she were attempting to soothe a wild horse. "My mistress is resting now!"

"Oh, I bet she is!" He hissed, raising a walking cane up high to gesture into the darkness of the house.

Behind Mr. Sinclair's reddened face stood Edwin, who remained inert a few paces off with a neutral, assessing expression. He continued to sweep his gaze back and forth as if cataloging all that he saw.

Lawrence stood at the foot of the stairs, peering both ways. Ophelia had disappeared. It seemed she went into hiding to wait until the chaos had blown over. Mr. Sinclair turned his face and saw Lawrence through the darkness. His eyes widened as their eyes met. He waved his hand quickly for her to come forward.

"Lawrence!"

"Mr. Sinclair," she said with a weak smile.

She stepped closer down the front hall and when she was within a few feet of the door, he pushed his way past Ms. Hettle and put his hands down on her arms.

"What brings you here?"

"Thank goodness you're alright!" he cried, still holding onto her as if to make sure she was real.

"Of course, I'm alright."

"You're coming with us now. You'll stay with us. You're not safe, Miss Stoner."

"No!" she exclaimed, stepping back and away from his grasp.

"No?" repeated Edwin from outside on the front porch. He continued to linger outside as if afraid to step foot in the house itself. She looked between the two men.

"Look, whatever you've heard isn't true! Ophelia is nothing at all like what you think. She's different, really!"

"We'll discuss this back home," Mr. Sinclair said, reaching for her elbow to pull her away. Lawrence wrenched her arm from his grasp.

"No! I can't," she yelled out automatically. "I won't go! I'm sorry, but I'm not leaving."

At this, Edwin finally took a step forward into the home. He seemed to study Lawrence closely. He ran his eyes over her form and zeroed in on her ghostly pallor.

"LJ," Edwin murmured. "Are you feeling alright?"

"I'm fine!" she laughed out, rubbing a hand over her arm. "Of course I'm fine."

"Miss Stoner-"

Mr. Sinclair opened his mouth to argue, but he froze. He turned pale and his eyes stared at something behind Lawrence. She felt the hair rise on the back of her neck, and the same needling sensation on her skin returned.

Mr. Sinclair's normally easy-going smile was nowhere to be seen, and he seemed decades older in that moment. He grabbed at the necklace around his throat like a life buoy. Lawrence already knew who it was, but she turned to look anyways.

Ophelia stood in the center of the foyer in the small ring of candlelight that flickered over her figure. She took slow, quiet steps towards the group, but stopped directly before the small spill of muted sunlight that hit the floor. Her nose scrunched up in disgust, as if she had smelled something foul. She then smirked and smiled pleasantly at Mr. Sinclair.

"Hello," she murmured out in a low, seductive voice. "*William*, isn't it?"

"It's you," he whispered.

His eyes remained wide and he took a reactive step back when she stepped closer. Ophelia then tilted her head away and her nose raised in the air, as if she were smelling something.

"Pa!" Augusta's bright voice called out from the distance.

Everyone turned and watched as Augusta rushed forward towards the house, her bright hair flying around her face. She was outfitted in her riding gear and had clearly come straight from the stables without changing. Her cheeks were flushed and she panted slightly as she came trotting up.

"What are you doing?!" she cried.

"Get away from here!" Mr. Sinclair turned to his granddaughter and waved her away, but she ignored him. "I told you never to come here! Edwin, take her away at once!"

Augusta caught sight of Lawrence and waved. She smiled apologetically as Edwin met her halfway and prevented her from getting any closer to the house.

"LJ! I'm so sorry about this! I tried to keep him, but they snuck away! I told Patrick to watch them, but he wandered off!"

"Augusta, stop!" Edwin herded Augusta away, practically picking her up and carrying her back to Canary Green.

"Pa!" Augusta yelled out from behind Edwin's form. "Come back home at once! Stop this nonsense!"

"What a *lovely* granddaughter," mused Ophelia with a wolfish grin.

Mr. Sinclair turned to her with fire in his eyes.

"YOU!" he shouted.

All of them, save Ophelia, jumped at the sudden shout. He pointed his finger at Ophelia, trembling.

"You stay far away from her, do you hear me? Mark my words. I will erase you from the face of this earth if you dare try anything. LJ, please. Come with us."

He waited for her, but LJ lowered her eyes and stayed put. Ophelia began to chuckle then. She laid a possessive hand on Lawrence's shoulder as Mr. Sinclair backed away towards the front door. He continued to stare at her and shook his finger at her.

"I know what you are. Monster! Devil! You killed them! You will pay."

He continued to glare until he left the house, stalking away without another look back. Lawrence hardly recognized the cheery patriarch in the man she had just witnessed. His accusations continued to ring in Lawrence's ears. Ophelia lingered in the hallway, but then turned on her heel.

"Close the door."

"Yes, ma'am," Ms. Hettle murmured, bowing as usual.

Once the doors closed, the house returned to complete silence and darkness once again. Lawrence continued to wait in the hallway until Ms. Hettle came up to her side. She gently touched Lawrence's elbow.

"Miss, are you alright? You must be shaken by that scene, you're shivering. Let me make you up a pot of tea."

Lawrence shuffled with Ms. Hettle towards the foyer. Standing behind the right balustrade, Greta did her best to stay hidden from view. Lawrence immediately caught her eyes and the two stared at each other in silence. She hadn't left yet, and by the way Greta turned her gaze back to the floor, Lawrence seemed to understand that Greta wouldn't be going anywhere.

"Miss?" Ms. Hettle repeated. Lawrence looked to her. "Would you like that?"

"She won't need anything of the sort. Get back downstairs, both of you," Ophelia dictated in her sharp voice.

Ms. Hettle immediately bowed and scurried off. She and Greta quickly made for the secret portrait entrance together. Ophelia stood at the entrance to the library and stepped aside, gesturing for Lawrence to follow.

"Lawrence."

When Lawrence entered the library, Ophelia sat waiting for her on the sofa. A cigarette burned between her fingers and she gestured for Lawrence to come forward. Lawrence went to sit on the couch opposite, but Ophelia waved for her to come to her side. Lawrence stood before Ophelia within arms reach, but did not go to sit. Her hands clenched slightly.

"What's that in your pocket?"

Lawrence looked down. From afar, it didn't even look like she had anything in her skirt pockets, but she knew exactly what Ophelia was talking about. She reached in and produced the invitation from Patrick. Ophelia watched from where she sat, her gaze tracking every movement. She held her hand out for it, waiting until Lawrence passed it over. Ophelia read it in silence, her hands curling around the edge of the paper.

"Another little gift from your mysterious walking partner?"

Ophelia tore the invitation in two, tossing them aside without a second thought.

"We could go together."

Ophelia snorted. She ground her teeth, her sharp jaw moving back and forth. She exhaled slowly out through her nose and tilted her head away.

"Don't be stupid, Lawrence."

"You made me believe we were equals," Lawrence said. "That we would respect each other and be honest. Yet, I have a feeling you've done nothing but lie to me for most of the time I've known you."

Ophelia's thin, arched brows raised a bit, and she crossed her arms. The jewels on her wrists clicked as she did so.

"Yes," she drawled offhandedly, as if mindlessly discussing the weather. She listlessly played with the jewels on her bracelets, picking at the gems with her fingers. "And how respectful *you've* been. Now, tell me who you've been going off to see in the mornings."

"A secret for a secret?" Lawrence countered, letting a flare of anger burst out of her unexpectedly.

Ophelia's cheek twitched. Silence descended between the two of them and hung heavy like a millstone. The tension in the air grew thick like a heavy fog. Ophelia's fidgeting hands ceased and she became still. Ophelia tilted her head up slowly.

"Go on then," she said in a low voice.

"He's just a friend. That's all."

Lawrence could see the tightening skin around Ophelia's eyes, displeased with the vague answer. Her fingers drummed along the top of her thigh, but she didn't say anything further. She then smirked.

"Ask away, my dear, but think very carefully."

"What are you?"

Ophelia reacted then, her head rising sharply at the question. She sneered and Lawrence caught sight of her sharp teeth once again. She stumbled back as Ophelia reached to grab her arm. Lawrence shied away from her touch and a strange look crossed Ophelia's face. She looked all at once lost, deeply wounded, and on the verge of tears. She didn't seem like the powerful, immovable figure Lawrence had always thought of her.

Ophelia slowly rose from where she sat and looked down at her. Lawrence fought the urge to lower her eyes, like the weaker animal would when faced with the apex predator.

"You seem to think you know the answer," Ophelia said, her voice deadly quiet. "That old fool next door had your mind twisted around before you even set foot in this house. You are just like the rest of them!"

Lawrence turned to leave, but Ophelia's hand shot out and grabbed her forearm. The cold digits dug into her flesh, and she let out a whimper of pain. Ophelia shook her lightly.

"Don't you forget that you're only here because of me! You were just a penniless, nothing artist living in a squalid little hut of sticks! Do you think anyone would have had any interest in your silly paintings, much less given you what I have? Do you think anyone would give you what I am willing to?"

She loosened her grip enough that Lawrence could wrench her arm from Ophelia's grasp. She rubbed her forearm where she could feel the bruises already starting to form into tender flesh. A few errant tears fell down her cheeks. Ophelia's furious expression faltered for a moment when she saw them.

Lawrence stormed out and raced up the stairs towards her room. She felt her neck prickle once she reached the top of the stairs. She looked back and saw Ophelia watching with a strange expression.

Chapter 16

Canary Green stood like a torch, a beacon at the edge of the water that illuminated the purple-blue summer sky of Bar Harbor. The warm air felt electric, buzzing with the new filament lights. The salty breeze from the Atlantic was carried in on the soft winds from the east.

A live jazz band played poolside, the noise echoing far and wide. The trill horn and reedy sax carried over the water and down the coast through the shuffling leaves of the trees and bushes. Men and women danced along the pool and gathered in little clumps around the estate's edges. Along the trim lawns and the wide oak hallways, people came and went, shuffling around endlessly, swaying in place, and then running off like errant children.

The people from the city came in waves that matched the timetable of the Bar Harbor train that went through the state and up from Boston and New York, Philadelphia, and Washington.

For hours, it seemed that hundreds of cars and taxis—a bus even—made their way down the Sinclair's driveway and back to the station on an endless loop. For once, though, the size of Canary Green matched its number of occupants, and it seemed perfectly suited to fit all its guests.

For the week leading up to the big party, several large trucks arrived daily with flowers and decorations. Extra help was called in from the neighboring towns for the full week. The extra hands spent the morning and night installing lights, stringing crepe streamers, and hanging glittering stars in all the rooms and hallways. All the carpets were beaten and steamed; the marble floors were mopped and waxed; and the cutlery and crystal were polished and set out in perfect little rows.

Food and drink were delivered the morning of the party. Cold items were put on ice, and the rest were stuck into the ovens to keep warm. Long tables held lobster and crab laid out on ice and lettuce, turkey crisped to a bronzed gold sat on bronze platters, and great arrangements of cold meats and jelly were laid next to oblong marble serving dishes of chilled salads and tiny *hors d'oeuvres*. In every room, sweating bottles of champagne, crisp gin and seltzer in silver bottles, and ice-cold beer were all brought in, smuggled from Canada, so it was of pure, good quality.

Three different bands were called in from the city and set up at different parts of the mansion. Sal Walker and his ten-piece jazz band played out on the veranda on a large platform with house lights on them at all times. Dancing girls accompanied them from Chicago and performed all night on elevated platforms above the crowds below. Before the first guests even arrived, the musicians were plucking and banging through the jumpy swing beats popular in the private clubs and speakeasies out west.

Once the sun began its descent, the lights were all turned on. They glittered spectacularly through the long night like a hive of lightning bugs. Hundreds of guests packed onto the property, and most were well on their way to being properly smoked.

As the people all moved on to their second and third drinks, the collective din of voices grew louder, randier, and more excited. Every voice competed to win out against the cacophony of the drums and snares. Men shouted across rooms, clapping hands and slapping shoulders with chums from their collegiate years. The women yelled, cheering at the top of their lungs, kissing new and old friends on the cheeks. People greeted each other as if they were being reunited after decades apart, when the truth was that they hardly knew each other's names.

As it was a costume party, everyone made great efforts with their looks. Simple hats and masks were not enough for this crowd. Cleopatra walked arm-in-arm with a green witch on one arm and a cowboy on the other. A mummy drank champagne straight from the bottle, teetering dangerously within close vicinity of the pool. Men in sparkling dresses with ruby lips shared cigars with women in pinstripe suits and thin mustaches drawn across their upper lips. A figure dressed as the evening star danced the foxtrot with a Founding Father right next to a young crow that slurped down an oyster in the corner with a court jester. It was a colorful parade of fabrics and painted faces, towering hair, and papier-mâché masks. And with every passing hour, the festivities grew more and more bacchanalian.

Lawrence arrived precisely one hour after the party was originally meant to start, and she was exactly on time. Her commute was short, crossing the opposite path and down the hill. She had crept out without a word and not a look back. She didn't know if Ophelia knew about her leaving, but she didn't stop her.

It seemed as if the Sinclair estate itself was its own sun, blazing with light and noise. It stood in direct contrast to the ominous quiet and dark of Ashmore, and she felt compelled forward like a fly to light. She approached from the side and went around to the front, following a long procession of cars and taxis that continued to pull into the long, gravel drive. She pushed her way through the front door and stumbled into the crowded foyer.

Lawrence stuck out in that she looked wrong in the sea of costumed characters. She had no time or chance to prepare so she came dressed in her normal black skirts and painters blouse. She went through the halls and up the stairs, following the music until it grew louder. She reached the main ballroom and headed out to the veranda, looking out over the lawn and pool below.

The bodies were packed in tight along the edges. Tables and chairs were dotted about and occupied by all sorts of people who constantly came and went. In the center, a space was drawn out for dancing, and couples shimmied and swung to the music. All the sudden movement and noise nearly overwhelmed Lawrence, sending her into a tizzy. She kept close to the walls, watching the others and keeping an eye out for a familiar face in the sea of people.

"Now, what are you meant to be then? A suffragette? A wistful portraitist who finds sustenance only in the ambrosia of Yearning and the nectar of Fantasy?" a familiar voice asked from behind.

Lawrence turned and came face-to-face with a very thick-armed dairy girl.

"Good lord, Patrick. Is that you?" she asked, laughing as she picked at his pale blue skirts.

She had him turn around to show off his elaborate costume. A tight choker wound around his tan neck, and white stockings went up his hairy legs. He carefully turned, keeping a hand on his powdered white wig that towered above him and added at least another foot to his sizable height. Moles and beauty marks in the shapes of stars and hearts adorned his stark white face. Lawrence laughed again as she brushed a hand down the thick stubble that poked out under the thick theater makeup.

"My, what a charming dairy girl you make."

"How dare you?" He sniffed, affronted. "I am Marie Antoinette, Dauphine of France. Not just any simple dairy girl, I'll have you know."

Lawrence bowed deeply with a dramatic sweep of her hand.

289

"My apologies, your majesty." She held up his dress skirts and looked under for a brief moment. "Goodness, look at your under-skirts. How ever did you find one that fit you?"

"Oh, you'll see we all take this very seriously. I've had this costume in mind for months now. I refuse to be upstaged by some cheap filly from the city."

"I doubt anyone will be upstaging you; you are the prima donna of the night, I think."

"*Merci beaucoup,*" he said with a flirtatious bow and horrifying French accent. He suddenly became serious then, dropping the accent entirely, and placed a hand on Lawrence's shoulder.

"LJ, you do know I'm dead sorry don't you? I feel horrible about letting it slip to the others. It's been eating me up, you know. I can't bear to think that you're walking around mad at me."

Lawrence wound her arm through Patrick's and patted him.

"Oh, Patrick, only if you forgive me for yelling and storming off on you like that," she said. She shook her head. "Nothing makes sense. I don't know what's real anymore."

"Since we're on the topic," he said, gesturing to a waiter to bring drinks over. "I'm half surprised to see you here. Not that I'm not absolutely buzzing with excitement that you are, but it seemed like you wouldn't. Especially after what Pa and Eddy did."

"Yes, that," she murmured, looking sideways and observing the other people in the room. He pulled her over to the wall and looked down at her.

"LJ, I want you to know that I had a stern word with Pa about what happened that day. It's absolutely inexcusable, but we know you understand. Surely you do. It's just madness."

"Yes," she nodded. "Perhaps not as mad as we thought."

"How do you mean?"

He turned away from her as a waiter arrived with a tray of drinks.

Patrick took two glasses for himself and shook his head, as if steeling himself for a great battle.

"It's going to be a long night."

Patrick downed both drinks in quick succession, setting the empty glasses aside without looking or caring where he placed them. He looked Lawrence over.

"This won't do," he said, gesturing to her plain clothes and un-adorned face. He guided her out of the room, skirts swishing with every step. "Come along."

It took less than a half hour, but Lawrence re-emerged from one of the private rooms as a new person. She wore a white, billowy shirt and trousers with a frilly white collar around her neck. A white felt cone hat sat atop her slicked-back hair, and her face was painted stark white. Black lines were painted on as brows, one quirked up and the other flat. Black tears went down the right side of her face down to the lips, which were an inky black line. Thick black cotton balls were stitched all over the hat and down the front of the shirt, and they were also placed at her wrists and ankles. People Lawrence had never met in her life smiled at her as she passed, complimenting her, which she only accepted with an awkward nod of her head.

Patrick waited for her at the bottom of the stairs, flirting with a young woman dressed as a colorful cockatoo. He brushed a finger over the hundreds of feathers stuck into her hair and said something that made the woman blush. The moment he saw Lawrence, though, he turned away from the girl and waved her over. The cockatoo let out an annoyed huff and turned on her heel, stalking away. Once Lawrence reached Patrick, he touched the frilly collar around her neck.

"Much better," he said with an approving nod. "Follow me, dear Pierrot."

The two walked together through the house. Patrick picked up a champagne bottle from a table as they passed, popping it. He took a big swig first and held it out to Lawrence, who followed suit. As they made their way through the crowd, Patrick loudly crowed at the top of his voice for the others to make way for the Queen of France and her court jester.

They paraded through Canary Green until they reached the second floor ballroom. At a little table by the veranda doors, Augusta sat with a small party of people around her. Edwin hovered behind her chair, a drink in one hand and a cigar in the other.

Augusta spotted the pair as they approached and let out a squeal. She rose from her seat with open arms.

"LJ! You came!"

She rushed forward and pulled Lawrence into a big hug. She then held her at arms length and looked her over with a beaming smile.

"A little French clown, how cute!"

Before Lawrence could say anything, Augusta pulled her into another bear hug, squeezing her tightly.

"Oh, LJ, you won't believe how sorry I am for what happened! I'm so absolutely juiced that you're here though! Oh, how glad I am you're with us again."

"Easy, Augs, you'll squeeze the life out of the poor girl," Patrick admonished, flicking her gently on the forehead to release Lawrence.

Once she was released from Augusta's grip, she took a few steps back and took in Augusta's costume. She tilted her head sideways.

"You are a rose?"

Augusta wore a green jumpsuit that went from her neck down to her wrists and ankles. All around her shoulders and face, splaying outward in large arcs, were several red petals of paper and crepe. Her face was bejeweled with black crystals, and her normally red, flaming hair was painted black with tar.

"Oh heavens no!" Augusta cried, holding her arms wide. She posed several ways, twisting her body around to show her costume from multiple angles. "I'm a poppy, of course!"

"I see it now; how foolish of me!" Lawrence apologized, kissing her lightly on the cheeks. She turned then to the ever-present looming figure at Augusta's side. "Senator Ernest, I presume?"

"Pax vobiscum," Edwin answered with a regal tilt of his head.

He was practically bare on top, with only the white and wine-red-trimmed robes of a Roman senator wrapped around him. Atop the crown of his head, a laurel wreath wrapped around his temple. A red circle had been painted in the center of his face in tribute to the god Mars. He didn't have his usual spectacles on, but held them in hand in case he needed them. Without them, his face seemed particularly childish and too open. He looked Lawrence in the eyes with a sincere look and a nod of his head.

"We are glad to see you here with us, *safe*, LJ."

Lawrence said nothing to that, but gave him a half smile and nodded. She thought of Ophelia then, and her heart gave a pitiful pang. She suddenly felt overwhelmed in the crowded room and the high collar of her costume felt as if it were suffocating her.

"Cheers to a wonderful summer!" Augusta cried, holding up a couple of glasses for Lawrence and Patrick to take. Desperate to take her mind off of Ophelia, Lawrence eagerly grabbed the glass.

Patrick leaned over to whisper to Lawrence. "I thought you didn't drink."

"I think a drink is exactly what I need," she said.

He smiled with a wink and they all held their glasses aloft and cheered.

The soaring trill of a trumpet signaled the end of a song and wave of cheers went up. The band leader called out their next song and urged for new couples to get out on the dance floor. Those who obeyed immediately began trotting around with their partners.

"Lawrence?"

Lawrence turned and Edwin came closer to her side with an expectant look. He reached towards her, but she was tugged away by her other arm and spun away towards the dance floor.

"Come on, clown girl, take me for a spin."

Patrick held his hand out to her. She looked back to Edwin, who waved his hand in understanding. Lawrence and Patrick melted into the crowd, spinning among the others. Lawrence laughed aloud as Patrick did his best not to trip over his voluminous skirts.

Once they got into rhythm, Patrick sought out her eyes.

"What's wrong, Stoner?" he asked, great sincerity in his wide, brown eyes. He grasped her hand in his and a brow raised. "Good grief, Stoner, you're chilled to the bone! I'm dying in this damned corset and all these layers. How do you ladies do it?"

"That must be why so many young ladies are abandoning their corsets and layers," she said with a shrug. *"La garçonne."*

She focused on her steps then, mindful not to trod on Patrick's feet. They swayed back and forth to the music. He rested his hand on her back and held her hand in his. For a few moments, it felt like she was absorbing his warmth. This was the closest they had ever been, but Lawrence's heart remained steady. She smelled his cologne and after shave and without meaning to, she immediately thought about how much more pleasant jasmine and smoke appealed to her.

"How's the painting coming along then?"

"Well, it was going quite well," Lawrence said with a far off look. When she didn't say any more, Patrick frowned.

"Not anymore?"

Before she could answer, a figure appeared by their side. A tall, slender figure in an elaborate layered costume like a Tudor monarch and a paper mask extended his hand out to Lawrence. He bowed slightly at the waist and tilted his head in silence. Patrick and

Lawrence stopped dancing and stared at the stranger in disbelief.

"Goodness, it's a king!" Lawrence laughed in delight.

"Henry VIII by the looks of it," Patrick said with a raised brow as he looked the man over.

The silent man gestured once again for Lawrence to take his hand with a tilt of his head. Patrick huffed a bit, his hand still in hers.

"Listen pal, we're still dancing. Wait for the next one."

The stranger was resolute, though, and stayed by their side. When they took a step to dance away, he followed, mimicking their movement. Lawrence laughed and released Patrick's hand from hers. She patted him on the shoulder.

"Gannaway, I think you've lost this one."

He held his hands up with an affable smile.

"Fine, I concede. However, you will have to make this up to me later, and believe you me that I will absolutely hold you to it Stoner!" Patrick cried.

He patted the mystery stranger on the back, which sent them stumbling sideways a bit, and shuffled off the dance floor in search of some drinks and new company.

The stranger held his gloved hand out for Lawrence to take. Once she placed her hand in his, he brought her body closer and wrapped his other arm around her waist.

"So, are you well acquainted with the Sinclairs then?" she asked.

The stranger remained silent, but tilted his head and shrugged. She laughed again.

"Surely, you're not intending to stay silent for the entire dance, are you?"

They whirled Lawrence around, answering her by saying nothing at all.

"Very well," she said with a sigh. "Perhaps then I may ask you questions, and you may shake your head. I'm sure you can do that much."

They nodded then and Lawrence smiled. She thought for a moment.

"Do you live in the area?"

A nod.

"Have me wet?"

Another nod.

"Oh! How interesting. I haven't met many people. That does narrow things down nicely. I wish you would let me know who you are. Perhaps once this is all over, you'll take some pity on me."

At that moment, Lawrence caught the familiar scent of jasmine and smoke. Even in the packed room of people, it carried through the fog to her like the beacon of a lighthouse. It was so clear and familiar, she couldn't help but gasp. Lawrence studied the crudely-made mask of the figure before her, as if expecting some clue that it really was who she thought. She leaned a bit closer.

"Ophelia?" she whispered. "Is it you?"

The figure tilted their head. They stopped dancing and reached for their mask to pull it away.

"Oh," Lawrence gasped, moving backward instinctively.

The young man from the newspaper office, William, smiled sheepishly at her. His cheeks blazed red and his floppy hair stuck to his sweaty skin.

"Sorry!" he blurted out. "I just saw you dancing with your friend, and recognized you. It's me, William. You put an ad out in our paper? I didn't mean to mislead you or anything like that."

"Yes, of course," she said, laughing lightly. "There's nothing to apologize for. How have you been William?"

"Oh, dandy," he said with another apprehensive smile. "How'd your ad do? I'm guessing pretty well since you're here."

"Not too bad," she said. She willfully omitted the fact that she had moved into Ashmore. She gestured to the room. "How do you know the Sinclairs?"

"Oh, my family have known the Sinclairs for decades. My great uncle used to be head butler here, but that was before. Anyways, they've always extended an invite to us to their parties. Good people."

Lawrence went to answer, but she felt her skin tighten and the hair on her arms raised. Ophelia was here. Another cloying wave of jasmine and smoke surrounded her and William raised his eyes to someone behind Lawrence.

"Oh, hello," he greeted in a friendly tone.

After the person didn't answer, Lawrence turned and came face to face with another imposing, masked figure.

This one wore a long, dark red suit with a large maroon cape folded over their arm. Two horns stuck out from a satin skullcap that covered their head, and a black, Japanese theater mask covered the upper portion of their face. The mask's features were exaggerated: its lips pulled back wide over a mouth of yellow tusks and teeth, the wooden nose was carved deep down the center, and wild white and red painted eyes covered the top. At the bottom, where the mask did not cover the chin or lips, the face was painted pitch black. The holes where the eyes should have been were covered, filled in with cloth.

"Oh, did you want to cut in?" William asked hesitantly.

The figure remained silent, but bowed their head once in affirmation. William backed away from Lawrence. He wiped another hand over his sweaty face, surrendering her over easily.

"Well, it was nice to see you again. Maybe we'll speak soon?"

He waited for a moment for Lawrence's answer, but she didn't even hear the question. Her sole attention was focused entirely on the new person in front of her. William eventually shuffled away, blending into the background with the rest of the party. She looked up into the wooden face, searching.

"What a horrifying mask," she said in a flat tone, staring into the demonic face.

The last song came to a close, and a round of applause went up. A single trumpet cried out and warbled, signaling the next song. The rest of the ensemble slowly joined in one-by-one, and the couples on the floor swayed to the slower tempo.

Ophelia didn't say a word, but moved forward and pulled Lawrence into her arms. Wrapped up in their embrace, Lawrence felt the chill of her skin through all the layers between them. Ophelia took control and they glided across the floor with ease.

They reached the center of the floor and Ophelia pulled Lawrence in closer, wrapping an arm around her waist. She held her firmly and brought her head down next to Lawrence's.

"Are you not glad to see me then?" Ophelia asked in a low voice.

Lawrence's breath stuttered and she let out a shaky breath.

"What are you doing here?" she asked in a hushed tone.

"It took you no time at all to figure me out," Ophelia said. The lips below the mask quirked up into a smile. "What gave me away? Or, is it that you see me so clearly that no disguise will ever work?"

Lawrence pressed her lips into a thin line as they continued to sway back and forth. Ophelia's lips frowned.

"You're upset."

"Why are you here?" Lawrence asked again. She looked down at the rest of Ophelia's costume. "You look like a man. You're wrong. I hardly recognized you."

"But you did."

"You didn't answer me," Lawrence repeated. She tried to pull herself away, but Ophelia kept a firm grip around her.

"What was the question?" she asked softly, her voice a gentle purr.

It was almost as if Ophelia had forgotten all about their argument, and even Lawrence questioned her own memory of how they had parted the day prior. She shook her head.

"What are you doing here?"

"What's wrong? Are you not happy to see me then?" She asked bitterly. Her grip momentarily tightened around Lawrence. "Because I missed you. I hated knowing you were over here without me."

"Really?" Lawrence muttered, her eyes narrowing.

She swallowed thickly and flexed her arm. The slight tugging ache in her forearm reminded her of the blooming fingertip-shaped bruises right under the fabric.

"I thought I was just a little nothing artist. I wouldn't have thought you'd have even noticed my absence."

"Of course I did," insisted Ophelia, the corners of her lips pulling down at the mere suggestion.

She slowly pulled back the sleeve of Lawrence's costume until her forearm was exposed. She gently brushed a gloved hand over the bruises and brought the arm up to her lips. She placed a gentle, cool kiss against her sensitive skin.

"You can't begin to understand how repulsed I am of my behavior. It was disgraceful. I don't blame you if you hate me. To think I have harmed you in any way sickens me. I would rather suffer a thousand worse pains than hurt you again as I have."

The fire within Lawrence burned out, and her heart twisted.

"I don't hate you, Ophelia," Lawrence uttered out with a grimace. "Of course I don't hate you."

"I hate myself for making you feel as I have. I should never have kept you cooped up as I did. It was wrong. I see that now."

"Is that why you came then?" Lawrence asked, her head tilted up. She searched the black eyes of the mask, but found nothing looking back at her. "What about everything else?"

Ophelia abruptly paused their dancing, and they stopped in the center of the dance floor as the rest of the couples continued to dance around and past them. None of the others paid them any mind, and they expertly avoided hitting them as they twirled and spun around.

"If you want the truth, come back," she said in a tone that brooked no arguments. Lawrence went to speak, but Ophelia continued first. "But make your decision carefully. Once you return, you stay."

Ophelia stepped forward and tilted her head down. She brought both hands up to cup Lawrence's face and gently caressed her face. She placed her cool, soft lips against Lawrence's and kissed her gently.

Lawrence's heart fluttered and her stomach tightened. She grasped Ophelia tighter to her. Ophelia tasted like dry wine and something richer like truffle that made her lips tingle.

In what felt like no time at all, Ophelia pulled away. The song had ended and the rest of the couples were clearing from the floor. Ophelia's hands lowered and she stepped away from Lawrence. She said nothing further as she took a step back and turned to go.

"Ophelia?" Lawrence called after her.

She continued to walk away, weaving her way through the crowd seamlessly and disappearing with a moment. Lawrence strained her eyes to look for her, but it was as if she had disappeared in thin air.

"Ophelia!"

Lawrence surged forward, looking back and forth through the crowd for a flash of red. So absorbed in her search, she almost didn't notice the arm that reached out in an effort to capture her attention.

"Lawrence?"

Edwin appeared in front of her, his toga robes gathered up in the crook of his arm like a proper Roman senator. He had placed his spectacles back on, smudging the perfect circle of red painted on his face.

"Edwin!" she cried in surprise. She continued to look around the room, searching. He peered over his shoulder to cast a sweeping gaze over the crowded ballroom.

"Are you looking for someone?"

"No," she replied, immediately.

"Good, may I speak to you for a moment?"

Lawrence immediately halted her search for Ophelia, taken aback by the request and his serious tone. He gestured for her to follow, and she trailed after him as they walked out from the dance floor to the veranda. He led her to a quieter corner on the balcony and leaned up against the stone banister. Edwin pulled out a battered pack of cigarettes and silently offered her one, which she took.

"How are you feeling?" he asked quietly, exhaling.

He stood in a shadowy corner and the embers from his cigarette illuminated his face in an orange glow. She stood a few paces away and shifted between her feet.

"Fine," she replied with a small shrug.

Edwin's eyes slightly narrowed as he took in her face and slightly hunched posture. He studied her as a doctor would a patient. His lips puckered together.

"You seem tired," he noted with a forced indifference. He gestured towards her eyes. "Have you not been sleeping?"

"Just been working," she said, tilting her head away out of his direct view. She inhaled slowly and let the smoke fill up her lungs until it burned. "Haven't been getting out much is all."

A stretch of silence settled between the two of them before Edwin cleared his throat lightly. "May I ask you a question, although, it might be a bit personal?"

Lawrence nodded.

"Have you been feeling a bit odd?"

"Odd?" she repeated.

In her mind, everything flashed through her mind from the very moment she had first woken up in her cabin with strange marks on her chest to the photo Greta had shown to her. A line of sweat trailed down her back.

"Yes, anything out of the ordinary," he explained. "Perhaps, some dizziness, paranoia, or lethargy? Sleepwalking?"

Lawrence reacted first, her face flinching at the mention of sleepwalking. Edwin immediately noticed and stepped forward.

"You have been, haven't you?"

"No!" cried Lawrence, laughing. She stuck the cigarette in her mouth with a shake of her head. "I know what you're alluding to, Edwin. I'm not falling sick like those others. You needn't worry."

He exhaled, the smoke coiling out through his nose like a dragon. He then stamped out his cigarette and looked out over the estate. He passively watched the party that continued on below them, clasping his hands behind his back.

Lawrence picked at her sleeves. "Is Augusta-"

"You know there have been more deaths?" he asked absentmindedly, cutting her off. She didn't say anything, but he continued on. "Down south. An older couple. One young woman has also gone missing as well."

His face remained grim. The red paint on his face highlighted the severe lines across his forehead. Lawrence remained silent and his eyes narrowed at her.

"Do you care?"

Lawrence frowned, taken aback by the sudden question that made her chest burn and stomach tighten. She shook her head, shrugging.

"What does that have to do with anything? Of course, I care, but I don't know those people."

"You asked once what it was I studied in college. Would you like to know?" he asked abruptly. Lawrence could only nod.

"I studied the occult, the supernatural, and parapsychology. Do you know what that is?"

She shook her head.

"It's about the possibility of the impossible, or what we think is impossible," he said, looking over his shoulder briefly before he turned around and leaned against the railing to face her again. He crossed his arms. "Your new friend is not what she says she is."

"I don't know what you're talking about," she said in a breezy manner. Although, as she spoke, she couldn't bring herself to look him in the face properly.

"Yes, you do," he countered in a firm voice.

A large lump formed in Lawrence's throat, but she remained silent. Her eyes flickered to the ground, and when she did look up again, Edwin stared at her with a strange, distant look in his eyes. Any friendliness she had seen in him had been entirely replaced with something at the edge of hostility.

"You could help us, Lawrence," he whispered. "She will never grow old. She will never die. She is as unchanged as a statue, forever stuck in time. She has more in common with the beasts and reptiles of an age long forgotten than she ever will with you. What do you think she sees you as other than a trifling amusement for this current century?"

"You're mad," she murmured, taking a step back out of his reach. He attempted to grab her, but she dove out of the way.

"Leave me be! You're wrong! You're all wrong."

"Lawrence!"

She rushed away from the balcony and re-entered the ballroom. She pushed her way through the crowd of people who continued to laugh and stumble out of the way. Lawrence staggered out into the hallway, turning both ways in search of Ophelia. She began to head off into one direction when a firm hand grabbed her around the bicep and pulled her close.

"There you are, my little clown!" Augusta shouted as she leaned heavily into Lawrence's arms. She pulled her into a tight hug and stuck her face into Lawrence's neck.

"Augusta-"

"Have you seen him?" She asked, her words slurring. "I haven't seen 'im in ages."

"Who, Auggie?" she asked, doing her best to keep her upright.

Augusta continued to sway violently and started to giggle. Patrick stepped out into the hallway, staggering slightly as he tripped over the edge of his skirt. He had lost the wig and parts of his white makeup had begun to sweat off, running down in streaks. He sidled up next to Augusta, leaning heavily onto the wall for support.

"Good Christ," he muttered. "Where am I?"

Edwin stepped out from the ballroom shortly after. He and Lawrence shared a brief look, but she turned her head away quickly. Patrick dragged Edwin under his arm and leaned on him. Even in his drunken state, he was stalwart and firm.

"Oh, Eddy," he crowed. "My handsome little scholar. Come, give me a hug."

"Gannaway, get off me. You're a thousand pounds," Edwin huffed, struggling under his friend's bigger size and stature.

Lawrence and Edwin were both held captive by their own separate jailers. Augusta continued to giggle and every time she swayed, Lawrence ended up being dragged along with her.

"Oh, come on, it's a party! You're being awfully tedious, even for you. Now, what is it that's on your mind?" Patrick asked. He held up his hand and brought his head close to Edwin's. "Animal, vegetable, or mineral?"

"Let me go, Pat," Edwin shouted, fighting to be heard over the noise of the music and people.

"Eddy, you haven't danced with me once! Do you hate me?" Augusta cried as she shoved Patrick's strong arm off of Edwin. She went right up to his face and fell into him as she tripped over her own feet.

"Don't be silly, Birdy. Of course, I don't hate you," Edwin said with a shake of his head.

"He *must* hate you, Augs. I've danced with you three times!" Patrick shouted. He then waved his hand towards Lawrence as she slipped away. "Where's she going?"

Lawrence pushed her way through the crowd of never-ending bodies. How Ophelia managed to get away so effectively was a true mystery. It was at the point of the night where everyone was collectively intoxicated in one way or another. The din of voices was now louder than the music, and it felt like some circle of hell with all the smoke and bodies pushing up against each other endlessly.

Lawrence managed to get to the foyer, but felt as if she had made no progress at all. She felt a slick line of sweat crawl down her back in the hot costume. She ripped away the frilly collar and tossed it aside carelessly. She ran a hand through her sweaty hair.

"*En garde*, civil!" cried a voice from behind.

Lawrence turned and for what felt like the first time in a long while, smiled in true pleasure.

From the staircase, Mr. Sinclair stood with a short sword and flintlock pistol in hand. From where she stood, Lawrence wasn't entirely confident they were simply props, either. Mr. Sinclair was dressed head to toe as a pirate with a long beard and eye patch included. He had rubbed kohl into his eyes and a stuffed parrot dangled precariously off his shoulder. He waved the sword wildly to push people out of his way as he made his way towards her.

"Mr. Sinclair!"

He faltered and Lawrence managed to catch him as he flew down the last few steps. She smelled the distinct scent of whiskey off his breath as he leaned in close.

"Is that really you?" he asked.

"Yes, Pa," she replied, helping him reach the main floor safely. She let him lean on her as they walked side-by-side down the hallway.

She worried for a moment that he would bring up their last encounter at Ashmore, and more specifically, Ophelia. However, as she studied the glazed look in his eyes, she realized he'd do nothing of the sort. She wasn't entirely sure he knew it was her specifically. He seemed at ease then, and Lawrence felt lighter herself. He laughed gaily and hummed in the moments of silence.

"Are you alright?" she asked.

"Well, once you're my age, it's not so much about how well you've been, but how well things have been maintained? Neutral zero is always the aim, my friend. Nothing too exciting, or it may very well be the end."

"Oh don't say that, please. It's too horrible to think about."

"You're absolutely right; no dark thoughts tonight!" he cried with another wide swing of his sword that got worryingly close to passing guests. "What a wretched host I am; you don't have a drink. Good thing I *am* the host. Gives you certain sway in what matters most. Lookee here."

Mr. Sinclair snapped his fingers, and a waiter came running over with a tray of coupe glasses full of fizzing champagne. He took two and handed one to her.

"Sante! Sante, my black and white friend!" he cried, clinking his glass against hers. He tipped his head back and drank his fill as Lawrence took a polite sip. She noticed the usual pouch of herbs was not around his neck. They were nowhere to be seen at all.

"Mr. Sinclair. Pa! Where has your necklace gone? Your herbs!" she cried, doing her best to capture his wandering attention. She waved her hand and gestured to the empty spot around his neck.

"Not the foggiest, my dear, not the foggiest."

"Aren't you worried without it?" she asked.

"Bill, you nance!" A man called out from the other side of the room. Mr. Sinclair whirled around from where he stood and laughed loudly as he caught sight of another gentleman close to his age dressed as Dionysus. They skipped forward like giddy schoolboys and clapped hands.

"Farewell, my dear," Mr. Sinclair said, walking off in an entirely new direction. He twisted around and waved his hand. "Do take care!"

"Mr. Sinclair!" she called after him, but he had gone off.

Alone now in the loud, raucous party, Lawrence headed out to the back garden. As she walked further from the lights and the noise, she had a little moment of clarity. She stood in the dark at the very edge of the estate and looked back from where she had come from. Lawrence felt separate, as if she were floating underwater and peering through a looking glass at a fascinating, alien world. She took a few deep lungfuls of breath and shivered.

* * *

As the sun emerged over the horizon, the party goers left in twos and threes. They broke off in clumps, staggering into town cars and falling into the back seats of taxis. Even more people simply slept where they had crawled to in their stupor, sprawled across benches or tucked under tables.

Lawrence had curled up in the library, snuggled underneath a table runner that had been piled up onto the floor. Traces of her costume and makeup remained on her, smeared and haphazardly removed. She woke with stiff, cold muscles that refused to stretch out. She let out a few scratchy, hoarse coughs as a slight ringing continued to echo in her ears.

Unveiled in the daylight, all of Canary Green seemed turned upside down. Streamers and lights went every which way like the webbing of spider's silk. Broken glass crunched underfoot and every table still upright contained at least a full ashtray and a half a dozen empty glasses.

Lawrence trudged out across the back lawn and took in some of the warm morning sun. She shut her eyes and tilted her head up, basking and facing towards the rays like a flower, desperate to absorb some of its warmth. She hadn't a moment to think of what had happened. She continued to think of Ophelia's offer to return, and that if she were to go, it would be absolute. Her heart continued to yearn, and she deliberated on the matter as she paced the lawn in solitude.

As she went to make another quarter turn, a horrible, bloodcurdling shriek pierced the silence. Lawrence froze for a quarter of a moment where she stood, with a foot still poised in the air, before she took off running.

She raced through the house, passing through the foyer and bounding up the steps as a door slammed open. Down the hallway towards where the bedrooms were, Augusta came flying out. She lost her footing and landed backward, scrambling away from the room.

"Augusta?" Lawrence called out to her.

She didn't hear, though, and sped past Lawrence. Her bright, charming face had gone pale and her eyes were wide and unseeing. They continued to flicker back and forth like a wild horse being cornered. Her mouth moved rapidly and she shook her head.

"No, no, no," she muttered continuously to herself.

She reached the top of the stairs and misplaced her foot. Augusta let out a quick shriek and a gasp as she went tumbling down the stairs. Her bright, coppery hair bounced as she rolled down a few stairs and slid the rest of the way to the first landing.

"Augusta!" Lawrence shouted in horror, hastening to her side. She fell to her knees and gathered Augusta up into her arms, taking care to cradle her head. "Augusta, what's happened! Are you hurt?"

"He-" she started, but stopped. She trembled, her hands shaking violently. Lawrence gathered them up into her own hands and pressed them close.

"He's not. I can't. I-"

"Augusta, listen to me," Lawrence said, speaking slowly. "What's happened?"

"What in God's name was that noise!"

Lawrence raised her head as Patrick appeared at the top of the hall. He yawned widely as he finished tying his satin robe around his waist. Streaks of makeup could still be seen around the edges of his neck and at his hairline. The moment he saw Augusta in Lawrence's arms, he sobered up and took to action. He bounded down the stairs and kneeled on Augusta's other side.

"You're so cold," Augusta murmured silently.

She wrapped her own thin fingers around Lawrence's. Augusta sucked in a sharp breath as tears gathered in her eyes. Fat droplets began to roll down her cheeks as she stared, unblinking at the space above.

"What's happened?" Patrick asked, looking to Lawrence.

"I don't know!" she cried.

The two of them turned as Edwin appeared at the foot of the stairs. His eyes went first to Augusta, lying still with tears streaming down her face. It seemed a strange sight, especially as she cried without making much noise at all. However, he observed for all of two seconds altogether before he darted forward up the stairs past all three of them.

"Edwin?" called Patrick. "What on God's name is going on?"

Edwin ignored him as he sprinted down the hall and headed directly into the room Augusta had come screaming out of. They listened with bated breath for some noise, a similar cry of shock or horror as Augusta's, but nothing came. Patrick and Lawrence looked to each other.

"Take her," Lawrence said, rising once she had handed Augusta off to Patrick.

Patrick murmured lowly to Augusta and brushed some of her disheveled hair out of the way. He patted her head gently and rocked her slowly as she continued to cry silently.

Lawrence went up the stairs and approached the bedroom. When she turned the corner and looked in, it was almost too much to take in at once.

The bed remained untouched, the covers still pressed and tucked in tightly. The armoire similarly had survived, but its doors had been thrown open haphazardly. The rest of the room had been overturned. The heavy sitting chairs before the fireplace were knocked aside, upturned as if they were nothing but dollhouse replicas. The coffee table had been reduced to splintery pieces, scattered all across the room. Books, papers, and little trinkets were strewn about as if a tornado had passed through just that room.

In the center of the chaos lay Mr. Sinclair.

Already his flesh had taken on its deathly pallor. A peaceful smile graced his features, and it truly did seem as if he were simply sleeping. He had on his costume from the night before, but instead of the sword and pistol, a metal stake lay within reach. Although there was not a scratch on his body or drop of blood to be seen, there was something undoubtedly violent about the general picture.

Edwin knelt by Mr. Sinclair's side. He didn't cry or make a scene. He simply stared at Mr. Sinclair in silence. His fists sat clenched on his thighs and they trembled slightly as his knuckles whitened. Lawrence hadn't made a noise or any movement, but Edwin knew she was there.

He slowly raised his head and turned to look at her. His red-rimmed eyes stared deep into her own. Misery and grief distorted Edwin's face. His lips spasmed and the skin around his eyes and cheeks twitched. He said nothing at all and simply turned away from her.

Lawrence walked away from the bedroom and Mr. Sinclair's body. She got away from Augusta and Patrick from where they were still situated on the stairs. She passed by the curious 'others' in the house who had been violently awoken by the screaming and short burst of chaos. They were hesitantly peeking around the corner and whispering in hushed tones, already speculating. Lawrence continued to walk, putting distance between herself and the house, until she reached the edge of the cliff and could go no further.

Chapter 17

William Sinclair was buried on the hottest, brightest day of the summer. It had rained the night before, so the ground was soft underfoot as the sun beat down from above. Most of the townspeople of Bar Harbor, and many more from further away, attended his service. They filled in the pews and lined up along the sides of the church. They bowed their heads as the hearse passed and remained solemn for the rest of the day.

Augusta led a small procession that broke away from the crowd consisting only of those closest to the family. Patrick walked rigidly beside her, expressionless. If one did not know him so well, they might misunderstand his lack of emotion for indifference. Lawrence and Edwin followed closely behind on their heels, heads bowed.

The mourners arrived to the family plot at the far edge of the estate, surrounded by large trees that acted like sentinels for the slumbering Sinclair family. There were at least ten stone markers already, and a freshly dug hole awaited Mr. Sinclair. His plot was situated under one of the many great oaks, closest to the garden and within view of the great sea beyond.

Lawrence stood by Augusta and let the pale, frail girl hold onto her for dear life. She had been quiet since the morning the body had been found, saying maybe ten words altogether at most. She made a small noise of surprise upon seeing the freshly carved marble headstone with her grandfather's name etched in. Edwin turned her way with a stricken expression, but stepped forward to help situate the coffin within its new home.

"They made that rather quickly, didn't they?"

Augusta's hoarse voice was hollow, as if she were simply letting the words leave her as she exhaled. Fresh tears fell from her puffy, red eyes. She leaned into Lawrence's side, averting her eyes as the coffin disappeared into the earth.

The four of them stood closest to the grave. When Lawrence raised her head, she caught Edwin's eye. They shared a brief look before they both turned away. Some words about life, death, and God were spoken before the first handfuls of dirt were thrown into the grave.

When the first clump hit the lacquered wood, Augusta abruptly turned on her heel. She gave Lawrence a final squeeze on the arm and walked away from everyone without a word or look back. After she left, the others lingered graveside and then drifted away as well.

Patrick took Augusta's spot by Lawrence's side. He clasped his hands in front of himself, his black suit creasing around the arms. The sudden loss and grief had had a profound effect on his boyish looks. His usually bright eyes had dulled and dark bags had formed under them. He bumped his arm against hers and offered up a plaintive smile.

"He really did like you," he murmured. "We all do. Augusta does. Edwin, well, who knows what the hell Edwin is thinking? I like you too."

He focused on the soft dirt below. He kicked up the loose turf and moved it about with the toe of his leather loafers. It muddied up the fine, soft leather, but he paid no mind to it.

"Thank you, Patrick," she whispered.

He nodded with a soft smile that slowly slipped off his face. He swallowed thickly.

313

"I don't know what to do," he whispered through a strained voice.

He smiled stiffly and sniffed as tears gathered in his eyes. He looked terribly young at that moment, and Lawrence saw a brief, flashing image of Patrick as a child. He looked like one then, his large shoulders curled in and head bowed.

"What do I do?" he asked again.

Lawrence grabbed his warm hand in hers. She shrugged and shook her head. "You're mourning, Patrick. I don't know if there is anything you *should* do."

"I feel like I have to do something, though," he repeated. "I feel like I'm forgetting something. He's in the ground now, so I guess it doesn't matter anyway. I think I forgot something. Maybe I didn't pick the right suit. I didn't know which one it was. They didn't tell me. I just picked one. I should have checked with Augusta. What do I do about Augusta?"

He rambled on as he thought, not really looking for an answer. It seemed like he was searching the universe for one as he raised his head heavenward, looking up into the endless blue sky.

"You picked the right one," Lawrence said, reassuring him. Even if she did not know the truth of it or not. "Augusta needs time. You need time. You all do. You should be there for each other. All of you."

He nodded his head, his eyes glazing over and staring out in the distance at nothing in particular.

"I'm going to take them away for a bit, I think," he said. "Her and Edwin. Both of them, I reckon, need some time away."

"Oh," she said, nodding.

It was a good plan, but she felt herself inevitably mourning the loss of her three friends. It paled in comparison to the grief she felt for the kindly neighbor, but she felt its sharp barbs all the same. She swallowed her own selfish feelings down and smiled at her friend, nodding her head in encouragement.

"I was thinking maybe Yosemite. Have you ever been?" he asked her, looking at her in earnest. Lawrence shook her head. "Neither have I. It's right here in our country, and I've never been. I think Augs will hate it while we're there, but she'll love it once we leave."

"That sounds lovely."

"You should join us," he said off-handedly.

He had suggested it so casually that Lawrence didn't even think to consider it as a real invitation, but he turned to her with a sincere look in his eye.

"Would you?"

Lawrence considered it. She could go. There was nothing stopping her, and she wouldn't have to say goodbye to her dear friends then. However, as soon as she considered it, she immediately rejected the idea altogether. Her heart kept her two feet planted firmly where they were, and she wouldn't be leaving Bar Harbor until she was ready.

"I can't," she explained apologetically.

"Ah yes," he said, nodding as he remembered her obligation. He turned back to her suddenly. "Can't you just give up on it?"

She didn't have to answer him before he turned away again.

"No, I suppose not. Wouldn't be right."

"Patrick, Yosemite will be lovely this time of year. You will write, though, won't you?"

He nodded.

"I wish you'd just join us. That's too bad," he murmured to himself. "I ran the whole idea by Edwin. He's been terribly difficult these past few days. We've all had a difficult past few days. He's been utterly useless. I don't give a damn anymore. He's got to stop being so pig-headed all the time. He's got to take care of the woman he loves-"

"That might be exactly what he's doing," Lawrence reasoned. Patrick gave her a strange look, as if he hadn't expected Lawrence to defend Edwin at all. "Patrick, you-"

"LJ."

She and Patrick turned to see Edwin stood a few feet away, arms clasped behind his back. Even immutable, predictable Edwin had been changed. If it were possible, he seemed more gaunt, and his eyes looked haunted. They were red, and the edges of his nose were irritated. He gestured to Lawrence.

"May we speak in private?"

"Patrick and I were talking-"

"Pat, will you please excuse us?"

He stepped forward and gave Patrick a firm nod. He continued past them and walked off towards Mr. Sinclair's grave, where he expected Lawrence to follow. Patrick chuckled and nodded. He stepped forward and gave Lawrence a brief hug, kissing the side of her temple.

"Take care, Stoner."

"You too, Gannaway."

Lawrence looked over to where Edwin waited for her under the oak tree. She dreaded it, but could not put it off any longer. She took slow steps and joined him, a few paces off. He leaned up against the bark of the tree, his lids heavy with despair and exhaustion. The crash of the waves and the whistle of the wind were all that could be heard. Edwin raised his head, watching Patrick's retreating form head towards the house. He looked at the swaying branches dancing in the wind, and Lawrence couldn't bear the silence any longer.

"Patrick told me he wants you all to leave Bar Harbor for a bit."

He nodded his head. "Yes."

"It will help Augusta, I think. It will help all of you. Although, I will be sad to see you all go," she said. "She will certainly feel better once she gets away from this place. Though, she may not want to return. I'm sure she will only associate this place with her grief for some time."

"I'll take her wherever she wants," Edwin said simply.

Lawrence studied Edwin with a soft smile. "You love her very much."

He didn't say anything, but an anguished look crossed his face and tears welled up in his eyes. He removed his glasses and wiped at his eyes roughly with the back of his hand. He was silent again for a stretch of time before he replaced his glasses and held his hands behind his back.

"I wanted to thank you for being there for Augusta. Well, for us."

He held his hand out and Lawrence took it, shaking it firmly. When she tried to pull her hand away, he held it firmly.

"Do you believe me now?"

"Not everything is because of ghouls and monsters," Lawrence said with an exhausted sigh, some ire and irritation creeping into her voice. She yanked her hand away, and his eyes narrowed slightly. "Sometimes people just die, and that's the end of it."

"Sometimes, but usually not."

"Enough of this, Edwin," Lawrence muttered, shaking her head. "Augusta has just lost her grandfather. She's devastated, and yet you continue this, this witch hunt! When will it be the end for *you*?"

"When she's dead!" he cried.

His sudden outburst of emotion caused Lawrence to startle. His face twisted and spasmed as he worked to contain himself once again. He walked away from her and ran a hand through his wild hair before he pivoted quickly and came back up to her. His voice was low and his eyes darkened.

"The world will only be safe once they're all gone! Then, the ones I care for will be safe. Truly safe."

"If she is what you say she is," Lawrence said, breathing heavily as they faced off against each other. "How does that make you any better? She's not just some cockroach for you to squash out. She's not evil."

"The difference is that she's killed innocent people, Lawrence. She killed Pa," he said, stuttering slightly as he spoke. He gathered himself once again, swallowing down his emotion behind a blank wall. "Exactly who has to die for you to believe?"

"There is no evidence of that," she ground out. "You're just blinded by grief."

Edwin reached into his pocket and produced Mr. Sinclair's necklace. The pouch was still intact, and the faint smell of herbs and flowers hit Lawrence, and her heart stuttered. The rope that held it together was torn apart and fraying at the point where it had been ripped apart.

"This is all the evidence I need. He would never have removed it unless it were ripped from his own neck."

"Stop-"

"I'm sorry, Lawrence." When she didn't answer, he shook his head. His eyes grew narrow as his lip curled. "For what I'm going to do to her, it will inevitably cause you some pain. I'm going to destroy her, Lawrence. Even if it's the last thing I do, I promise you."

Lawrence's heart seized at the dark promise. Panic became a vice grip around her lungs, squeezing the breath from her. When she looked into his eyes, all she saw was his anger and pain. There would be no reasoning with him. Strangely enough, she felt her own anger extinguish. She settled her lips into a thin line and nodded.

"Take good care of yourself Edwin, and the others."

She turned and began to walk off, but he called out after her.

"Whatever you think you feel for this creature, doubt it! They've got no heart to love. They just want to possess you. She'll destroy you! That's not love! Do what's right!"

Lawrence went so far as to clap her hands over her ears as she rushed away. Anything to put as much distance between the two of them. He continued to watch her from under the oak tree.

"I am sorry Lawrence!" he cried out after her. "I'm going to kill her, no matter. You would do well to stay out of my way!"

She continued to rush away until she saw Ashmore in front of her, looming in the distance, dark and finite in its stature and size. It looked like a great red boulder that had crashed onto earth, stuck precariously on the edge on the top of the hill. Lawrence went forward towards the lanterns out front, which called to her like a siren song.

* * *

Ashmore had not changed, but it felt alien to her. She had knocked to be let in, but Ms. Hettle did not come to greet her as she had before. Instead, the front door pushed in on its own.

She entered into the darkness, better prepared now for what she could not see. She knew what she was returning to. The door shut behind her, and Lawrence stood in silence at the bottom of the stairs. She listened, turning her head both ways like a curious cat.

A bump above caused Lawrence's head to whip up towards the second floor. She listened, waited. Then, another bump.

Lawrence raced forward, gathering up her skirts and surging up the stairs. Without any hesitation, she tore down the wing forbidden to her and stopped before the large double doors. Looking back once over her shoulder, she pushed down the handle and slipped inside within one fluid movement.

The room inside was pitch dark. Three separate layers of curtains had been laid over each other to keep all possible light out. Lawrence went to them first, pushing them away to let in the light. Her breath left her in one loose exhale as she looked around.

As Greta had said, the main room was just a farce. It was empty. The walls remained bare, devoid of any of the murals or paintings featured in all the other rooms. The wooden planks underfoot were unstained and rough. With every step, the heels of her shoes clicked against the raw, wooden floor planks. There was a staleness to the air that caused Lawrence's nose to scrunch up. This wasn't it.

Lawrence left the fake bedroom and stood in the hallway.

She faced the tapestry of the god and pulled it back. There, she faced another smaller, rickety door. She grabbed the ring handle and pulled. All at once, a coppery stench hit her that was hard to ignore. She hid her nose into the inside of her elbow before she continued on into the unknown.

She took slow, timid steps like a child first learning how to walk. She toed her way forward through the darkness, one hand extended out, reaching and searching. Her foot found the first obstacle in her way, and she tapped it lightly. A small crate lay overturned, a mound of melted wax on its surface. She grabbed a discarded taper candle and felt around until she found a loose box of matches. She lit one, the sudden flash of light blinding her for a moment.

Lawrence stood outside a small circular room, many degrees colder than the rest of the house. Her own breath came out in a fog in front of her face. Along the wall lay a long, rectangular box the approximate height and size fit for a human. Pushed up against the opposite side of the room sat an armoire, the two doors kept tightly shut with a chain and fish-shaped padlock.

Her foot squelched on the floor. Something sticky underfoot caused her to look down. A long trail of blood stretched from the entrance to the locked cabinet. New blood sat on top of old blood, dying the stone crimson. Lawrence inhaled sharply, her cry of horror caught in her throat.

The chain wrapped along the handles of the cabinet twinkled lightly, echoing around the room. Lawrence froze where she stood, lifting the small candle higher. Another small rattle rang out as the left door strained lightly against the metal bind, pushing. A low moan came out through the sliver of opening.

"Hello?" Lawrence whispered, inching forward closer. "Is something in there?"

Another moan, low and guttural. The door shook again. Something inside was trying to be let out.

Lawrence went forward and inspected the fish padlock. It wasn't a true lock, but a contraption secured by a metal pin that went through its body.

As she went to reach for it, a hand shot out next to her head and slammed the door shut. Lawrence let out a gasp and dropped the candle in hand. It rolled along the bloody floor for a moment.

Lawrence's back pressed into the front of the cabinet as Ophelia brought her body closer and wrapped her other hand around the column of Lawrence's throat. She brought her face closer until they were nearly nose to nose. Even in the dim light of the single candle below, Lawrence could see how Ophelia had changed.

She had aged ten years in the course of a few nights. Her normally lustrous, glowing bronzed skin looked sallow and crepey. Lines had formed around the crease of her mouth and along the high plane of her brow. She looked tired.

"What are you doing in here?" she asked, the cool fingers tightening briefly.

A chill went through Lawrence at Ophelia's empty, hollow voice that echoed through the room.

"Ophelia," she breathed out.

"I can't allow you to see what's inside," she explained in a matter-of-fact way. "You won't see me the same, and I'm afraid I can't allow for that to happen."

A ragged, pitiful sound fell from Lawrence's lips as the first tears fell. She wrapped her hands around Ophelia's wrist that led to the hand that continued to encircle her throat. She knew it wouldn't make a difference if it really mattered, but she tried all the same.

"Oh god," she whimpered. "They were right."

"Who, sweet one?"

"You killed him," she whined. "Oh, god!"

Ophelia hushed her lightly as she continued to cry. The thumb along the side of Lawrence's throat moved gently, as if settling a wild animal. Ophelia brought her face close and pressed her nose against the soft skin of Lawrence's neck, inhaling deeply. Ophelia smelled her as if she were a flower or rich wine, something to be savored.

"Why," Lawrence groaned. "Why did they have to be right?"

Ophelia lifted her head, but said nothing.

"Why couldn't you just have been—" Lawrence shook her head.

"I am still me," Ophelia responded easily. "It doesn't change anything. It doesn't have to. I've not lied about anything else to you Lawrence. We could still carry on just as we were."

"No," Lawrence sobbed, shaking her head. "You killed them! You killed them all, Ophelia. They were right, and I didn't listen!"

A sudden realization came to Lawrence then and she pushed Ophelia away, who surprisingly let herself be moved. Lawrence went to the collar of her dress and pulled it down, ripping the fabric as she exposed the bare skin to her. There still remained the distinct scars along the top of her breast and at the side of her neck where she had been bitten.

"You were going to kill me. You still are, aren't you?"

Ophelia remained silent but lowered her head. Lawrence couldn't tell if it was shame or something else. Lawrence's breath started to come faster until she felt like she couldn't breathe. The walls of the room were coming in closer. She let out a cry and put her hand across her chest.

"You're going to kill me too."

Ophelia came alive then, reanimating suddenly. She clasped Lawrence's face within her hands.

"No!" she cried, shaking her head. "After you left your card with Hettle, I did go to you. Once I saw you, though, I knew. All it took was one look for me to see that you were meant to come here. Don't you understand? You're the one I've waited all this time for. I never have to be alone again. *You* never have to be alone again. Do you think I would ever let harm come to you, Lawrence? I'd rather die than harm you."

Ophelia held Lawrence's hands within her own and brought them up to her lips to press kisses to her fingers. Lawrence tried to pull her hands away, but Ophelia had the strength of a grizzly bear, and it was as useless as trying to break free from iron shackles. The joints at Lawrence's elbows and shoulders began to strain as she fought. There was no doubt in her mind that she'd sooner pull her own arms out before she could ever break free from Ophelia's grasp. She calmed and settled, and that was cause enough for Ophelia to look at her once again.

"Lawrence?"

"Take your glasses off," Lawrence ordered, her voice firm and unyielding. "Let me see your eyes."

Ophelia paused for a moment, and Lawrence was sure she was going to refuse. She leaned back and away from Lawrence. She removed her glasses and pocketed them quickly, but she kept her head turned down. When she turned back to Lawrence, she opened her eyes slowly. Lawrence gasped and pushed herself back further into the cabinet, the sharp prodding of the chain and wood detailing grounding her.

"Your eyes!" she breathed out, horrified and mesmerized at the same time. "Oh my god!"

They shone like starlight and burned like hellfire. So captivating and alluring, the moment Lawrence looked into them, she couldn't tear her own eyes away. She felt the burn in her own pupils, and the sharp sting was like hot pokers and stinging nettles. Hot liquid began to weep from the corner of her eyes, and Ophelia quickly pressed her icy palms over Lawrence's face.

"Stop!" Ophelia cried. "Turn your eyes away!"

Even after her eyes were covered, Lawrence saw a white light. It was only then that she realized the pain she had felt was nothing at all. It had actually been lessening the longer she had stared in Ophelia's eyes.

Taken away from the sight, Lawrence's eyes continued to sting and burn. Ophelia's chest heaved as she dabbed gently at her face. When Lawrence opened her eyes, blinking rapidly, she saw the blood-stained cloth disappear into Ophelia's pocket. She had already replaced the dark glasses over her eyes. The sudden rush of paranoia and awe began to dissipate.

Ophelia monitored her closely, but when Lawrence didn't speak, she stepped forward.

"Lawrence!" she cried. "Ask me whatever you want, and I'll answer it now. I'll be honest with you if you just give me a chance. That's all I ask."

"Honesty?" whispered Lawrence. "You promise me honesty? Why should I trust anything you say?"

Ophelia's jaw ticked, but she straightened her spine.

"It is true. All of it," she began abruptly, her voice deceptively calm. "I was responsible for all those deaths sixty years ago. All the ones from then and now have met their end at my hands. It's not murder."

"What about John?"

Ophelia's face morphed, the delicate brows rising in her genuine confusion. "Who?"

"John Humphries. The man I told you about. The man whose death the detective was investigating."

Ophelia paused for a moment before she gave a quick nod of the head.

"Yes. I killed him not because I needed to, but for my own pleasure. That is the only one I confess any crime for. I would do it again too, if given the chance."

Lawrence covered her face with her hands as hot tears sprang up that stung her sensitive eyes. Her hands began to tremble.

"Do you know what he wanted to do to you? Do you understand?" Ophelia asked, and her voice grew heated. Her hands clenched as she stepped forward, jaw clenched. "I only gave him what he deserved!"

"Oh god," Lawrence whispered.

"How many others do you think he hurt, hm?" Ophelia asked, her voice quick in her excitement. As she sneered, her teeth glistened in the dark. The impressive row of double canines winked in the dim light.

"Do you think you were his first time trying? I doubt it."

As her head tilted, something shifted within Ophelia's appearance. Her demeanor became more savage, and Lawrence felt as if she were stuck in a room with a wild animal. The wolf had shed its sheep skin, but it already had its jaw around her neck. The veil returned over Ophelia's features, settling until the humanity reappeared. She swallowed and turned her head away.

"I am not a monster," Ophelia murmured. "Should I be sorry for something I had no more control over than you? I cannot help that I am this way."

"Innocent lives were taken. If that is not a monster, what is?"

"And you know this?" She asked abruptly, her voice a whip in the quiet room. "They were all faultless and sinless then? Who are *you* to judge *me?*"

She pushed away from Lawrence, showing her back to her.

"Can I help it if I need them to survive? Why must I answer for their lives, but you humans can kill all sorts of animals without the oppressive burden of your morality being questioned at every turn? They're just dumber animals than you all. They've no rights. Certainly, they must not think or feel! Just because God has created life you deem inferior to your own, what consequence is it to you of their souls?"

Ophelia breathed heavily as she spoke, her chest heaving as she threw her arms out. "What are humans to me but worms?"

Lawrence looked around, her eyes straining to adjust to the dark room. She had nothing to protect herself with. She felt her time was coming then, and she'd just be another corpse in the ground, a tick added to the tally of bodies left in *her* wake.

"Even in war," she spat the word out like it was filthy and left a sour taste in her mouth. "Humans kill each other without prejudice in pursuit of their own selfish goals, but God is suddenly all forgiving, then, is He? All those men who faced their own kind and shot them, drove knives through the hearts of strangers on orders of men they've never even seen, will all be welcomed to His kingdom without question." She scoffed.

"I don't want to hear your philosophy about these things," Lawrence murmured. "You killed people I knew. People I cared about."

"I didn't let them suffer," she said, shaking her head as if she abhorred the thought of it. "I'm not cruel. Like I said, I had the same amount of choice in being this way as you did in being born. Why were you born now and not a hundred years from now? Why a human and not a fish? Why a woman and not a man? If you keep asking yourself these questions, you'll drive yourself mad. All we can do is accept who we are and live honestly to the truth of our being."

Ophelia grabbed Lawrence's hand suddenly, and although she had felt her several times over, it still shocked Lawrence how cold she truly was. How lifeless. Lawrence's own little warmth leeched out at the spot where she grabbed her, as if she were pulling out the life from her through that point of contact.

"You can understand that. I know you do. You know what it's like to live in a world that won't accept you for exactly who you are. You can't help but be who you *really* are. I understand you. No one will understand you as I do."

"Are you saying we're alike then?"

"More than any other two beings can be without existing as one," Ophelia said, nodding her head in complete earnestness. She tilted her head. "When you eat your roast beef, did you know the cow that was butchered? No, it was done far away, where you don't have to see the blood and the mess. You don't ever think about it because you don't see it. It'll be just like that."

Lawrence understood her then. They were all just animals, livestock. In the grand hierarchy of the animal kingdom, *she* was something separate, greater. They were simply below whatever she was. Yet, Ophelia was there, opening the door and offering her a place by her side.

"You want me to turn the other way? Allow you to carry on to kill indiscriminately? Despite what you may believe, we are feeling, thinking beings."

"Do you know there are certain humans who believe trees and plants can feel pain?" retorted Ophelia. "They think they are complex in their own ways. Are deer and other mammals villains, then, for eating and grazing on what they must to survive?"

Ophelia breathed in deeply as she wrung her hands together. She looked sideways, as if desperately looking for the right thing to say.

"No, maybe that comparison is unfair. How about the wild animals that maul and attack smaller ones? A lot of them go after the young and weak, especially because they're easier to get at. They're not wrong. Why am I? I only kill what I need to survive. You're only hurt because they're your familiar species."

Ophelia reached toward Lawrence, but she shied away from her touch. Ophelia grimaced, her face contorted in pain.

"I know you are afraid of me," Ophelia murmured. "You're the only human I've shown this part of me. I don't want there to be anything between us. I am telling you how I feel because I cannot bear this any longer, to be so close to you and so far away."

The silence between them stretched on. It created a wide chasm that seemed to grow with each passing moment.

"How old are you exactly?" Lawrence asked. Ophelia only shrugged.

"Did you kill Mr. Sinclair?" she asked, studying her closely.

"No," she answered, shaking her head. "I swear to you."

Ophelia's face remained composed, unyielding. Not a single tic of emotion or betrayal of unconscious reflex showed on her marble-like features. Lawrence let out a low breath. Whatever she had pent up was released then. A hot torrent of tears fell down her face. She exhaled sharply and pushed her palms into the sockets of her eyes as she wept.

Ophelia gingerly pulled Lawrence into her arms, encasing her inside, trapping her. Her arms were steel bars, wrapped in velvety softness. She brought her face down to Lawrence and pressed her soft, cool lips against hers. She whispered to her, repeating the words like an oath.

"Forget all about them. They don't matter, Lawrence. They don't matter," she whispered. "It'll just be you and me in this life now. No one else matters."

She kissed her again, softly. Lawrence felt the sharp tip of a canine, but just as it nicked her, Ophelia drew away. She looked down at Lawrence with a soft smile that nearly took her breath away.

"It will become easier. You'll be surprised at how easy it is."

Ophelia stepped back, pulling Lawrence by the elbow to take her away from there. Lawrence hesitated, looking over her shoulder to the armoire that had remained silent until then. Ophelia caught her hesitance and came to murmur into her ear.

"You don't have to look," she whispered, gently caressing her hair. "Just look away."

Lawrence lowered her eyes and turned her back on the locked cabinet. She let Ophelia guide her away. With a knowing, fearless step, Ophelia led Lawrence through the pitch black hallway. They reached the door, but Ophelia stopped and turned to her a final time.

"Never come back into this room, Lawrence. Promise me." Ophelia's face was hidden in shadow, but Lawrence heard the unspoken dark promise in her words if she disobeyed.

"I promise," she said with a nod that sealed it all.

They emerged from the darkness to the silent corridor. A small part of Lawrence expected to see Ms. Hettle hovering close by, wringing her hands and fretting, but she was nowhere to be found. The small trek to Lawrence's room seemed to stretch for miles. She had made a choice now, and there was no going back. As the door to Ophelia's room closed, so had the previous chapter of her life.

Ophelia was a killer, yes, but not a monster. Not to Lawrence. She had met men more monstrous by leaps and bounds. Surely someone capable of such love could not be a being of evil. So, when Ophelia led her into her own room and pulled Lawrence into her arms, she held onto her like she was her own life preserver.

She felt the power in her arms and felt the solid weight of her body as it lay on top of her. There was something distinctly different, though. Something hollow, like holding a large marble vase against her body instead a being of flesh and blood.

Ophelia had undressed her gently, freeing her of the long skirts and blouse with a fluid ease. Her own slip dress joined them on the floor shortly after. She laid Lawrence down gently within the bed, the black lenses of her specs showing Lawrence her own self exactly as Ophelia saw her.

Ophelia buried her head into Lawrence's warm skin, kissing wherever she could reach first. Whenever Ophelia's sharp canines pricked her skin, a thrill of fear and excitement went through her. Wherever they grazed, the skin raised in bumps and Ophelia's soft lips would follow quickly after, brushing over the same location.

No food nor drink would ever give Lawrence greater pleasure than Ophelia. Her first thoughts when she rose to the last one before she lay her head down to sleep would be of her only. They lay together until dawn came and went with its brightness.

Chapter 18

The long days of summer passed, but Lawrence spent them within the dark. She rarely left the house. There was no need to.

Canary Green sat empty as the days turned to weeks. The usually active doors were closed, and the wide windows were shuttered. There was something unnatural about seeing the grand house shut up in the middle of summer, but the whole air of the estate had changed.

At the start, Lawrence kept to her routine and woke early, alone and cold in her own bed. Even when Ophelia would join her as they went up for the evening, she would always be gone before the early morning hours. With every later hour Lawrence stayed awake to keep Ophelia company, the less daylight she saved for herself.

For a couple days of days here and there, Ophelia would slink away from their bed and disappear without a word. Lawrence slept on her own on those nights, or rather, for as long as she could get herself to sleep. She never asked Ophelia what she was doing or where she was going, because she knew. It didn't matter anyways as Ophelia would always come back, triumphant and energized.

On those nights she would return, Lawrence ignored the sharp tang of iron and death that hung around Ophelia like a heavy cloud. She'd simply turn her head away. Those people were nothing to her. They didn't matter. Ophelia did.

Still, there were more than enough hours still for Lawrence to continue on her portrait. Through it all, she had not forgotten it. For any hour she was not with *her*, she passed in front of her easel.

"You haven't had me sit for you for some weeks now," Ophelia had said in passing one evening. Ophelia had taught her all sorts of games like Senet and chess, which they used to pass the twilight hours. Ophelia traced a hand over the covered easel. "Are you done with it then, my love?"

Lawrence shook her head, exhaling. "Not at all. I can carry on by myself now."

"You don't seem very enthusiastic. Are you unsatisfied?" Lawrence shook her head in response. "Bored then?"

"Not at all," Lawrence said with a smile. "I've just been a little preoccupied as of late."

"Oh, is that so?" Ophelia replied with a wry smile. She sat by Lawrence and intertwined their fingers together. "And with what then?"

"Enjoying. I'm learning to enjoy life. That's my purpose now. I shall enjoy things endlessly until the end, whenever that may be."

So in those early days Lawrence still continued on the portrait on her own, chipping away at it with commendable dedication. She progressed steadily into molding and forming the main figure, adding layers of color and the first highlights. As she continued, the brushes she used grew finer.

Rich, marine blue joined ochre to make the deep satin shadows within Ophelia's beaded dress. Bronze sap and umber outlined the dark background that faded into obscurity behind the brilliant, lustrous seated figure. Lawrence took great care to make each gem in Ophelia's necklace glisten. The rubies in her ears dripped down like fat drops of blood.

It was as if the viewer had entered into a room unknowingly and caught Ophelia unaware. She was seated, but angled slightly with her face pointed out with a serene expression and restrained smile with the corners tilted up. Her usual glasses remained in place even in oil.

Lawrence lit a cigarette and stood at the opposite end of the room in observation. She analyzed her work as a whole and there was no doubting it was *her*. The likeness was there, but she couldn't help the nagging, gnawing feeling that there was something essentially wrong.

She smoked as she stared blankly at her work. She didn't feel the time pass, and didn't notice when someone entered the room to stand behind her. Off instinct alone, she knew it was not Ophelia.

"It's grotesque," a voice murmured lowly.

Lawrence looked sideways. Greta stood a few paces behind, just a step inside the library. Her eyes were blank and steely as they stared at the canvas. A deep cut ran along the edge of her face, irritated and already puckering where it began to scar. Greta's face twisted as she sneered at the portrait.

"Your face," Lawrence pointed out in alarm. "What happened?"

Greta quickly turned away from Lawrence, hiding the cut from view. She remained silent, lips set into a thin line.

"I thought you would have been long gone by now. Yet, you stay."

Lawrence's voice sounded tired even to her. She offered Greta a chair to sit, but she shook their head. She clasped her hands tightly and took a step away from Lawrence.

"I tried," she said. "I didn't even get off the property. Now Hettle keeps an eye on me day and night. Well," she said with a scoff. "As best she can." She stepped forward a bit.

"I suppose you and I are damned. We've both made a deal with the devil the moment we agreed to enter this god-forsaken house."

"I don't know what you're talking about," Lawrence murmured, turning back to face her easel. She quickly lit a cigarette to keep her hands busy. Her head spun and her throat burned in protest.

"Yes, you do," Greta stated plainly. She let out a sigh. "I know what you two do. I know what you are to her. Do you help her with the bodies?"

"Shut up!" Lawrence cried, slapping her hands over her ears. Greta looked at the portrait with unveiled disgust.

"It should be burned to hell, and you both along with it!"

Greta rushed forward like a charging bull, reaching for one of the palette knives on Lawrence's side table. Once Lawrence understood what it was she meant to do, she reacted without thought.

"No!" Lawrence cried in horror, throwing herself between Greta and her work.

She grabbed Greta's arm to keep her from destroying it. Lawrence hung off the limb, slapping wildly in a frantic effort to keep her away. Greta let out a noise of exasperation and pulled Lawrence's hands away. She then dragged her up and around like a rag doll. Greta brought her thick hand down across the side of Lawrence's face, and she fell to the floor in a pitiful pile. Greta had the strength of a mule, and she felt every ounce of it as her vision rattled.

"You're as guilty as she is! Perhaps even more!" She growled. "Maybe all I have to do is get rid of you, and she'll finally leave this place."

Lawrence grabbed the side of her tender face and scrambled back to get out of the cook's reach. Greta stepped forward, as if ready to make do on the threat, but stopped and shook her head in derision.

A noise out in the hall disrupted them. A door opened and closed, and shoes walked across the hallway, echoing through the house. Greta turned back to look down at Lawrence with a final shake her head.

"It's going to eat you alive."

Greta quickly slipped out of the library, but Lawrence stayed at her spot on the floor. The tears that rolled down her face momentarily cooled the tender skin on her cheek. She wiped her tears and pressed her face against the chilled marble side of the fireplace.

When the room stopped spinning and the ringing in her ears abated, Lawrence went straight to the drink cabinet and poured herself a generous glass of wine. She took several healthy gulps until her senses dulled and quieted the din of accusing voices in her mind. Once she had finished that glass, she poured herself another. By the time she had finally drunk enough, she no longer saw Greta's twisted, horrible face spitting at her in venom, and it gave her a small moment of peace.

A cool hand brushed against her temple, brushing away the sweaty tendrils of hair stuck to Lawrence's forehead. Ophelia kneeled by her side, laughing her twinkling laugh.

"Drinking yourself silly out of boredom, are you?"

Lawrence pushed herself up onto her elbows and blinked her eyes open slowly. Her eyes were bleary and she stank of smoke. The stinging red mark across her face had long faded. She sniffed a few times and fell backwards. Ophelia picked up the full ashtray within arm's reach to Lawrence and set it aside.

"It smells like the engine room of a ship in here."

Lawrence remained silent, but Ophelia saw the strange look that crossed her face. She brushed another cool hand across her forehead.

"My love, is something the matter?"

"I don't want to see the servants ever again. Tell them to stay out of the way."

"Did something happen?" Ophelia asked, her voice hardening slightly.

Lawrence shook her head. Ophelia's brows knit together, but she just nodded and let the issue go.

Thereafter, Lawrence never did see them. They must have come up at some point as she noticed the little changes—the bed sheets were changed, glasses were taken out to be cleaned, the fire was made up for the evening. Lawrence saw the little indicators of their existence, but they were absent enough that she could imagine them as the specters living under the floorboards.

Her easel continued to sit, undisturbed, in the library. After determining no real damage had been done, she covered it with the tarp and set the half-finished portrait aside. Lawrence's paints and brushes, cleaned and dried, sat on her little work table, ready for her whenever she decided to return. A fine layer of dust collected over the top as she never did.

Whenever Lawrence did look at the corner of the library where the painting sat in wait, she could never bring herself to walk over and actually do anything to it. She once sat at her stool, but only to stare at the covered canvas. She couldn't even bring herself to look at it.

After a few minutes of simply watching, almost waiting for something under the tarp to come out for her, she abruptly stood and walked away. Even if she did want to work on it, her ability to concentrate and sit still for any length of time grew shorter and shorter.

Lawrence neither worked on it nor put it away out of sight. The painting felt like a living thing, like a caged bird hidden under a blanket being forced into slumber, and it mocked her every day.

* * *

She didn't feel any pinch or shock of pain as she had before. Lawrence opened her eyes and remembered only feeling so incredibly tired. She thought it strange, as she had just been sleeping, but she felt she could rest her head again and sleep another full night's sleep.

A dull throb began to pulse at the side of her neck that grew stronger and stronger until it beat like a drum. She tried to raise her hand to touch it, but her arm refused to move. It felt as if all her limbs were weighed down. Lawrence's whole body felt sluggish, moving slow like she was underwater. Her throat pinched and she smacked her lips together. How badly she wanted a cup of water.

A sniffling, shuddering cry came from within the dark room.

Lawrence used all her strength to turn her head sideways and saw a figure sat on the floor with its back to her. She recognized Ophelia's smooth back and the short hair as she ran a hand through it. Her shoulders continued to shake as she wept. She brought her knees up and shoved the palms of her hands into her eyes.

"Ophelia?" she tried to croak out, but it came out only as a breathy sigh. Nevertheless, Ophelia heard and her head jerked up.

Lawrence felt the warmth of liquid trailing down the side of her body as it wet the blankets below. She smelled the sharp scent of blood all around her until it was all she could smell. With every passing moment, it cooled, but it never quite reached the chilling temperature of her own body. She shivered and her fingers locked up, refusing to move.

Ophelia rose and came closer to Lawrence, bringing her face to hers. With only the hazy candlelight to see and her own consciousness coming in and out, Lawrence wasn't entirely sure if what she was seeing was real or a dream.

Ophelia quickly replaced her glasses on her face and ran the back of her hand across her chin. Dried blood covered Ophelia's mouth and the edges of her lips were downturned as she stared down at Lawrence with something akin to pity or despair.

"What-" Lawrence began to ask, but she stopped. Her throat hurt too much to speak.

"Shh," Ophelia hushed her gently and placed a gentle kiss to the corner of Lawrence's mouth. She brought a damp rag over and placed it against the side of Lawrence's neck. "Go back to sleep, my love."

Ophelia continued to dab at her neck, wiping all over Lawrence's body. Lawrence wanted to sit up and ask why she had been crying. She wanted to drink some water and move her body freely, but she could do none of that. So, she laid back and fell back into sleep as Ophelia washed her and continued to apologize under her breath.

Chapter 19

In the middle of summer, once they had known each other for longer than they had not, Ophelia instructed Lawrence to get ready in her nicest outfit.

True to her promise, Ophelia quietly put in a large order of lace slips and satin dresses. Silk stockings and leather heels, velvet coats and thick wool sweaters, and dresses in every color for every possible occasion appeared in Lawrence's closet.

Whatever clothes Lawrence came to Bar Harbor with, her few dresses and thin coat, were all discarded. She couldn't remember when it had exactly happened, but they were all gone one day. It felt silly, but it felt as if a part of her had been thrown away. However, the first time Lawrence had worn her new chiffon shift dress, Ophelia had cooed and praised how lovely she looked. With each endearment, Lawrence's sadness over her old clothes had lessened until she forgot about it entirely.

The changes continued.

Ophelia took to brushing out Lawrence's long hair that fell to the bottom of her waist. She handled the tresses with such reverent care, it warmed the deepest parts of Lawrence's soul. One particular evening, though, Ophelia held a handful of the hair and observed it with a thoughtful look on her face.

"Your hair is so very long and lovely," she remarked.

Lawrence looked at Ophelia through the reflection of her vanity mirror. Before she could reply, Ophelia opened up a drawer and pulled out large shears. She held them aloft and gestured to the long strands.

"Will you let me?"

"What?" Lawrence said in confusion. Inexplicable panic shot through her. "You want to cut my hair? Why?"

"It just seems so terribly cumbersome to have it so long," replied Ophelia with a shrug. "Besides, it's the style now. You'll look absolutely darling. Don't worry, I know what I'm doing."

"I've never cut my hair before," murmured Lawrence, lost in thought as she stared at her long hair.

A sudden shiver of anxiety speared through her at the thought of losing all of her hair, and she fought the urge to rip herself out of Ophelia's grasp. Ophelia read her expression with pursed lips.

"You don't trust me?"

"It's not that," Lawrence insisted. She stared for a moment longer, but then nodded, reluctant. "I suppose it's just hair."

Ophelia smiled, appeased. "Exactly. Now, relax. It'll be over in a moment."

Without hesitation, Ophelia took up a large chunk of hair and callously cut it off with a few grinding snips. Lawrence's long tresses fell to the ground in piles, gathering in little mounds. Lawrence gripped her shaking hands tightly within her lap and held her breath until it was over.

It felt like a great fur coat had been taken off. Her head felt a few pounds lighter, but her chest tightened with every passing moment. Once it was all over, Lawrence's hair barely reached the bottom of her chin. With the final cut, Lawrence let out a sigh and gave Ophelia a shaky smile. Ophelia, though, didn't notice as she studied her handiwork. She then gave a little nod.

"Much better. "

Ophelia helped pluck Lawrence's eyebrows until they were thin little arches. She painted her lips in dark stain and patted rouge on her soft cheeks. It all felt too much, but with every little change, Ophelia would smile and remark over what an improvement it was. It filled Lawrence with happiness to please Ophelia, but her own chest felt a little hollow.

It wasn't until Lawrence walked down the hall and passed a mirror, did she really see how much she had changed. She nearly shouted in alarm, taken aback by the reflection of the strange, well-dressed woman that had passed by. Lawrence barely recognized herself.

Just like the caterpillars that shed their silky cocoons, or the swans that pluck off the brown fluff of their youth in exchange for white, lustrous feathers, Lawrence felt unlike herself. She was sure it was a passing silliness of hers, just as she had felt sad over her hair and clothes, and she would learn to fill in her new shoes with time.

So when Ophelia instructed Lawrence to dress nicely, she picked one gown out of the many that now sat in her closet. With an unpracticed hand, Lawrence picked out jewels and did her best to mimic the heavy makeup Ophelia had shown her how to do. She waited for Ophelia in the library, sat by the fire to keep warm. Within a few moments after the clock chimed, Ophelia strode into the room in a suit, hands in her pockets.

"My god, what are you wearing?" Lawrence shouted, eyes widening once she saw Ophelia.

She had on men's trousers, a dark vest and tie, and a double-breasted coat that hid her lean, feminine figure under its thick layers. She had a long overcoat draped over one arm with a black Homburg in the other hand.

"How do I look?" she asked, ignoring Lawrence's question.

She lowered the tenor of her voice slightly, and it almost deceived

Lawrence. She knew her so intimately that she knew it could be no one else but Ophelia. To anyone else, though, she would simply be a beautiful, young man. She had even gone so far as to tape a thin, fake mustache over her top lip.

"How do you look?" Lawrence repeated, still taken aback and amazed at the transformation. She stood from where she sat and surveyed her up and down. "Well, let me have a proper look at you."

Ophelia turned, smirking as Lawrence took a turn around her as if she were a prized sow at auction. Lawrence hid her smile behind her hand and chuckled.

"You look like a French aristocrat, or no, you look like Valentino! That's it; you look just like him."

"I'll take the 'Latin Lover' over a Frenchman," Ophelia said languidly as she smoothed down her slicked-back hair. "We should get going, or we'll be late."

"You're going out?"

"*We* are going out to dinner," corrected Ophelia. She quirked an eyebrow up. "You do want to leave this place, don't you?"

"You're taking me out of here?" asked Lawrence, her eyes wide in wonder. Ophelia smiled again, pleased.

"Well you have been very good."

She took a step forward to pull Lawrence by the elbow, but Lawrence dug her heels into the floor. "You can't go out like that! You're wearing pants!"

"Plenty of women wear pants, Lawrence; don't be so old-fashioned," she pouted. "Besides, no one will know I'm a woman unless you tell on me. Let's be a proper couple for once."

"What, just because you want to hold hands out in public you're willing to risk it?"

Ophelia shrugged, but shot her a teasing smile and wink. "I didn't go to these lengths for some hand holding, Lawrence. I expect a little more for my efforts."

Lawrence blushed, but didn't say anything to that. She gestured to the tailored outfit.

"Where did you get these clothes anyways?" she asked.

"You never know when you might need a man's suit, so I keep a few on hand. If you ever care to see what the world looks like through a man's eyes, just say the word. It's quite *enlightening*."

She held her arm out again for Lawrence to take, and led her out to a waiting car on the drive.

There was something exceptionally freeing about being in public with Ophelia in disguise. For the nights they did go out, they went several towns away where no one would know them, and they were just another couple then.

The restaurants they dined in were dark, and none of the workers made a point to linger or ask too many questions. Ophelia paid well, and if it brought any attention to them, it was only that we were to be well taken care of.

Naturally, curious onlookers caught on and a few whispers began to circulate about the young, well-off couple. They were reserved, attractive, and mysterious, which was the perfect fuel for gossip and intrigue.

The mysterious couple would arrive in the evening and sit in the dark corners facing out to the rest of the room. They'd drink the nicest bottle of wine, smoke a little bit, and then leave before anyone could try and get to know them.

'They must be from someplace far away,' said the young people, as they gathered in little groups and tittered away like hens in roost. 'I think the man must be a film star of some kind. He looks so exotic!'

Lawrence might have even been flattered or enjoyed it to some degree if she weren't so nervous about being found out. Whenever she felt eyes tracking their movements, the hair would rise on her arms and she'd fidget in her seat. Ophelia would then place her cool hand over hers and brush her lips across her temple to calm her.

Although Ophelia had no need or desire to eat, Lawrence still did. However, she began to leave more on the plate with every passing day. Lawrence could no longer stomach the sight of meat; one particularly rare, bloody steak sitting in its own bloody juices was the final straw. Food no longer brought Lawrence any joy. She sometimes felt the pang of hunger on her side, but she would let it sit and gnaw at her.

When the excitement of going out to those dinners began to fade, Ophelia invoked Lawrence's excitement once more by bringing her to secret bars and private establishments, hidden away in cellars and private homes from prying eyes. There had once been a time when seeing such things would have made Lawrence's eyes go wide as the doors and shelves were pushed out of the way to reveal dark dens of sin and pleasure.

That was what they did together. Ophelia had promised to show her life, and more importantly, how to enjoy it. To her, life was something to be savored, like a sweet wine or rich chocolate. Once one amusement was drained up or no longer provided any sweetness, the next pleasure was sought out. Willful ignorance and selfish gratification bound everything together and made everything possible.

Yet, there is undoubtedly some consequence to that overindulgence. Just as a tooth rots and decays from sweets, so does the human soul. Lawrence felt her own soul withering at times, but she ignored those sharp pangs of warning and continued on. The days continued on until they began to melt and fuse together, muddied by all the drinking and intoxicating fumes that surrounded them constantly.

When Lawrence contemplated what was to become of her, she could only think of it in relation to Ophelia. Her future was no longer hers alone now, and all avenues, both pleasant and horrible, included them together as a unit. That enough should have given her enough joy, but it was empty. The hollowness within Lawrence persisted until she felt like a wooden doll, going through the movements of life without a clear reason why she was doing them.

Chapter 20

Lawrence added another log to the fire and knelt by it, nearly touching the grate. It should have burned her, but she barely felt its heat. When she continued to tremble, she poured herself a large glass of wine, which did work a bit better and loosened some of the stiff muscles in her legs and back.

She raised her hands up to her blouse and undid the top buttons, fingers trembling as she did. She looked down at her bare torso. There were the old sets of scars along her breast and torso that had gone pale and healed over thicker, but nothing new. She let out a little sigh of relief. Ophelia had made a promise to her and she felt guilty for assuming the worst.

It wasn't in her imagination though. Lawrence felt terrible, and it only seemed to be getting worse. She'd sweat and struggle to breathe from merely standing or walking for a few minutes. Her body ached from the moment she woke, and she only felt reprieve when she finally lay her head down to rest. As of late, she began to struggle to hold onto her cigarettes and her fingers would fumble whenever she went to light them.

The door to the library opened, but she didn't immediately turn. Ophelia had gone out on one of her necessary trips, but Lawrence hadn't expected her to be back so soon. She smiled nonetheless as she felt peace knowing she wouldn't be alone any longer.

"Back already?" she murmured, turning and expecting to see Ophelia. She inhaled sharply as she saw Detective Declan step in.

He tipped his head in greeting, the edge of his thick mustache twitching slightly.

"What are you doing here? Who let you in?" she gasped out, struggling to rise to her feet. He watched her with interest, eyes narrowing.

"You look a bit worse for wear, Ms. Stoner. Late nights?"

"Ms. Aldane isn't home now, you'll have to come back later," she stammered out, swallowing thickly.

She tried to look past the detective's shoulder for Ms. Hettle, or anyone, but saw nothing in the dimly lit corridor.

"That's alright," he replied smoothly. "It's not her I need to see. I'm here for you."

"Me?" she repeated, her voice pitching in surprise.

He nodded, taking a step forward. Lawrence staggered back, grabbing a nearby table as she nearly lost her balance.

"You had the chance to tell me what happened on the night John Humphries went missing," said Detective Declan. "I know everything. I know all about your little trip out to the secret club. I have a witness willing to testify that they saw you with him all night, *drinking*. I also have another strong witness who says they have enough evidence to prove you've had a hand in a number of the other mysterious disappearances and deaths that have been occurring. You're a danger to society, and I'm going to be the one to bring you in."

"What!" she cried, stumbling back further. "That's wrong. I haven't done anything like that. You don't understand, he was hurting me. *He* took me into the alleyway."

"So, you don't deny going to that secret club with Mr. Humphries and drinking?"

"Well, no," she stammered. "That's not the point!"

"Oh yeah?" he said, cutting her off. "Who's to say you're not the one that lured *him* there?"

"What?" she said, taken aback by the very idea of it. "Why on earth would I do that? He's the one who brought me. I didn't even know about that place!"

"You're a stranger from out of town who no one knows or knows anything about. One night, you arrive alone to a restaurant and sit there in wait for quite some time. It's only until Mr. Humphries comes up to you in kindness that you engage and invite him to sit with you. After a few minutes of conversation, you push him to take you to a fun little joint you've heard about."

"No!" she yelled. "None of that is true!"

"It doesn't take a genius to realize that all these deaths hadn't started occurring until you showed up either. If you cooperate and tell the police exactly what you did to all those innocent souls, I will personally vouch for you not to get the chair."

Lawrence paled as the Detective stepped towards her. He wrapped a meaty hand around her forearm.

"Ophelia!" Lawrence yelled out at the top of her voice.

The detective shook her roughly.

"That'll be no use! The cook already told me she's not here."

He pulled her by the arm, dragging her closer to the door. She dug her heels into the ground and tried to pry his hand off, but he stayed latched on. They continued to struggle closer and closer to the door when the detective turned back to her abruptly.

"Quit that! The more you struggle, the harder this will be."

The door to the library quietly opened. Lawrence's eyes widened when she Ophelia slip in, but when she went to call her name, Ophelia raised her finger to her lips. The detective had yet to see her.

"Close your eyes, love," said Ophelia. "Go on."

"What?" Detective Declan turned to look.

348

Lawrence hesitated for a moment, but quickly shut her eyes.

She flinched as a spray of something warm splattered across her side, hitting her across the torso and face. The detective let out a strained groan and a final exhale as his hand momentarily tightened around Lawrence's arm and then fell away. His weight pulled away from Lawrence's side, but she didn't open her eyes. She continued to stand there, waiting.

A cold hand wrapped around Lawrence's neck and a soft bit of cloth wiped across her face. She slowly blinked and looked around the empty room.

Detective Declan was gone.

All that remained of him was his hat, which had fallen onto the floor, and a spray of blood. Lawrence looked down at her hands and saw the bright crimson already beginning to cool across her skin and dress. Her vision grew hazy and she felt bile rise in her throat.

"Ophelia?"

Ophelia picked up the hat from the floor and turned it over in her hands. She smoothly moved to the fireplace and tossed it inside. It crackled before catching fire, pulsing with light as it quickly burned. She turned back to Lawrence with a smile.

Lawrence looked at her in horror. She held up her hands, still covered in blood.

"What did you do?" she asked in a low whisper.

"What are you so upset about?" Ophelia asked with a frown.

She came forward and gathered Lawrence's hands in hers. She placed a gentle kiss on the inside of her palm and licked up some of the blood.

"Ophelia," she breathed out, watching in horror as Ophelia licked up more of the blood with delight.

Ophelia licked her lips as if enjoying the sweetest wine. Lawrence nearly gagged at the sight. Her brows pushed down together as she struggled to speak. Ophelia absentmindedly picked lint off the edge of Lawrence's ruined blouse and caressed her face.

"Come, come," Ophelia said in a gentle, mothering tone. She took a seat on the sofa and patted the space next to her. Lawrence looked around one last time before she stepped forward without a word and joined her.

* * *

They lay together at night, their bodies facing each other atop the soft duvet on Lawrence's bed. They never went to Ophelia's wing, and Lawrence never returned to Ophelia's room, as promised. As Ophelia lay by her side, she removed her glasses, but kept her eyes shut. She had her cold hands over Lawrence's in a gentle grasp.

"Why are you always so cold?" Lawrence asked in a low whisper.

Ophelia remained silent and her body remained still. At last, she answered.

"I don't know."

"Do you feel cold?"

"I don't feel anything."

Lawrence's brows puckered together as she frowned, disturbed by the thought. Whether Ophelia had considered her words when she answered, she wasn't sure. She gulped down the little lump that instantly formed in her throat as tears suddenly pricked at her eyes.

"Have you heard the legend about Te and Hemera?" Lawrence asked, her voice remaining a hair above a whisper.

Ophelia's mouth pressed into a thin line, but she kept her eyes closed and her face neutral.

"That's not going to happen to us," she said. "Don't think like that."

"What *is* going to happen?" Lawrence asked. "I'm going to die—"

"Stop."

"—and I'm going to move on without you. How can I do that?"

Lawrence let out a gasp as her tears fell down the side of her face, running like a waterfall against a cliffside as they soaked her cheek against the pillow.

"How am I supposed to move on without you and leave you behind? You're going to keep living, and you'll never join me on the other side. We'll never move forward together after this life."

"It's not going to happen like that," Ophelia insisted, grabbing Lawrence's hands blindly. "Don't think like that, Lawrence. I'm not going to let you die."

"You can't stop that, Ophelia. It's going to happen."

"Stop it, Lawrence. I'm going to find a way. We will. Together."

Ophelia's voice was fervent in her oath, but Lawrence saw how her jaw had set. The muscles along her throat shifted as she swallowed. She chose not to say anything else. There was no answer to it. Even if Ophelia did have a solution, she didn't know if it was a real one.

Although the thought of dying filled Lawrence with dread, she felt less afraid of it than before. She had once been afraid of being forgotten, unknown, and unloved. That had all changed. For as long as *she* lived, she would not be forgotten. That was clear enough to her.

She couldn't help the gnawing, nagging feeling that there was a greater reason for how dreadful she felt. Whether it was what she suspected or simply because Greta had been right all along, all Lawrence could reconcile was that she was tired. She let out a heavy exhale and shut her eyes.

"I hope there's nothing after this life," Lawrence murmured. "I hope there's nothing. I just want to rest."

"Don't make such vows, Lawrence. You deserve to go to Paradise. If I were any less selfish a being, I would let you go, but I'm not."

Lawrence smiled lightly, knowing Ophelia couldn't see it. She traced her hands across Ophelia's perfect, untouched face.

"I wonder how you'd look old. I'm sure you'd still be lovely. It's odd, I never saw myself dying as an old woman. I suppose I may have some prophetic insight."

Ophelia's mouth twisted.

"Stop thinking about dying, Lawrence," she instructed her in a firm voice. "It's morbid. You're young, and we have all the time to find a way to stop it. I'm not going to continue on without you. If, at the end of this all, there is no way, then that's the end of it. Wherever you go, you'll have to take me with you. The day you die is the day I die. That's all."

Her promise was simple, but sincere. Lawrence felt sure that no two people had ever felt as much for each other as they did. They understood each other better than people understood themselves. She placed her hands on the side of Ophelia's face.

"Will you let me see your eyes again?"

"No, Lawrence."

"I won't look for very long. Please."

Ophelia considered the request for a moment, and let out a little huff. She gradually opened her eyes, and Lawrence stared into their brilliance. The paranoia was not as strong then. She looked into blazing starlight and saw the core of the hottest fire within its depths. She felt dread and delight in equal measure as a rush of euphoria hit her. Lawrence felt as if she saw something like the final light one saw before they died. She stared until she felt the warm liquid seep from the corner of her eyes. Ophelia shut her eyes once more, and Lawrence wiped away the blood herself.

Chapter 21

Rain pelted against the windows and the chill in Ashmore increased tenfold on that dark day. Lawrence lay on a chaise, wrapped tightly in blankets like a mummy. Ophelia had wordlessly carried Lawrence down in her arms. She set her down where she lay and tucked her in tightly, kissing her temple once she was settled.

Ophelia didn't ask if Lawrence wished to play any games or read anything. It seemed she knew Lawrence wasn't up to it. So once Lawrence was set up, Ophelia took a seat by her side and took up a book on her own.

Under the blankets, Lawrence drifted in and out of sleep. Pressure on her chest squeezed like a tight band, making each breath a bit more difficult than the last. She flexed her fingers and toes as best she could, fearful that if she stopped they'd simply freeze up and stop moving altogether.

"My love?"

Lawrence cracked an eye open. Without moving her head, she looked around the room. The fire had burned down and her blankets had been moved. Ophelia's book sat on the table, opened to a different place than where she had been reading earlier. Lawrence hadn't even realized she had fallen asleep, or how much time had passed.

"How long was I asleep?" she asked in a hoarse voice.

Ophelia kneeled by her side and pressed a glass of water against her mouth, tipping in some of the cool liquid. Ophelia studied Lawrence closely with her lips pressed into a thin line. She brushed a thumb under her left eye.

"Not very long," she murmured. "Are you hungry?"

Lawrence shook her head. She had no interest in food at all despite not having eaten for quite some time. She didn't exactly remember when the last time she had eaten been. She asked for more water, drinking the rest of it at once. Ophelia took the empty glass and set it aside.

"I'm still so tired," Lawrence murmured. "Don't you think something's the matter?"

"How do you mean?"

Before Lawrence could answer, Ophelia's head rose, tilting towards the door. After a moment, Lawrence heard the sound of footsteps approaching. They stopped in front of the library doors and gave a couple short knocks. Without waiting, Greta pushed into the room with a silver tray in her hands.

Lawrence's muscles along her shoulders tensed and her heart began to race. Sweat accumulated in her palms, and she turned her head away as Greta came closer. The cook came up to the two sofas and set the tray down on the table.

"Greta, was it?" Ophelia enunciated the cook's name slowly. Her fingers drummed against the sofa in a slow rhythm. "I would have thought you'd have learned to listen to a few basic rules by now."

Greta swallowed, but kept her chin upturned. Her eyes trembled, but she grit her teeth and stood firm with her hands behind her back in deference. She let her scarred face be seen by the two of them.

"Of course not, ma'am," she replied in a saccharine tone. "I wanted to thank you again for the lesson. I won't forget it."

Ophelia remained silent, but the corner of her mouth quirked up quickly. Greta's own lips twitched, but she schooled her expression quickly.

"However, it was such a chilly day with the rain, and our resident artist looks a bit worse for wear."

Her voice was flat as she turned her head to look over to where Lawrence lay. When she saw the state Lawrence was in, she smirked. Lawrence could feel the heat of her gaze on her, but she couldn't turn to face her.

"Just thought a nice cup of tea would help."

"Get back downstairs," Ophelia commanded in an icy tone.

Greta bowed silently with a nod of her head and turned on her heel to go. Lawrence continued to hold her breath until she heard the library door open and close. Ophelia wrapped a gentle arm around her, helping Lawrence up into a sitting position.

"I am sorry about that," Ophelia murmured to her, reaching for the porcelain teapot. "I had given them explicit instructions never to come up here while we were here. *That* one has been a thorn in my side since she got here."

"What happened to her face?" Lawrence asked in a timid voice. Ophelia's brow rose, but she shrugged. "You didn't have anything to do with that, right?"

"Are *you* ever going to tell me what she did to you?" Ophelia asked in return.

Lawrence felt her face pale even further, and Ophelia nodded in confirmation. She then looked to the closed door through which Greta had left with a displeased expression.

"I see."

"Don't be silly," laughed Lawrence weakly.

She tried to lift her cup, but it trembled in her hand. Ophelia took it from her and poured out two glasses. Lawrence thanked her as she took back the cup, holding it between both hands.

Lawrence brought the cup up to her nose. It was something herbal, dark, and aromatic. She hadn't smelled anything like it before, but it was lovely. The cup felt scalding hot between her two icy hands, but feeling the pain was better than feeling nothing at all.

As Lawrence raised the cup to her lips, Ophelia shot up and out of her seat. With a speed Lawrence couldn't register at first, Ophelia came forward and slapped the cup out of her hand. It shattered on the ground with the tea splashing everywhere.

"What are you doing!" Lawrence cried.

Ophelia's face contorted into a strange expression and she spit on the ground. She suddenly gagged, doubling over. She clutched her stomach and let out a low groan. Lawrence reached an arm out towards her, struggling to pull her back to the couch.

"Ophelia?" she cried in despair. "What's happened? Tell me what's wrong!"

Ophelia let out a low exhale that became a groan. She staggered forward and opened the lid of the tea to sniff it. Her brows drew together and she snarled, throwing the pot into the fireplace where it shattered into the flames. Lawrence flinched at the sudden fit of anger.

Ophelia brought her fist down onto the heavy oak table, and a hairline crack immediately went down the center, splitting one of the delicate rose filigree inlaid within. Ophelia turned to Lawrence and held her hand out to her.

"I need you to help me, dear," Ophelia muttered, her voice eerily calm. Lawrence shakily rose and went under her arm to support her. "Help me upstairs, will you? Thank you, my dear."

They rose and Lawrence's knees immediately buckled. Ophelia's weight on her side felt like a column of solid marble. Cold sweat immediately broke out on Lawrence's brow, and she cried out in pain.

"Ophelia, will you please tell me what's happening. Are you sick?"

Lawrence's voice wavered as the two of them stumbled forward, swaying dangerously from side to side. With every passing moment, Ophelia leaned on Lawrence more heavily. Her weight was like an anchor, dragging her down with each step. They reached the foyer, and Ophelia stumbled to her hands and knees.

"Ophelia!"

After a moment, Ophelia pushed herself up and they took each stair slowly. When they reached the top, Ophelia leaned against the banister, breathing heavily and swallowing as if she were about to be sick over the side. Lawrence guided her to the room and laid her on the bed.

Lawrence held Ophelia's hand tightly in hers as a few tears fell. She couldn't say anything as she searched Ophelia's face for some answers. She felt totally helpless. Ophelia had been a constant, a being of complete strength. To see her suddenly so weak shook Lawrence to her core. She brought Ophelia's hand up to her lips and pressed a kiss to the inside of her palm.

"I'm not dying," Ophelia murmured, her voice low and strained. "Don't worry."

"Ophelia, tell me what's happening. I'm going mad here!"

"I have to say," Ophelia gasped out with a sardonic smile. "I didn't think she had it in her. I underestimated her."

"Who?"

"The-the cook," Ophelia mumbled, her eyes shutting. "Poisoned... tea."

With that, Ophelia fell into a deep sleep and it was like keeping vigil over a corpse. Her body grew stiff and still, and reminded Lawrence of the tomb effigies of kings and queens. Ophelia's rigid, bronzed skin seemed to turn gray before her eyes. Lawrence traced her hands over her face, and it felt like cold marble. She was struck by such a dreadful feeling of loss and worry. Although Ophelia had told her not to worry, that was all she could do. She lay down by Ophelia's side and took up one of her hands; she held it closely to her body as she waited.

When Lawrence awoke, she was alone in the room.

A soft indent where Ophelia's body had been was all that was left by her side. She quickly rose and went in search of her. Lawrence covered the entirety of the first floor, but could find no trace of her.

Lawrence headed to the sun room last, stopping before the double doors. She took a deep breath and cracked the door open a fraction. The bright sunlight flooded in, and she flinched away from it.

She stood there for a moment and turned to leave when something just outside caught her eye.

The strong winds from the sea cut into her like tiny razor blades as she stepped out into the garden. Most of the flowering trees and shrubs were now withering away; their petals and needles falling and rotting on the ground. The season was coming to an end.

At the edge of the pond, a small cloud of insects buzzed around the bank. Birds huddled together and landed near something that bobbed along the water. Lawrence took slow steps forward, her feet sinking into the soft mud.

Immediately, the strong, sharp scent of rotting meat and sickly sweet fruit hit her. She smelled rotten eggs and something mustier that had been fermenting in the sun and water. Lawrence gagged and stuck her nose into the corner of her elbow. She coughed a few times, turning away until she spotted what was stuck within the marshy reeds and lily pads. A tangle of dark hair and purple, bloated skin appeared among the algae.

She staggered back with a gasp, falling into the soft dirt on her back and hands.

Greta's body continued to bob up and down in the water, turning slightly with the soft current. Some of the fish and insects had already gotten to her, biting and nibbling at any open patch of skin. The body turned on its side and Lawrence clearly saw what had become of the poor girl. Already her face had puffed up and become mottled, decaying quickly in the water and sun.

Lawrence's breaths came out in short pants. Whenever she tried to inhale, the breath she took exited from her just as quickly until she struggled to breathe at all. She clutched her throat and tore away the top layers of clothing that seemed to choke her relentlessly. Panic clouded her vision and she crawled away from the water, fighting to breathe properly as the edges of her sight began to grow dark.

A warm hand gently rubbed circles on Lawrence's back. When she raised her head, Lawrence saw Ms. Hettle crouching by her side. She continued to pet her softly and breathed deeply in a slow, rhythmic pattern until Lawrence could match it. When her breathing and racing heart finally calmed, Lawrence wiped the tears from her face with the back of her muddy hand. She lay her head against Ms. Hettle's thigh, pressing her forehead into it to ground herself.

"How do you do it?" she asked. Ms. Hettle's face twisted in her misunderstanding, but Lawrence shook her head. "You know what she is."

Ms. Hettle nodded her head once, her face set into a grim expression. She might not have been proud of it, but she had somehow accepted it. Lawrence felt lost, cast adrift in a sea of doubt. Whatever innocence she had falsely managed to preserve had been stripped away the moment she came face-to-face with the reality she had tried so hard to avoid. The hollow space in her side where her soul had been had sprung a leak, and she felt it leaving her.

"How do you deal with it?" she asked again, imploring.

"I haven't really. I'm dealing with it, same as you are," Ms. Hettle replied.

She reached into her dress pockets and produced a small handkerchief for Lawrence to take. Lawrence took it, murmuring her thanks, and dabbed at her face.

"I made my choice, and now, so have you."

"Ms. Hettle," Lawrence said. The old woman turned her face to her, giving her full attention. "Why didn't you tell me?"

The housekeeper hesitated for a moment, but the corners of her lips turned down. She helped Lawrence to her feet, and the two of them huddled together as they stumbled back into the house.

"It wouldn't have mattered," Ms. Hettle said, surprising Lawrence with her candor. She patted Lawrence on the arm. She frowned deeper when she felt how cold Lawrence's skin was. "It's all been about you. It's all been for you. That's all. Come on, let's get you warm."

As they walked together, Lawrence struggled putting one foot in front of the other. Before they walked very far, Lawrence had to stop and catch her breath. The short trek had already winded her. She leaned up against the side of the house.

"I feel a little funny, Ms. Hettle," Lawrence said. She turned sideways to the elderly housekeeper, watching her face for any reaction. "What do you think it could be?"

Ms. Hettle's thin lips settled into a line, but she merely shook her head. Once she brought Lawrence back into the library, she got her situated into her usual place by the fire and quickly disappeared.

When Ophelia reappeared later in the evening, smiling demurely and looking as lovely as ever, Lawrence lowered her head into her hands. Whether Ophelia had any indication of knowing whether Lawrence had found Greta's body or not remained unclear. She came up to Lawrence's side and kissed her slowly.

"What happened to Greta?" Lawrence asked in a low voice.

Ophelia turned sideways and the corners of her lips lifted slightly. Lawrence waited, expecting her to answer, but she never did.

* * *

Lawrence sat before her easel, unsure and shy to be back at her seat after so long away. It felt unnatural. She had a thin blanket wrapped around herself, tucked in like a bird. The cloth covering was puddled on the floor and the canvas stared back at her.

For the first time in weeks, Lawrence rose early. She crept downstairs to the library after the sudden urge to see the portrait hit her. She needed to see what had brought her there in the first place. She could no longer pretend.

Lawrence pushed the blanket off her shoulders and went to her side table. All her brushes and tools had collected a thin layer of dust over the top. With slow hands, she poured out thinner and squeezed out fresh paint onto her tablet. She picked up a wide, coarse brush and dipped it into a taupey, beige color.

With an unprejudiced hand, Lawrence painted over all of Ophelia. She removed her from the painting until only a beige block remained. She buried Ophelia under a new coat of paint, and only she would know the original was there.

Lawrence barely let it sit to dry before she went on to the next brush and picked up the first color. She quickly sketched out Ophelia again, seeing her so clearly in her mind's eye that she wouldn't have needed a model anyways.

She placed the first blocks of paint where her chin would be. Then, her sharp, angled cheeks. Her full lips. Her eyes. Lawrence shut her own as she tried to remember how they looked. No words could describe them. Even her own mind and memory felt unreliable. Nevertheless, she continued on until even through the canvas, she felt the burn of those alien eyes.

Whatever fine dress Ophelia originally wore was removed. All the jewels that crowded her slender neck and the rubies that dangled from her ears were taken out as well. All the little details that distracted, served as a sort of costume to what Ophelia really was, were removed.

When the clock on the mantle chimed, alerting Lawrence that the new day had come, she finally set down her brush. She had no time to fully finish it, but its main subject was mostly done, and that's what mattered most. That awful, irksome feeling that something had been wrong with the original painting finally subsided. Lawrence had finally done justice to Ophelia; she saw then the reality of what Ophelia really was.

Ophelia's nude form appeared to be in motion, emerging from a place of hiding within a secret garden. Just like the snake that slithered out in Eden, Ophelia appeared suddenly, equally as beautiful and captivating as her surroundings.

Her beautiful, unadorned face stared straight ahead; the corners of her lips were pulled up in her usual smirk. Along the edge of her beautiful lips, her double canines poked out, glinting in unseen sunlight. Ophelia's painted eyes glowed even in the dark room, and Lawrence almost felt as if she had painted Ophelia into existence. The eyes glistened with an unnatural, ethereal light. As if Ophelia were a sort of Medusa, Lawrence felt calcified and rooted to the spot as Ophelia's likeness stared back at her. Unfinished, blossoming camellias surrounded her body. The edges of the rough canvas remained bare and raw.

A sudden, overwhelming violence and hatred swelled up within Lawrence and she grabbed the nearest palette knife. She raised her arm up as if to strike at the canvas.

Just as it seemed she would bring her hand down to ruin her work, she stopped.

Lawrence lowered her head, letting the knife drop from her fingers. It hit the rug with a thud and tumbled away. She went to lay down on the rug and waited, waited until she could finally sleep.

Chapter 22

"Come now, Lawrence, get up."

Ophelia stood over Lawrence, peering down at her with a disappointed look. She finished tying her tie and smoothed a hand down the front of her vest.

"I can't," Lawrence said, licking her dry lips.

Lawrence remained in bed, tucked in under several blankets. Her muscles seized up but she continued to shiver. From the moment she woke up that day, she felt a sharp, familiar pain on the right breast, but she hadn't had the chance to look at it. She didn't have to look.

"Don't be silly, Lawrence. You can. Get up now. I'll help you dress," Ophelia said, her jaw ticking slightly as she took in Lawrence's bedridden state. She ran another hand over her slicked-back hair and sighed.

"All you've been doing is lying around and sleeping. When you aren't doing that, you smoke endlessly and drink yourself into a stupor. We haven't gone out for nearly two weeks. Enough!"

"Ophelia," Lawrence gulped. "Please don't be cruel."

Ophelia sighed and set her hands on her hips. She drummed her fingers and bit the inside of her cheek. She took a deep breath in and sat by Lawrence's side.

"I'm sorry, Lawrence. I'm sorry. I know you haven't been feeling well. You're going to feel better soon, though. Don't worry."

Lawrence nodded, her hands gripping the blanket close to herself. Ophelia loosened her tie, settling in. Lawrence let out a grunt and worked to gesture to the bedside table where a little crystal carafe of whiskey sat.

"Would you pour me a glass?" She asked. "It'll warm me, and if you help me dress, I'll be ready to go."

"Really?" Ophelia's face brightened, and she gave Lawrence a disarming smile.

She poured out a healthy glass and helped Lawrence sit up to drink. She then lifted Lawrence to her chair at the vanity, brushing out her short hair and applying makeup like she was her own personal doll. She pushed off Lawrence's nightgown and dressed her quickly, wrapping her in a cocoon fur coat to keep her warm.

Lawrence took a final look at herself in the mirror and was taken slightly aback at her own reflection. Her face had seem to gone a flat, grayish tone and the thin skin revealed the spidery veins right below the surface. The dark bags under her eyes had deepened to a purple and the hollows of her cheeks gave her a skeleton look. Ophelia caught her looking, but the moment they caught each other's gaze, she smiled and placed a gentle kiss to the side of Lawrence's neck.

They arrived to a local restaurant in Derby, keeping to themselves as usual. They were deep into their second bottle of red wine with a full ashtray as they passed the hours waiting. Ophelia had wordlessly placed two tickets on the table by Lawrence's hand and shot her a wink. A traveling theater troupe was passing through the town.

"It's a German one," murmured Ophelia, looking over a thin pamphlet that advertised the troupe. "Why are the Germans always so abysmally sad? Listen to this: 'In this grand, mythological epic by Herr Linden, we follow a fantastic story about love, betrayal, and the dark faces of men. Christina Chessam as soprano plays Gisele, the witch, and Dovid Mendhel as tenor portrays Frederik, the lover.'"

"Sounds quite romantic; what's wrong with it?"

"I have a funny feeling this Gisele girl will not live to see the end of Act Three," murmured Ophelia.

"Don't be so pessimistic." Lawrence tapped her cigarette, flicking away some ash into the tray. She smiled dreamily, eyes half-lidded. "It could have a happy ending."

Ophelia snorted. "I doubt it."

"We'll put a bet on it then."

"I thought you didn't gamble," Ophelia smiled, intrigued. "Very well. What do you have to offer me?"

Lawrence tipped her head back as she thought about what to lay down on the line, but her thoughts were interrupted suddenly as a voice rose up from the table closest to theirs.

"Have you heard the news? It's horrible!"

The feminine voice pitched high, and it was impossible not to listen. Lawrence peered sideways at the table. A young woman and her beau had arrived to the table one over, shrugging off their coats. The woman leaned in close as she greeted her friends, a look of panic across her pretty features.

"Percy and I are leaving as soon as possible. There is something spreading, I'm telling you! There's at least twenty or thirty dead already!"

"My god," said one of the seated men. "I warned you all, didn't I? We're getting another visit from the 'Spanish lady'. It's just what we need."

The man shook his head, grumbling to himself.

"Oh David, don't even joke!" cried another woman.

Lawrence sat still, twisting an emerald ring, gifted to her by Ophelia, around her forefinger. She glanced sideways at Ophelia to assess how she was reacting to the news, but she remained passive as always. She placed her hand on Lawrence's. For once, they were nearly the same temperature.

"Ignore it, Lawrence."

Lawrence quickly ashed her cigarette. She took up her cigarette case and fiddled with it, opening and shutting the metal clasp over and over. Her fingers fumbled over it, and it nearly clattered to the table, but Ophelia swiftly caught it before it could. She then abruptly stood and held her hand out for Lawrence to take.

"Let's go; we will be late."

They traveled to the edge of town where the troupe had set up their caravans and tents. A large crowd had already gathered, and the two of them took their seats at the edge of the crowd, away from the others. The stage was a bit haphazard, built in the morning and expected to be taken down by the next. Stakes were driven deep into the ground, and torches were set up all around the venue and the seats.

The audience waited patiently, the soft murmur of conversation in the background as the red curtains remained tightly drawn. A violin suddenly played, the sharp twang disrupting every conversation. The crowd fell silent. The curtains were wheeled back on a squeaky pulley, and the play began.

Ophelia paid little attention to the play, leaning over regularly into Lawrence's side to whisper and kiss.

"Will you pay attention?" Lawrence whispered with an admonishing smile and a light wave of her hand.

"I *am* paying attention."

Lawrence hushed her, leaning forward to watch the actors on stage. Their costumes were albeit a bit poorly put together, and the makeup was thickly caked on, but their talent was indisputable. Lawrence couldn't remember the last time she had seen a live act, and it completely enthralled her. The crowd laughed and cried along with them. The beautiful love songs entranced Lawrence and made her heart flutter.

In the third and final act, things began to change. Love had been proclaimed, duels fought, and now the tragic heroine was being tied to a pyre in the center of the stage. She sang pitifully about her lover and how glad she would be to reunite with him shortly in the afterlife. Logs were added to the pyre, and the angry townspeople united in the chorus, declaring her a witch and adulterer and condemning her to hell.

"Oh no," Lawrence moaned, frowning as she prepared for Gisele's inevitable end. Ophelia's brow rose and she grunted.

"Predictable."

"It's so tragic," Lawrence murmured, her face twisted in despair.

"Her lover has been killed. What other purpose does she have? She will join him soon, and they will be together again. What could be tragic about that?"

"She doesn't know, though, does she?"

"Know what?"

"If they will be together," Lawrence murmured. "After, I mean. None of us know."

There was a pause as Ophelia considered how to answer. Lawrence felt her eyes on her, even through the dark spectacles. She chose not to reply and instead turned her head away.

On stage, a sudden, great shriek echoed out through the field where they sat. The woman on the pyre wailed pitifully, and the townspeople cheered. With a great whoosh, green flames exploded out across the stage with a large cloud. The flames lined the front and back of the stage, and even torches dotted throughout the crowd erupted with the same emerald fire. The crowd cheered in delight at the fantastic feat of pyrotechnics. Lawrence laughed as well, clapping lightly.

Ophelia rose from her seat with an abrupt gasp, staggering back from the fire as it seemed to be everywhere. She held her arms close to herself, clutching her chest as her mouth fell open into a silent scream. Her chair fell to the ground, and although Lawrence reached for her, she shoved her away and ran off.

"Ophelia?" Lawrence called out after her, but her voice was drowned out by the roaring applause. She abandoned her seat and followed after.

Night had fallen hours earlier, and the troupe had set up in the middle of a field. Lawrence squinted her eyes to see in the dark. She walked further away from the stage and crowd, searching between the dark caravans and tents for any sign of Ophelia. She ducked her head and looked across the flattened field, but saw nothing. The applause continued on behind her, growing fainter as she continued on her search.

Lawrence walked blindly, her eyes roaming back and forth in the dark. She left the campgrounds and went to the edge of the forest, peering into the darkness. She staggered forward, tripping over unseen vines and roots. Every joint protested and her muscles strained the further she exerted herself. She passed a great tree and caught, out of the corner of her eye, a huddled figure against the bark. Lawrence dropped to her knees and caught Ophelia around the shoulders.

"Ophelia!"

Lawrence examined her face, but her covered eyes seemed focused elsewhere.

Ophelia shivered, but not due to cold. She continued to hold herself tightly as she finally seemed to notice that Lawrence was there with her. The sudden drastic change in character, the fear, was unlike her.

"Ophelia, what is the matter? You ran off as if the Devil himself were chasing you."

"Yes," she replied heavily.

She removed the tie around her neck and loosened the top of her shirt, as if it were suffocating to simply wear it. It could have simply been Lawrence's impression, but it felt as if she had aged. She tucked her legs in closer to her body. Lawrence rested her hand on Ophelia's back, rubbing it.

"What happened?"

"I can't-I can't talk about it," muttered Ophelia, shaking her head.

"Tell me," Lawrence implored.

"I was just afraid," she said, taking up one of Lawrence's hands and kissing it affectionately. She gave her a weak smile. "I apologize for abandoning you. I wasn't in my right mind. Will you forgive me?"

"I will forgive you if you tell me why you were so afraid."

"Don't make me talk about it."

Lawrence studied her, wanting to press the issue further, but finally nodded. Ophelia shut her eyes, exhaling slowly as she gathered some strength. She stood from the forest floor, brushing away the dirt and debris that had gathered on her expensive suit. Ophelia grabbed Lawrence's hand and pulled her away, practically dragging her along.

They didn't return to the troupe grounds, instead leaving directly and returning home. Even when they reentered Ashmore, Ophelia continued to pull away from Lawrence. She was quiet for the rest of the evening, thoughtful and detached. They climbed into Lawrence's bed in the early hours, and she pulled Lawrence into her arms, holding her tightly.

In the dark room and the quiet, Ophelia finally spoke.

"I once had a dear friend who was quite like me. He was whatever I am. We had known each other for years, and he was about as close to being family as one could be. His name was Amoun."

Ophelia whispered the name as if she didn't wish for his ghost to overhear. Lawrence was suddenly reminded of the photograph Greta had once brought to her, and she remembered the striking face of the young man that sat next to Ophelia. He had an arrogant smirk in the photo and a confident pose that reminded her a bit of Patrick.

Lawrence turned over in bed and went to the side table. She reached in and pulled out the photo, holding it out for Ophelia. Ophelia looked over once, her brow furrowing when she saw what Lawrence had in her possession, but she didn't ask how she came to have it.

"Is that him?" Lawrence asked, already knowing the answer.

She gestured with her head to the man. Ophelia sighed, and Lawrence watched as her throat moved slightly. She nodded. Ophelia faced the ceiling, speaking upward towards the heavens.

"He was terribly bright, clever, and incredibly foolish. He thought he would live forever and that he was untouchable. He was not, it turns out. The last I ever saw of him, he was burned on a similar pyre to what we saw this evening to the same green flame. I don't think I'll ever forget his screams," Ophelia said, her voice hollow and emotionless. A few errant tears fell down her cheeks, and she shivered.

"Why did they kill him?" Lawrence asked.

"Did they need a reason?"

"Surely they had one," she murmured.

"Men, Lawrence," muttered Ophelia, her tone becoming dark. "Stupid, hypocritical men who act in fear and malice rarely look for a reason. If they do have one, it is usually a stupid one. Men are evil, Lawrence. Maybe you do not understand that fully, but you will come to such conclusions on your own in time."

"Surely not all men, Ophelia," Lawrence whispered. "If he were like you, I imagine they felt he had to die. Is murder not justified in this instance?"

Ophelia froze beside her, and she turned to her slowly.

"Is that all I am still to you then, a murderer?" Lawrence didn't answer. "What they did was not murder; it was something entirely different. The problem with humans is that they only have one word

370

for murder, and all instances of it fall under that one crude word. Context and feelings are not subject to consequence. That's all they care about."

She paused for a moment as she balled her hands into fists.

"What if you were to kill in defense of yourself? A man robbed you, beat you, and put a knife to your throat. When all seemed lost, you then turned the knife on him and killed him. Are you just a murderer too, then? Does that feel fair?"

Even if she were to come up with a clever argument, something to say about the inherent evilness of all murder, Lawrence could not think of one. It felt as if she could never be right against Ophelia. She lowered her eyes.

"That's not this case, though, is it?"

The two of them turned away from each other, saying nothing further on the subject.

"I thought your kind couldn't die," Lawrence murmured, thinking out loud. Her voice echoed in the dark, silent room.

Ophelia turned to look at her, a strange look crossing her face. Her mouth puckered together slightly and her jaw set. She then turned away fully, and that was the end of it.

* * *

Lawrence stood at the foot of the grand staircase at Ashmore. She raised her hands before her face, turning them frontwards and backwards. She didn't feel any pain. She didn't feel cold. She didn't feel anything.

She felt as if she were stuck in a viscous honey, all of her senses muted and dull. The house was dark as usual, but a single light from the second floor beckoned her up. She took each step slowly, passing by the weeping statue on the landing.

Lawrence stood at the intersection of the hallway and looked down the West Hall where the light came from. The tapestry that covered Ophelia's hidden bedroom was pushed aside and the rickety door stood wide open.The soft, glowing light from within appeared to pulse and grow brighter. She stepped forward, floating into the dark as the door silently shut behind her.

She entered Ophelia's room, and it looked much the same as the first time she had discovered it. Now, though, she could clearly see the long box that served as *her* resting place and the dark armoire with its chain. In the casket, loose dirt and flowers were packed in, almost like a sort of mattress.

Lawrence crept forward, looking for anything out of the ordinary. Why had she been called back to this room where she had promised never to return? Her eyes fell on the armoire. This time, though, the chain was unlocked and only loosely tied around. She took a few small steps forward, listening.

She reached out and grasped the fish lock that kept the chain in place. Even as her heavy limbs moved slowly, Lawrence was able to pull out the pin with ease. The heavy chains fell to the floor with a thud, and one of the doors opened slightly. Lawrence reached forward and pushed aside the door. She gasped and staggered back, nearly falling as she saw who lay within.

Patrick's pale, lifeless body lay crammed inside, wrapped up crudely in a dirty tarp and held together with rough ropes. The once-brilliant red scarf he had given Lawrence was dirtied and wrapped around his mouth as a sort of gag. A sudden sob escaped Lawrence and she threw her hand up over her own mouth to stifle her screams.

Long cuts crisscrossed along the bare skin visible on his neck and arms. Dried blood and dark bruises mottled his skin. Although he seemed dead, his chest rose and fell slightly, and short little moans came out muffled behind the scarf. Once the cabinet opened, he inhaled sharply and began to cough. His eyes flew open, darting around wildly, and his head shook.

"Patrick?" Lawrence called to him, but he didn't seem to recognize her.

His pupils flitted back and forth, searching behind Lawrence. The usual spark in his eyes had died. His broad frame seemed uncharacteristically shrunken down.

"What are you doing here?" she whispered. "What has she done to you?"

Lawrence quickly untied the scarf, tossing it aside. She grabbed his hand and held it in hers. His skin was frozen and his fingers were stiff, as if he were already freezing up. He didn't respond to her, but muttered incoherently under his breath.

"Patrick!" she whispered to him urgently, tugging on his arm to pull him from the closet. "I'm going to get you out of here. Can you walk?"

She tried to undo the ropes and pull him out, but he refused to move. She tried shaking him, but he remained unfocused and sedate.

"Patrick," she whined. "Please! You have to help me get you out!"

His eyes widened until all the whites around his pupil were visible. His unfocused gaze sharpened, staring at something directly behind Lawrence. He then struggled feebly against the ropes, but it was no use. He shook his head.

"Lawrence!" he cried out in a hoarse whisper. "Run. Run!"

"What?"

She felt it then. They weren't alone anymore.

Her skin broke out in goosebumps and the hair rose on the back of her neck. A shadow fell across the both of them. As her head turned, she met two bright, glaring eyes staring at her from the dark doorway.

Ophelia took a step forward into the light.

Her teeth were bared like a wild animal and she held her hands out in front of her, the nails seeming to grow into long talons. Her mouth was stained red with blood and a long trail of crimson ran down her front. Lawrence opened her mouth, but no sound came out.

Ophelia let out a low growl and lunged forward.

Lawrence fell backwards in her dream, and it felt as if she fell several stories, but she woke with a start in the safety of her bed. She looked to where Ophelia's side of the bed remained empty.

The pain in her body returned and her stiff joints ached with every slight movement. She felt the chill now deep in her bones and her head pounded. She swallowed through the gritty dryness in her throat, and laid her head back against the cold, sweat-soaked pillows.

Lawrence pushed herself up with a grunt. It wasn't her imagination. The pain could no longer be ignored. With shaking hands, Lawrence reached up to the collar of her nightgown and pushed it down.

She looked down at her bare chest and let out a pained sob. Right at the top of her left breast were four new marks that throbbed, matching the beat of her heart. Something within Lawrence broke, and she wanted nothing more than to lay back down.

Despite that, Lawrence pushed out of bed, stumbling a bit as the blood rushed to her head. The room began to spin, and she grabbed onto the side of the bed as she made her way towards the door. Her feet dragged, sliding forward in a slow, rhythmic thump. Lawrence made her way to the door leading to Ophelia's room. She pulled at the handle, but it refused to budge.

"Open. Must open. Patrick," Lawrence murmured under her breath. "She's got Patrick."

She continued to mutter incomprehensibly, pulling at the locked door.

"Miss?" A soft voice appeared at her side, and she slowly turned to look.

Ms. Hettle grabbed Lawrence's hand and pulled it away from the door. She let out a gasp and rubbed Lawrence's hands together to warm them.

"Oh, Ms. Hettle," Lawrence murmured. "Patrick. He's in there. He's inside. I have to save him."

"Miss," she pleaded, her voice barely above a whisper. She tugged at Lawrence's arm to pull her away, but Lawrence wouldn't let her. She shook her head.

"No, I have to help. He'll die. Let me in."

Ms. Hettle hesitated for a moment, and it seemed she might just turn and leave her there, but she shook her head.

"I can't," she whispered. "I don't have the key. She's already so angry. So angry."

"Please," Lawrence pleaded. She forced her fingers to grab hold of the older woman's hand and grasped her as tightly as she could. "Courage. Courage, Hettle. Please."

Ms. Hettle's head lowered. "I, I can't."

Lawrence let out a sigh and leaned against the wall as she worked to catch her breath. The pounding in her head grew so severe that she barely registered Ms. Hettle's words. Her vision wavered and she licked her dry lips.

"Please," she mumbled.

"She killed Greta," Ms. Hettle whimpered. "I let her take Greta as long as she didn't take me. I let her take my dear Helena. Anybody but me."

Ms. Hettle began to moan and cry, holding her frail hands over her face as she hastily wiped away the tears. Her face settled, and she looked to the locked door behind Lawrence. Her expression changed, and it seemed as if clarity had finally left her.

"Dead," she whispered and lowered her head again. The emotion had leaked away from her voice and a calm, passivity settled over her.

"All dead."

Ms. Hettle raised her head and seemed to realize Lawrence was still with her. She grabbed her by the elbow and brought her towards the stairs.

"Come, we must hurry!" she whispered. "She might come back any moment."

She let Lawrence lean on her all the way down, taking each step slowly as Lawrence grunted with each step. When they arrived to the landing, Lawrence lost her footing and fell to her knees at the foot of the statue.

"Oh!" Ms. Hettle cried out, reaching out to try and help her back up.

"Don't stop," Lawrence murmured under her breath. "Have to go. She's got Patrick. Patrick."

Lawrence continued to mumble incoherently as Ms. Hettle guided her towards the front door. She reached into her pocket and pulled out a ring of keys. With a deft, practiced hand, she unlocked the front door and pulled it open.

"I wish I had never left my sister," Ms. Hettle murmured. "Get far away, miss. Far away where she won't find you."

Lawrence stopped at the threshold and looked back at the housekeeper. She attempted to grab the housekeeper's hand, but succeeded only in swatting at the air in her direction.

"Come with me. Let's go, Ms. Hettle."

Ms. Hettle smiled and patted Lawrence's cheek. "Sweet girl."

She pushed Lawrence out and shut the door after her. Lawrence crossed the patio and stumbled down the long drive. She looked back only once, remembering how she had once seen Ophelia in the window so long ago. She turned and continued on, moving forward.

* * *

Lawrence landed on the front steps of Canary Green. The doors remained shuttered and the windows were dark. She didn't think about any of that, though, as she stopped before the door and brought her hand down against the front.

"She's got him. I have to save him. He's there," she mumbled.

She fell down, unable to stay upright any longer. Lawrence couldn't remember how she even made it there in the first place. She laid her head to rest against the ground, shutting her eyes to rest. A door opened and closed, and footsteps raced around.

"Oh, Eddy! Come quickly! Bring her in at once! Martin, get the fire in the drawing room going! Call Dr. Mordray!"

A pair of strong arms lifted Lawrence from the ground, shifting her in their arms as they carried her inside. She smelled a familiar cologne and aftershave. They settled her down on the sofa, tucking her in tightly under layers of blankets.

Lawrence's eyes fluttered open briefly and she saw an old family portrait above the fireplace. There were two stately figures and a young child: the mother in a black dress and pearls, the father in a well-tailored suit with a firm jaw, and a young boy with a vacant frown. There was something distinctly familiar in the features of the impish young boy.

"He doesn't like to sit for portraits," she muttered under her breath.

"What was that?" a voice asked. "What did she say?"

"I couldn't understand," another responded. "She's been speaking nonsense."

"Oh, Martin, did you call for the doctor?"

When Lawrence woke once more, she had been moved into a room she did not recognize. The door then opened, and although she couldn't turn her head, her eyes shifted sideways.

Augusta stood in the doorway. She was largely unchanged, but grief had left its mark on her permanently and her eyes held a sadness.

Once she spotted that Lawrence was awake, she let out a gasp and rushed forward with a sob.

"LJ!"

She sat by Lawrence's side and leaned forward to pull her into a hug. Lawrence let out a groan, and Augusta let go of her immediately. She set her back down gingerly.

"Oh, dear."

"Is that really you?" Lawrence asked in a hoarse voice.

Tears welled up in Augusta's eyes and she smiled brightly, nodding. She petted Lawrence's head and rubbed her hand down Lawrence's arms.

"Oh, of course it's me LJ. I'm so glad to see you."

"Me too," she whispered in a voice too quiet to be heard.

"Is she awake? Stoner?" A booming voice called out from outside the bedroom.

Augusta twisted in her seat as Patrick burst into the room. Lawrence's breath left her in a rush when she saw her friend standing there before her. He had changed slightly; his hair was a bit shorter and his face a bit thinner, but much of his energy had returned with the time away. He smiled brightly and trotted forward. He came to the other side of the bed and grabbed Lawrence's hand in his. She felt the warmth of his body, and he flinched slightly when he touched her skin.

"Jesus," he muttered. "You're cold as ice, LJ. What the hell's happened to you, Stoner?"

"Pat!" Augusta whispered in an admonishing tone. "Don't say that!"

He ignored her, though, and mussed Lawrence's short hair. "My God, LJ, look at you. I'd have passed you in the street and kept on going. Look what you've done to your hair!"

"You're here," Lawrence murmured. "You're not in the wardrobe. You're alive."

"What?" he asked, chuckling a bit as he patted her hand with his.

His smile faltered a bit as he shared a concerned look with Augusta. When he looked back down at her, he smiled again and patted her on the head.

"What's been going on, Stoner, huh? When you didn't write back, we thought something might have happened."

"Write?" she repeated.

"Yeah, you daffy duck," he said. "We sent letters and postcards, almost every other day! Augusta alone keeps the post service busy, you know."

"Letters," repeated Lawrence in a daze. "You wrote me."

Augusta bit the inside of her cheek and inhaled deeply. She abruptly got up from the bed and busied herself with re-tucking Lawrence in, fussing over her like a concerned mother hen. Patrick stared down at Lawrence, his face settling into a grave expression. He bit the inside of his cheek and took a seat at the edge of the bed.

"Well, Stoner?" he asked with a soft smile. "You look a bit run down, old girl."

"To be honest," said Lawrence, licking her dry lips. "I do feel a bit rotten, Gannaway."

"No kidding?" he laughed. "Cause you look like you've been dragged by the heel from here to Bunker Hill."

Lawrence laughed, but it came out hollow and weak. It dissolved into a coughing fit that racked her entire body. Augusta's eyes widened a bit and she floundered, unsure of how to help. Patrick kept Lawrence steady, his lips thinning into a firm line as he waited for the worst of it to pass. She settled back into the pillows, her breath coming out in a reedy exhale.

"When did you come back?" she asked the two of them. "Why did you come back?"

"Well, lucky for you, we pulled in shortly after you took a dive on the front porch, and well, Augs couldn't stand the west anymore. Besides, there's nothing out there but tumbleweeds and grizzly mountain men with no sense of humor whatsoever. In all honesty, though, it was actually Eddy who insisted we return. Said something about 'moral obligation to vanquishing evil'."

"Lawrence," Augusta interrupted Patrick, looking at her with an imploring look.

"Lawrence?" she repeated with a bemused look. "This must be serious."

"You're leaving with us," Augusta said. "We know the most excellent doctors who've gone to the top schools in the country. They're going to have a look at you, and they're going to make you all better."

Movement by the door caught Lawrence's eye.

"Edwin," Lawrence said.

Patrick and Augusta turned to look at Edwin, who stood in the doorway. He held his hands in his pockets. A light stubble had begun to grow across his sharp jaw, and although he didn't smile, he nodded his head at her. Augusta turned back to her with a watery smile. She cleared her throat lightly and crossed her arms.

"So, that's the end of it. Don't you dare try to say you won't come with us. I won't hear of it." Augusta sniffed delicately and took a handkerchief out of her pocket, dabbing at the corner of her eyes. "I'll be glad to leave this place once and for all. I really am so glad to see you, LJ. Really, so happy."

She suddenly began to cry, but laughed as she did so. "I'm not crying because I'm sad! It's the stupidest thing, really. I just start crying randomly sometimes; I don't understand it."

"Pat, will you take Birdy and get her something to eat? She hasn't had a proper meal all day," said Edwin, stepping further into the room.

"I'm not hungry!" she snapped. She blew her nose, sniffling.

Patrick tapped Augusta on the side of the head. "Come on. I think

I overheard Martin muttering something about a ham."

Augusta gave Lawrence a peck on the cheek and Patrick smiled down at her. Once she and Edwin were alone, the two of them stared at each other in silence. He scuffed his shoe along the floor before he stepped closer to the bed and pulled something out of his pocket: a small bag of herbs identical to the one Mr. Sinclair used to wear around his neck. Lawrence felt a strange sense of relief at seeing it. He hung it directly over where she lay, the pungent smell settling around her like a fog.

"Thank you," she said at last.

His eyes flickered up to her for a moment before darting away. He stuck his hands back into his pockets and paced away from the bed, heading to the windows, where the curtains were still drawn.

"Will you please open them?"

"It's dark out."

"I don't care," she replied. "Please. Open them."

He drew the curtains aside, and Lawrence felt a weight lift from her chest just being able to see the dark sky. The stars above twinkled, blinking like a lighthouse.

"I'm sorry, Lawrence," Edwin said at last. He turned to look at her in sorrow and pulled off his round glasses to run a hand over his face. "I loathe the terms on which we parted ways. I should not have said such things to you. Memories of the things that were said have been plaguing me for the past months. That, among other things."

"I am sorry too, Edwin," Lawrence whispered.

Her throat began to hurt the longer she spoke, and she felt she was approaching her limit. Whether through intuition or his knowledge on these things, Edwin immediately went to the table and poured her a glass of water. He held it up for her and tipped it back slowly as she drank. She nodded her head in thanks.

Edwin stood at her bedside, looking down at her. He settled his hands at his waist as he studied her. His eyes went from her face to her neck, her hands, and then back up to her face. His lips thinned. He disliked what he saw. He held his hand out towards the collar of the nightgown Lawrence had been changed into.

"May I?"

Lawrence gave a subtle nod. Edwin's slim fingers swiftly unbuttoned the top and he peeled it away. With a clinical assessment, he pressed his almost burning hands across a few of the bite marks that littered her skin. Once he was done, he quickly buttoned her top up again and held up Lawrence's stiff arm, feeling her pulse and pressing the skin in several places.

"I'm dying."

Edwin's head remained lowered, and he didn't meet her eye. Lawrence shut her own eyes and smiled ruefully.

"Has she killed many more?" she asked.

"The governor has been made aware of the situation," he replied in a calm, sedate tone. "They'll most likely either put the town into quarantine, or at the very least, put a travel ban on the areas affected by this sudden 'flu.'"

Lawrence nodded. "I deserve it. You tried to warn me, and I didn't listen."

"LJ."

"I knew what she was, and I still loved her," she whispered. "Well, love. I still do. I chose to stay because I wanted to. I wanted her, and I turned a blind eye."

Edwin cleared his throat lightly, and his Adam's apple bobbed when he swallowed.

"It was quite nice," he whispered, as if confessing or confiding to Lawrence. "Not to have to think about it. To not have to worry, constantly. For that little bit of time we were away, I just didn't care. It was selfish, but I did it because I wanted to."

"You're not selfish, Edwin," she said. "You're the least selfish person I know."

"Then, you don't deserve what she's done to you either." At her look of confusion, he continued on in explanation. "I know better than most what she is, and what a danger she poses, but I left anyway. I felt lost and angry when Pa—" he trailed off as the memory of Mr. Sinclair's passing returned, and he ground his knuckle into his thigh. He then shook his head. "—I just wanted to be with my friends, and be without worry. Selfish."

He turned to her with a pensive smile. "So, between the two of us, I am more at fault."

"Have you ever killed something like her?" she asked. Edwin didn't answer, but gave a small shake of his head. "Then there is no fault. She would have just killed you like the rest, and Augusta wouldn't be the same. Neither would Patrick."

Edwin chose not to respond to that, but turned to her with a curious look. "Why did you leave then? What changed?"

"I had a dream," she said. "She got Patrick. I was so sure, so sure it was real. I had do something."

Edwin's brows pulled together and he bit the inside of his cheek. He reached forward and placed his warm hand over hers.

"Thank you," he said in all earnestness, looking into her eyes. "Pa always had the best intuition, and he knew you were a good person."

"I'm not," she argued.

"You made a choice," he said, ignoring her. "You could have stayed. You could have kept your eyes closed to it all, but you didn't. I don't take your love lightly, Lawrence."

Edwin patted her on the arm. "Rest. You'll need to be put on a new diet; red meat, liver, spinach, beans, fruit. All of it to help your body start making fresh blood. We'll need to bind your limbs tightly to encourage blood flow. When you're able to travel, we'll take you far away, Lawrence. I promise."

Lawrence could only smile weakly and nod at Edwin. She didn't believe it was possible, but she liked how hopeful and reassuring her friends were. She had been sequestered away into a dark hole, bleeding inwardly. The bright warmth of friendship had already begun to heal those little fissures. Now, it was simply a question of whether or not it was too late.

Chapter 23

Lawrence remained in bed the first few days after unceremoniously arriving back to Canary Green. Under Edwin's strict orders, her legs and arms were bound tightly in cloth wraps and she was fed small amounts throughout the day.

At first, the changes were imperceptible. Lawrence appreciated the attentive care her friends gave as they nursed her back to health, but it felt like a futile task. Near the end of the week, though, the pounding in her head ceased and she no longer felt the bone-deep ache that had made it difficult to walk. She stayed awake for longer stretches of time, and the ease of her limbs began to return slowly.

She had anticipated for Ophelia to come raging into Canary Green. Lawrence watched through the open window with bated breath, half expecting for it to shatter and for her to sweep in at any moment. But, that never happened. Ophelia never appeared and it seemed as if she weren't simply up the hill, a short walk away. A part of Lawrence hurt at how she had simply left without a trace, but another felt as if a great weight had been lifted off her shoulders.

Once Edwin gave his approval, Augusta had Lawrence wrapped up tightly and brought downstairs. 'For her own health and sanity,' she had argued. So, Lawrence lounged on a long chaise in the sun room, surrounded by every sort of potted plant and bush that could only survive in the controlled heat of the greenhouse. The table close by held her prescribed meals that consisted of different organs, green vegetables, and a sweating, crystal carafe of water. Augusta sat close by, fanning herself as a light sheen of sweat covered her brow and pert nose.

"Did you finish your portrait?" she asked suddenly, turning to look sideways at Lawrence in question. "I realize I hadn't asked."

Lawrence swallowed first, pushing past the lump that formed in her throat. "No."

Augusta gave her a sad smile and nod. She reached over and placed her hand over Lawrence's. "It makes you do crazy things, doesn't it?"

Augusta didn't say what, but Lawrence understood. She lowered her eyes and nodded.

"How are *you*, though, Augusta? Has anyone asked?"

Augusta smiled serenely. "People have only just stopped asking. I was starting to go a bit loony with how careful and cautious the boys were being, treating me like some porcelain doll. Just between the two of us, though, I don't think they understand. They're angels, of course, and I adore them dearly, but they don't understand. Sometimes, I think they believe I'm just a silly little girl that can't handle anything real. It's okay if they think that. I don't mind it really. I wish I was. I lost both my parents when I was young and I've lost the only other family I had. I'm alone now, but I have been for some time."

Lawrence opened her mouth to argue, but Augusta shook her head with a pleasant smile.

"No, don't misunderstand. I know I'm not really alone. What I mean is different. It's hard to describe when there aren't words to explain it. I'm a very lucky girl. I know that. It's awful and wrong how lucky I am." She lowered her voice as if whispering a deadly secret to Lawrence. Her eyes shined and flickered about as if worried some greater power could overhear them. "Sometimes, I think the universe knows just how lucky I am and is just taking back in equal measure. Balance, and whatnot, you know?" She chuckled when she saw the concerned look across Lawrence's face. Augusta patted her friend's hand. "Don't worry, you don't need to be afraid for me. Life is fragile and short, but how wonderful it can be. I haven't quite made my peace with it yet, but I've decided to keep on living. If only to see how it all turns out."

Augusta shot Lawrence a cheeky smile, raising her cup up to her lips. She looked out the window, basking in the sun like a content cat. Lawrence studied her friend and felt a deep warmth of respect and awe filling up within her. She hadn't considered the depth of feeling Augusta could feel, and realized how wrong she had been. She reached out to lay a cool hand over her friends. Augusta perked up and leaned closer with another bright smile.

"Augusta, will you promise me something?"

"Anything, darling. Anything!"

"I haven't finished the painting, but I have worked on it. It's not what it was originally, or what I thought it would be, but it's true. It shows the truth, and if you ever can, I hope you can have it."

"Oh, dear," Augusta said, nodding fervently. "Where is it? I'll cherish it forever."

"It's in there still," Lawrence said, nodding her head back in the general direction of Ashmore. Augusta's lips pursed, knowing already the futile nature of Lawrence's request.

"If you ever find a way to get it. Do. Please. I want you to have it. I trust you. Will you promise me?"

"Oh, LJ," Augusta sighed, tearing up slightly. "Of course. I promise."

"Good, now will you help me up? I think I need to rest."

* * *

The clock on the mantle ticked slowly, each passing second reverberating around the silent room. Edwin leaned against the mantle, watching the clock like a hawk, his eyes flickering every few moments to the door. Augusta in turn watched him, her forehead creasing every so often. She would raise her glass to her lips, only to lower it again. Any moment there was a little noise, or it seemed that the door would open, the three of them would perk up until they realized it was nothing at all.

Lawrence sat on a nearby chaise, propped up with pillows and a throw blanket across her lap. A tray of food sat untouched by her side.

"I'm sure that dolt will be here in a moment, and we'll laugh all about this ridiculousness," Augusta said with an airy, forced laugh, cutting the silence. Her eyes trembled and her hand shook as she brushed a stray curl from her face. "He always does this. He just storms off on his own at all hours of the day. It's quite silly. I've always told him not to do that. I'll be having words with him when he's back. Goodness, look at those clouds coming in. Oh, dear."

Augusta stood and paced over to the windows. True enough, dark clouds gathered in the horizon over the far waters. A clap of thunder boomed and Augusta jumped slightly. She turned and looked to Edwin, who seemed to make a decision in that moment. He strode from his spot by the fireplace and headed to the door.

"Eddy, stop!" Augusta cried. "You can't go on your own. I'm going too."

"Birdy, no," he said. "Stay here with LJ. Pat may return before I'm back. I'm just going to take a quick turn around the block. That's all."

"Edwin Ernest, don't you dare take a step towards that door!"

He immediately froze where he stood. Augusta rushed to Lawrence's side, patting her hand.

"LJ, dear, will you be alright? We're just going to pop out for a moment. Just a moment."

"I'll come with you," she said, moving to push the blanket off of her. Augusta quickly stopped her, tucking her back in.

"Don't be silly! You're still on the mend. We'll be back soon. Two shakes of a lamb's tail! You stay right here!"

"Alright," Lawrence said with a nod, patting Augusta's arm. "Be safe."

The two of them left in a flurry, rushing out the door together. Another clap of thunder, this time closer, boomed outside. The windows rattled slightly and the first drops of rain hit the windows. Lawrence looked out at the dark sea as it began to rain properly. She watched the door for a minute longer, half expecting and half praying for it to open suddenly and for Patrick to come bounding in with his strong walk and cocky smile like a proud rooster.

A terrible thought suddenly struck her, fizzling through her as if *she* had been hit by lightning. Her spine went straight and her breath became rapid. Lawrence quickly moved the blankets aside, pushing herself up from the chaise. She crossed the room and entered the front lobby. Martin appeared at the foot of the stairs and quickly approached.

"Ma'am, you're not meant to be up," he said, keeping up with her as she continued towards the front door. "Ma'am, really. I must insist you let me escort you back to the drawing room. You can't go out there, it's pouring rain!"

Lawrence ignored him, pushing past the front door. She crossed down the gravel drive as the rain began to pick up. Martin continued to call out after her, but she hardly heard it. She only thought for a moment on where she had to go, but her feet moved first.

She headed towards the trail that led up to Widow's Weep.

Lawrence nearly slipped as she reached the trail; the dirt began to turn to mud in the pounding rain. She trudged through as the cold mud caked onto her feet and ankles. She stopped for a moment as she reached the hill. Ashmore Hall rose before her, and her heart clenched at the sight. Lawrence put her head down and continued to trek up. Short locks of hair plastered onto her face and the long dressing gown clung to her frame, weighed down with the weight of the rainwater.

She had neared the top of the cliff when her foot slipped. She staggered, nearly falling sideways down the perilous drop into the water. The side of the trail had been wiped clear, falling off directly into the water. Lawrence's stomach dropped, and she fell to her hands and knees. She crawled over to the edge and looked out over the side. She let out a cry of anguish, dropping her forehead to the earth.

"No!" she cried, slamming her hand down against the grass. "Oh god, no. No!"

She whimpered again, but pushed herself up and went to look again.

There, at the bottom, Patrick lay strewn across the rocks. His face was angled up, but his eyes were closed as if he were merely sleeping. A large gash cut across his face, and parts of his skin were mottled with bruises. His left leg and arm were twisted around awkwardly, bent in an unnatural way. The ocean water crashed against his body, and when it ebbed, his hair and body shifted with the movement.

The world spun, and her mouth went dry. Lawrence doubled over, vomiting into the grass below her. Her hands pulled at the grass as her throat and eyes burned.

"Lawrence!"

She looked over her shoulder, squinting against the pelting rain. Down the trail, Augusta and Edwin rushed forward together, approaching as they fought against the whipping wind and rain. Lawrence shook her head, desperate to make sure they didn't come any closer.

Augusta cried out to her. "What are you doing out here! You'll catch your death!"

They came closer, but slowed once they saw the position she was in. Edwin's face fell. Augusta's eyes widened before she let out a horrified shriek and fell to the ground.

"Oh god," Edwin said.

Even against the crashing waves, the rain, and the distance, Lawrence heard Edwin as clearly as if he were standing next to her. He set his hands on his hips and then ran a hand through his hair. He catapulted his glasses far into the ocean and crouched, pushing his palms into his eyes.

"Shit! Goddammit! No! No!"

He shot up then and stalked off. Edwin went to the closest tree and began to punch it until his bare fist began to crack and bleed. Augusta remained on the ground, nearly catatonic. She continued to stare off at nothing in particular, hands fisting into the sparse grass, as if to keep from floating away.

Lawrence turned away, looking briefly back again at Patrick's body, and then turned further to look up at Ashmore. The lights continued to flicker on the porch, and she felt the familiar tingle across her skin. Even through the covered windows, she felt *her* burning stare.

* * *

The bright, full moon rose high in the clear, cloudless sky. Lawrence stood at the window of her bedroom and tugged down the small sachet of herbs that hung at the top. She tossed it aside and pushed the window open wide. She then took a seat and waited.

Lawrence woke with a start when an icy hand caressed the side of her face. Ophelia stood before her, bent forward with her face close to hers. Lawrence stared at herself in the reflection of Ophelia's glasses. It seemed so strange to see her again. While the time away from each other had been brief, it had felt as long as several months or years.

Lawrence studied Ophelia's face, remembering her features. She inhaled the usual scent that followed around her in a cloud. Her heart raced and weeks of memories of being wrapped up in that scent came to mind. Ophelia smiled down at her, the four sharp fangs glinting at her.

Lawrence had expected for her to be angry, to fly at her in a wild rage. Instead, Ophelia smiled serenely and took a look around the bedroom. She went to the bed, her nose scrunching as she neared and saw the bag of herbs that still hung over where she lay. She turned to Lawrence and pursed her lips, turning away again.

"Are you really so amoral?" Lawrence whispered, watching as she continued to wander around the room. "Do you hold nothing sacred? How could you hurt Patrick? What had he done to deserve this?"

"Patrick." Ophelia repeated the name as if working to remember where she had heard the name before. Her jaw flexed slightly in the flickering light. She paused then and nonchalantly shrugged.

Lawrence dropped her head and covered her mouth with her hand as a cry escaped her. She brushed away her tears as Ophelia dropped into the seat opposite, languidly crossing her legs.

"Now, now, don't cry, love," Ophelia said in a biting tone with a smirk. "Will it make you feel better if I were to tell you he only suffered for as long as he fell?"

"My god, you're sick!" Lawrence yelled. She shook her head and turned away from her.

"Oh, Lawrence, how long will you continue on this charade that you're secretly a very good, pious person who values the sanctity of life? Please." She shook her head as she tilted her chin upward, as if in observation of the ceiling. "You and I are more alike than not. That's why we get along so well."

"We're nothing alike."

"On the contrary," Ophelia said in her smooth, velvety voice. "You were getting so good at ignoring how many people I killed. I did kill quite a lot. It was getting easier, wasn't it? Just as I said."

"Not at all," Lawrence said in a cold tone. "It killed me. It was eating away at me. Every single death."

She looked to Ophelia then, desperately searching her cold, impassive face for some flicker of guilt or remorse.

"Why did you have to eat children?"

The corner of Ophelia's mouth ticked up. "Why do you lot sometimes eat veal? Sometimes, you're just in the mood for it, aren't you?"

"You were wrong," Lawrence said, shaking her head. She turned her head away as she muttered lowly. "You *are* a monster."

Ophelia was there before her in the next moment. It still took her breath away how strong and fast she sometimes could be. She let out a gasp as Ophelia slammed her hand down onto the back of the chair, next to Lawrence's head. The wood cracked and the table nearby trembled a little.

"So, now what? You think you're going to just leave me? Is that it? Where are you going to go, Lawrence?" She laughed drily, amused. "Back to your little hut by the water? Freezing at night and boiling hot during the day? Will you stay there until you starve to death, all *alone?*"

"Stop," Lawrence whispered, fresh tears gathering in her eyes. "Stop being like this."

"When you've decided to stop this silly little game of yours, I'll be waiting. I've entertained this little distraction, but I'm growing tired of it. The longer you wait, the more painful I make your friend's deaths, and you will have no one to blame but yourself. Make your choice, Lawrence, but remember, there is nowhere for you to go where I can't find you."

Ophelia let go of the back of Lawrence's chair and sidled away, breathing heavily as if pulling herself together. She let out a loud exhale as her fists clenched by her side.

"Why did you kill the cat?" Lawrence asked abruptly.

Ophelia's thin eyebrows rose at the abrupt and seemingly random question. For once, she did seem a bit guilty as she lowered her eyes and crossed her slender arms. She didn't have a good answer. No matter how well Ophelia could have reasoned or explained herself away, there would never have been a good answer.

"I thought you had loved me," Lawrence murmured.

"Of course, I love you," Ophelia retorted in an incredulous tone. She shook her head at the mere ridiculousness of the question. "Love doesn't begin to encompass the depth of my feeling for you. A singular, simple word will never suffice. I have waited centuries for you, and I would wait several more. I have no answers for what I am or what will become of me, but I know that when I saw you there for the first time, I felt again. This cold, useless organ in my chest fluttered, and there is nothing on this earth I wouldn't do to preserve that. A few trifling humans will not interfere. So, if its an apology you want, then fine. I do apologize. I apologize for how I've hurt you. I'll even apologize for killing your friends and the damned cat. I've taken for granted how deeply it'd affect you. I promise, I'll let you develop friendships in New York."

"How very bighearted of you," Lawrence muttered. She shook her head, calmly and more poised than she felt. "You'd never let that happen. You've isolated me in every way. Every person I've come close to, let in to my life in any way, has met their end."

"Hmm," Ophelia nodded. "An interesting pattern, yes."

She began to count off her fingers. "The diner girl, the cat, the pig, the detective, the old man, the cook, and now this young man."

"What?" Lawrence raised her head with wide eyes. "The old man? What are you talking about?"

Ophelia remained silent, but leveled her with a look. The corner of her mouth quirked up for a second, but she schooled her expression within the next. Lawrence felt her heart shrivel up, and whatever small bit of warm feeling she had left for Ophelia seemed to leak from her. Its exit was painful, though, and she dropped her head down. She couldn't bear to look at her. Ophelia sighed.

"I'll be waiting for you. Don't take too long, love."

Ophelia approached the window.

"I never thought it'd be me," Lawrence whispered. Ophelia froze at the window, ready to depart. Her fingers, which usually tapped against her arm went still. She faced the wall, but Lawrence knew her full attention was on her. "That was foolish. *I* was foolish. Of course I was next. That's only natural, isn't it? That's all you know how to do. To consume. You just consume until there's nothing left. Then, you move on."

Ophelia's head tilted toward her slowly, like a jungle cat turning to face its victim. Her expression shifted slightly, but Lawrence felt her skin prickle again. She seemed to study Lawrence, looking at her face properly. It seemed as if she were finally taking her seriously. The room somehow felt as if it got colder, and she took a step forward.

"You're wrong, my love," she said, strolling forward until she reached Lawrence's chair. She slowly lowered herself once more until she kneeled before Lawrence, and gave her a benign smile. She pushed away some of the stray hair from Lawrence's face, and brushed a cold finger against her temple.

"You're entirely wrong to think I'd let you go to death. Don't ever worry about that."

She rose then and left Lawrence, disappearing from the room and bringing the darkness with her. A heaviness lifted, and it seemed as if the lights that had been forced into dimness were now able to shine to their full strength. Lawrence let out a loud breath as fresh tears fell from her eyes.

Chapter 24

The moon made its descent and in turn, the sun rose, bringing forth a dusky dawn. Lawrence remained in her seat by the window, looking out at the coast. She knew what she had to do, and knew it very likely that she would die.

It sounded brave, accepting her fate and going forward into the unknown with some measure of calm, but she *was* afraid. She could not accept it so easily, and secretly wished she could live a little longer. Everything within her screamed to simply leave and run far away. She felt such great terror at her impending death. She hadn't lived nearly as fully as she wanted to, but she had forfeited all rights to that.

The paths of life that had once lain out before her, with all its twists and turns, openings and new opportunities, were now closing up and becoming dark before her eyes. Not so long ago, she may have regretted that deeply and felt bitter about the truth of it; but, she knew what she had to do. Mr. Sinclair had been right all along. She hadn't gone out looking for it, but purpose had come and found her. Although it was late, no one would suffer further from Ophelia's hand. If even one life was saved, that would make it worthy.

A short conversation she had once had with Ophelia came to mind in those hours of silent contemplation. It was a short conversation, one of the hundreds or thousands they had, but she remembered it as clearly as if they had just had it. They were sitting together under the green gazebo at the earliest hours of the morning as they drank and shared a cigarette.

Ophelia took a drag and handed the lit cigarette back to her, their fingers brushing lightly as she passed it off. She exhaled. "There's no point discussing it."

"Of course there's a point!" Lawrence cried.

"Why?"

"All lives have a purpose. They must. It is up to the individual, though, to determine what that is. Although it will vary from person to person, one's purpose is no greater than another's." Lawrence shook her head as she spoke, deeply impassioned by the idea. "Only dim or shallow people have no interest in determining their life's purpose."

Ophelia let out a snort, turning her head skywards to the dark heavens.

"Philosophers waste away their lives sitting on rocks with their eyes turned upward," she sighed, taking the cigarette back. "What was the point of their living then if they never actually participated in their own lives? They simply commented on others."

"That is their purpose, then."

"Not everything has to have a meaning, Lawrence," Ophelia replied with a heavy voice. "It might simply be that humans are beings with the unfortunate ability of awareness. That, along with thumbs, has given them the misguided notion that they are somehow better and therefore must have some higher purpose. The reality might simply be that they are just beings that came to be, and they will one day no longer be. That might also be a possibility, too."

"That's too horrifying to consider, I think," Lawrence murmured.

No doubt she had frowned, upset at the idea, because Ophelia then laughed. She pulled Lawrence to her and kissed her, holding her hand and placing another gentle kiss on her knuckles.

"What would my purpose be then, do you think?" Ophelia had asked her suddenly.

"If I don't know my purpose for being, I doubt I'd know yours," Lawrence said, laughing.

"Exactly," she murmured. "For something that will never die, that is the epitome of all that is wicked and unholy, what must my purpose be?"

"You're not wicked, though, surely?" Lawrence argued. "You're simply living."

A passing look of pride and contentment crossed Ophelia's features for a moment. She then shrugged nonchalantly, as if it were just one of many possible theories.

"You know there are some worms that live in the guts of animals and feed off of what they eat until the animal dies? They're parasites. Their whole existence is just pain and misery brought to the being of another creature. They can't help it, though. It's simply what they are. Perhaps that's what my purpose is, then. For all that is good and right, I am the counterbalance. I keep people from getting too comfortable. I'm the reason they lock their doors at night and keep their children from wandering too far."

"You're not like that, though," Lawrence said with a vehement shake of her head. "You can't think that, really. Surely, you could do something positive with your long life."

"Perhaps," she murmured. "Although, why should a salmon swim with the current when its instinct tells it to go upstream?"

Lawrence laughed again then. "You simply know too much about nature, and I don't know enough. I can't tell if everything you're saying is real or not."

Ophelia smiled, and the tips of her sharp teeth poked out under her crimson lips. "It's real."

Lawrence understood her better now.

Only arrogant, troubled souls waste their entire lives searching for the truth that will inevitably never become available to them. They will waste their hours, days, and weeks pining for their youth and innocence as they are fixated on their mirrors, watching for every graying hair and wrinkle that appears on their brow. It was simply better to be. Those who didn't dwell on these silly questions were all better off. One ought to simply live as one saw fit to do, and that itself was the fulfillment of purpose.

Lawrence had fixated too much of her short life on legacy and greatness. She let fears and trivial heartbreaks dictate too much of her choices. She had been too afraid of dying, unaware of what lay beyond. What memory or influence could she leave that would not inevitably be forgotten about? If she were dead and nothing was promised after, it would not matter much anyway.

True cruelty was just to be alive and aware of it, only then to have it be taken away.

Ophelia had promised that she would not let her die. She would find a way for them to be together forever, frozen in time as the rest of the world continued to move forward. There were no doubt thousands, maybe hundreds of thousands or millions of souls whose lives Ophelia had taken in order to survive. Lawrence could not fathom living in such a way.

Although they had not known each other for very long, and in the full span of Ophelia's existence, it was a laughably small blip, Lawrence felt that she knew Ophelia wholly, and only a few passing words could not do her justice.

Ophelia was wild and impetuous, like the dark waters and crashing waves against the cliffside. At the same length, she was cool and calculating, moving slowly and only striking at the precisely right moment. She was just like the snakes that slowly wrapped themselves around their victims as they squeezed the life out of them. Lawrence, though, also knew how brilliant and warm Ophelia was capable of being. She was a being full of yearning and affection, but also capable of incredible cruelty. How lonely she must have been for centuries, walking through the world on her own and being forced to remain in the shadows.

From her window, Lawrence watched as Edwin left and returned on his morning run. She rose from her seat, her joints popping with the movement. She wrapped a thin shawl around her shoulders and went down to the library. A servant making up the fire quickly stood when Lawrence entered. She curtsied and gathered up her tools and coal bucket, ducking out of the room. Lawrence went directly to the wall and pulled on the shelf, revealing the short corridor that led to Edwin's study.

Edwin sat at his desk, hunched over as he finished running a towel over his damp hair. A book lay open on the desk that he read while he did so. He turned to look at her once she entered, but only nodded. She sat on the short sofa in the same spot where Mr. Sinclair had sat that morning she had eavesdropped on their conversation.

"You run outside?" Lawrence asked. "What's the point of that, I wonder?"

"There are some studies that say it's quite good for your health," he explained. "Gets the blood pumping. I enjoy it. Helps me clear my head."

Lawrence took one of the cigarettes off the table and worked to light it. Her fingers fumbled with the lighter until Edwin came over and gently took it from her, lighting her cigarette with a steady hand. She nodded her thanks.

"Perhaps one day everyone will be running outside together like a pack of gazelles."

Edwin chuckled as he went to the dying fire and used the fire poker to prod at it, bringing it back to life. He then took the seat opposite to Lawrence, crossing his thin legs. He had a forlorn expression and puffed eyes.

"How is Augusta?" she asked at last. He inhaled deeply as his eyes squinted and he swallowed thickly.

"Sleeping now," he replied in a hoarse voice. "Hopefully."

"And you?"

At that, he shrugged. She offered the cigarette to him, and he took it. He inhaled sharply and quickly wiped his red-rimmed eyes as a few errant tears fell. His hand trembled a bit as he raised the cigarette to his lips.

"You were always right," Lawrence said flatly.

He didn't react at all; in fact, it seemed to hurt Edwin to hear her admit that. She picked at some dry skin on her lip until she tasted the coppery tang of blood fill her mouth. She continued.

"I found out shortly after the party what she was, and I didn't care. I believed her when she told me she didn't kill Pa. I knew she killed, though. She even killed in front of me, and I chose to stay anyway. I chose to turn my head away from the horribleness and pretended it wasn't happening. I didn't want to believe it was real because I—" she paused for a moment as she exhaled and held her arms over her chest, as if hugging herself. "—I love her. I love her so much. Even now."

She bowed her head and spoke as if in confession. He listened quietly like a priest, without any judgment. Lawrence shook her head, holding her hands out in front of her.

"What would you do? If it were Augusta?"

"I'm sure I'd be sitting where you are now," he said quietly.

"I'm going to kill her," she admitted in a low whisper.

His expression remained thoughtful as he looked up towards the ceiling. He didn't jump to stop her or yell at how ridiculous an idea it was. He understood, perhaps better than anyone else could.

"She's expecting me back," Lawrence explained. "I'm the only one who can get close to her. If only you tell me how to do it, I will."

"I would if I could," he said. "There's no definitive answer to what will work. Besides, you're still far too weak. You're certainly not going on your own. No, I will go. This is something I'm meant to do. I've prepared my whole life for it, after all."

"She'll kill you."

He nodded, calm and accepting the fact of it. "Most likely. I will be surprised if I live."

Lawrence shook her head vehemently.

"You can't," she said. "You can't do that to Augusta. Not after what happened to her grandfather, and now Patrick? She'll not survive if she loses you too!"

"And you think it will be any easier for her to lose you?" he asked in a serious voice. He studied her, incredulous at how little she valued her own importance.

"You can't seriously compare the two of us and what we mean to her, can you," she argued. "You can't go after her yourself, Edwin. You will fail, and you will die. And it will be for nothing."

He smiled sadly, shrugging as if to say there is no other way. The two of them fell into silence. Lawrence licked her dry lips, leaning to the side as she looked around the small study.

"Do you have poison?"

"Poison will do very little against her, I'm afraid."

"It will slow her down, though." He looked to her with a curious, inquiring expression, but she merely shook her head. "Trust me. I saw."

He eyed her with a bit of interest, but nodded his head once. He abruptly rose from his seat and went to a cabinet, undoing the complex lock with a practiced, deft hand. Inside, dozens upon dozens of small vials and bottles stood lined up in immaculate rows. He began to pick them up, reading the labels in search of something in particular.

"Something tasteless, if possible. Otherwise, she'll know."

He nodded mutely and continued to search. He pulled out a small vial and held it up, shaking it before he set it on the coffee table.

"Odorless, tasteless, painless, but strong. It may only slow her down, but that can kill a hundred men, easily."

Lawrence picked up the small vial and studied it, rereading the complex name before she set it back down. The glass fit neatly within the palm of her hand, and would be easy to conceal.

"Good. What makes a green flame?" she then asked.

His head cocked to the side with a curious expression.

"I beg your pardon?"

"What would cause a flame to burn green instead of the regular red and orange? Is it a specific sort of wood, maybe?"

Edwin thought for a moment, tilting his head upwards and closing his eyes as if searching through an unseen archive within his mind.

"Copper sulfate? Boric acid? When I was a boy, we'd sometimes sprinkle borax over the fire for fun. Not very strong, but it made a pretty green color."

Lawrence chewed on her lip as she thought. She had no way of knowing if that would be enough. Would she need to recreate the exact fire the theater troupe had created? Edwin immediately sensed how important this particular detail was, and he leaned in as he returned to his seat.

"The copper won't necessarily burn on its own, but will burn brighter and perhaps even stronger if we introduce some accelerant and light that first." He ran a nail across the inside of his fingers as he thought. "Why?"

"We went to see a play one night," she explained. "A traveling troupe had put on a German play, a romantic tragedy." Lawrence scoffed lightly as she shook her head.

"Anyway, in the third act, the woman was burned at the stake. All around us and on the stage, green flames lit up. It was actually quite spectacular. Ophelia ran off suddenly into the woods like a frightened deer."

"A green flame?"

She nodded her head. "She said a friend of hers was killed in a similar way."

"A friend?" he repeated, interested. A calculating gleam entered his eye as he adopted his assessing, academic demeanor. Lawrence nodded once more.

"Just like her."

His eyes narrowed imperceptibly, and he suddenly rose from his seat. He grabbed a book from the shelf, flipping through it quickly. He developed a thoughtful look, as if he had never even considered this possibility.

"It all has to go. All of it. It's the only way," she murmured.

"Better safe than sorry," he agreed.

Edwin seemed to realize what he was saying and set the book aside. He sat by Lawrence and clasped his hands together in his lap. He struggled a bit, but smiled tightly and clasped his hands together. He ran a hand down the short stubble on his jaw and chuckled.

"Patrick had you all figured out from the start. He told me, 'That LJ girl is a real American. Poor as dirt with no family or name to rely on. Yet, she perseveres. She's a good egg, but she's lonely. I've only ever seen such lonely eyes in your face, Eddy boy. What can we do for her, do you suppose?'"

Lawrence chuckled softly. "He mentioned something about taking me under his wing when we first met. I suppose he liked to collect broken things in an effort to fix them."

Edwin immediately shook his head, disagreeing. "Not broken. Patrick never pretended to be anything he wasn't. He admired you greatly for your courage and genuine spirit. And, he understood what a lonely endeavor living can be."

A fresh, unexpected wave of tears rose up from within Lawrence, and they streamed down her face before she had a chance to wipe them away. No matter how quickly she dashed them away, fresh ones continued to fall. Edwin watched for a silent moment before he reached forward, offering her his handkerchief. She thanked him silently and dabbed at her eyes.

"I'm awful," she murmured. "I'm evil for what I've done, or what I didn't do."

"What's that?"

"I stood by, and let all those people die. First Teresa, the detective, Greta, Mr. Sinclair, and now Patrick. She did all those things, yet a part of me still loves her. Is that not evil?"

"I would think in spite of loving her, you're choosing to do something about it. That's not evil." He scoffed and crossed his arms in front of his chest. He pressed his new pair glasses up, as they had slid down his nose. "I've seen plenty of evil, LJ, and you, quite frankly, don't come close."

Lawrence opened her mouth to argue, but he shook his hand. He then placed it across his chest.

"You had asked me what I'd do if it were Augusta, and I were in your place. Of course, I'd like to think I'd be doing what you're doing now, but I don't know. I can't even imagine it, thinking I'd do the right thing. I might have done nothing too."

"I pray you never need find out," whispered Lawrence.

"Thank you."

In the library, a door opened and a few soft footfalls approached the study. In the next moment, Augusta appeared at the doorway to the study and looked between the two of them. Her brilliant hair stuck out in tangled curls. Her red, swollen eyes continued to water, and she looked dead on her feet. She saw Lawrence's face then and turned to Edwin sharply.

"You've been making her cry? What did you say, Eddy?"

"No, Birdy. We've just been talking is all. That's all, really," he replied immediately, rising as she entered. He gestured for her to sit, but she continued to stay where she stood.

"Talking about what?" she asked in a suspicious voice.

Lawrence looked to Edwin, letting him decide if he wanted to tell her. Edwin smiled gently at Augusta and stood before her. He brushed a hand down her wild hair and placed a gentle hand on her shoulder.

"LJ needs our help with something. Maybe you can help her, Birdy."

"Oh?" She looked to Lawrence with wide, expectant eyes. "Of course we'd help you, darling."

Lawrence looked at Augusta as she felt affection bloom in her chest. She would never be able to repay the kindness. Even if she were to live another hundred years, she felt it would never be fully repaid. She smiled sadly.

"You don't even know what it is I'm going to ask you."

"Does it matter?" She grabbed Lawrence's hands in her own and leveled her with an earnest look. "You're not going to do something silly like try to leave us, are you?"

Lawrence felt the hot prick of tears at the corner of her eyes, and to keep them from falling, she laughed and pulled Augusta in for a hug.

"Thank you, Auggie."

"For what?"

"I don't know, caring, I suppose."

"LJ here will be joining us once we leave here," Edwin said definitively.

Augusta's eyes brightened for the first time in what seemed like years, and she smiled.

"I've told her we're amenable. What do you think, Birdy?"

"Anywhere!" she said, nodding in agreement. She turned to Lawrence. "Where do you want to go?"

Lawrence knew she wasn't going anywhere, but she smiled anyway. She pretended to think and then shrugged. "I don't know. How's New York?"

"It's nice," commented Edwin with a nod of his head.

"That's settled then, off to New York!" said Augusta with a clap of her hands. She became re-energized as she had something new to focus her energies towards. "I'll have to discuss with Martin about getting the house shut for good. I can't bear to be here. Perhaps we just sell it. Anyways, that's a thought for another day. We'll have to pack, and decide where to stay. Oh, goodness."

Augusta continued to speak, more to herself, about all the preparations that had to be done for their trip to New York. She paced and turned, leaving the study to get started immediately. Edwin watched her go with an amused look, turning back to Lawrence with a somber expression.

"You could leave her?" Lawrence asked quietly. "She expects both of us to leave with her."

"I will have an easier time knowing you'll be with her," he admitted.

He turned his back for a moment, and Lawrence took the opportunity to reach down and pick up the vial from the table. She slipped it into her pocket before he turned back. Edwin looked back at her with a polite smile, unaware of what she had done.

"It all could have been different, in another life."

"In another life," she said, nodding.

Lawrence stepped out of the library and Augusta stood in the hallway talking to Martin. They both glanced over briefly once

Lawrence appeared. Augusta finished her instructions and Martin nodded briefly, glancing over the young woman in tender concern before he turned to carry out his orders.

"You really shouldn't be up," Augusta chided Lawrence lightly, looping their arms together. She dabbed at her nose. "You must promise you'll stay in bed for the rest of the day."

She escorted Lawrence back to her room, and when they stood in front of the door together, Lawrence turned to her suddenly. Augusta studied her face like a small child trying to decipher the mood of their parents. She grabbed Augusta's hand in hers and rubbed them affectionately.

"You've been a wonderful friend, Auggie. The best. You will live a life full of ups and downs, and I know it will be a long one. You will grow beautiful and old. You're going to have so many beautiful little wrinkles and lovely gray hair, and you're not going to die until you've lived a full and wonderful life, and you've had enough of being alive. Do you understand me? Maybe in our next lives, we will meet again. Otherwise, if there is another side, I'll be there to greet you as you greeted me when I first came here."

"Lawrence!" Augusta cried, throwing her hands up to the sides of her head. She shook her head as if she refused to listen. "Stop talking like that! We're not saying goodbye, at least not for a long, long time. Now, you're growing old *with* me. We're all going to go away together. Let's go far away. We can live in a chateau in the mountains. I'm dead tired of the sea. I hate it! Let's never look at the sea again for as long as we live. We'll have a lovely house far away in the mountains where we'll be together, just us four. We'll bring Patrick's ashes up with us. He always wanted to live somewhere crazy. He told me once. Think of how lovely the mornings will be in the mountains. No one will bother us there. We'll do that, won't we?"

She gripped Lawrence's hands tightly, and her lip quivered as she looked to Lawrence with so much hope. Lawrence couldn't help but nod.

"Of course, of course," she said with a smile.

Lawrence brushed a stray hair off Augusta's shoulder. Lawrence gave Augusta a final kiss on the cheek and went into her room.

She lay her head down to rest for a short while. From where she lay, Lawrence watched the bright, clear day pass outside. The wispy, thin clouds drifted by, and a sudden gust of wind rattled the thin pane of glass in the window. The first cold winds of fall had arrived.

Perhaps she should have done more in those final hours, but she could not think of what would be worth doing. By then, the time had come to move on, and she had lost the hours anyway.

Once evening arrived, Lawrence went down the stairs. She immediately heard Augusta's voice carry through the halls.

"What do you mean? You aren't going anywhere!"

"I'm just going to step out for a moment," Edwin's softer voice replied. "Just a moment, really, Birdy. Don't worry."

"No!" she cried. Lawrence heard Augusta's voice waver slightly as panic crept in. "You can't leave, Eddy. Don't you dare think of leaving!"

"Birdy, don't cry," he said in a soft, cajoling voice. "Come here."

Lawrence passed through the hall with soft, soundless steps. She reached the front door and placed a hand on the doorknob. A throat cleared itself lightly behind her, and when she turned, she saw Martin a few feet away with a tray in hand.

They shared a silent look, and Lawrence nodded her head. He seemed to somehow understand, and bowed back to her.

Lawrence slipped out into the cool, evening air and left Canary Green for the final time.

Chapter 25

Lawrence stopped at the midway point between Canary Green and Ashmore. She looked out at the trail she often walked, and the exact place where she had found Patrick's body over the edge. When she saw Ashmore again, it was almost like returning home in a strange way. It stood before her like a mountain, dark and colossal against the blue-blackening sky. A bright, wide moon rose above, illuminating the roof tiles and brown-red brick.

There was a strange quiet to the area that felt unnatural. She didn't hear the usual chirping bugs or crashing waves against the rocks beyond. All Lawrence could hear was the crunch of her shoes against the gravel and her own heavy breaths. The nights had grown just cool enough that a faint puff of breath appeared as she exhaled, fading in a moment on the faint breeze.

She let herself into the dark house. She peered into the dark recesses and hallways, as if waiting for Ophelia to pop out at any moment. Even for Ashmore, it was unnaturally quiet.

As soon as she fully stepped in, the front door slammed shut.

Lawrence whirled around and saw a slender hand across the door; the connecting arm and the rest of Ophelia's body remained obscured in shadow.

"Welcome home."

"Ophelia."

When Lawrence stepped back, treading carefully, Ophelia matched her pace. Each of her steps mirrored Lawrence's. As Ophelia stepped into the first small pool of candlelight, Lawrence saw her properly.

Her face seemed dull and her features seemed even sharper, as if the bones below were pushing against the skin at her elbows and cheeks. Dark lines underlined the thin frame of her glasses, and her dark hair seemed flat and lifeless. She observed Lawrence with an unreadable expression. In the light, Lawrence saw the smeared, dried blood that covered the bottom of her chin, neck, and front of her dress.

"What have you done-"

Before she could finish, Ophelia rushed forward and was on Lawrence in a split second. Lawrence let out a small sound of shock as Ophelia's fangs pierced her skin. She struggled weakly at first, pushing at Ophelia's iron-clad grip as she drank. After what felt like hours, but in truth was only a few mere minutes, Ophelia let Lawrence go, wiping at the dark blood that stained her mouth.

Lawrence grabbed at her neck, gasping and gurgling as blood continued to bubble out of the gash in her neck. Almost immediately, the weakness returned to her body. Whatever small progress in her health that had been made was undone. The cold seeped back in, and it felt as if the gravity on her body doubled in that short span.

"There we are," drawled Ophelia, smacking her lips in satisfaction. "No more running."

Lawrence went down to her hands and knees and came face-to-face with a body. Ms. Hettle's small corpse lay halfway between the opened door to the drawing room and the hallway. Lawrence reached out and traced a gentle hand down Ms. Hettle's cold face, pressing away some of the white hair that had fallen loose from her bun.

"The old lady surprised me," Ophelia said. "Came into my room with a knife." She let out an amused snort. "Didn't think she had it in her."

Lawrence pressed her palm against Ms. Hettle's face one last time before Ophelia picked her up, cradling her close to her chest. She inhaled Ophelia's signature scent as she was brought into the library and set down on the sofa. Ophelia leaned down over Lawrence, bringing their faces close together, and kissed her deeply. Lawrence tasted the sharp taste of her own blood that made her want to vomit.

"What's wrong, love?" Ophelia asked her in a sweet voice.

Lawrence hadn't realized it, but a few tears had begun to fall. Ophelia used a finger to wipe them away, her head tilting slightly as she studied Lawrence's face.

"Nothing," she said, shaking her face.

Lawrence saw her unfinished painting, unveiled, where it still sat on the easel. Ophelia's portrait stared back at her, the blinding eyes a beacon in the dim room. Ophelia noticed where she was looking and went over to it.

"Ah, yes. When did you decide to change it? You didn't tell me," she pointed out. "I don't think I've ever been portrayed in such a way. You flatter me, my dear."

"I just wanted to show the side of you I saw," answered Lawrence. "This is how I see you."

Ophelia shot her a sly smirk over her shoulder, stepping forward to study the painting a bit closer. "You're almost done. Perhaps you will finish it when we bring it with us to New York."

"New York," Lawrence repeated in a soft, distant voice.

She had nearly forgotten about how she was meant to join Augusta and Edwin. Ophelia took a final look at the painting and returned to Lawrence's side. She placed a gentle kiss on her shoulder and sat by her side. She crossed her long legs, holding Lawrence's hand in hers. Her cold thumb traced the vein on the inside of Lawrence's wrist, feeling the unsteady pulse.

"I've a small townhome near the park," Ophelia explained. "You'll be kept inside while you change, but then you will have all the time in the world to paint."

"Change?" Lawrence repeated dumbly. Ophelia nodded. "Don't I have a say?"

"You do, unless you say no," Ophelia said, laughing lightly.

"What if I were to just die?" Lawrence asked softly, searching Ophelia's face. "Would you carry on without me?"

Ophelia didn't answer, simply lowered her head. She brought her hands together as if in prayer and turned away from her for a moment, as if subconsciously. She sighed and rose from the sofa, frustrated.

"Why bother asking such a pointless hypothetical? We shall not be without each other ever again, so there is little point wandering aimlessly down these endless avenues of thought, isn't there?"

"Just us?" Lawrence asked.

"Just us. Only us."

"Am I never allowed to have anything else then? Anybody else?"

"Am I not enough?" Her sharp voice lashed out like a whip, and Lawrence couldn't help but flinch at the sound. Ophelia then quieted and tapped her slender fingers against her arm, sighing. "I'm learning, Lawrence. I am. After so, so many years alone, it's hard to remember what it's like, but I'm trying. I'm trying for you, Lawrence. Don't you see that? I already apologized for how I acted. I told you I only did it out of jealousy and petty fears, but it was all for you. And, you just don't understand!"

"It was for me?" repeated Lawrence, incredulous. "Killing those I cared for was for me?"

Ophelia began to pace before Lawrence on the sofa as she ran her hands through her short hair.

"You laughed and smiled with that girl on the pier. You barely knew her, but I heard all about how close you were! Then that old man, and the detective! They all just want to take you away! I was just trying to keep you with me!"

"For as long as you say you've been alive, you've certainly a lot to learn."

"And how long, exactly, do you think I've been *alive*?" Ophelia asked, turning on her heel to address Lawrence. She began to stalk forward slowly.

"I neither know nor care."

Ophelia stopped before Lawrence, leaning forward until she had no choice but to lean back. Ophelia placed a hand on the back of the sofa, caging Lawrence in.

"Do you think if I sat and thought about it for long enough, maybe even I could remember? I don't. I may have very well crawled out of the mud with the rest of the snakes and lizards that existed for centuries, just as I have. I don't even remember how it all started," she said wistfully. "I remember the last few hundred years, though those memories are getting a bit hazy as well."

She pushed away from Lawrence and went to stand in front of the fire. This was her chance. Lawrence pushed up from the sofa, staggering a bit as she continued to bleed a bit from her neck. She went to the cabinet full of dark bottles and crystal glasses. She looked over her shoulder, saw Ophelia had her back turned to her still.

She quickly poured out two glasses of wine, reaching into her pocket and palming the small vial of poison. Without thinking any further, she dumped an equal portion into both glasses. She palmed the vial again, slipping it into her skirt pocket, and turned to join Ophelia by the fireplace.

"What's this?" she mumbled halfheartedly.

The flames flickered and danced in the reflection of her dark glasses. Lawrence held out one of the glasses, holding her breath until Ophelia took it. She brought it up to her lips, but lowered it again.

"This is old."

"It doesn't matter, I don't think," Lawrence said breezily. "If this is how it will be, then fine. Let's not leave this place in anger. I forgive you for it all. All of it. And, I love you. Despite it all."

Ophelia's eyes narrowed for a moment as she seemed to consider her words. She seemed satisfied, though, as she then smiled brilliantly and pulled Lawrence in for a deep kiss. The sudden, unexpected show of affection took Lawrence off guard, and a few tears fell quickly. Ophelia brushed them away.

"No more tears, love. I can't stand it."

Lawrence couldn't help it; she did cry as she watched Ophelia take the first sip. She waited for some reaction, but none came. Ophelia took a long pull of the wine, and Lawrence looked down at her own glass. She took a small sip, and then a bigger one. Edwin was right, as usual. There really was no scent or taste. Lawrence even doubted for a moment that she had put the poison in correctly, but she had.

Lawrence watched until Ophelia finished her glass. She continued to observe the clock on the mantle, watching as the minute hand continued to tick towards the hour.

"You keep looking at the clock; are you expecting something to happen?" Ophelia asked in mirth with a dry chuckle.

"Yes," Lawrence nodded. "I am."

She reached into her pocket and pulled out the empty vial. She held it out in her palm. Ophelia plucked it out of her hand, holding it between two fingers. Her brows furrowed together as she raised it to her nose to sniff.

"What is it then? Scent?"

"Poison."

The air between the two of them stilled. The fire continued to crackle. Ophelia slowly looked over at Lawrence. Surprisingly, she

416

smiled. She held her near-empty glass up to her nose a couple of times and began to chuckle.

"Interesting," she murmured. "This is not anything you could have gotten your hands on, surely. Where did you get it from?"

"Does it matter?"

Her Cheshire grin widened a fraction. "Oh, I'd like to know."

"Edwin Ernest," Lawrence said. "I think you should know his name."

"I'll keep it in mind," she said with a nod. "You know, my love, no amount of poison will ever really do anything. I will be sick for a while, but I will not die."

"Yes, I know."

"My goodness," she said, turning the vial over. She let it slip between her fingers and fall to the rug with a light thud. "Did you put it all in my glass? A vial that small, it must be quite strong."

"No, don't worry. It was divided equally between the two of us."

Ophelia stopped then, the amused expression on her face disappearing in an instant. She looked between Lawrence and her glass, which was now nearly empty.

"Lawrence," she muttered. "Lawrence, what did you do?"

She snatched Lawrence's glass from her hands and smelled it. She tossed it away, and it shattered into a million pieces as it collided against the wall. She rushed forward to Lawrence, grabbing her face in both hands and studied her face closely.

Lawrence began to feel a pleasant numbness start at the tips of her fingers and toes. It started to spread, inch by inch. Edwin was right yet again. It did work fast.

Every bit of pain and cold she had felt as Ophelia had spent the weeks draining her, left her. Aches that she had grown used to, simply because they never went away, eased. Lawrence had always thought death would have a feeling, or a taste. That wasn't it at all. She smiled.

"I did the right thing."

"Are you mad?" she cried.

Ophelia began to try and pry Lawrence's mouth open, but she turned her face away. She wrapped an arm around her, holding Lawrence firmly in place, as she stuck fingers down Lawrence's throat. She began to gag and cough, but all that came out was some tainted wine and blood.

"Oh god! What have you done, you stupid girl!"

Ophelia screamed as she pulled Lawrence towards the couch. She too began to feel the effects of the poison as her legs hardly moved, and she stumbled forward. Ophelia continued to try and make Lawrence vomit, but she continued to turn her head away, even as the sides of her mouth began to bleed where Ophelia's hands gripped and tore at the skin with the sheer force of her hand.

With every passing moment, Lawrence's body was growing numb. She felt very calm, as if lying on her back on calm, warm waters. Everything around Lawrence slowed. Her limbs and body felt heavier, and her lids began to droop. She coughed a few times, and Ophelia's brows rose. A warmth trickled down her chin, and she knew it was blood.

"No, no," Ophelia muttered.

She brought her wrist up to her mouth and used her sharp canines to cut deep into her skin. It sounded like shattering stones or chipping glass. Dark, oozing blood like tar and oil came seeping out of the gash. Ophelia held her wrist up to Lawrence's lips and tried to tip in her blood. Lawrence turned her head away, though, using all of her strength to keep her lips in a firm line. Ophelia whined, desperate.

"Drink, Lawrence. Please! I'm begging you. Please."

Lawrence didn't answer. She didn't think she could if she tried. She merely shook her head with a serene, sedate smile.

"I will force it down your throat!" Ophelia growled, grabbing the sides of Lawrence's head. She bared her teeth and went to do just that when the library doors burst open.

Edwin rushed into the room, raised a large hunting rifle, and aimed right for Ophelia's chest. She let out an animal growl just as he pulled the trigger. The rifle boomed and Ophelia went flying off the top of Lawrence. She collided with the second sofa, tumbling backward as the wood cracked and splintered with the impact.

Edwin rushed to Lawrence's side then, looking down at her aghast.

"Lawrence!" he cried. "What did you do?"

She couldn't answer him, then, but her eyes flickered over as she saw Ophelia slowly begin to rise from behind the shattered sofa.

"Edwin," she struggled out in a wheezy voice.

He looked over just as Ophelia straightened out, cracking her neck. The skin where the bullet had hit her looked splintered and little seams of her dark blood began to ooze out. She raised a hand to the superficial wound with a sneer. She then doubled over slightly, gagging and dry-heaving.

"You," she grunted out, raising a finger to point at him. "I knew I recognized you."

Edwin aimed his rifle right between her eyes. She simply smiled, snickering.

"I've heard all about you and your friends. I should have killed you first."

"You should have," he said, nodding his head sharply once. "This is for Patrick Gannaway, George Sinclair, and every other innocent soul you've ripped away before their time."

"Ugh," Ophelia grunted out as she struggled to walk as fluidly as she normally did. She spat out on the floor in disgust. "I'm going to ensure your suffering."

She let out another low growl and rushed forward. Unable in her weakened state to move as fast as she was usually able to, Ophelia met Edwin in the center of the room. He fired his rifle once, and then twice, but she managed to dodge both of those shots.

Ophelia grabbed the hot barrel of the gun, ripping it from his hands. She bared her teeth like a hellcat and lunged for his neck, but he swiftly turned and kicked her in the side. She let out a shriek. A small knife had clicked out from the tip of his shoe, hidden within the thick sole. Ophelia grabbed at her side, staggering sideways.

Ophelia pulled her hand away, watching as a bit more of her black blood oozed out from the new wound. She snarled and whipped to Edwin. He began to backpedal, but she advanced on him quickly and grabbed him around the throat.

She threw him, and he went flying backward towards the closest shelves of books. His lower body caught against the back of the sofa where Lawrence lay, tipping it over, as he hit the bookshelves.

"Lawrence!"

Ophelia rushed to her, patting her cheek to keep her awake. She pressed her ear to Lawrence's chest, listening. She bit into her arm again to feed blood into Lawrence's mouth, but Edwin came up from behind, dagger in hand. He brought it down into Ophelia's back, and she grunted.

Ophelia released Lawrence, raising to face Edwin, who limped backward. She leaned over and vomited wine and black blood. She coughed, wiping her mouth with the back of her hand. She let out another guttural growl and advanced on him, grabbing Edwin by the throat and lifting him up. His legs kicked and flailed, but not matter how hard he pulled at her hand, he couldn't loosen her grasp. His face began to turn purple. Ophelia ripped off her glasses with her other hand, tossing them aside.

Edwin shut his eyes tightly, but she slammed him back against a wall and pinned him in place. She grabbed his face and pried his eyelids open, forcing him to stare into her eyes. Edwin let out a groan at first, but then began to scream in pain. He struggled and screamed like a poor rabbit stuck in a bear trap. Lawrence flailed on the floor, unable to even lift her own head anymore. All feeling below her waist had left her, and she began to struggle with every breath.

"LJ!" Augusta cried out from the doorway of the library.

She hadn't yet spotted Ophelia and Edwin, who were pushed up against the wall. Augusta came rushing forward to Lawrence's side, pulling Lawrence's head into her lap.

"Lawrence! What happened. Oh god, you're bleeding!"

"Don't touch her!"

Ophelia came staggering up behind Augusta and grabbed her by the hair. She flung her backward, sending Augusta sliding across the floor until she collided with the nearest bookshelf. Augusta landed in a small pile on the floor, crying out only once upon impact.

Augusta rubbed the back of her head, noticing then Edwin's prone body a few feet away. She let out a cry of distress and scrambled forward on her hands and knees to him, cradling his head in her lap.

"Oh my god, Eddy! Eddy, please wake up! Oh god, you're crying blood! Eddy!"

"Birdy," he gasped out in a wheezy, hoarse voice. "I can't see. I can't see, Birdy."

"Oh, Eddy!" Augusta cried, tears streaking down her face. She used her delicate fingers to wipe at the blood that trailed down his face. "It's okay. You're going to be okay!"

"Birdy," Edwin said in a hurried voice. "The fire. You have to light the fire!"

"I can't," she whispered in a trembling voice. He wrapped his hand over hers, pressing it against his cheek.

"You can," he insisted. "I know you can. Go, now!"

Augusta hesitated for a moment, her eyes flickering over to where Ophelia stumbled over to Lawrence. She pressed a swift kiss to his lips and stood. She disappeared from the room, flying out without another look back.

Ophelia leaned over Lawrence, groaning and coughing up more black blood. It ran down the front of her chin and dripped onto the front of her bloodied dress.

"Lawrence," she whispered in a hoarse, reedy voice. "Please."

She tried to raise her wrist up to her lips, but fell into another coughing fit. Ophelia grabbed Lawrence's face in her hands, forgetting to cover her eyes. Ophelia was the last thing Lawrence saw as her eyes burned out, and she sighed out a final time through frozen lips.

Ophelia's eyes widened and she let out a shriek that rattled the windowpanes. Lawrence's irises had exploded and blood trailed down her eyes as her body became limp. Ophelia let out another cry, pressing her forehead against Lawrence's still chest.

"Why," she whimpered. For once, she stared deep into Lawrence's eyes without the protection of her glasses, but Lawrence's gaze remained elsewhere. She ran a hand down the side of Lawrence's face, caressing her.

"How could you do this to me? How could you leave me?"

She began to cry pitifully, holding and hugging Lawrence's body in a close embrace. She shook her lightly, as if that would be enough to bring her back.

Through the windows, bright, green flames began to crackle and glow against the glass, catching quickly on the old wood of the house. When the first windows in the library cracked and exploded, Ophelia flinched. Her eyes widened further at the sight of the green flames, and she let out a shout of alarm. She gathered Lawrence's body up in her arms.

Her own weakened body immediately stumbled, and she staggered to regain her hold over Lawrence. She only made it a few steps before she nearly fell again. Ophelia grabbed Lawrence's wrists and dragged her from the room. She completely ignored Edwin where he lay, focusing all her remaining energy on pulling Lawrence towards the front door.

Augusta stood between Ophelia and the entrance, a lit candle in her shaking hand. She had already spread copper powder and gasoline all over the front hall. Ophelia stopped. She spotted Augusta and sneered at her.

"Get out of my way!" Ophelia snarled.

Augusta's eyes trembled slightly as she kept her gaze fixed on Lawrence's body, but she held the candle higher.

"May you burn in hell for all eternity."

Augusta threw the candle down, and the second it landed on the first line of powder and gasoline, flames shot up with a great burst. The green flames spread quickly through the front hall, circling Ophelia until she had no choice but to stagger backward.

Augusta wasted no time and dashed into the library. Ophelia let out a string of curses and dragged Lawrence up the stairs, making it as far as the foyer before she collapsed, unable to go any further. Ophelia sat propped up by the weeping woman statue with Lawrence in her lap. Her muscles began to lock up, until she could only watch as the green flames began to consume the house around her, inching closer and closer to where she sat.

Augusta dragged Edwin from the library. She had wrapped his body in blankets to protect him from the flames, even as her own skirts caught on the green flames they dashed through. She gave a final forlorn look to Lawrence in Ophelia's arms, and left the house.

Ophelia's body began to seize and spasm sporadically until her breath became labored. She let out a snort and looked down at Lawrence. She pressed a kiss to her temple and shut her eyes. She wiped away some of the blood from her chin and leaned backward.

The house became an inferno, burning for hours until the first rays of sun appeared. Even then, the black plume of smoke that rose above the raging fire went on for days. Everyone in town hiked up the hill to watch it burn. No one lifted a hand to stop it, though.

Augusta held Edwin in her arms as she watched, too. Her face and skin were burned, and a good chunk of her hair had been scorched, but she didn't care. She didn't brush away any of the soot or blood. She held her loved one in her arms, and she cried. She cried for her grandfather, and for Patrick, and for Lawrence. She had always been too kind to be alive. Augusta watched and cried until hands and arms came, and forcibly pulled her away.

When that final morning came and the smoke cleared, Ashmore Hall was gone.

Final Word

Thank you again for picking up this book. I do hope you enjoyed.

If you'd like to read the **epilogue**, you may download for free online at my website: **smnamkoong.com**

Sign up for the mailing list if you'd like info on future releases.

www.ingramcontent.com/pod-product-compliance
Lightning Source LLC
Chambersburg PA
CBHW020008120726
47903CB00004B/1187